HIGHLAND DOC'S CHRISTMAS RESCUE

SUSAN CARLISLE

FESTIVE FLING WITH THE SINGLE DAD

ANNIE CLAYDON

MILLS & BOON

First Published in Great Britain 2019
by Mills & Boon, an imprint of HarperCollins*Publishers*
1 London Bridge Street, London, SE1 9GF

Highland Doc's Christmas Rescue © 2019 by Susan Carlisle

Festive Fling with the Single Dad © 2019 by Annie Claydon

ISBN: 978-0-263-26993-2

MIX
Paper from
responsible sources
FSC® C007454

This book is produced from independently certified FSC™ paper
to ensure responsible forest management.
For more information visit www.harpercollins.co.uk/green.

Printed and bound in Spain
by CPI, Barcelona

HIGHLAND DOC'S CHRISTMAS RESCUE

SUSAN CARLISLE

MILLS & BOON

To Dallas
I'm proud of the man you are,
and your father would be also.

CHAPTER ONE

AS THE TAXI rolled up the rise Cass Bellow looked out the window at the snow-blanketed Heatherglen Castle Clinic in northern Scotland. Why had she been sent here?

More than once she'd questioned her doctor's wisdom in transferring her to this private clinic for physical therapy. Weren't there plenty of other places in warmer climates? Particularly in her native US. Or, better yet, couldn't she have just gone home and handled what needed doing on her own? But, no, her doctor insisted she should be at Heatherglen. Had stated that he sent all his patients with extensive orthopedic injuries there. He declared the place was her best hope for a full recovery. Finally, at her argument, he'd bluntly told her that if she wanted him to sign off on her release she must complete her physical therapy at Heatherglen.

As the car came to a stop at the front door she studied the Norman architecture of the building with its smooth stone walls and slate roof. The place was huge, and breathtaking. There were more chimneys than Cass had a chance to count. This place was nothing like what she'd expected. Though it was early November, festive Christmas wreaths made of greenery and red bows already hung on the outside of the lower floor windows. They further darkened her mood.

When she had been given the search and rescue assignment assisting the military after an explosion in Eastern Europe, she had never dreamed she'd end up in traction in an army hospital on a base in Germany. Her shattered arm and leg had finally mended, but she needed physical therapy to regain complete use of them. Now she'd been sent to this far-flung, snowy place to do just that. All she really wanted was to be left alone.

She opened the cab door and wind blasted her. Despite the heat coming from the still running car, she shuddered. As Cass stepped out, one of the large wooden castle doors, decked with a huge Christmas wreath full of red berries, opened. A tall man, perhaps in his mid-thirties, with the wide shoulders of an athlete stepped out. With rust-colored hair and wearing a heavy tan cable sweater and dark brown pants, he looked like the epitome of what she thought a Scottish man should be. As he came down the few steps toward her, he smiled.

"Hello, you must be Ms. Cassandra Bellow. I'm Dr. Lyle Sinclair, the medical director here at Heatherglen. You may call me Lyle."

His thick Scottish brogue confirmed her earlier thoughts. Yet she was surprised by the way the sunny cheerfulness of his voice curled around her name, nudging at her icy emotions. Irritated, she pushed that odd notion away. This doctor was far too happy and personable for her taste. Her goal was to do what must be done with as little interaction with others as possible. She planned on nursing her wounds in private.

"Yes, that's me." To her satisfaction her flat, dry tone dropped the brightness of his smile a notch. If she could just get to her room and collapse she'd be happy. Her right side was burning from the ache in her arm and the agony of putting her full weight on her right leg.

"Flora McNeith, the physiotherapist whose care you'll be under, couldn't be here to greet you and asked that I get you settled in." Concern filled his face. "Do you need a wheelchair? Crutches?"

"No, I can walk on my own. Run, that's another thing." She pulled at her jacket to stop the biting flow of air down her neck.

A light chuckle rolled out of his throat and over her nerve endings. "I understand. Then let's get inside out of this weather." He looked up at the sky. A snowflake landed on the dark red five o'clock shadow covering his cheek.

Cass averted her eyes and gave the cobblestone drive, cleared of snow, a searching look. It was farther than she wanted to walk, yet she wouldn't let on. The three steps up to the door looked even more daunting.

All she needed was fortitude to make the walk and climb those steps. She had plenty of that. Soft snowflakes continued to drift down as she took a deep breath and steeled herself to put one foot in front of the other. With another silent inhalation, she started toward the entrance. Dr. Sinclair walked beside her.

She managed the first two steps with no mishap but the toe of her short boot caught the edge of the last one. Grabbing at air, Cass finally found the fabric covering Dr. Sinclair's arm. She yelped with the effort to hold on. Being right-handed, she'd instinctively flailed out that arm and immediately regretted it. Pain shot through it, but not as sharp as it had been weeks earlier. She gritted her teeth, thrusting out her other arm to ease the fall.

Instead of tumbling onto the steps, her body was

brought against a hard wall of human torso. The doctor's arm circled her waist and held her steady. Her face smashed into thick yarn. A hint of pine and smoke filled her nose. For some reason it was reassuring.

"Steady on, I've got you." His deep burr was near her ear.

Cass quickly straightened, getting her feet under her even though pain rocked her. She refused to show it, having already embarrassed herself enough. Her lips tightened. "I'm fine. Thank you."

Glancing at him, she got the weirdest impression that the concern in his eyes had nothing to do with her physical injuries, as if he was able to see her true pain. That was a crazy idea. She shook that odd thought off and focused on where she was.

Taking a third fortifying breath, Cass stepped into the massive foyer.

No way was she going to let him see the effort it took to keep walking. She'd lived through much worse. She'd always been self-sufficient. Weakness wasn't in her vocabulary. As a young girl she had learned the power of being emotionally strong.

Still, that brief human contact had been nice.

There were two enormous cement urns filled with pine and berries on either side of the doors. Cass looked further to see the stone arched beams of the ceiling then on to a grand staircase. On the floor beside it lay a pile of pine wood. Here she was in this strange place for the holidays when all she wished for was home. She would get her arm and leg strong again as fast as she could, then return to America to grieve her loss in private.

"Are you sure you're okay?" The doctor stood too close as if he was afraid she might stumble again.

"I'm fine." The words sounded sharp and overly loud

in the cavernous entrance hall. If she could just get to her room, she could nurse the excruciating throbbing in her arm and leg. She would be limping by then as well.

"On our way to your room, let me tell you where a few things are. This is Admissions." He waved a hand to indicate a room off the hall. "Louise, my administrative assistant, and I have our offices there. She's out this afternoon as well. You two can sort out the paperwork in the morning. I'm sure you're tired."

Cass was beyond tired. The effort it had taken her to travel from Germany to Fort William then the drive north had worn her out. She hadn't recovered anywhere near as much as she wanted to believe.

"Over here is the dining room." He walked across the hall and stood in a wide doorway.

Cass joined him. Despite her physical distress, she loved his accent. It was soothing, for some reason.

The room he wanted her to see was long and wide with a dark barrel ceiling sculpted out of wood from which hung large, black iron chandeliers. A fireplace Cass could stand up in filled the wall on the far end with flags arranged overhead. The walls were partially covered in wainscoting. Above that were a few male portraits in impressive frames. A huge table, surrounded by imposing matching chairs, capable of seating at least twenty people, stood in the center of the room. An oriental rug in blue and red lay beneath it. The only thing out of place was a pile of greenery on the floor in one corner and a few boxes stacked beside it.

He must have noticed the direction of her gaze. "Pardon the mess. We're in the process of decorating for Christmas."

Cass pretended he hadn't spoken. Not even the holidays could heal her broken heart.

Dr. Sinclair was saying, "All meals are served here, unless there's a reason the resident is incapable of joining us. We dress for the evening meal. It's at seven."

"Dress? As in diamonds and tux?"

Chuckling, he shook his head. "No. More like no workout clothes allowed. The idea is for the residents to use their skills and have something positive to look forward to. We work on the principle that if you don't use it, you lose it."

She glanced at him. He really was quite handsome in a rugged way. "Like?"

"Fastening a button, passing a bowl or even manipulating a fork." He turned toward the central hall.

"I have no trouble with any of those so why must I attend?" She joined him.

"Because we want our residents to feel like they're part of our family, which they are," he said over his shoulder as he started down the hall.

She had zero interest in being sociable. All she wanted was time to herself to think about what she would do next, where she wanted her life to go. How she could get past the mass of emotions churning inside her. Could she continue working in search and rescue? Work with a new dog? Learn to trust another man?

Maybe she could just make sure she wasn't around when it was dinnertime. This place sounded more like a prison than a clinic. "Hey, do you mind telling me why I was sent here?"

That got his attention. "So you can regain your mobility."

"I know that. I mean why here in particular? Couldn't I have gone to a clinic in America? What makes this place so special?"

He shoved his hands into his pockets. "As I understand it, your orthopedic doctor believes this is the right clinic for you."

She stepped toward him, pinning him with a direct look. "What led him to believe this specific clinic was the right place for me to complete my physical therapy?"

Dr. Sinclair shifted his weight and raised his chin. "I'm not sure what you're looking for but our residents have an uncommonly high success rate of making as complete a recovery as possible, and by recovery I mean holistic recovery. Our state-of-the-art clinic features a peaceful atmosphere conducive to healing…" he waved a hand around, indicating the castle "…and our canine therapy has proved to be fundamental in facilitating that recovery as well. Does that reassure you?"

Canine therapy. Cass took a step back, her chest constricting. She couldn't deal with this right now. It was too soon after the loss of her dog and partner, Rufus. "I'm not interested in canine therapy."

Her German shepherd-wolfhound mix partner had been with her for four years. She'd had him since he was a puppy. She'd even gone to Germany to pick him up from the breeders. They had trained together at a search and rescue school in California. They'd understood each other, trusted one another.

Now he was gone. Despite him being an animal, the hurt of his loss was more acute than the pain of broken bones or her ex-boyfriend's assessment of her ability to maintain a relationship. She and Rufus had been all over the world together, crawling in and over disaster sites that others only saw on TV while drinking their morning coffee. As a team, they had been a part of tragedies that no one should ever see or experience. Gratitude and guilt filled her in equal measure.

She felt the doctor's keen observation and focused

on his mild expression. He turned and started down an adjacent hall to the left, saying, "This way to the lift."

Cass glanced at the staircase in relief then followed, taking careful steps to ensure there wasn't a repeat performance of what had almost happened outside.

He looked over his shoulder. "As our residents improve, they use the stairs whenever possible."

Cass once more eyed the daunting set of wide steps made of gray marble. "And that's mandatory?"

Dr. Sinclair gave her a grin. "'Mandatory' is such an unfriendly word. Why don't we go with 'greatly encouraged'? It's part of the graduation program to be able to walk up and down the stairs, but we don't require that until you're ready."

Did her relief show on her face? "What makes you think I'm not ready?"

"Maybe the tight line of your lips that indicates that little stumble outside hurt more than you wish to admit."

Cass grimaced inwardly. The man had an acute sense of awareness. Could he see that more than her body pained her? That her heart hurt? Cass hoped not. She was nowhere near ready to share her feelings. "I don't hurt."

"Liar." He gave her a flash of a smile. One she was sure made people want to confide in him, which she wasn't going to do. As if he knew what she was thinking, he said in a gentle manner, "You do know it isn't weakness to admit you're in pain or that you need help. That's what we're here for."

She'd had enough of this. All she wanted was to get to her room. "Who're you, the resident shrink?"

They walked out of the elevator and started down a wide hallway lined with portraits. A few decorations were already in place here and there. A red carpet runner muffled their steps.

"No, but as clinic administrator and emergency medical doctor I help develop the patients' therapy. All the doctors here work together to form patient plans. Recovery is as much mental as it is physical."

"So you think I have emotional issues?" Cass certainly did have them. She couldn't keep her job without a dog, and she wasn't sure she could handle having another one. To possibly lose another best friend would be too much, too painful. To get close enough that someone or something mattered was more than she wanted at this point.

Lyle's…wasn't that his name?…mouth quirked as he stopped to face her.

"Why, Ms. Bellow, in some ways I think everyone has issues. So don't go thinking you're special. Here we are." He pushed open a thick wooden door. "Your room belonged to the lady of the castle."

Cass couldn't deny it was a grand room. Its large canopy bed was hung with seafoam green curtains and covered with a matching spread. Beneath a bank of windows was a seating arrangement of a loveseat and two cushioned chairs. A chest, which she guessed held a TV, was nearby and on the opposite wall was a large fireplace with a fire already burning. The gleaming oak floor had a plush rug in the center of it. The festive fairy had been at work decorating in here as well. There was greenery along the mantle and groups of candles on tables. If she must be in this clinic, then she had won the lottery for the perfect room. She could hide out here in comfort.

"One of the staff should've put your luggage in here." He looked around. "There it is. Great." He pointed to the far side of the room where there was another door. "Through there is your bath. You'll find a hot tub, which I encourage you to use often. I'll leave you now to settle in. You don't have to be at dinner tonight. A tray of food will be sent up. Breakfast is between six and eight in the dining room. I'll let Flora know you've arrived. She may not have a chance to check in with you this evening, but you can expect to see her first thing in the morning. One of the staff will come and collect you at seven for breakfast. Is there anything you need before I go?"

Cass had slowly wandered around the room as he spoke. "I don't think so."

"If you have any questions, just pick up the phone. Somebody is on duty twenty-four hours a day. I hope your stay is a positive one."

Before he could say more a man appeared in the hallway behind him. "Lyle, you said to let you know when Andy Wallace arrived. The ambulance is at the back entrance. I'm on the way after the wheelchair now."

"Thanks Walter. I'll go down." Lyle turned to her. "See you around, Ms. Bellow."

Later that evening after dinner, Lyle bowed his head against the howling wind as he walked to his cottage. Seeing the once strong, always smiling Andy Wallace with sunken eyes and needing a wheelchair had made for a tough last few hours.

Andy was older than him. They had only been acquaintances growing up. Still, Lyle could remember Andy and Nick, Lyle's best friend Charles's older brother, laughing and always into something. Now Andy was a shell of that person. After an IED had exploded under his Humvee in Afghanistan he was a patient in a clinic started in honor of Nick. The irony was sickening.

Ms. Bellow wore the same sad expression as Andy. That look implied the weight of the world lay on her slender shoulders. His staff had their work cut out for them with those two. He and Charles, the Laird of Heatherglen and a doctor as well, had discussed both patients but Lyle suspected there was more to Cassandra Bellow than was on paper. She didn't even try to hide her desire to be elsewhere.

That resolute and dejected air about Cass indicated a serious psychological injury, but she carried her issues like a backpack they were so obvious. Maybe being at Heatherglen would help her with not only her physical problems but with what was bothering her heart and soul as well.

He recognized that look in both his residents because he'd seen it in his own eyes every time he'd shaved while serving in the Royal Army Medical Corps. All the men in his family had been expected to make a career in the armed forces and he hadn't disappointed. As one of his father's two sons, Lyle himself had been encouraged, then expected, to join the army. The importance of serving had been drummed into him his entire life. Yet medicine had pulled at him. To find a happy medium he'd combined the two.

Despite that compromise, he'd found the discipline and unwavering devotion of military life wasn't for him. He wanted to concentrate on caring for people in the way he loved best, personally. To his father's disappointment and ongoing puzzlement, Lyle had resigned his commission and returned home, remaining in the reserves.

His father still hadn't given up on the belief that Lyle

would return to active duty someday soon. Every time they were together the subject came up. Now that his father's health was declining, the pressure had grown. If Lyle resumed active service, he could make his father's last few years happier, make him proud. But the exchange would be that Lyle would be miserable.

Charles had been in the process of setting up the clinic when Lyle had returned home from overseas. He'd asked Lyle if he would consider being the administrator, as well as run the emergency centre for the surrounding villages. Lyle had accepted and never looked back. He had found where he belonged. Still, his father's disappointment weighed on him.

The decision to return to the military hung there. Then there was his obligation to the clinic...

While he'd been in the Middle East that hopeless look he recognized in Cass's and Andy's eyes had grown in his own after receiving his "Dear John" letter from Freya. He had been caught in a net with no way out. Freya had called a halt to their relationship while he had been thousands of miles away, unable to talk to her face to face. For months the pain had been like a gnawing animal in his chest. It wasn't until he had returned and started work at the clinic that he could at last breathe and see the relationship for what it was.

Lyle continued along the snowy, muddy path toward his cottage. He knew this walk by heart. The moon was large tonight and he didn't need his torch. From experience he was sure his housekeeper had left a fire laid. The thought of lighting it and a warm drink kept him moving. Thankfully he had a full belly from the meal he'd shared with the residents before leaving the clinic. He wasn't required to dine at the castle, but Mrs. Renwick was a much better cook than he was. Since he didn't much enjoy eating alone, he ate most of his meals at the clinic. And just as he'd expected, the two newest residents hadn't been in attendance.

Going through some paperwork in his office the next morning, he allowed his thoughts to wander to Ms. Bellow. He had gone to Andy Wallace's room to make sure he was comfortable and had spoken to the overnight nursing staff about him. Yet despite his curiosity about Cass, Lyle hadn't searched her out. Because she wasn't under his direct care, he couldn't think of a reason to do so. Flora would have her case well in hand. Still, he felt compelled to see Cass.

She'd whetted his curiosity for some reason. Something about her sharp, self-assured tone and unwillingness to show her obvious pain made him want to understand what was going on behind those gloomy eyes. He'd felt her fragility when she had leaned against him. All bones and skin, as if she had lost weight. Being injured would have caused some of that but she was *too* thin. He felt the odd need to protect her, reassure her. Not that he would let that show. Still, just before lunch he couldn't stop himself from walking to the physical therapy department.

Lyle found Flora, with her dark head down, working at her desk. He knocked lightly on the door.

She looked up and smiled. "Hello, Lyle. What can I do for you?"

"I just wanted to check in on Cass Bellow. I haven't seen her today." He put his hands in his pockets.

"She was here for therapy this morning." Flora put down her pen. "She was ready to start when I arrived."

He leaned against the doorframe. "Great. When we met yesterday, I was afraid she might be resistant."

Flora shook her head a little. "If there was a problem it was with her working too hard. She acted determined to be finished with her recovery well before the prescribed time. I had to remind her that she could hurt herself further if she pushed herself too hard."

"I'm sure that you'll see she takes it slowly and easily." Lyle took a step into the office. "By the way, did you tell her there's animal therapy as well? I got the impression it was a surprise to her when I mentioned it. I don't think she was told by her doctors in Germany that it's a central part of our program here."

Flora's eyes darkened with concern. "I did mention it but was called away before more was said."

"I'll speak to Esme. If Cass doesn't show up at the canine therapy center, then I'll talk to her."

Flora nodded. "Good."

"I told Cass the residents eat together, and she didn't look any happier about that."

Flora picked up the pen and tapped it on the desk once. "You and I have been at this long enough to know how to handle an uncooperative patient. We know physical issues often include adjusting to a new way of life." She lifted her shoulders and let them drop. "Why would Cass be any different?"

"Agreed. What about Andy Wallace? Have you had your session with him?"

"I'll see him this afternoon."

"Let me know how it goes. I don't think he's in any better frame of mind than Ms. Bellow."

Flora grinned. "We don't get all those great accolades for being the best therapy clinic for nothing."

"You have a point." He nodded his head at the door. "I'm on my way to get a sandwich for lunch. Care to join me?"

"Thanks, but I need to finish some paperwork for the boss."

Lyle chuckled. "And he appreciates your efforts. See you later." He left, walking to the dining room to pick up some food before returning to his office. Lyle planned to continue checking up on Cass and Andy for a few days until he was satisfied with their compliance, then he'd back away.

After lunch, Cass sat in her room by the fire, rubbing her thigh, glad therapy was over for the day. It had been grueling. Less from what she had been asked to do and more from her pushing herself. She had broken into a sweat and had clenched her teeth more than once not to cry out as pain had shot through her leg. Flora had warned her to slow down. It had been strenuous and stressful at best. Even her arm had resisted a couple of the exercises.

Making matters worse was the discovery Cass had made that she had stamina issues. The hospital stay in traction had taken a lot out of her. She'd always been fit, had worked out regularly with ease. Now she just felt frustrated. Regaining her strength wasn't going to happen fast enough.

That morning she'd been up and dressed by the time Melissa, a staff member, had knocked on her door. She had slept well the night before. Sleeping in the hospital hadn't been ideal. The peace and quiet of this country castle did have its appeal.

She had on some of the few clothes she habitually kept packed in her to-go bag. The knit sweatpants and T-shirt would have to do for workout clothes. When she and Rufus had caught the transport plane to Eastern Europe, nowhere in her plans had she thought to prepare for weeks of being in a hospital or being in a physical therapy clinic in Scotland in the winter.

Melissa had escorted Cass by elevator to the ground floor. There she had been led to the dining room.

"I'll return in a few minutes to show you to the physical therapy department," Melissa had said.

There hadn't been anyone else in the room. Cass had been thankful for that. She'd gone to the buffet and helped herself to a boiled egg and a slice of toast. She had just finished her second glass of orange juice when the woman returned.

"Flora's ready for you."

After placing her dishes on a tray, Cass followed Melissa down a long hall off the main one. They entered an area that looked like a gym where exercise equipment faced a bank of three large windows. In another corner of the spacious room were mats. Two high padded tables sat in the middle.

"You can have a seat on a table and I'll let Flora know you're here," she'd been told.

Cass scrambled up on the table with more effort than she liked.

A leggy, dark-haired woman wearing what looked like the latest fashion in exercise clothes soon joined her. Dressed in a hot pink jacket over a black top and leggings that came to mid-calf she made Cass feel extra-frumpy in her outfit. The woman even wore makeup.

She offered her hand, "Hi, I'm Flora McNeith. It's nice to meet you, Cass. I apologize that I wasn't here to meet you yesterday. I'm sure Lyle took good care of you."

"Who? Oh, yeah, the doctor."

She chuckled. "Most woman consider him more memorable than that. We should get started on your therapy."

Over the next hour Cass showed Flora the range of motion in her leg and arm. For the first thirty minutes they concentrated on her leg and the last half-hour on her arm. Flora applied a cold compress before working with either part of her body, then a warm one after.

When they were through Flora said, "I'm sending you to the whirlpool for half an hour. After lunch someone will show you to your afternoon therapy at the canine therapy center."

She didn't give Cass time to respond before she turned to another patient who had entered the room. Cass had no intention of going to the canine therapy center. She wasn't ready to be involved with a dog again, any dog. Wasn't sure she'd ever be ready. Why had her doctors in Germany insisted on sending her to this clinic when they knew her background? Maybe they had thought it would be what she needed since she had been a dog handler, but she wasn't emotionally ready. She would just make it clear, without explanation, that she wouldn't be going to the canine therapy center.

As she walked toward the door marked "Whirlpool" Cass groaned. She almost cried with pleasure as she slipped into the hot swirling water. Today she had taken the first step towards her complete discharge and regaining her life. The one that didn't include Rufus.

After her trip to PT she'd stopped by the dining room long enough to grab a sandwich, leaving the soup behind. With food eaten, a warm shower taken and clean clothes on, Cass now had a nap on her agenda. She would be perfectly happy spending the rest of the day in her room.

She woke with a start when there was a sharp knock on her door. "Coming." Cass opened it to find a staff member there. This time it was a young man.

"I'm here to show you the way to the canine therapy center."

"I'm sorry but I don't feel like going." What she really meant was she *wasn't* going.

The man studied her a moment as if he expected her to say more, then nodded. "I understand."

Cass settled back in the chair and looked into the fire. She knew her abilities and strengths. The wound of losing Rufus was too raw. Her emotions in general were stretched to snapping point. She couldn't cope with the thought of interacting with a dog even if it was supposed to speed up her recovery.

She loved her job, but could she ever return to it, ever get so involved with another animal that she risked reliving this almost unbearable suffering? What if it wasn't a dog? Could she ever open up enough to anyone again to take the chance of losing her heart?

CHAPTER TWO

LYLE STOOD OUTSIDE Cass's door. She had refused to go to her canine therapy appointment. From the information he'd received from Flora she'd been more than game to do the work in physical therapy. Why was she balking at the rest of the program?

It was important. He and his colleagues had been highly successful in using canine therapy in the recovery of their patients. Cass needed to participate. He had read in her paperwork that she'd worked as a dog handler for search and rescue. Certainly she wasn't afraid of dogs. If anything, he would have thought that she would be eager to meet her assigned dog.

Lyle rapped on the door twice.

He heard a voice call, "Just a minute." Then a few seconds later the door opened.

Cass was dressed in a T-shirt, a zip-up hoodie, jeans and socked feet. She only came as high as his shoulders. She pushed at her short blonde hair, her tone demanding as she said, "Yes?"

"I understand that you don't want to go to your canine therapy appointment." Frustration with her resistance made him sound sterner than he'd intended.

"You understand correctly." She stepped back into the room.

He moved to just inside the doorway. "It's part of the program here. Everyone's required to participate."

"Why?" She stood feet slightly apart as if preparing for a fight.

He lowered his voice. "Because we've found that people recover faster when part of their therapy involves a dog. It's almost crucial to full recuperation. Why don't you let me show you the way to the center?"

"No, thank you." She put her hand on the door.

His brow rose. Did she intend to close it on him? "Are you in pain? Do I need to speak to Flora?"

A look of something close to panic filled her eyes. "No, I'm just tired. I don't feel like it today."

He checked his watch. It was too late now for her to go anyway. She had already wasted half her time. "Okay, that's understandable. Rest is good. Take the remainder of the afternoon off. I'll see you at dinner."

She made no comment as she closed the door.

Lyle had to back out into the hall to avoid having the door shut in his face. When was the last time he'd been thrown out of a room? He couldn't even remember one. People didn't treat him like that, yet Cass had effectively done so. He shook his head. She would be a tough nut to crack.

It was almost dark when Lyle started for home. Cass hadn't been at dinner. Neither had she ordered a tray. He had left his meal long enough to go to her room, determined he'd be less understanding this time. If she couldn't follow the clinic protocols, she would be transferred elsewhere.

There was no answer when he knocked on her door. He tried three times before he called her name. Finally, he opened the door a crack and listened for the shower running. Nothing. He called again then stuck his head in to look. Cass wasn't there. First thing in the morning he was going to confront her when she showed up for her PT session with Flora.

A short time later Lyle turned to go through the gate leading to his cottage when he saw a dark shadow of a person down the way. They were sitting on the fence. Who was it? He was acquainted with most people around here but didn't recognize this person. The locals knew better than to sit outside at this time of year. His conscience wouldn't allow him to go home without first checking on the stranger.

He didn't wish to scare whoever it was, so he approached slowly. Still, there was no movement. Were they so deep in their thoughts they didn't hear him walking up? He stepped closer. He still couldn't tell if it was a man or a woman. The person didn't move. He went nearer, close enough he could touch them. Just as he was about to, they turned and looked at him. *Cass!* He had assumed she was safely in the castle somewhere, if not already back in her room. He would have never thought she might wander out into the night and cold. What had possessed her to come outside?

All she wore was a thin jacket. Her hands were shoved into her pockets. She wasn't dressed adequately for this weather. She should have on a woolly hat and scarf and a thicker jacket. "What're you doing here?"

She looked away, toward the last of the dying light.

"Are you okay? It's much too cold to be sitting here."

"I had to get out. I've been cooped up in a hospital for weeks. I needed some fresh air." Her words were so soft he leaned forward to hear them.

Lyle glanced in the direction she was looking and saw nothing that should hold her attention. He could only guess that her thoughts were so deep she had no idea what danger she was in. Could she even find her way back to the castle?

But first things first. "How long have you been out here?"

It took a moment before she answered, "I don't know."

Had frostbite started? He needed to get her out of the cold.

"Why're you here, Doctor?" Her voice sounded stronger.

That was encouraging. Much more like herself than her first few words. He pointed. "I live just down the lane there."

"Oh." Cass glanced over her shoulder then shrugged as if disinterested.

"I went to your room looking for you during dinner. I thought by now you would've come out of hiding and gone to your room for the night, prepared to ignore any knock on your door." He took a seat beside her.

This time she really looked at him. "What gave you that idea?"

"The expression on your face when I told you that you'd be expected for dinner in the dining room. I guessed you weren't planning to come. However, I didn't expect you to run outside to get away."

She pursed her lips and nodded. "Yeah, I don't think I'm gonna make those communal meals. And I'm not running away."

"We're not going to discuss that now. What we need to do is get you inside and warmed up." He stood.

Cass didn't move. Instead, her attention went to the sky once more. "Don't worry about me. I'm all right."

Lyle's brows drew together. He was sure she didn't

appreciate the full effect of his reaction because of the dim lighting. "So you're knowledgeable enough about the area that you can get around without getting lost?"

Cass straightened and glared at him. "I work in search and rescue. I assure you I can manage to get myself back to the castle."

There was spunk in her voice. "That remains to be seen. You're obviously ignorant of the danger of being out in this weather without adequate clothing. I'm not taking any chances on losing one of our residents to exposure. Right now, you're going to the closest warm place and that's my cottage. When you're defrosted and dry, I'll walk you back to the castle."

It wasn't until that moment that Cass registered she was bone cold. How long had she been sitting here, staring off into space?

"Come with me. My cottage isn't far." He offered his large gloved hand, palm up.

She stared at it a moment. Was she acting crazy, like he already thought she was? Cass took his hand just long enough to slide off the wall. He turned and she trailed after him. They didn't go far before they entered a small clearing with a two-story stone cottage sitting in the middle. Trees surrounded it. A light over the door was on and another burned brightly in the window. Someone was expecting him.

"Is your wife going to mind you bringing a wayward patient home?"

"If I had one, she wouldn't mind." He walked to the door and opened it, then turned and waited for her to enter.

Cass stepped in, giving him room to follow. They stood in a small hallway. He waved a hand toward a room off to one side as he closed the door and began removing his coat. "Go on in and take off your shoes. They must be wet. I'll have the fire burning in a minute."

She entered what must be his living area. There was a small couch and a large leather chair situated close to the fireplace. The seat of the chair had a dip in it. It was obviously the doctor's favorite spot. A lamp and a stack of books sat on the floor beside it. A desk with papers strewn across it was against the wall with a window that faced the front lawn. Behind the desk stood a wooden chair. On the other side were shelves full of haphazardly placed books and a few framed pastoral scenes on the wall. The room had a very masculine feel to it. The man certainly owned his space. Cass found that comforting and reassuring in some odd way.

Lyle soon joined her, minus his outer clothing and shoes. He was in his socked feet, which made him seem even more approachable. "You don't have your shoes off yet? You need to get that jacket off as well. It looks like it's soaked through."

Cass started to remove a boot. "I can tell you spend a lot of time telling people what to do."

"You can thank my father and time in the army for that." He pulled a box of matches off the mantel, knelt and lit the fire. It soon came to life. "You really don't have any idea how long you've been outside?"

Cass considered pretending she hadn't heard the question. She'd gotten lost in her thoughts, her disappointment and grief, but the last thing she wanted to do was confess why she'd been out there. "No, I'm not sure."

He stood. "You really are going to have to be more

careful around here. It's easy to wander somewhere you shouldn't. With or without snow."

Although she hadn't yet gotten her boot off, Cass removed her coat. It was heavier than usual. He was right. She hadn't noticed how wet she had become.

The doctor reached for it and she allowed him to take it. Going to the desk, he hung it over the back of the chair, which he then pulled closer to the fire.

"Do you regularly bring patients home to sit by the fire?" She dropped one boot to the floor.

He grinned. It was a nice one. The kind that made her want to return it. "No. I'd have to say you're the first. But then I only do it for people sitting on my fence who are obviously about to freeze to death."

Shivering, Cass removed the other boot and let it drop beside the first one.

He pulled a colorful knit throw of orange, browns and tan off the back of the leather chair and draped it over her shoulders. She pulled the edges around her. Warmth filled her immediately. After letting it seep in, she removed her wet socks and spread them on the hearth. With a sigh, she stretched her ice-cold feet out toward the flames. Rubbing her stiff damaged leg, she got comfortable on the small sofa.

"I'll go and brew a pot for tea." Lyle started out of the room.

"The English and their tea," Cass murmured.

"I heard that. And I'm Scottish. Not English," he said with a clipped note.

Cass winced. She'd just been chastised. Her mother would be displeased with Cass for being rude, no matter what the circumstances.

He looked over his shoulder. "I forget you're American. Would you prefer coffee? I think I have some in the back of the pantry." He waited, an expectant look on his face.

She mustered a slight smile. "No, tea is fine. You've already gone to a lot of trouble for me."

"No trouble." He left the room.

While listening to him moving around in another part of the house, Cass laid her head back against the cushion of the sofa and gazed into the flames. The feeling was returning to her feet. She wiggled them. This was nice. The most peaceful she had felt in weeks.

Lyle returned with a small tray. On it were two steaming mugs, a milk jug and a sugar bowl. "Do you take yours with sugar and milk?"

"I don't know. My coffee I like with both."

"Then let's try it that way." The doctor mixed the ingredients in and handed her a mug.

She wrapped her hands around it, letting the heat seep into her icy fingers.

He sank into his chair with his mug in his hand. The chair fit him perfectly. "How're you feeling now?"

"Much better. I had no idea how cold and wet I was."

Leaning forward, he rested his elbows on his knees with the mug between his palms. "You really need thicker socks and boots. There's a good shop in the village for those."

"My sturdy boots were cut off and discarded when I was taken to the medical tent. I went straight from the tent to the hospital and from the hospital to here. When I can, I'll buy another pair. And maybe replace my cellphone." She had said more than she had intended.

His brows went up. "Medical tent? I had no idea. Do you mind telling me what happened?"

"It wasn't in my file?"

He pursed his lips and gave a noncommittal shake

of his head. "Yes, but I'd like to hear it about it from you. I think you need to talk."

"Being a shrink again, Doc?"

"It's Lyle, and I was going more for being your friend." He leaned back, looking completely comfortable. "If you don't want to talk about it that's fine."

Now she was being put on the spot. If she didn't tell him something he would think she was a head case. "There's not much to tell. I was searching for a girl lost in the rubble of a building after a major explosion in Eastern Europe. It had been two days and there wasn't much hope. I found her alive but in the process a wall fell on me. So now you have it." Cass had been careful not to use the word *we*. She didn't want to talk about Rufus. She refused to break down in front of this stranger, no matter how nice he was.

"Wow, that's some story."

And he hadn't heard it all. Wouldn't ever as far as she was concerned. "Yeah, makes for a great party story."

He gave her a direct look. "I think it makes you a pretty impressive person. Your type of work can be both rewarding and very depressing."

He was right about that. His piercing empathy made her conscious of her vulnerability. She wasn't used to people seeing through what she said that clearly. The men she'd had relationships with certainly hadn't—including Jim, her latest disaster. Now she had scars on her body. How would men react to them?

Lyle put the mug down. "How're your hands and feet feeling now?"

Relieved he'd changed the subject, she answered, "Instead of being numb they feel like needles are being pushed into them."

"That's good. The feeling is returning."

Giving him a wry smile, she brought the mug to her lips again. The warmth flowed through her, matching the heat in the room. "So how come the administrator of the prestigious Heatherglen Castle Clinic is living way out here in the woods?"

Looking over the edge of the mug, he gave her an indulgent look. "In the daylight it's not that far out. This was the gamekeeper's cottage. When I returned from serving in the Middle East I needed a place to live. Turned out this came with the administrator's job."

"I don't see you as the military type." He didn't strike her as a squared shoulders, stand-at-attention kind of man. His smile was too quick, his manner too easygoing to fit into that strait-laced world.

"Aye. I was born and bred to it."

The words were flat, suggesting that hadn't been a completely good thing. There was more there but she didn't ask. It wasn't her business and she didn't like him prying into hers, so she wouldn't.

"You were overseas?"

"Aye, two tours in the Middle East."

"That couldn't have been much fun." She was sure that was an understatement.

A dark look came over his face. "It wasn't."

He must have seen stuff similar to what she had in her work. She would never have guessed they'd have anything in common. Cass didn't want to talk about the similarities in their backgrounds. Instead she would rather lock it away and not think about the past. Or the pain. "So you were raised around here?"

"Yes. In the village of Cluchlochry. My parents don't live far from here. Where're you from?"

His tone led her to believe he loved the area. "Indiana, but I live in Montana now."

He raised his eyebrows and nodded approvingly. "I've been there. Beautiful scenery."

"It is. That's my favorite thing about it. But even with all the snow, it's pretty around here as well."

"In the spring it's like living inside an emerald it's so green." Reverence made his Scottish accent more pronounced.

Did it do the same when he whispered in a woman's ear when he desired her? Heaven help her! *That* wasn't a thought she should be having. Where had that idea come from? She swallowed hard and wiggled her toes. Surely it was the fire making her skin so hot.

"Let me have a look at those. I want to make sure you don't have the beginnings of frostbite." He went down on one knee in front of her.

"Look at what?" Her mind had been in a completely different place. "Oh, my feet. I don't think that's necessary."

He gave her an odd look then patted his thigh. "But I do. Put your foot up here."

With reluctance she did as he requested. Lyle's leg was firm beneath her bare sole, his corduroy pants soft.

He cradled her heel gently in the palm of his hand. All his touches were functional and professional, yet a streak of response zipped through her. She pulled back and sat straighter, watching the top of his head with its light, curly red hair. Were those coils as soft as they looked? She almost reached out a hand. Almost…

"Wiggle your toes for me."

Her head jerked up. It took her a long second to comply.

His fingers traveled over her toes. She pulled back but he held her foot securely. He raised his head, a slight grin on his lips. "Ticklish." It was more a statement than question.

"A little." It sounded childish to admit.

Cass groaned inside.

"There's no sign of frostbite here. That's good." He placed that foot on the floor. "Let me see the other one."

Cass didn't even try to resist this time. She gave that foot the same attention as the other, but without tickling her. For some reason that disappointed her.

"Wiggle," he commanded.

She did.

"Good." He rose from the floor and moved to pick up one of her socks. "These are still damp. You really are going to have to get some thicker ones when you buy those boots if you plan to take walks. When the snow melts it can get very muddy. I'll get you some dry ones to wear back to the castle." He left the room.

It was past time for her to get back to the clinic but his place was so cozy, so comfortable. Too much Lyle's space. She shouldn't be having such a reaction to him. This wasn't the time to add more conflicting emotions to those she already had.

He soon returned and handed her a pair of thick, very masculine navy socks. She had no doubt these would keep her feet dry. He took his chair while she pulled them on. Immediately her feet were warmer."

"These feel great. Thank you. I'll have them laundered and returned as soon as possible."

He poked at the fire, making sure the screen was secure around it. "No hurry. I know where to find them if I need them."

Cass reached for her shoes. "I think it's time for me to be going. I've taken up enough of your evening."

Lyle didn't disagree with her. Instead he rose and

went into the hallway. With her shoes now on, Cass reached for her damp coat.

"Wait. You need a dry coat as well." He had one in his hand, holding it open for her. She slipped her arms in and he settled the heavy jacket on her shoulders. There was that same smell she had caught when she'd first met him. The coat swallowed her whole but it was like being wrapped in his arms. Although that was an unsettling and unrealistic notion, it was nevertheless a reassuring one.

Lyle pulled on his own outdoor clothing while she waited. He studied her a moment. "You need a hat, scarf and some gloves as well." Disappearing upstairs, he returned with a handful of woolen items.

"I can't take these. Surely you need them." She offered them back to him.

He shook his head. "I have a drawer full. My mother knits these."

Cass ran her hand across them. The wool was so soft. "It feels wonderful."

"Try on the hat. It may not be tight enough, but it'll be better than nothing." He watched her expectantly.

Cass pulled the dark tan hat over her head, tucking in stray hair around her face. She still held the scarf. "I'll be all right without this."

"No, you won't." His stern look stopped her from further argument.

Cass wasn't used to having people tell her what to do. A bit irritated, she wrapped the scarf around her neck. It too smelled of pine and wood smoke, like him. Those scents would forever remind her of Lyle.

She forced that thought out of her head and focused on tucking the ends of the scarf inside her borrowed coat. "Your mother does a beautiful job."

"Thank you. What I can count on is that you'll stay warm in them. These gloves will be far too large but they will work for right now. You'll need to buy some of those as well. Now, come on, it's time we got you back to the castle."

She inhaled. There was that scent again. Yes, she needed to get out of here. Something about Lyle and his home made her wish for things better left alone.

CHAPTER THREE

LYLE OPENED THE door and the bitter cold embraced her. Cass pulled the scarf a little tighter around her neck, glad to have it. Lyle closed the door behind them, blocking out all but the porch light.

It was cold and darkness had taken over. As they walked further away from the house she could see the stars shining brightly. She paused in awe. It was beautiful.

Cass had been to many places in the world, but few compared to how amazing it was here with the moon and the stars…and the peace. In the distance there was a rise with what looked like the ruins of an old building on its crest. She pointed. "What's that place?"

"That's the old castle keep. The first laird of Heatherglen build it. It's a tumble of stones now but you can get a beautiful view of the valley, including the village, from up there. There's a path to it, but I don't recommend you go off on your own. The path can be a bit tricky in a number of places."

"Are you worried about me wandering away?"

He searched her face for a moment. "I'd like to hope not, but based on the facts I have so far, I feel like you might."

"I repeat, I was a member of a search and rescue

team." One that was broken now. She no longer had a partner.

He pulled a flashlight out of his pocket and turned it on now that they were way from the cottage. "I understand that, but surely you've always had help."

She'd always had Rufus. Had relied on him to return them back home safely. Now she had no one. At this particular moment Lyle was fulfilling the role Rufus had had in her life. Still, she wasn't sure she could ever let herself truly rely or care for anybody, whether dog or human, ever again.

"Search and rescue is an interesting vocation. How did you get started in that?"

"When I was ten my younger brother got lost in the woods while my family was on a camping trip. He was gone almost twenty-four hours. My parents and I were terrified we would never see him again. The search and rescue people saved the day. Later on in college I realized I wanted to help people like my family had been helped." She paused. Why was she telling this virtual stranger all of this? What about Lyle had her talking so much?

He matched his pace to her slower one. "You and your kind are special people. I worked with a few of you while I was in the army. Did you do your training there?"

"No. I didn't start that until after college. While I was in school I worked at the vet clinic at the university. I was there most weekends as a volunteer. Some of the dogs were retired search dogs. After working with them I had no doubt what I should be doing."

"It sounds like an exciting way to make a living." He sounded truly impressed.

Sometimes it could be too exciting. She had no interest in reliving the last few months of her life. "It can be, but it also has its downsides. It's awful to see people desperately searching for loved ones or learn that a family member can't be saved."

"I know what you mean. War can do devastating things to a body. Trying to piece it back together can be the stuff of nightmares." His sincerity convinced Cass he understood all too well.

In spite of her determined efforts to conceal her private hell, she was feeling uncomfortably vulnerable yet again. "I'd rather not compare notes on what we've seen." Her last assignment was at the top of the list.

"You're right. Some things are better left in the past."

Cass couldn't agree more. She'd had enough issues generated in the recent past to last her a lifetime. She wobbled when she stepped into a snow-covered dip in the ground.

His hand nestled in her elbow. "How's that leg feeling?"

"Like a building fell on it and it had more PT than it liked."

"I bet it does. You're doing too much. A walk outside might have been over the top." He moved the torch so that it illuminated the snow in front of her.

"I'm handling it." She was, just barely though.

"I spoke to Flora and she said you might have overdone things today."

She pulled her arm from his hold. "Are you going around checking up on me?"

"That's part of my job." Nothing in Lyle's voice was apologetic.

Cass stepped as far away from him as the path would allow. "Well, I'll have you know I don't need a babysitter."

"I'll keep that in mind. I also understand you're in a

big hurry to leave us. You know, you can hurt people's feelings with that attitude."

When was the last time she had been teased? Her personality didn't make people do that often. "I'm not as interested in people's feelings as I am in getting my leg and arm well again. You do know I could've made it back by myself. All I had to do was come out the gate and follow the fence back."

"That may have been so, but I couldn't take the chance of you getting lost. It looks bad in the press for the clinic to lose a patient."

No matter how she tried to push him away, or how close she came to rudeness, he seemed to take it in stride. She had to appreciate his sense of humor and self-assurance. He had an ability to make her smile even when she didn't want to or feel like it.

A whimper from somewhere up ahead caught Cass's attention. Her senses went on full alert. She searched the ground for who or what was making the noise. Her reaction came from years of being vigilant at her job. Unable to see clearly in the small amount of light, she angled her head to listen. There it was again.

Lyle turned his flashlight toward a hedge nearby. The sound came again. It was animal, not human. This time Lyle stepped in the direction of it.

"Do you hear that?"

"Yes." She didn't move from her spot. The noises brought back painful memories. Like the ones Rufus had made just before he'd died.

"It's an animal in trouble." Lyle took small steps toward the shrubbery, making the light arc back and forth. The whimper came again, and he focused the beam in that spot. "It's a dog."

Cass's chest tightened. She couldn't deal with a dog right now. Even a stray.

"Hey, buddy, do you need some help?" Lyle asked in a tender, soothing tone. His shoulder moved as if he were reaching out a hand.

There was a growl.

Cass still remained rooted where she was. She couldn't make herself step forward.

"We can't leave it out here in the cold. It looks like it's starving." Lyle reached out his hand again.

Another growl.

Lyle spoke over his shoulder. "If I can get it to come to me I'll take it to the canine therapy center. Esme will check it out and see about it."

Cass forced herself to take a step closer. She looked over Lyle's back to where the light was directed. He reached forward once more.

The dog snarled, showing its teeth.

"It doesn't look like it's going to let me take it. I can't just leave it here. I'm afraid it'll freeze before morning."

Cass was shocked back to reality. The animal was so obviously undernourished. It shook in the cold. Its big brown eyes had a pitiful, fearful look. Cass's heart lurched. She had to do something. Everything in her that made her vulnerable to getting hurt again reached out to this pathetic animal. She didn't want to care but couldn't help herself.

Lyle didn't understand Cass's standoffishness. After all, she had worked with a dog. He glanced back at her. She just stood there, staring at him and the dog. "I don't recognize it as anybody's around here. I know them as well as I know their owners."

Finally, Cass blinked and stepped forward, but there

was little enthusiasm on her face. "Let me see if I can help." She went down on her knees, paying no attention to the wetness that must be seeping into her jeans. Removing a glove, she reached out her hand, letting the small scruffy dog smell her.

The dog slowly extended its nose. It obviously liked Cass far better than him. It crawled out from under the hedge and came to Cass. Just a puppy, it was small with muddy matted hair. One of its ears stood up while the other flopped. It had an oddly patterned coat, making it look of mixed breed. Cass lifted the dog to her chest.

Lyle stood. "It figures. I've always been far better with people than animals. It likes you."

Cass gave him a dry smile. When she struggled to stand he helped her.

"The canine therapy center is right down this way. Not far. Just behind the castle. It used to be the stables. It's just through the woods." He led them back to the path. "We'll take it there. Esme will see to it."

Cass didn't say anything as she came to stand beside him. As they walked she held the dog close but not overly so. Was she afraid of the dog? Or was there more going on? Lyle would have thought she'd be the first in on a rescue.

Soon they reached the center. The lights were still on. "Esme must be keeping another late night. I'm glad I didn't have to call and get her out in the weather again. She's the veterinarian. This therapy center/veterinary center is Esme's brainchild." He hurried ahead and held the door for Cass.

She moved in past him.

"Esme, it's Lyle," he called as the door closed behind him.

"Hey, be there in a sec," came Esme's voice from another room.

She soon appeared with a broad smile on her face. Her short blonde hair was disheveled, as if she had been running her hands through it. "What's going on?"

Lyle nodded toward Cass, who still held the dog. "We have a patient for you."

Esme looked at the dog then gave Cass a questioning look.

"Esme, this is Cass Bellow, one of our new residents. She hasn't made it down to meet the dogs yet, so you haven't met her."

"Welcome, Cass. So, who do you have there?" Esme reached for the dog.

It growled.

"Aw, I see you have that special touch," Esme said, speaking to Cass. "Bring it back here and I'll give it a look." Esme led them down a short hall into an examination room. "Put it on the table."

Cass did as she was told.

Esme went to touch the dog again and it rumbled a complaint deep in its chest.

"I'll give him something to ease his anxiety." Esme went to draw up a syringe of medicine.

"Apparently Cass has that special something with animals." Lyle looked at her, expecting to see a positive expression, but instead she appeared distraught. What was wrong?

Esme quickly and efficiently gave the dog an injection. It soon rested easily in Cass's arms. "You can put him on the table now. He shouldn't be any trouble."

Cass placed the dog on the metal table and backed away. "I think you have this now." She looked at him. "I can find my way back to the castle from here."

Cass was out the door before Lyle could stop her.

"She seemed in a hurry," Esme murmured as she started examining the dog.

Lyle agreed. That accompanied intense curiosity about the stricken look on Cass face as she'd fled.

The next evening Lyle entered the dining room. A number of the residents were already there and engrossed in conversation. Cass wasn't one of them. He hadn't seen her since the night before. The few times he had left his office during the day she hadn't been anywhere in sight. After her reaction to the dog he'd been very interested in how she was doing.

Everyone was seated at the table and the food was ready to serve when Cass entered the room. Relief washed through him. He had feared he was going to have to go and find her and he hadn't been looking forward to the conversation that would have taken place.

She was dressed in a simple white button-down shirt and jeans. On her feet were the same boots she'd worn the night before. Her hair was brushed back and it didn't look as if she had any makeup on. There was a fresh, simple air about Cass that appealed to him. Something he was completely unprepared for.

For too long he'd held onto Freya because she had been something safe and secure in a world he'd been unable to control. He had been too young, too unsure of life and couldn't see that before he'd gone overseas. Still, the way their relationship had ended had colored how he viewed potential partners. He was gun-shy, and he'd be the first to admit it. The next time he got involved with a woman he wanted it to be a mature, mutual lifelong commitment. That certainly couldn't be with a resident who would soon be gone and had her own life thousands of miles away. He needed to stop any kind of thoughts like the ones he was having now.

"We're glad to have you join us," he informed Cass as he stood and pulled out the chair next to him. Smiling, he added, "I was worried I might have to go out in the weather to hunt you down."

She gave the therapy dog belonging to the resident on the other side of her a long uncertain look before taking the offered seat. "It isn't because I didn't think about skipping out."

"I'm glad you changed your mind."

She gave him a direct look. "Hunger pangs changed it for me."

He nodded. "Whatever the reason, I'm glad you're here. Let me introduce you to everyone."

"You don't—" She didn't finish the sentence when those at the table turned to look at her.

"Everyone, this is Cass." Lyle then went round the table, giving each person's name. They either nodded or said hello to her as he went. She offered them all a tight smile.

The food was served family style out of large bowls and platters, passed around the table. Cass only took small amounts of a few items. At this rate she would never gain back the weight he suspected she had lost.

"I thought you might like to know that the puppy we found last night is doing well. Esme said he's fine except for being underweight. He should make a full recovery."

"That's good." She started picking at her meal.

Cass wasn't helping much with making conversation. Lyle made another effort. "She's going to ask around and see if anyone claims him."

"That's nice." Cass took a bite of food as if she loathed doing it.

Roger, the man sitting on the other side of her, asked her a question. Cass gave him a two-word answer. Apparently, she didn't want to carry on a conversation with anyone. But she needed to. If he had ever seen someone badly in need of interaction, it was Cass.

He tried another approach. "I see the residents and staff have been busy in here today. It looks festive."

Cass looked around as if she was seeing the room for the first time.

How could she not react to the greenery and red bows hanging from the chandeliers, along with the large matching centerpiece of green boughs, velvet bows, and crimson balls? Or the mantel filled with decorations? In his experience it was the kind of stuff women loved.

Other than her hesitant look at the dog beside her, she appeared unaware of everything and everyone. He'd forced Cass into noticing him, but only for an all-too-brief moment. For some reason he wanted her to initiate an interaction with him. He wanted her to like him.

Lyle transferred his attention to Alice, who sat on his other side. Maybe giving Cass space would help open her up a bit. He and Alice carried on a lively conversation about the upcoming village Christmas market beginning this weekend. They went on to discuss some of the other events planned for the festive season, like the annual Christmas festival at the castle, and the live nativity in the village.

"I was told there would be a tree lighting in the village and a parade in a few weeks." Alice's eyes lit up with excitement.

"There is and they even include some of the dogs from the center."

He glanced at Cass a few times during the discussion and caught her listening. When she saw him looking, she focused on her food again. He decided to try to draw her into conversation once more. "Cass, do you like craft markets?"

Her head jerked up. "I…uh… I do."

"Then you'll want to be sure and catch the minibus into Cluchlochry on Saturday morning. The village has a pretty impressive one. Great place to buy Christmas presents."

"I'll think about it." She pushed back her chair. "Right now I need to go for a walk before it gets dark."

"Hey, before you go could I speak to you for a moment in private?"

Her expression said no. Yet she answered, "Okay, but just for a minute. I really want to walk."

"I promise not to take up too much of your time." He rose when she did and followed her into the hall. "Why don't we go to the lounge?" With a hand he directed her down the hall. She headed that way and he joined her. They turned a corner and entered another hall. At the first doorway, Lyle opened the door to the large room with numerous sitting areas. A fire roared in the fireplace in the center of the main wall. Windows filled the opposite side.

"Why don't we have a seat?"

"I'm starting to feel like I'm being brought into the principal's office. You could have gotten on to me about not going to canine therapy again today in the hall outside the dining room." Cass sat on the edge of a cushion of the closest sofa.

"I could have, but I'm more interested in finding out why you're so resistant to the idea of canine therapy. Especially since I know your job entailed working closely with a dog. I assume you at least like animals a bit. I noticed you were slow to help with the dog we found and left the center as quickly as you could. I read in your file that you lost your partner." He didn't miss the stricken look that flickered in her eyes. "Is that what the problem is? I'd like to help. The staff here would like to help."

Cass shot to her feet. "I don't want your help or anyone else's. If you want me to go to canine therapy, fine. I'll be there tomorrow."

"There you are." Charles walking toward them stopped anything further Cass might have said.

Lyle came to his feet. "Hi, Charles. I'd like you to meet Cassandra Bellow. She's one of our newest residents. Cass, this is Dr. Charles Ross-Wylde. Also the Laird of Heatherglen and Esme's brother."

Charles smiled at Cass. "It's nice to meet you. Please call me Charles."

"Hello. You have a lovely home…castle." Cass's words were tight and formal. She glanced toward the door.

Charles chuckled. "Thank you. You're American, aren't you?"

"I am."

"You must be the woman who works in search and rescue?" He gave her an earnest look. "Interesting job."

"It can be." Cass looked toward the door again. "Why don't I let you two talk?" She slipped away.

Lyle watched her go. He had no doubt Cass would keep her word about going to therapy. How much she would get out of it was another question. He'd just have to trust that the dog she was paired with would do what was needed to help her heal.

"Lyle."

He looked at Charles, who was grinning at him with twinkling eyes. "What?"

"You like her, don't you?"

"Why would you say that?" Lyle didn't want to discuss his confused reactions to Cass Bellow. Not even with his best friend Charles.

He laughed. "Because I called your name three times before you answered!"

Lyle wanted to groan. Now Charles would ask questions every time he saw him. "Did you have something important you wanted to talk to me about?"

Charles looked at him with a knowing smile on his lips. "It isn't as interesting as Ms. Bellow but we need to talk about Andy and his progress."

"Ah. Why don't we go to my office to do that?"

Cass was still stomping and swinging her arms in exasperation when she reached the main road after the long walk down the castle drive. How dared Lyle treat her as if she were a disobedient child? She was doing her physical therapy. Aware of what she needed, it wasn't canine therapy. But he wasn't going to give up.

She'd gone to dinner like he wanted, wasn't that enough? She would go to the canine therapy center tomorrow all right, but her participation in the therapy would be minimal and uncooperative. That should keep him off her case.

"Be strong," she said to the trees, and shoved her hands into her jacket pockets. When her brother had been lost, her mother and father had hugged her too tightly and had constantly reminded her they all had to remain strong. Afterwards Cass had used the mantra "Be strong" whenever she'd felt helpless. Even now, years later, she was using it to defy that feeling.

"Be strong!" she yelled to the sky.

She'd been strong when Jim had broken her heart,

then soon after that when she'd learned that Rufus was gone. She'd been strong when the doctors had warned her she might never regain full use of her crushed arm and leg. She had been strong during the grueling hospital stay. During her agonizing physical therapy sessions here. Only it didn't matter how strong she was. Nothing changed. She was alone with no one to lean on.

The sound of a vehicle coming up the road drew her attention. The driver was going too fast for the icy conditions. As it came around the curve the back end went one way and then the other. The skid landed the front end of the car in the stone wall between Cass and the road.

She hurried out the castle gate and over to the car with her heart pounding, ignoring the ache in her leg. The engine was still running even though the hood was crumpled. The hot air of the radiator hitting the cold air created stream, making it difficult to see.

Cass reached out to touch the side of the car with a shaking hand. She'd not done any rescue work or even given anyone medical attention since her last assignment. Now here she was faced with an accident without the support of her partner. Could she do it? Would she break down and cry? She inhaled deeply, bracing herself. "Stay strong."

She ran her hand down the side of the car to keep her bearings as she worked her way to the driver's door. Cass pulled it open. She could, would, get through this.

The driver groaned, his palm pressed to his forehead.

"Are you okay?" Her instinct and training kicked in. "Don't move. You could have more injuries."

"I'm fine." His words were slurred.

She placed a hand on the man's shoulder. "I'm an

EMT. I know what I'm talking about. More help will be here soon."

The man pulled his hand away from his head. Blood covered it.

"Don't move," she said firmly. "Keep your head back. I'm going to reach in and turn the engine off." She found the ignition key and turned it. The steam dissipated.

There was a moan from the back seat. She had someone else to check on. If she only had a cellphone to call for help. Hers had been damaged in her accident and she hadn't had time to replace it yet. Surely the driver had one. "Sir, do you have a phone? Tell me where it is, don't try to find it yourself."

The man gave her a weak yes and told her it was in his jacket pocket. Cass carefully reached inside his pocket and retrieved it.

Cass quickly dialed 999. When a person answered, Cass gave the call handler all the necessary information. She then stepped to the rear passenger door. Pulling it open, she found crumpled in the footwell a lady of around sixty. "You're going to be fine. I know you're in an uncomfortable position but try not to move."

The woman groaned, but Cass knew from the sound she was barely conscious. Using her fingers, Cass searched for a pulse in the woman's neck. She located one but it wasn't strong.

A voice she recognized as Lyle's said from behind her, "Don't move her. She may have concussion."

Cass said over her shoulder, "I've already told her that. And I've already called for help."

"I know. I must have called right after you."

She needed to get the man's bleeding under control. "Do you have any supplies?"

"No. I was on my way home when I heard the crash."

Cass stood. "You see about this woman and I'll look for a first-aid kit."

She worked her way to the front passenger door. Opening it, she searched the glove compartment for anything they could use. All she found was a stack of napkins. Those would have to do.

"Cass, we need to lay this lady down on the seat so I can examine her properly," Lyle said.

"Okay, take these napkins and have the man hold them to his head. I'll crawl in the back and help lift the woman up."

Lyle accepted the napkins and applied them to the man's head. "I need to get him to the clinic to stitch him up, but first we need to take care of this woman. She's lost consciousness."

Cass had been busy climbing into the backseat on her knees while he talked. Her leg rebelled at the position but she continued. She reached under the woman's arms and locked her hands across her chest. To Lyle she said, "Ready?"

"On three. One, two, three."

Cass pulled the woman against her chest. As the woman's back came up on the seat, Lyle grabbed her ankles and lifted. Soon they had her lying across the seat. She moaned and her eyelids flickered.

"Will you check her pulse and heart rate while I see if she has any internal injuries?" Lyle asked, as he started pressing on the woman's midsection.

"Her heart rate is steady but not very strong," Cass reported.

"Okay. So far I can't find any additional injuries." He continued to examine the woman.

A minibus pulled out of the castle gate and drew up alongside them.

"We need to get them both up to the clinic where I can give them a thorough evaluation." Lyle continued searching for problems.

Cass looked at the top of his head as he worked. "Shouldn't we wait on an ambulance?"

"That'll take too long. It has to come from Fort William. We're the emergency care for this area."

"Really?"

Now he met her look. "Rural area. That's how it is."

That made sense.

He was an impressive man to assume the responsibility for so many lives.

The staff member who had been driving the minibus joined them.

"Ron," Lyle said, "we need to get these people to the clinic ASAP. The man should be able to sit up front. We'll need the stretcher for the woman."

Ron nodded and headed back to the minibus.

Lyle backed out of the car. "Cass, would you please continue to monitor her while I have a look at the man?"

"Okay." Cass picked up the woman's wrist and placed two fingers on the inside. It took a second but she located a pulse. Still shallow but steady.

"I'm going to get this man into the minibus," Lyle called. "You good there?"

"Yes." Cass remained focused on the woman, trying not to think about her own recovering leg and arm as she began to worry about the injured woman being exposed to the cold. "Bring a blanket if you've got one."

"Will do." A few minutes later Lyle returned, pushing a gurney with Ron's help. "It's going to take all of us to get her loaded."

The two men positioned the gurney right outside the door.

Lyle handed her the blanket. Cass spread it over the woman. He tucked it around her legs. "Cass, if you'll support her head and shoulders while Ron and I get on either side of her and lift her out, I think we can make it work."

Cass wasn't looking forward to the pain she was sure would rocket through her leg and arm from the exertion. That didn't matter. Caring for the hurt woman was more important. Cass worked her hands under the woman's shoulder blades and supported her head with her upper arms. "Ready."

"Okay Ron. One, two, lift!"

Slowly the two men maneuvered the woman over the seat onto the gurney. Keeping the woman's upper body and neck as straight and stable as possible, Cass crawled across the seat and out the other door. By then electrifying pain was coursing through every nerve of her leg. Her arms and back were convulsing under the strain. When she tried to stand, her traumatized leg gave way. She grabbed the gurney. Though it wobbled on its wheels, she managed to balance on her other leg.

"Damn," Lyle swore as he reached for her. "I can't believe I got so caught up in what was happening I forgot you were a recovering patient. Sit down." He guided her to a seat of the vehicle. Giving her a stern look, Lyle ordered, "Stay there while we get this lady loaded."

Cass hated to admit it but she was relieved to sit. Her eyes were watering from intense pain. As she took a moment, emotions swamped her. Her loss of direction, missing Rufus, the fog of her future all came down on her. Sorrow tightened her chest.

Lyle gave her a concerned look. For a second Cass

feared he would question her but instead he said, "Ron, let's get this woman strapped down and loaded." Mere moments later he returned to her. "It's your turn."

Clenching her jaw, she stood. No matter how sick and unsure she felt inside, Cass refused to let it show, even if she had to struggle to do it. She feared Lyle was too perceptive and had already guessed. Cass said with more confidence than she felt, "I can walk."

"Maybe so, but you aren't going down on my watch." He wrapped an arm around her waist and guided her to the back of the vehicle.

Hot awareness of his strong sturdy body zipped through Cass as Lyle held her tight. Unable to stop herself, she leaned against him. After hesitating a moment, she rested her arm around his middle back and hobbled to the minibus. She couldn't ignore the sensations simmering in her core any more than she could ignore her agonizing leg.

Lyle held her steady until she reached for the frame of the door. Cass was climbing into the minibus when she was lifted off her feet and placed gently on the floor. She looked over her shoulder. "Thanks."

"No problem. Have a seat and move down." Lyle wasted no words. He was all business.

She did as she was told, scooting down to the end of the small bench seat. Lyle joined her. Their bodies touched all the way along one side. Strangely she wanted to rest her head against his shoulder but she resisted the urge. She refused to show any more weakness. What would Lyle think of her if she had given in to that impulse?

Ron close the doors. They were soon moving. Lyle's attention remained on the woman on the gurney, which was locked to the floor with straps. She still hadn't regained consciousness. Lyle took her pulse as they rode. He gave Cass a nod.

From what Lyle had said, Cass assumed that they were headed to the castle. By the winding of the road she could tell she was right. After making a big circle, Ron backed the minibus to a stop. Seconds later he opened the door.

Lyle climbed out with one agile move. "You stay put," he told her. "I don't want you to fall. Someone will be out to get you." He didn't wait for her response before he and Ron unhooked the gurney and rolled the woman inside.

Cass forced herself not to shake. Memories of lying in the rubble of that building flooded back. The sound of her calling Rufus's name and him not answering. The waiting until someone could get to her. Panic rose when Lyle didn't come. Pain throbbed through her body. She needed to get out of here.

She searched the area she could see. It was a part of the castle she wasn't familiar with. The vehicle was backed up to a small loading dock with two double doors. Her impatience grew to be an almost living thing. She had to do something. What if Lyle needed her help? Just as she was about to rise, Ron came through the doors, leaving them swinging. He gave her a glance then hurried down the steps nearby. Her heart dipped. He must be going after the man up front.

With Ron and Lyle concentrating their energies on the injured people, it would be some time before someone would come to assist her. She decided she wasn't in so much pain that she couldn't get herself inside.

Giving her leg a rub, she pushed up off the bench, making sure she didn't use her right arm. It took effort. With a tight jaw she made it to her feet. She slowly moved out of the minibus, steadying herself by pressing her hand on the side of it. Just as she was stepping off, the doors swung open again and out came Melissa, pushing a wheelchair.

She positioned the wheelchair just outside the van doors and stepped inside. "Lyle sent me out for you. He said you wouldn't stay seated long. I guess he was right."

Cass didn't like Lyle thinking he knew her that well, but she couldn't deny he was right. She took a step forward, trying to keep as much weight as possible off the leg. Cass couldn't deny the wheelchair was welcome.

"Here, let me help." Melissa supported Cass to the chair and assisted her into it.

With Cass secure, she pushed her inside. They entered a large emergency examination room complete with all the most up-to-date equipment. Cass was fascinated. She'd had no idea this area of the clinic existed. There were many facets to Dr. Sinclair and his "clinic".

Lyle stood beside the older lady, who still lay on the gurney. Thankfully she was now conscious and talking to him. Ron was busy cleaning the driver's head wound at an exam table nearby.

"What can I do to help?" Cass asked, putting her hands on the arm of the wheelchair, preparing to stand.

Lyle gave her a piercing look of reprimand. "Nothing. You've done enough. You need to take care of yourself."

"Surely you need some help." Cass looked from him to the man Ron was seeing to and back.

Another member of the nursing staff rushed in. Behind her came another.

"We have plenty of help. Melissa, please see that Cass gets to her room. I'll let Flora know what's happened. She may want to examine you. Melissa, Cass actually might also benefit from some time in the hot tub." Lyle's attention returned to his patient.

Seconds later Cass was being wheeled out of the room. It didn't take Melissa long to get her up to her room and hot water running in the tub. Cass gratefully slipped into the whirling water, looking forward to the relief it would bring her leg and arm. She'd survived her first emergency without Rufus. It had been a sad moment but somehow an encouraging one. In a small way, Cass was moving forward.

Lyle was ready for some rest but he needed to check on Cass first. The ambulance from Fort William had arrived to take the injured woman to the hospital. Lyle had stitched the gash on the man's forehead and sent him home with family members. After a quick check on Cass he was headed for his cottage and bed. The adrenalin spike of handling an emergency had worn him out.

He knocked lightly on Cass's door in case she was already sleeping. After waiting a minute and getting no answer, he turned to leave. He would see her tomorrow.

The door opened a crack. "Yes?"

He could only see a sliver of her but it was enough to tell that her hair had been pushed back and her face was freshly scrubbed. She looked adorable and unsure at the same time.

What was it about her that captivated him? That pulled at him like no other woman he knew did. Was it her strength? Determination? Her vulnerability? He needed to solve the puzzle and move on. Cass wouldn't be here long and he wasn't going to waste his emotions on anyone he didn't intend to keep forever. He'd already gone down that road.

The dirty street behind him was graveled with disappointment and heartache. He had vowed the lane ahead would be paved with the love and loyalty of a woman who wanted him as much as he did her. A lifelong partner. The next time he fell in love, he would get it right.

He shoved that fantasy aside and concentrated on what he was there for. "How're you doing?"

"Better after a hot bath."

"Good. You were impressive out there, Cass. You stayed in control. I know you must have been in pain. You should have said something. More than that, I should've thought." Guilt filled him. "I'm sorry."

She opened the door wider. "Hey, I'm an EMT. I'm trained to help."

"True, but you're also a patient here. I should have remembered that." She looked cute in her T-shirt with her pink-tipped toes.

"I'm fine." For once her eyes weren't clouded with hidden feelings. In fact, there was a hint of a smile in them.

"I'm glad. Then I'll let you get some rest." He needed to go. Right now. He started down the hall.

"Hey, Lyle."

He almost kept going, but curiosity got the better of him.

"You were pretty impressive out there too."

He smiled. It felt good to have someone praise him, especially Cass. He was confident in his abilities, but it didn't hurt to have others notice. His father certainly hadn't. "Thanks. Sleep well, Cass."

CHAPTER FOUR

CASS'S HAND SHOOK as she wrapped it around the handle of the glass door of the canine therapy center the next afternoon. She had said she'd keep her appointment and she would. But she wasn't looking forward to it.

The thought of having anything to do with a dog made her want to break down and cry. The pain of losing Rufus was still too raw. It might be silly for a grown professional woman to feel this way, but she didn't care. Rufus was gone. Some part of her clung to the irrational hope he would be waiting with his tail wagging when she returned home. No other dog could replace him.

She would do what she had to, then hurry to her room for a good cry.

When she jerked the door open the young man sitting behind the desk started. This was the same high-ceilinged room with the rough board walls where she and Lyle had brought the puppy a couple of nights before. He'd said it used to be the stables and she could now see that. The other night all that'd filled her mind was that she had a dog in her arms.

"Can I help you?" the man at the desk asked.

"I'm Cass Bellow. I'm a resident at the clinic."

He looked down as if checking a list, then back at her. "Oh, yes, we've been expecting you." As he got to his feet he added, "Come with me. Margaret assists with the canine therapy program. She's back here."

Cass forced her feet to move and followed him down a hall. It wasn't the same one Lyle and Esme had led her down to the examination room the other night. The man pushed through a swing door. Cass entered a room furnished with easy chairs.

A dark-haired woman was down on her heels next to a woman seated in an easy chair holding a small black dog of no pedigree. Cass recognized the woman in the chair from the dinner table at the clinic. Lyle had introduced them, but Cass didn't remember her name. Shame pricked her. She hadn't even tried.

"Margaret, this is Cass Bellow," the man announced.

The dark-haired woman looked at them, stood and came toward Cass with one hand outstretched. She smiled. "It's great to finally meet you."

Was that her subtle way of reprimanding her for not showing up for her earlier appointments? The temptation to run grew.

"I help Esme with the canine therapy here at Heatherglen," Margaret continued.

The man quietly left the way they had come in.

Staring at the small dog that was enjoying the woman's gentle pats, Cass's chest tightened. She wasn't ready for this. She had no interest in doing *anything* with a dog.

Margaret was saying, "I thought you might like to meet Muffin. He's a sweet little dog. He'll be your companion during your stay. Let me get him and you can get acquainted." She stepped through a side door.

Cass stood, knees shaking, in the middle of the room, looking everywhere but at the other woman. She didn't want any responsibility for a dog for the next month.

Especially one named Muffin. Her breathing became shallow. Her mouth turned dry. She shifted from one foot to the other. The need to leave intensified. This was too much. A meltdown was building if she didn't get out of there. She wasn't ready, might not ever be. What if she became too attached to the ridiculous Muffin? She would be leaving soon. All this pain would be there again.

Without thought Cass bolted for the door and up the hall to the front room. She had to get out of there. Ignoring the man behind the desk calling her name, she shoved the door open and stumbled into the cold air. Sucking in a deep breath, she kept going, heading toward the castle. By way of a side door she'd found yesterday, she slipped inside unnoticed.

Instead of going to her room, where someone would surely look for her, she headed for the conservatory. While exploring she'd also found an alcove hidden behind some large palm plants and banana trees with only a small sofa. There she could lick her wounds in private.

Relief washed through her when she found the floral fabric-covered settee empty. She sat, pulling her legs up under her and wrapping the coat Lyle had loaned her tighter. When would the pain go away?

She had no idea how long she had been sitting there staring off into space when she heard, "Cass?"

Lyle.

She stiffened. How had he found her? It didn't matter. She had no intention of explaining herself. Why couldn't he just leave her alone? "Go away."

He just stood there.

Finally, she murmured, "How did you know where to find me?"

"I saw you come in here. When I had a call from the center I knew where to look."

Great. She'd believed she'd made her escape. Her focus remained on the green spots showing in the snow that was melting outside. "So now you're riding to the rescue."

Lyle came to sit beside her. "I'd just like to help. Be a friend. I was told you looked upset."

Maybe if she ignored him he would go away. Instead of him taking the hint to leave, he settled further back into the cushions, his big body almost touching hers. They remained like that for a while, neither saying anything.

"You're not leaving, are you?" Cass stared at the dust motes dancing in the sunbeam streaming through the glass.

"Not until I know you're okay." He stretched his legs out and crossed his ankles.

She huffed. "Let me assure you I'm not going to harm myself."

"I didn't think that but it's good to hear."

He settled back as though he was content to stay the rest of the day. As the silence between them grew so did her temper. She hissed, "What do I have to say to get you to leave?"

For a moment she thought he was ignoring her. When he did reply, concern laced his voice. "I'd like to understand why you're determined to have no part in our canine therapy program, especially since you work with a dog all the time."

Could she tell him? Would he understand? Was that the only way to get him to leave her alone? If he knew, maybe he would see to it she didn't have to go to canine therapy.

She opened her mouth to tell him about Rufus but the words stuck in her throat. If she said it out loud, then it would make it true. She didn't want that. Couldn't live with that. She closed her eyes tight. Maybe if she said it really fast she could get it out. "Rufus, my partner, died. Now I don't know if I can be around a dog all the time."

The moisture she had been banking for days seeped out of her closed eyelids. She took a deep breath in an effort to stop the sob welling in her throat but it didn't work. Instead she doubled over in agony. As she tried to catch her breath Lyle ran his large hand across her back in a comforting stroke.

Then he cupped her shoulder and pulled her against his chest. She buried her face in his shirt, her fingers clutching his sides. All the emotions she had held in check since the day that wall had collapsed flowed freely. The pain deep within her consumed her. Rufus was gone. Life as she'd known it had gone with him.

Lyle held her close, rubbing her shoulders and back. "Let it all out," he whispered.

Cass did. All the raw feelings she'd held in check for weeks flowed, leaving her nothing but a heaving shell. She couldn't stop the pain, fear and sorrow from escaping.

Lyle continued holding her and murmuring soft reassuring words while she clung to him.

She had no idea how much time had passed when she woke with a start. Disorientated, she still had a sense of safety. Slowly it dawned on her she was still in Lyle's arms.

Embarrassment flooded her. Placing her palms on his chest, she pushed into a sitting position. Yet one of his hands remained on her back.

"I'm so sorry for that ugly scene," she heard herself

saying. "I don't know why I fell apart like that. It isn't like me."

"I'd imagine it was because you needed to. You've been under a tremendous strain." He shifted, putting his hands on his thighs.

She missed the reassuring weight immediately. Lyle was right, there was a lot of stress and emotion involved in her profession. She should be able to handle it. But where Rufus was concerned she was lost. Cass wiped at his sweater. "I've made a mess of your clothes."

"I don't mind. I'm glad I was here to help." He sounded as if he meant it.

"So part of your job description is to have patients cry all over you?" Cass managed a weak smile.

He looked at her tenderly. "Not all patients. I have to say you're a special case."

Warmth gradually replaced the coldness running through her. Lyle was a nice man saying all the right things. For an instant she wished he wasn't a doctor speaking to a patient.

"I knew about you losing your dog, it was in your file. But I had no idea that going to canine therapy would be so difficult for you. You've had a tough time physically and…" he paused "…emotionally. Flora, Esme and I didn't recognize that. I'm sorry. Would you like to talk about what happened? I'm a good listener." His words were encouraging, not demanding.

Cass shook her head, both in response and to clear it.

He waited a few moments then asked, "When did you learn the details of what happened?"

"I realized the wall was falling but I had no idea…" She swallowed. Her throat was tight and dry. Inhaling, she fought through the final pang of denial. "I didn't find out Rufus didn't make it until I woke up in the hospital. When I asked about him, one of the nurses had to ask around for the information."

Lyle put his arm around her shoulders again and gave her a supportive squeeze. "I'm sorry. It shouldn't have happened like that."

Cass continued to look at the windowsill. It was such a large one. Almost big enough to use as a seat. "No matter when I was told, or how, it wouldn't have made... the terrible truth any easier to hear."

"Maybe not, but at the very least the news should have been given to you in a sensitive manner." He sounded irritated on her behalf. "Will you tell me about your dog?"

She didn't want to, but he deserved to know why she'd just sobbed herself into an exhausted sleep all over him. "Rufus was more than my dog. He was my partner and best friend."

And her longest relationship. He been there more than once when a relationship with a man had ended. Those guys had either been intimidated by a woman who handled such an emotionally demanding job, or they didn't like her leaving for weeks at a time on the spur of the moment. For a couple of them her relationship with Rufus had been a bone of contention. They'd wanted all her attention and hadn't understood the uncanny connection between her and her canine partner. Now she had physical scars that they might find offensive, too.

Jim, the latest and the man she'd believed was The One, had felt her job was too risky. It had been nice to have someone worry over her at first, but it had soon started to feel restrictive. Despite their breakup he'd been kind enough to call her while she'd been in the hospital, but it had soon turned into a conversation that was more about him telling her *I told you so* than about his real concern for her. There had been no sympathy on his part for Rufus. She'd thought at one time they might have a chance at a real life together. Sadly, she'd really cared for Jim but there was no hope of that after their conversation.

Lyle removed his arm. She wanted it back. It was comforting. "How long was this dog your partner?"

"Four years. He was two when I got him. We spent the first eight weeks in training. He was born in Germany. Most good rescue dogs are. The Germans are known for breeding them to be work dogs. In fact, most of his commands I gave in German." It felt better, and was easier, to talk about Rufus than she'd imagined.

"Interesting." Lyle waited.

She looked at him. His expectant expression suggested he was truly interested in what she was saying. Yet she couldn't imagine him actually caring.

"How did you train together?"

"Are you really interested?" What if he was just asking to keep her talking as part of her "therapy"? None of the men she had known before him had cared one way or another. Why would he be any different?

"Aye. I wouldn't have asked if I wasn't." His voice carried concern. It had been so long since she'd heard that in a man's voice, it struck a deep chord within her.

"I had to do a written test and have a physical. Then I had to have a home visit so the powers-that-be knew I could care for a working dog. An animal like Rufus can cost as much as ten thousand American dollars so handlers are vetted closely. That kind of money can't be wasted. Rufus had to have a physical as well, and learn obedience basics and detection, especially body odor recognition. It was pretty intense for both of us."

"A powerful bonding experience for you both."

Cass's chest tightened from the memories. They had indeed bonded. She had loved the dog, heart and soul. At least Lyle *seemed* to understand. "Though he was only four, he was getting old for a working dog. Rufus was going to have to retire soon. I had already put in the paperwork to take him after he was done."

"Going to canine therapy was almost like punishment for you. You should have said something." His distress was evident in his voice.

She looked away in horror. "And embarrass myself, like I did a few minutes ago?"

Lyle took hold of her hand. His was large, secure… comforting. "You haven't embarrassed yourself. It's okay to be human."

"Yeah, but blubbering all over you is a bit too human."

He leaned closer until his shoulder touched hers. "I didn't mind. I'm just sorry I kept pushing you into canine therapy."

"I figured you'd seen it in my file." She winced at how pitiful she sounded.

"Yeah, but that didn't mean I understood how close you were."

Great. He probably thought she had really gone off her rocker. "I don't know if I can handle being around a dog right now. I'll be leaving here in a few weeks and I, uh, just can't risk becoming attached to another one." What she wasn't telling him about was the heavy guilt she carried over the fact that Rufus had sacrificed himself to save her life. If he hadn't barked, she would have never looked up to see the wall starting to fall. Or that he'd jumped and pushed her out of the way. It had been a split second between her life and Rufus's death.

"I understand completely," Lyle said sincerely. "Would you consider an alternative kind of therapy, if we can come up with one? Maybe just helping out at the canine clinic. Not having a specific dog assigned to you."

She was doubtful it would work but she could try. At least he was trying to work with her. Somehow she had to get past this grief, rebuild her life emotionally and move on. Yet her heart protested with a fresh pang even as she said with caution, "That might work."

"If it doesn't, then we'll try something else." His sincere tone and expression convinced her he would at least listen if she complained. Lyle's comfort was the first she'd had since Rufus had died. She was going to hang onto it.

He let her hand go and shifted away. "Do you feel up to a bite to eat?"

"I don't want to go to the dining room."

"It's too late for that." He tilted his head toward the glass.

Cass was shocked to find it was dark. How long had they been sitting there? "I'm so sorry. I made you miss dinner."

"Not a problem. Mrs. Renwick will have left me something in the kitchen. Let's go see what we can find."

"I think I'll just go up to my room." She wanted to get away. Regain her composure.

"Nonsense. You must be hungry, and I could use the company while I eat."

She had kept Lyle from his hot meal. She owed him. "Okay, I can do that."

"Not the most excited acceptance I've been given to a dinner invitation, but I'll take it." He stood.

Cass liked his sense of humor. He seemed to take life as it came without too much angst. She lacked that ability. Her way of meeting life's challenges now consisted of worry, fear of failure and the guilty conviction she hadn't done enough to make a difference. She wanted to save everyone, give them what her family had received. The chances of achieving that desire were slim to none, but still it was her goal. Now she was just a mass of nerves, help to no one. Not even herself. Squaring her shoulders, she said, "I'll try to do better in the future."

He offered his hand. "That's what I like to hear. That old tough Cass. You had me worried there for a while."

Lyle still thought she was tough? She would have thought he would have seen her as the opposite after the last few hours. She took his hand just long enough to get to her feet. "How's that?"

He put his hands in his pockets and rocked back on his heels. "I don't handle crying females well."

"I'm sorry I made you uncomfortable." She couldn't meet his eyes.

"Hey, I'm glad I was here to help. Now, let's go and get some dinner." He started toward the hall and she joined him.

Lyle led the way to the kitchen. His heart went out to Cass. She was distraught over the loss of her dog. He knew well the empty hole loss could leave in your life. He had felt it intensely when Freya had left him. When he'd told Cass that he didn't handle women crying well, he hadn't been kidding. All he'd done was hold her.

The fact that he'd liked having her cry on his shoulder was a bit unnerving. What had begun as a professional obligation to check on a resident in crisis had ended in a very personal act of compassionate empathy.

Was he drawn to her because he could sense her private suffering? Whatever it was, Cass held some sort of spell over him. One he didn't mind being captivated by.

Cass followed him quietly to the kitchen, seeming fine with doing so. They walked through the now silent dining room to the swing door beside the fireplace. He held it open for her as they entered the large commercial-style kitchen.

"Have a seat at the table." There was a small wooden one next to two corner windows in the large room. "I'll see what I can find in the fridge."

Her chair scraped over the tile floor as she took a seat.

Opening one of the doors of the very large fridge, Lyle announced with deliberate cheer, "Ah, we have roast beef and vegetable soup. How does a sandwich and a bowl of hot soup sound?"

"That's fine."

He glanced over his shoulder. "Again, I was looking for a little more enthusiasm."

A fake smile contorted her lips as she swung a fist overhead. "Great!"

He grinned. "That's more like it."

"Can I help?"

"Sure." He started pulling bowls and a platter off the shelves. When Cass reached him he handed her a few of them. She carried them to the table. Lyle followed with the rest. "You unwrap the containers while I get plates and things together." He searched cabinets and drawers for what they needed, making a couple of trips to the table to put everything down. She was halfway through removing the plastic wrap from the bowls when he said, "Now I'll warm up the soup if you'll make the sandwiches."

"All right."

He pushed the uncut loaf towards her. "I'd like two thick slices."

"Noted." She picked up a bread knife and start cutting.

Lyle ladled soup from its storage container into a saucepan and turned on the stove. As he stirred, he watched Cass work.

Standing, she placed two slices of bread on a plate and buttered them. That done, she unwrapped the rest of the containers. Next she cut slices of roast beef, laying them on the bread. She finished with condiments and lettuce.

Cass's movements were concise and efficient. She had a no-nonsense way about her. Her blonde hair swung over her cheek and she pushed it back with impatience as if she had no time for things to get in her way. She cleaned up as she went. He got the distinct impression she took responsibility for herself and expected others to do the same for themselves. It must have been a rare event for her to let someone witness her raw emotions. Strangely, he was honored he had been the one there for her.

Lyle carried the steaming saucepan to the table and poured the soup into the bowls he'd found earlier, then returned the pan to the stove.

As he came to take his seat at the table Cass inhaled deeply. "That smells wonderful."

He grinned. "I can take credit for it being hot but not for how it smells."

She returned his smile and his heart made an extra thump. He filled the two tall glasses with milk. "Those sandwiches look good."

"I can take credit for how they look but not how they taste." Cass was trying to mimic his accent.

They both laughed as they settled onto their chairs.

She gave him a shy glance. "I don't do Scottish well, do I?"

"I'm going with it needs work." He looked at her over his sandwich just before he took a large bite. He appreciated the sparkle in her eyes that had replaced the earlier dull sadness.

They ate in silence for a few minutes before Cass let her spoon rest against the side of the bowl. "Do you know how the woman we helped is doing?"

He nodded. "I spoke to her doctor this morning. They kept her in overnight for observation, but she seems to be fine."

Cass lifted a spoonful of soup to her mouth. "I'm glad to hear it. How about the man?"

"He'll come in next week to have his stitches removed." Lyle took another bite of his sandwich.

"You really are a jack-of-all-trades, aren't you?" She appeared fascinated.

He rather liked that idea. In fact, he liked her. It had been too long since he'd let himself be drawn to a woman. It would be short-lived, of course, as Cass would be returning to the States soon, but why couldn't he enjoy her company while she was here? It would certainly make his Christmas more interesting. "I wouldn't exactly say that I'm Santa, spreading cheer, but I try to help out where I can."

They finished eating and Lyle started cleaning the table. "Even with my special powers I'd better do the washing-up if I don't want to get on the wrong side of Ms. Renwick."

"I'll help," Cass said in such a firm tone he didn't dare argue.

Together they covered the food and returned it to the refrigerator. His hand brushed hers as she handed him a bowl and he saw color bloom in her cheeks. Despite her tough exterior, her face couldn't conceal her attraction to him. Her gaze met his before she quickly returned to the table to pick up their plates.

Instead of joining him again, she went to the sink and turned on the water. Now she was trying to hide from him. With that in mind, he did his best as he finished clearing away to give Cass space while she washed up. He was aware enough of her to realize she was trying to avoid more contact between them. Was she attracted to him? Was she noticing his every move, as he did hers?

Cass turned toward him, her hip resting against the counter. "Didn't you say that Ms. Renwick leaves food for you?"

"She does, but that doesn't mean she isn't particular about how her kitchen is kept." Lyle stacked the bowls in the cabinet.

"So, if I'm not careful I'll end up on her wrong side?" Cass hung a dishcloth back just as it had been when they'd come into the kitchen.

"I wouldn't worry about it too much, she's really a softy at heart."

Despite his assurance, they stood at the door and gave the kitchen one last look before they exited the room.

"I don't think we've left anything out of place," Cass said as the door swung closed behind them. "My mother is just as particular about her kitchen."

"I'm sure Ms. Renwick will be pleased." That was the first time she'd revealed a personal detail without being asked. He was delighted she had begun to open up.

Cass led the way through the dining room and continued into the hall, where she stopped and turned. Her eyes flickered up to meet his gaze then down to the floor just as quickly. "Thanks for supper…and for, you know…" she glanced up at him in a self-conscious manner "…a while ago. My…uh, meltdown."

She looked so apologetic he crammed his hands into his pockets to keep himself from hugging her. "Not a problem."

"I'll give the canine therapy another try." There was determination in her words.

"And I'll speak to Flora and Margaret and see if they can work something out so you won't have to work with one particular dog."

Cass gave him an earnest look. "I'll do what I can to make that work. I really do appreciate you letting me cry on your shoulder."

To his complete astonishment, Cass placed a hand on his shoulder, came up on her toes and gave him a quick kiss on the cheek.

Pleasure zipped through him. When he saw Cass's shocked face seconds later with its charming pink cheeks he was mesmerized. This tough woman appeared flustered. Her eyes had gone wide in surprise before she blinked a couple of times and looked away. She shook slightly and he feared she might fall. Lyle reached for her.

Cass stood close enough that he could smell the fresh scent of her hair.

"I'm sorry," Cass murmured.

Lyle lowered his head to hear her words, bringing

his lips closer to hers. He watched them, the soft full pads that looked so delicious.

"That was inappropriate. I shouldn't have done that." Cass glanced at him then away.

"I'm not," he said quietly. "I rather liked it."

Her eyelids fluttered closed, then her gaze met his. They stood there watching each other for precious moments. The tip of her tongue made a flicker of an appearance. Lyle wanted a taste, just a small one, of that glossy moistness on her bottom lip. He lowered his head and placed his mouth over hers. Cass remained still in his hands. Lyle took the kiss deeper.

Cass returned it for a second before she slipped out of his hands and whispered, "Goodnight."

Lyle watched her walk away. Disappointment filled him. Everything in him wished he could stop her without frightening her. He wanted more than a chaste meeting of lips. It hadn't been nearly enough. He sought a full, no-holding-back kiss from Cass. There was an attraction between them he wanted to explore. It had been a long time since he'd experienced such a driving need to kiss a woman breathless.

CHAPTER FIVE

CASS WALKED TO the canine center the next afternoon still astounded she had foolishly kissed Lyle. Making her embarrassment worse and her pleasure more, Lyle had actually looked pleased she had kissed him.

But she didn't do that sort of impulsive thing. Ever. She thought through her actions first. Never had she fallen apart like that in front of anyone. To do something so rash only showed how open the wound was that made up her life. Then there had been her crying jag. Until last night she had held it together despite all she'd been through. Talking about Rufus had broken her.

Lyle had been incredibly kind when she'd really needed someone. Beneath his attention she'd opened up like never before. He'd listened without judgement instead of running away. Lyle acted as if he cared, understood her loss.

Cass shook off that admission.

She'd kissed Lyle. What had she been thinking? She hadn't been, instead she had just reacted. It had been a stupid, careless move. Being here at the castle was about therapy and making a full recovery, not romance. Her heart couldn't handle those emotions right now. Even if it could, what did she imagine would come of it? Nothing, that was all that could happen.

As she entered the canine therapy center, Margaret greeted her at the door as if she had been waiting for her. Instead of taking her into the room where she had been the day before, Margaret escorted Cass into another one where the dogs were housed in pens with fenced runs. Cass shoved her shaking hands down into her coat pockets. She didn't want anyone to see that her hands were trembling.

Margaret stopped in front of the first cage. "The dogs on this side of the building are the ones we call the 'reimagined' dogs. They're working dogs that we get from all over the world. When they're too old we take in the ones we can, retrain them and give them new purpose. Esme also has a breeding program for specialized therapy dogs for epilepsy and diabetes patients. We train from puppy age until they are just over a year old. Those dogs are Labrador retrievers, Labradoodles and golden retrievers."

Cass nodded.

"Now, this is Oscar. He's a sweet dog and has been paired with Mr. Ellis."

"I've seen them together some." Cass recognized the small black and white, wire-haired dog, along with a number of others. They'd all been paired with patients at the clinic.

"And you should remember this one. He's the dog I understand that you and Lyle brought in the other night. We're calling him Dougal."

Cass nodded. Dougal suited the little dog. Rufus had already been named when Cass had got him, but his name had suited him too.

They moved to the next pen. The dogs were getting larger as they went.

"This is Morrow. He used to be a guide dog."

He was being "reimagined," much as Cass was working to do with her life. If she didn't return to search and rescue, what was she going to do? Could she accept a new partner and try again? A sick feeling welled up in her, but she forced it down with a clenched jaw. She'd already made a spectacle of herself in front of Lyle. She *would not* do the same in Margaret's presence.

Margaret kept moving down the aisle, introducing Cass to dogs as they went. Cass battled to remain calm rather than listening until Margaret said, "…and he was a search and rescue dog. A good one, I understand. But he went blind in one eye and that ended his career."

Cass's attention remained riveted to the light-gray-furred German shepherd lying quietly in the back corner of the cage.

"He hasn't adjusted to being here as we would like. I think we're rather dull to him after his exciting life." Margaret's voice was sympathetic.

Cass empathized with the dog's pain. She, too, was out of her comfort zone for reasons beyond her control.

"Now, this is McDuff. Everyone's favorite." A big dog with shaggy fur and wide brown eyes came to greet them.

Cass reached out to him without thinking. He smelled her hand, fluffy tail wagging.

"Now that you've met everyone I'll show you where the supplies are and tell you some of your duties. I have to admit you're the first resident to offer to help us with dog care and I'm very glad to have you. We don't have enough help."

Margaret showed Cass the room where food was stored, the grooming area and where cleaning tools could be found. She explained what Cass needed to do and on which days of the week. "Also, we would like you to walk any dogs that don't currently have assignments. That's the list on the board over here." She walked to the wall where a clipboard hung. "Currently there are just three dogs. You're free to take them outside for a walk on the lead or a run in the outdoor pen."

Cass would turn them out in the pen. Leash walking was more than she was emotionally prepared for. Too personal, too risky. She might start caring.

"You think you'll be okay with the work?" Margaret checked her watch.

Cass nodded. This she could do. She would be active instead of sitting around with a dog in her lap or on the floor beside her. Surely she wouldn't get attached tending to all the dogs on a daily basis. Having one assigned to her was the danger. She could feed them, walk them, and clean their cages and meet her therapy requirements then move on. All she had to do was make up her mind to do what she had to do. For some people that type of work might be beneath them. But it was the perfect means for Cass to ease back into interacting with a dog without the temptation of completely committing.

Over the next hour she fed and watered the dogs. When it was time to enter the search and rescue dog's cage, she had to read his name on the sign because she'd missed it when Margaret had said it earlier. She hesitated. Hero didn't scare her, instead he reminded her too much of herself. He remained in that corner as if he wanted to shut the world out. Was that what she was doing?

"Hey, fellow, it's nice to meet you. I understand we've been in the same business. I'm sorry to hear about your eye. That's tough." She moved to fill his food bowl. He watched her closely as she worked. Cass filled his water bowl from a bucket. He came up on his haunches as if he might be thirsty. "Come and get it. I won't hurt you."

"He mostly speaks German."

Cass heart clinched. Just like Rufus.

"I should have told you that." Margaret stood outside the cage. "But I'm sure he appreciates your soothing voice. I've been watching. You're good with the dogs."

"I've been around them all my life." Cass unlocked the cage.

"It shows. It's time for you to go." Margaret held the gate to the cage open. "I don't want to wear you out on your first day. I'll see you tomorrow."

"Okay. I need to put some things away before I go." Cass walked back toward the storeroom.

"Can you see yourself out?" Margaret called, heading the other way.

Cass placed the bucket she carried on the floor. "I can."

"Good. You did well today, Cass." Margaret gave her a smile and left.

Hopefully each day would get easier.

Three days later Cass was on the minibus to the village with five other residents. She looked out the window at the beautiful and fascinating countryside. She'd seen much of the world and, even covered in patches of snow, this place appealed to her. Her doctors had been wise to send her here.

Going to the canine therapy center still didn't fill her with excitement but it wasn't as difficult as it had been on the first day. She'd managed to interact with the dogs while remaining emotionally removed from them. She was pleased to see that Dougal was growing stronger each day. His odd appearance with some weight on him was beginning to make him look cute. The only dog that did disturb her was Hero. He still remained standoffish. Cass was trying not to let it bother her, yet it did.

Today she wasn't going to think about dogs or therapy or even the past. Instead she was going to enjoy her trip to the village. She didn't know what to expect of Cluchlochry, but she was enchanted from the moment she stepped off the bus. It looked like a scene from a Victorian Christmas card. Wreaths of fresh greenery with bows were on every building door and window. The main road was just large enough for two small narrow vehicles to pass. Her large American SUV would never be able to make it.

The sun was shining this morning, promising a warmer day than usual, and she was glad she'd left Lyle's scarf and hat behind, not wanting to have to carry them.

In the center of the village just feet from where she'd stepped off the bus was the cobblestoned village square. She followed the crowd to a building she'd overheard was called the community center. There were a number of tents set up outside, but Cass found the majority of the stalls inside. The individual areas each had their own holiday decorations. It was like entering a winter wonderland. Excitement filled her at the thought of some retail therapy. She wasn't much of a "girly-girl" where most things were concerned, but she did love a shopping trip. The van had come in early enough that the crowd was still comfortably small. Visiting the stalls should be fun.

She planned to buy boots and socks today as Lyle had suggested that first night. However, she would wait until later to shop for them to avoid carrying them around any longer than necessary. After she was finished at the Christmas market she would ask someone where to do shoe shopping. For now, she was going to see what the market had to offer.

The first stall she came to held handmade wooden figurines. Behind the table sat an older, grizzled man with the air of an outdoorsman. He glanced up for a moment then went back to whittling.

Cass picked up an angel and admired the workmanship. The texture was smooth and there was attention to detail. The face had the kind of expression befitting an angel. It was old-world craftsmanship at its best. Her mother would love any of the items on display. She would return to buy something for her mother before she headed back to the castle. Hoping she would make it home before Christmas, she planned on being prepared to celebrate with her family.

When they'd heard she was injured they had wanted to come to her in Germany. She had convinced them not to, assuring them she was going to be fine. Once she'd been sent to therapy she had persuaded them she would be home sooner if she concentrated on getting better. What she hadn't said was that she needed time to recover emotionally so she wouldn't fall apart in front of them, as she had with Lyle.

Cass paused at every stall, fearing that if she didn't she might miss something. At this rate she wouldn't see all the market today and would still climb back on the bus with an armload of purchases. However, she needed to get some local money to buy things. She went outside to the street and searched for an ATM sign. Soon she had some pounds in her pocket. Conscious of smiling for the first time in a long while she went to the nearest stall.

This one offered handmade Christmas-tree ornaments. Cass was enthralled. Each one unique, they were made out of natural things like nuts, twigs, and pine cones. They would be perfect on a tree. Once again she resisted the impulse to buy and moved on to the next display.

There she found leather goods of quality craftsmanship. She continued walking, merely looking at some stalls and handling items at others. Coming to town had been a good decision, even though she had initially intended only to buy new walking boots and socks. Nevertheless she was having a nice day. Even the bustle of the growing crowd made her feel more alive. She had needed this kind of therapy.

Spying a sign with the words "Aileen's Knitting" on it, she made her way over. It was past time to return Lyle's hat and scarf but Cass wanted to get her own before she did so. And some gloves.

The stall had two tables and a number of hat racks filled with hats and scarfs of every color. Cass went to one of the tables and ran her hand over a few of the items of outerwear, even trying on a couple. She studied herself in a mirror hung on a stand to see how she looked. The pale pink and gray striped scarf and matching solid pink hat she especially liked.

A plump middle-aged woman sat behind the table next to a small heater. Her needles clicked as she spoke. "That looks lovely on you."

Her Scottish brogue was so thick Cass had to concentrate to understand her. "Thank you. Your work is beautiful. And so soft." Cass pulled the cap off and picked up another in the same color but with a rosette on the side. She studied it.

At that moment a familiar masculine shoulder pushed a door open just behind the woman. Lyle entered, carrying a box. He turned and the door closed. She must have caught his eye because he looked at her with surprise. A smile curved his lips that made her middle flutter. "Well, hi, there. I see you took my suggestion about coming to the market."

Her face warmed. This was their first encounter since they had kissed. Surely if she acted like it hadn't happened, he would as well. "Yeah, I'm doing some shopping therapy, like the doctor ordered."

Lyle looked over the box at her. "I wouldn't say I ordered it, but I'm glad you came."

She nodded toward the box. "I see you're moonlighting. You don't have enough jobs already?"

He chuckled as he rested the corner of the box on the edge of the table, continuing to hold it. "It's more like helping my mother out. Muscles and all that."

Cass knew those muscles well. She had felt those strong arms around her and the firmness of his chest when she'd pressed her face against it. She glanced at Lyle's mother, who watched them with pronounced interest, her knitting momentarily forgotten.

Lyle's head turned as if following Cass's line of sight. "Mum, this is Cass Bellow. She's one of our residents at the castle. Cass, my mother, Aileen Sinclair."

Cass was unsure how to respond. Lyle's mother was looking between the two of them as if she suspected something Cass was refusing to admit to herself. A second too late to sound natural, Cass finally managed to get out, "It's nice to meet you. Your work really is lovely. I wish I had your talent."

The door opened again and a tall man who was undoubtedly an older version of Lyle joined them with a box in his hands. "Aileen, where do you want this?

"Over in the corner will be fine." Lyle's mother pointed to the one opposite hers. "I don't want it near the heater."

The man put the box down as instructed and turned to Cass. Something about his bearing made Cass want to stand at attention and pass inspection yet he looked in poor health. His was gaunt, far too thin for his height. There wasn't a sparkle in his eyes like Lyle's. His skin had a grayish tint to it. Lyle's father was sick.

"Sir, this is Cass Bellow. My father, retired Colonel Gregor Sinclair."

Still resisting the urge to salute, she settled for, "Hello, sir."

"Hello, young lady." The older man offered his hand. Cass put hers inside his. He still had a firm grip, but his fingers felt fragile in hers.

She looked at Lyle's parents. "It's nice to meet you both."

"You're not from around here, I can tell," Lyle's father said.

Cass chortled. "Is it that obvious? No, I'm from America. Montana currently."

Lyle's father nodded. "I worked with many Americans while I was in the military. Good sorts. I expect that Lyle will be working with some as well when he returns to active duty."

Her look swung to Lyle. Was he going to join the army again? He seemed to love working at the clinic.

Before she could ask, he took the hat from her hand. "This will look nice on you."

She unwrapped the scarf from her neck. "I think so

too. I'd like to get both of them, and the gloves as well.
They're too nice to pass up. Plus I need to return yours."

"You do?" Lyle's mother gave him a questioning
look.

"Cass didn't have a chance to prepare for our Scottish
weather before she was transferred here." Lyle turned
to put his box on top of the other one as if discourag-
ing more of his mother's questions.

Cass pulled out her cash, counted out the correct
amount indicated on a sign next to the mirror, then
handed it across the table.

"Thank you, Mrs. Sinclair. Maybe one day I'll learn
to knit and make something half as lovely as your work."

"If you'd like to learn I could show you. Lyle could
bring you to the house some day for lunch." Lyle's
mother looked from Cass to her son, a small smile on
her lips.

Was Aileen's maternal intuition working overtime?
Cass shook her head. "Oh, no, I didn't mean to imply
you should teach me."

"Nonsense. I'd love to give you a lesson. And at this
time of the year knitting is about all I'm doing anyway,
with the Christmas market going until the season is
over." The clicking of the needles started again.

Cass didn't know what to think about Aileen's invitation but she said the polite thing. "Thank you."

"Would you like a bag for those?" Mrs. Sinclair
asked, a nod of her head indicating the knitted items
Cass held.

Cass glanced down. "No, I think I'll wear them."
She stuffed the gloves in her pocket, looped the scarf
around her neck again and pulled the hat snugly over
her head. "It was nice to meet you Colonel and Mrs. Sinclair." Giving Lyle a swift look as she turned to leave,

she added, "Bye." Hesitating a second, she turned to look at Lyle. "Would you mind giving me directions to where I can buy some boots?"

"Why don't I show you instead?" he offered.

"I don't want to put you out. I'm sure your mother needs your help." Cass didn't need him thinking she was using that as a ploy to spend more time with him.

"I'm good for now." Aileen waved a hand. "While you're gone, Lyle, why don't you stop by McKinney's Pub and get Cass one of their pies?" She looked directly at Cass. "Best meat pies you'll find anywhere."

Lyle stepped around the table and came to stand beside Cass. His hand touched her back briefly and was gone. He called over his shoulder to his mother, "I'll do it."

They worked their way around the people coming and going as they walked in the direction of the door. A couple of times Lyle put a gentle hand in the small of her back while guiding her through the crowd.

"That hat and scarf color is very flattering on you," he said. "Reminds me of when you blush. Your cheeks turn that shade." He grinned as their gazes met. "Like right now."

The compliment gave her a luscious warm throughout her body like a hot drink heating her from the inside out.

They exited the building and turned left down the street. As they continued walking toward the other end of the village green they approached a monument. It consisted of a tall narrow shaft encircled by steps. On top was a small statue.

"What's this?" Cass stopped and studied it.

"It's a Mercat Cross. They have been used in Scotland since the eleven-hundreds to distinguish the right by the monarch to hold a market or fair. They were symbols of authority. There're aren't many of them left now. We're rather proud of ours."

"That's interesting." She liked learning historical facts about places she went.

"They're not only places for merchants to meet but places where state and civic proclamations would be made. Even to this day in Edinburgh the town crier will still make proclamations on occasions."

She looked up to where the statue stood on top. "I would love to hear one sometime."

"Maybe you will one day."

Cass doubted that. She wouldn't be here long enough for that to happen.

They moved on in comfortable silence until they made their way through the crowd and out into the open again.

"So how have your last few days of working with the dogs gone?"

Cass glanced over at him. "Don't you already know? I figured you've been checking up on me."

Lyle chuckled. "I have, but I'd like to hear from you."

She appreciated his honestly. "It's going better than I expected. I admit it was tough to get started, but I'm getting used to the dogs and them to me."

"I'm glad to hear that." He did sound pleased, as if her happiness really mattered to him.

She couldn't say she was happy yet, but she'd moved the needle that direction. "You're not really surprised, are you?"

"Not really. Canine therapy has proved very effective. Even on those who are resistant." He gave her a knowing look.

"Is that your way of saying I told you so?" Somehow she didn't mind if he did. This was the best she had felt since before the accident. Her thoughts weren't so dark anymore.

Lyle stopped in front of a shop built of brown timber. The upper half of the door had four window panes. A Christmas wreath hung low beneath the glass. Attached above the door was a swag of greenery entwined with red ribbon. On either side of the door were display windows filled with boots, coats and other outdoor wear. All of it was arranged to create the impression of presents under a Christmas tree.

Lyle opened the door for her. "The shoes are at the back on the right."

Cass followed him down a narrow aisle lined with high shelves stuffed with items. The dim lighting added to the alluring atmosphere. The place smelled of wood oil and pine. Cass inhaled, taking it deep into her lungs. It reminded her of Lyle. She was enchanted with the shop. In fact, she was charmed by everything about the Heatherglen area, including Lyle. What was happening to her?

They arrived at the back of the shop. There in one corner was a small wooden bench along with boxes of boots piled on the floor.

Lyle stretched to his full height and looked over the shelves. "Apparently Mr. Stewart isn't around. We'll have a look at these and he should be back soon. He must have stepped out for lunch. I have experience with this so we'll just help ourselves."

Cass lowered her chin, eyeing him dubiously. "You've been a shoe salesman?"

He gave her an indignant look. "I worked here when I came home on school breaks."

"Oh. So you *are* a jack-of-all-trades."

He stepped toward the boxes. "I wouldn't exactly say that, but I can handle reading shoeboxes. What's your size?"

"Eight and a half, US." She sat on the bench.

Lyle nodded and studied them a moment. Moving a couple, he pulled one out. "I hope I made the European to American conversion correctly. Give these a try and we'll see."

She took the box from him and opened it. Removing her shoes, Cass pulled the new boot on her right foot. She stood and wiggled her toes. "Nicely done. Feels good but I would really rather have them in black."

"I aim to please. Let me see what I can find." Lyle shifted around a few boxes. With a bright smile on his handsome face, he handed her a box.

Cass sat on the bench again and started trying on the second boot.

"What's your favorite color?" Lyle asked, his back to her as he straightened boxes.

"Why?"

"You need some good socks." He studied her with visible curiosity.

She continued trying on her new boots. "Blue."

He moved down the wall and seconds later handed her a pair of thick socks. "These'll keep your feet warm and wick the moisture away. I promise you'll like them."

Cass removed the boots and her socks then pulled on the new ones. "I can already tell the difference." She flexed her foot then slipped her foot into the boot. Nice. Quickly she pulled on the other boot and laced them both up.

Standing, she walked back and forth a couple of times, testing the feel of the footwear. "You know, if you ever decide to give up medicine you could have a future as a personal shopper."

Lyle gave a regal bow. "Thank you. I have to say with complete confidence that's the first time anyone has suggested that to me."

They both laughed.

When was the last time she'd laughed like this? How had she not noticed it slipping away?

She liked Lyle's relaxed view of life. With his job and military background she marveled he wasn't up-tight and domineering. Instead he seemed to accept life as it came and made the most of it whenever he could. Cass needed more of that in her world.

Lyle had a way of making her smile, and she also needed more of that right now. However, she must not start depending on him to make her feel better. She had to depend on herself. She had to regain her strength. Be strong.

If she opened up to him any further, leaving him would be a new trauma, one she knew she couldn't handle. Her job certainly didn't lend itself to an easygoing and emotional personality. Even when she was at home her focus had been on working with Rufus to keep them both sharp. Had the men in her life been right? Did she live too closed off? Had been concentrating on her job and Rufus more than she should have?

"You want to keep those on?" He picked up the box.

"I believe I will. Start breaking them in." Cass picked up her other shoes and placed them in the box while Lyle held it. She met his gaze. "By the way, what's your favorite color?"

"Green." His eyes didn't waver. "I'm particularly fond of the shade of green of your eyes."

Her breath caught. "Are you flirting with me?"

"What if I am?" He took the box and set it on the bench. "I've been thinking about that kiss."

A tingle ran through her. "You shouldn't."

"What? Think about it or think about doing it again?"

"Both, " she squeaked.

"Why?" His voice turned gravelly, went soft. Lyle stepped toward her.

Because she was damaged. Because she was scared. Because she couldn't handle caring about anything or anyone again. "Because I'm leaving soon."

"Cass, we can share an interest in each other without it becoming a lifelong commitment. I'd like to get to know you better. Couldn't we be friends? Enjoy each other's company while you're here?"

Put that way, it sounded reasonable. Lyle moved so close that his heat warmed her. Why was it so hard to breathe? She simmered with anticipation. His hands came to rest at her waist as his mouth lowered to hers.

She didn't want his kiss. That wasn't true. Until that moment she'd had no idea how desperately she did want Lyle's lips on hers. Her breath caught as his mouth made a light brush over hers. He pulled away. Cass ran her tongue over her bottom lip, tasting him.

Lyle groaned and pulled her tight against his chest. His lips firmly settled over hers. Cass grabbed his shoulders to steady herself. Slowly she went up on her toes, her desire drawing her nearer to him. Sweet heat curled and twisted through her center and seeped into her every cell. She'd found her cozy fire in a winter storm.

The sound of the door opening brought both their heads up. Their gazes locked with each other's.

"Hello? Is someone here?" a man called.

"It's Lyle, Mr. Stewart. I'm in the boot section."

"Please don't do that again," Cass whispered, and stepped as far away as the small space would allow. She couldn't deal with the feelings swarming in her. This wasn't what she needed or wanted. She needed to figure out her life, not complicate it.

Now that she'd really been kissed by Lyle, she wanted more. *No!* And she couldn't handle the feelings his kiss had kindled in her. This was too much at the wrong time. Panic welled in her. She shook her head. Letting something grow between them would only turn into disaster. She didn't want to hurt Lyle, and she couldn't endure another heartache.

He studied her for a moment, then picked up the box, placing it under his arm as if nothing earthshaking had happened. "Let's go and pay for these then get one of those pies."

That suited her just fine. She could pretend nothing had changed as well as he did. Head held high, she followed him two aisles over to a wooden counter. A middle-aged man with white tuffs of hair, rosy cheeks and a white beard stood behind it. He could pass for a Santa Claus.

"Well, hello. How're you, Lyle?" Mr. Stewart gave them both a wide smile.

The man's accent was just as thick as Lyle's mother's.

"Fine, thanks, Mr. Stewart. We've been helping ourselves to some boots. I was just going to write you a note and leave the money."

"Give me a second to set this down." The older man placed a brown bag on the counter. "I went to get a meat pie before they were all gone. I look forward to Mrs. McKinney's pies all year."

"I hope you left some for Cass and me. We're on our

way there next." Lyle leaned toward the bag and inhaled deeply. "Mrs. McKinney makes the best."

While the men were talking, Cass managed to get her purchase paid for. She and Lyle exited the shop. The sun was shining but clouds were gathering.

"It looks like it'll snow again tonight," Lyle commented. "We need to go this way." He indicated to the left. "McKinney's Pub is down this way."

Cass shook her head. "I'm not really hungry. I think I'll just look around some more then go back to the castle. I appreciate your help with my boots."

Lyle said nothing until she looked at him. "Cass, I didn't mean to make things uncomfortable between us."

"You didn't."

He searched her face for a long moment. "Then you won't mind joining me for lunch. You don't want me to have to eat alone."

She pursed her lips. "Somewhere in there I think there's a touch of emotional blackmail."

He quirked a brow, his grin devious. "Could be. Live dangerously and join me."

She was doing that by just being around him. Her body still hummed with awareness, but she did owe him. He'd been nothing but kind. More than once Lyle had gone far beyond what was necessary. Helping her with her new boots was just one of the small things. Still feeling unsteady after their kiss, she was afraid that remaining in Lyle's presence might further break her tightly strung nerves. It was risky to her well-being for her to say yes. "If you're going to insist."

A winning smile lit up his face. "I am. You know how I hate to eat alone. This way."

They didn't walk far before they came to a building

with an elaborate sign stating that it was McKinney's Pub above the door. "Here we are."

Cass turned the doorknob and pushed the door open, to find a room with a dark timber-beamed ceiling, stone-flagged floor and a handful of wooden tables and chairs unoccupied. Men were standing at the bar with drinks and talking. She glanced back at Lyle to see him duck to enter.

"Why don't you go see if you can find us a table near the fire while I place our order?"

"Okay."

"Before you go, would you prefer beef or pork?" Lyle asked.

"I don't know. You make the call." She didn't often let others decide anything for her. Being with Lyle was definitely having an odd effect on her. For some reason she trusted him not to let her down.

"Okay. One more thing, hot drink or something cold?"

"Hot, definitely hot." She shivered. "I can't even imagine drinking something cold." Cass reached into her pocket. "Here's money for mine."

Lyle looked offended. "Put that away. I'll get this."

"I don't expect you to buy my lunch." She couldn't continue being indebted to him. "You're always doing something for me."

"You can return the favor sometime. Now, go and find us a seat." He started toward the bar.

"You don't need my help carrying the food?"

He shook his head. "I can handle it. You find us a place to sit before they're all taken."

"All right." Cass made her way to an empty table to one side of the roaring fire in the fireplace. She turned a chair toward the flames and sat down, stretching out her hands to the warmth. A couple of minutes later she looked around to see where Lyle was.

She quickly found him among the people at the bar. With his height and broad shoulders he stood out among the others. His hair was mussed but it matched his easy-going personality. Lyle was every bit as appealing to look at as he was to talk to. She was getting in deeper and deeper the longer she was with him. As hard as she tried to push away, the greater the pull he had on her.

Soon, carrying two drinks with steam wafting from them, Lyle joined her. He placed them on the table. "You got us a perfect table. How did you manage that?"

Cass shrugged and picked up her mug. "Lucky, I guess."

Lyle picked his mug up as well. "This is hot punch. I think you'll like it."

She took a sip. "Mmm…"

"I like it when you make that sound," he said, just for her ears. "You did it a while ago when I kissed you."

"I did not!"

Lyle gave her a wicked smile that said, Do *you want to bet?*

Heat that had nothing to do with the punch surged through her. "You shouldn't say things like that to me."

"What, the truth?"

Much to her relief, they were interrupted by a young woman placing two plates on the table.

Lyle said politely, "Thank you." The woman gave him a shy look and hurried away.

It appeared Lyle sent most women into a tailspin by just being nice. Cass had imagined he only had that effect on her.

She watched as Lyle used a napkin to pick up the perfect brown half-moon pastry. He closed his eyes and took a bite. His eyelids dropped as an expression of pure bliss washed over his face. He slowly chewed. Something low within Cass tightened. She shook off the vision of Lyle naked in bed, wearing that same expression. How could just two kisses cause such an idea to pop into her head?

Instead of concentrating on her traitor of a mind, she followed Lyle's lead and picked up her pie. She took a small bite of the flaky pastry. It melted on her tongue as the taste of tangy beef hit her taste buds. She closed her eyes and enjoyed the moment. Did she have the same look on her face as Lyle? She opened hers to find him watching her closely, an intense flame of desire in his eyes. Oh, yeah, she had.

His voice turned husky as he said, "You should look like that all the time."

"How's that?" Cass dared to ask, unable to take her gaze off him.

"Angelic, as if you had found nirvana."

Emotion that had nothing to do eating meat pie and everything to do with the fire in Lyle's eyes flashed through her. This caring and comforting man wanted her. That knowledge was empowering.

"Hello, Lyle." a woman's soft voice said from behind Cass.

The pleasure lighting Lyle's face went out, leaving a blank look with a hint of surprise. The woman was important to Lyle. Cass turned to see her. She had vivid blue eyes and was heavily pregnant. A sick feeling filled her stomach. Who was the woman to Lyle?

The last person Lyle had expected to see was Freya. He hadn't seen her for some time. Through his mother and father, he'd learned that she had married and moved to

Fort William. He was truly glad for her, but that didn't make the surprise of seeing her again any less nerve rattling.

He laid his food down and stood. "Freya."

"It's nice to see you, Lyle." She sounded hesitant, as if she was afraid of his reaction. "How are you?"

"Well. And you?"

Her hand went to rest on her protruding middle. "I'm doing fine."

Lyle felt a sharp, piercing pain. They had talked about and planned on now many children they would have. There had been so many dreams they'd shared. He mentally shook his head. Those were long gone. Their relationship had been doomed the minute he'd boarded the train for training camp. He knew that now, but back then he'd been too caught up in pleasing his father by joining the army and the image of his fiancée waiting on his glorious return to see reality. Knowing his own mind and what he wanted out of life hadn't entered the equation. Much less fighting for it.

Freya glanced at Cass, who was observing them with interest. Was Cass thinking the child was his? "Freya." He nodded toward Cass. "This is Cass Bellow. Freya is an old friend."

"Hello," Freya said with a small smile as the two women studied each other.

A man not much taller than Freya but with huge shoulders joined them. He studied Lyle then Cass before giving Freya a questioning look, his brows making a V at his nose.

Freya cleared her throat. "This is Angus, my husband."

Lyle extend his hand. "Lyle Sinclair." It took a second before the man's eyes widened in recognition, then narrowed.

Angus shook Lyle's hand briefly, then put his arm across Freya's shoulders in a statement of ownership. To her he said, "Your parents are waiting."

Freya gave Lyle a sad, apologetic look. "It was nice to see you, Lyle."

"You too, Freya." He watched them walk away. That had certainly been interesting. Why had the meeting left him feeling so disconcerted? He'd got over Freya years ago, yet it still shook him to see her again. At one time they had been so close. Now there was a fence between them so high that they would never be able to climb it. Her husband's actions and facial expression made him question how controlling and overly jealous he might be. Was Freya truly happy?

"I think it's time for me to get back to the castle." Cass stood. "I promised Flora I would help with some of the decorations today instead of formal therapy."

Lyle blinked. How had he forgotten Cass was there? She must think him an idiot. "But we haven't finished our meal."

She gave him a curious look. "I have. Thank you for the pie. I should go."

"I'll walk you to the minibus." He needed to answer the questions hanging between them.

Cass waved for him to sit down. "No, you finish your lunch. I can find my way. I'll see you back at the castle."

Before he could order his thoughts, she was gone.

What was Cass thinking? Imagining? Had she seen what had once been between him and Freya?

CHAPTER SIX

BACK AT THE castle Cass debated whether or not to return Lyle's coat and other belongings that evening or wait until she saw him during work hours. Surely he needed his clothes. Yet her growing curiosity about the history between him and Freya made her cautious about seeking him out. It really wasn't her business, and yet she couldn't dismiss the distinct impression that something between them had caused Lyle great pain. Or was the baby the issue?

She knew Lyle well enough to know he would take responsibility for a child he'd fathered. Having a family of his own would be a serious matter to him. So was the baby his?

As hard as Cass had tried to maintain her emotional distance from Lyle, she cared about him. He had made it impossible for her to remain uninterested. Not only did she find him attractive, he had also proved he was a good man. So here she was, caring about him, concerned for him.

The feeling he needed someone to talk to also nagged at her. She owed him. Maybe she could help.

With her new socks and boots on and wearing her own jacket, which she'd found a few days ago laid out on her bed, she bundled Lyle's coat, socks, scarf and hat in her arms and made her way out of the castle. It would soon be dark, so she had tucked her flashlight safely in her pocket for the return trip.

At the gate leading into his yard she stopped. Was she being too forward by coming to his home like this? What would he think about her just showing up? Still, the need to see him, be there for him if he needed to talk, neutralized her apprehension. Her outlook on life had improved so much since he'd let her spill her problems to him. Maybe tonight he needed someone to listen to his troubles. She owed him and cared about him enough that she should at least be here for him. They were friends.

Pausing in the act of knocking on the door, she had the uneasy feeling her "honorable" thoughts about Lyle needing her were just an excuse to see him again. He had friends, colleagues, even his parents to confide in, so what had possessed her to think he required her?

As if of its own accord her fist hit the door. Breath held, she listened for movement inside, half wishing Lyle wasn't home, half hoping he was. All of this was so against her nature. She'd always known her own mind. Why was she doubting herself now? Why had she started acting like a silly schoolgirl around Lyle?

She had stepped off the porch to leave when the door opened. Her heart beat faster as she straightened her back.

"Cass?" He sounded both startled and pleased.

Did he think she was seeking his interest by showing up like this? Was she? "I, uh, wanted to return your things now I have my jacket back and a new scarf and hat." She thrust them into his hands before turning away.

"Would you like to come in for some coffee?" He asked, sounding hopeful.

She looked at him, even less sure about being there. But hadn't she been eager for Lyle to invite her in? "Could we make that tea?"

He chuckled. "Of course. Come in."

Inside, Lyle helped her off with her coat. As he did so, his hands rested on her shoulders for a moment. She missed the heaviness of them the second they were gone. She had the impression he wanted to keep an appropriate distance between them. Wasn't that what she'd all but told him she wanted? Especially after their kiss in the shop. Or did she want that?

"Come and join me in the kitchen," Lyle suggested as he moved through the door opposite the living room.

"Let me take my boots off first. They're pretty muddy." Cass sat on the small bench underneath the coat rack and removed them, then followed him.

Lyle was already at the stove with the kettle in his hand when she entered. He placed it on the element and leaned against the counter. "I see you're wearing your new socks again."

"Yes. They're the best I've ever worn. I plan to buy a few more pairs before I leave for home." Cass settled into one of the wooden chairs at the small round table in the middle of the room.

"Flora tells me that if you continue making the progress you have been, it'll be sooner rather than later." He opened a tin filled with biscuits and placed it on the table before returning to the cabinets.

She reached for a biscuit. "I'm pretty determined to get through this as quickly as possible."

Lyle glanced over his shoulder, studying her for a moment. What was he thinking? He returned to removing mugs from an upper cabinet and added tea bags to them. "I noticed that."

Did it bother him that she so was eager to leave the clinic? Cass looked around. "I like your kitchen."

"Thanks." He put a bowl of sugar and small pitcher of milk on the table. The kettle switched itself off as the water was boiling. Lyle poured the steaming water into the mugs before setting one in front of her and the other at the place beside her, rather than across from her. He took a seat.

She liked him being close enough to touch. Maybe she had imagined he was trying to keep distance between them.

Lyle pushed the tin in her direction. "Have another if you wish. It's interesting you like my kitchen. These old cottage kitchens have charm but they're often difficult to modernize. I've been led to believe women like to have the latest and greatest to work with."

Cass added sugar and milk to her tea. "That sounds like you're speaking from personal experience."

"Yeah. Freya always wanted one of those new brick houses with all the glass."

A zip ran along Cass's nerves. He had made it that easy for her to ask about Freya. Still, she hesitated to pry. Would he be upset if she did? Cass watched him. Lyle studied his tea. "Would that be the Freya I met today?"

"That's the one." A pensive look remained on his face. "I think I owe you an explanation."

"Why?"

"Because I was kissing you and then a pregnant woman who I'm sure you figured out shared a past with me shows up. It didn't make me look good."

"You didn't—don't—owe me an explanation." No matter how much she wanted to hear one.

"Maybe not, but I'd like to give you one anyway. The baby isn't mine. I haven't seen Freya in over a year. She was my girlfriend when we were teenagers. I asked her to be my wife the night before I left for basic training."

"Now I understand the look on her husband's face." It had been jealousy.

Lyle nodded. "Yeah, I'm not his favorite person, I imagine. But he has nothing to worry about. It's been over for a long time."

"What happened?" Cass hissed in dismay. "I shouldn't have asked that. It's not my business."

He finally met her look. "It doesn't matter. I don't want to have any secrets from you."

What was he saying? That sounded too much like he wanted a relationship more intimate than friendship. Their kisses had certainly been a step beyond mere friends.

"I received the classic 'Dear John' letter. By the time I was able to come home months later she was already married."

Cass placed her hand over his hand resting on the table. She had been right. He did need to talk. "I'm sorry that happened to you. You deserved better."

He turned over his hand and held hers. "It was a rotten feeling at the time but far better than marrying the wrong person."

She couldn't disagree with him, but it must have been a horribly painful experience. To feel so helpless. She knew that all feeling too well. In too many areas of her life.

"It took me some time, but I realized that we would never have made it. Ours was a young immature love and an engagement based on me leaving, not on something lasting. I promised myself that the next time I asked a woman to marry me, we would both be mature enough to know what we were doing, and that we understood what real love is." He let go of her hand.

"Enough of this serious talk. Here I am dragging up my long-gone past while your tea is getting cold."

Cass took a sip from her mug. "I knew something big had gone on between the two of you. I just wasn't sure what. Her husband made a point of making it clear where she belonged."

"I noticed that as well. I hope she's happy. My mother said this is her second child." He bit into a cookie.

"I must admit I was curious. In fact, half of the reason I came tonight was that I thought you might need to talk. You helped me by listening so I thought I could return the favor."

He gave her a thoughtful look then grinned. "I see. And here I was thinking you wanted to spend more time with me."

Just like that Lyle had changed the atmosphere. He knew how to ease a tense situation.

She returned his smile. "Please don't let anyone tell you that you lack an ego."

His grin turned suggestive, causing her middle to quiver. "I'm not sure that was a compliment, but I'm going to choose to take it that way."

Cass huffed in humor. "Does anything keep you down long?"

"I try to keep a positive outlook where I can. I learned long ago that life was easier that way. How do you see the glass? Half full or half empty?"

She winced in her mind. Most of her life she would

have said half full but right now she wasn't sure she could. "Can I get back to you on that?"

Lyle watched her far too closely for comfort. "Sure. I just want you to know that I'm here for you."

"Thanks. I know I showed up at the castle with a chip on my shoulder. I'm trying to do better."

"From all I've heard, you are."

Cass pushed away from the table. "I should be going."

"Do you have to? Stay awhile and I'll walk you back later." His face was hopeful.

She ought to leave. Hadn't she already stepped over the line by coming here? Yet she did want to remain longer. "I guess I could."

"Great. Would you like to watch TV, play chess or maybe do a puzzle?"

She blinked and laughed. "Wow, you know how to show a woman a wild time."

He carried their mugs to the sink. "What can I say? Most of my excitement comes from accidents. I'm not planning one to impress you."

"I'll be more than happy to settle for a puzzle. I haven't done one of those in a long time." That seemed like a safe enough activity.

"During the winter months I keep one going all the time. It's in the living room. Go on in and see what you can do. I'll be in after I finish here." He turned to the sink.

Cass did as he suggested. A fire was burning. She found the table with the puzzle laid out on it behind the sofa. It had to have been there the other night but she had been so out of it she hadn't noticed. The puzzle was a picture of a lioness and her cub. A difficult one at best. She sat in the chair, adjusting the lamp over the table to shine it where she wanted it.

Lyle entered to find Cass sitting in his chair at his puzzle table. Something about the sight seemed right. She looked like she belonged, fit in his world.

Her head remained lowered. The glow of the fire reflected off her hair. He longed to brush his hand across it. Test its softness. Pulling another chair close, he joined her.

"So this is how you spend your evenings?" She picked a piece up and tried it. It didn't fit. She put it down and went for another.

"Not every evening." He wished Cass would put as much energy into getting to know him as she was into working on the puzzle. Was he really that desperate for a woman? No, it was more about the sensations Cass stirred in him. Sensations that had lain dormant for a long time. The same ones he'd been afraid to show for so long.

"I would think a hot young doctor would be too busy with the ladies at the pub to spend time doing puzzles." She put a piece in and made a tiny sound of joy, and it sparked something in him.

What would it be like to kiss her again? That thought was all it took to set his blood humming. How would she react if he tried to kiss her right now? Would she push him away or tug him closer, like she had at the shop? He had to stop these runaway thoughts.

Focus on the puzzle, he told himself. Concentrate on finding that one missing piece. Maybe if he did that, he'd forget the sweet smell of Cass's hair moving just inches from him, or the breathiness of her voice when she spoke or the soft touch of her hand as it brushed his when they both tried to fit a piece into the same space.

Minutes ticked by, the longing in him growing, groaning with the seconds. To stop himself from reaching for Cass, Lyle stood and went to the fireplace, using the need to put another log on the fire as an excuse. With his back to the warmth, he watched her. She truly was striking. Every fiber of his being was on alert for the least hint of encouragement.

Cass looked up. "Hey, are you going to leave all of this to me? This is such a great picture."

"I like the one I'm seeing." His gaze met hers and held.

Cass's head dipped to the side as if she was making a decision. Moments ticked by as they watched each other.

Lyle cleared his throat. "Cass, I've been thinking of little else but kissing you again. If you don't want that to happen then it might be better if you go."

She blinked. "Go?"

Lyle chuckled softly as he stepped toward her. "Or stay? That's up to you." When Lyle reached her, he lifted a strand of her hair and let it drift through his fingers. He didn't miss the hitch in her breath.

Taking her by the shoulders, he brought her to her feet and against him. The chair turned over with a bang but neither of them gave it any notice. His lips found hers. They were as soft and pliable and welcoming as he remembered.

There was no uncertainty on Cass's part this time. Her arms circled his neck, pulling his head closer as he took the kiss deeper. She moaned low, wiggling against him and sending his desire into orbit. Her mouth opened without his request and her tongue eagerly met his in a sensual dance.

With his desire for her increasing by the second, he buried his fingers in her hair. Cass gripped his shoulders as his mouth left hers to leave kisses along her jaw and up to her ear. She did a super-sexy wriggle against his taut length when he planted a kiss behind her ear.

Cass cupped the side of his head and guided his mouth back to hers, then kissed him deeply. His body throbbed in appreciation. Cass ran her hand over his chest and down to his beltline. There she pulled his sweater up and his shirt out of his pants. Seconds later his skin rippled with the pleasure of her hand moving over it.

Lyle had to touch her, all of her. He lifted Cass to the back of the sofa and stepped between her legs. Finding the edge of her sweater, he stripped it from her and let it drop to the floor. He kissed her temple. "I've dreamed of doing this for so long."

"You have?" Her whispered words held a note of wonder.

He looked into her eyes. "I have."

The smile that lit her eyes and curved her mouth was suggestive and stimulating, promising delights to come. Excitement set his blood on fire.

Cass reached for his sweater and started to remove it. He stepped back just enough to whip it off. As she balanced on the sofa back, her hands went to the bottom button of his shirt. She unfastened each one with astonishing speed, pushing the material to either side, exposing his chest.

When she licked her lips, he was almost undone. Only with self-control that he wasn't aware he possessed did he manage not to flip her over on the cushions of the sofa and have his way. But Cass deserved better than that. She was someone who merited the best he could offer, and he vowed she would receive it. He cared too much about her for their joining to be anything less.

Lyle watched her face as her index finger traveled across his chest, around his nipples, then followed the line of hair disappearing beneath his pants. She let that naughty finger dip inside his waistband and tugged him to her. Her eyes were wide, questioning.

He found her lips again. When she pushed his shirt off his shoulders, he finished removing it without his mouth leaving hers. More than once he'd seen the fire in Cass. Her intensity for life was momentarily banked but he hadn't been prepared for this profound craving to explore her passion. He wanted, needed, to see more of her, touch more of her, to experience all of Cass.

Pulling her shirt up, he ran his hand over the smoothness of her back until he found the edge of her bra and followed it around to her breast. His hand covered it. She stilled. Her breathing had turned into panting. Satisfaction filled him when just the brush of his thumb made her nipple harden, pushing against the material of the bra. He quickly found the back clasp and released the barrier. Pushing it away, he caressed her skin until he found her breasts once more. Cupping one, he judged its weight. Perfect.

Cass leaned back slightly against his arm. Her eyelids were half-closed and her lips swollen from his kisses. She was gorgeous. Stunning. Her lips parted. Heat shot through him. He pushed her shirt out of the way and covered her nipple with his mouth. Cass moaned. Her fingers ran through his hair as she held him close.

He twirled his tongue, teasing her nipple until it stood high. Cass made a crooning sound. When it turned to a coo, Lyle's heart sored. Pleased with himself, he moved to the other breast. As he achieved the same results his desire matched hers. Holding her securely around the waist with one arm, he leaned her back to view the full landscape. Cass lying out before him was beautiful scenery to behold. Eyes satisfied, his mouth feasted on her full breasts until she forcibly pulled his lips to hers.

As her flesh meshed with his, the aching in his body became raw pain. He pulled away, helping her to sit up straight. He steadied her with his hands on her waist. "Cass, are you sure you want to do this? Do you want to go upstairs? You decide."

To his alarm and disappointment, she pulled her shirt down over the mesmerizing view. Just as he let go of her waist so she could move away she said in a soft sexy voice, "I've always wanted to see your bedroom."

Lyle grinned. "Always, is it? I like the idea of that." He offered his hand, palm up. "Then let me give you a tour."

Cass floated more than walked up the narrow stairs behind Lyle. His firm hand clasping hers reassured her of his desire. She didn't want that to ever wane.

Even so, this impulsive decision to share Lyle's bed was reckless and far out of character. Yet this newfound freedom was intensely exciting. Anticipation tingled along every nerve. Lyle's touch, his smell, the flames of desire in his eyes all drew her to him. Being with him made her feel wonderful. Made her forget her losses. Dream of the gains. She wanted these precious moments and as long as he was willing to create them, she would take all he offered.

Tomorrow she would worry about the repercussions.

Right now, she was going to enjoy feeling, being alive as never before and leave her fear and hurt outside in the cold.

Lyle's bare back was wide, solid and strong. He was

everything she needed in life right now. Was she using him? Maybe, but she would see to it he received as good as he gave. Because of him she had remembered how to give and felt whole for the first time in weeks.

At the top of the stairs he turned right down a small hallway and entered a dark room. Not letting go of her hand, he continued to lead her across the floor. Her socked feet sank into a plush rug seconds before a click heralded light. A lamp sat on a small wooden table beside a large impressive bed. The dark headboard almost reached the ceiling while the matching footboard rose a few feet above the mattress. A quilt in browns and tans covered it.

Lyle turned to her. "Are you still sure you want this?"

Cass cherished his thoughtfulness. She cupped one of his cheeks. "Oh, yes." Going up on her toes, she kissed him.

That was all the invitation he seemed to require. Pulling her tight against him, Lyle tumbled with her to the bed. She winced.

Lyle said a harsh word under his breath. Raising himself so that he could see her, he asked. "Did I hurt you? I'm so sorry." He made a move to leave her.

She pulled him back. "Just a little tender. But I'm all right. How about kissing me?"

Lyle smiled. "With pleasure." His lips found hers.

As he kissed her his hands explored and caressed her waist and hips before lightly trailing between her legs. By the time they pulled apart, her center beat like a drum keeping rhythm with their heavy breathing.

Lyle rolled to his side, supported his head in his hand, and studied her. His other hand went to the hem of her shirt and beneath it. She shivered when his fingers found skin and skimmed along it. His heated gaze met hers. "Shh… I want to see all of you."

She looked away. "I have scars from the accident…"

Lyle's lips found hers briefly. "Even those. They're part of who you are now. The amazing person you are."

Cass had never thought of them like that. Her fear had been that they would be one more turn-off for men. She tried to relax as Lyle pushed her shirt and bra up, exposing her breasts. When he wanted to remove her shirt, she lifted off the bed enough for him to do so.

"More beautiful than I imagined."

She studied him in wonder. He'd been thinking about her, imagining her without clothes? The revelation was like a balm to her battered emotions.

Lyle gave her a gentle kiss before moving to one breast, then the other. "So sweet." He rotated her so he could see the injury on her arm then gently kissed the area. "I'm so sorry you were hurt."

Moments later his hand moved to the button of her pants and undid it. It took him no time to find the aching need at her center and slide a finger inside. She squirmed. Instead of giving her the relief she yearned for, his caress heightened her burning need.

"Lyle…" she crooned. Her gaze met his.

He kissed her deeply and continued his ministrations. Stopping, he tugged at her pants. Cass lifted her hips, assisting him in the process before kicking them to the floor. Lyle ran his hand along her right thigh. He paused over the puckered skin, then leaned toward it.

She shifted away. "Don't. It's so ugly."

"Shh… Nothing about you is ugly."

Lyle lightly kissed the area then his mouth moved to hers as his nimble finger entered her again. As it teased, his tongue mimicked the erotic dance.

Cass forgot everything but the sensation Lyle was creating in her. Cass's body tightened as the longing built, pleading for release. When she reached the limits of her endurance her body took over as if leaving her behind. She closed her eyes, flexed her back and tightened her legs around his hand, slipping into the land of wonder and delight that Lyle had built just for her.

Lyle's kisses gentled. He gave her one quick peck before he left her. Cass opened her eyelids just enough to see him shuck his pants in one swift movement. He stood strong and proud. Her breath caught in her throat at the beauty before her. She had caused this reaction in him. With that knowledge came a sense of amazement and power. Lyle obviously wanted her as much as she did him. He opened the drawer on the bedside table and removed a package, tore it open and rolled the condom on. Stepping to the bed, he looked down at her.

Cass opened her arms. Lyle came to her and she pulled him close. Her legs opened and he entered her slowly. She accepted all of him, but just barely. He eased out of her snug core, then plunged in again. Taking his head in both hands, Cass brought his mouth to hers. She loved kissing him. Loved how he made her feel—happy and healthy once again. Lyle increased his pace. The friction grew, building on itself. That growling need she'd known before returned with a vengeance.

Her eyes widened as she broke off their kiss and stared into Lyle's blazing ones. "Oh."

There was a lift to the corners of his mouth as she went over the edge of pleasure again.

Returning to herself, she saw the tension in Lyle's face that made his cheekbones more pronounced. His eyes were still locked with hers, but his attention was elsewhere. He thrust into her, faster and stronger.

Throwing his head back, he let go a throaty groan as he found his release.

Cass's eyes slowly closed as Lyle shifted to her side, still breathing heavily. He intertwined his fingers with hers. Like their lives had become.

Could she let them remain so?

Lyle returned to bed to find Cass napping under the covers with her head on his pillow. Her scent would linger there when she was gone. Fulfillment filled his chest, made his heart light. Cass had come willingly and given without reservation.

He eased in next to her and pulled her close. She was warm and sleek along his side. After murmuring something unintelligible she settled like a kitten beside him. He brushed her hair from her face. Her lashes rested in a dark semi-circle long her cheek.

With Cass he'd found the most pleasure he'd ever experienced. He'd had relationships since Freya but only Cass had managed to capture his attention so fully that he thought of her more often than his job. No matter what he was doing, she slipped into his mind. Even after she'd left the pub this afternoon, he had been more concerned about her reaction than his own to seeing Freya.

Cass shifted against him. He looked down to find her watching him. "Hey."

A shadow of uncertainty filled her eyes. "Hi. I didn't mean to fall asleep on you."

"I'm not complaining." He hoped it would happen often. His body was already coming to life. Leaning down, he kissed her.

Cass stopped him from taking it deeper and further with a hand to his chest. "I'd better go. I don't want to miss the head count at the clinic."

Lyle wanted her to stay but he wouldn't make her. Still, he had to protest at her leaving. "They don't do a head count, do they?"

She smirked. "So asks the man running the show."

"I'm not a dictator."

Cass sat up, bringing the sheet along to cover her. To his disappointment. Was she still self-conscious about her scars? "I know that. In fact, next to my father you're the nicest man I know."

Lyle's chest tightened. Having felt his father's disappointment most of his adult life, to hear Cass say that touched him. He felt valued. He put his hand behind her neck and brought her lips to his. "Thank you. I think that might be one of the nicest compliments I've ever received."

"You're welcome. Now I'd better get going."

By slipping off the bed and snatching up her clothes, she gave him no time to argue. "Bathroom?"

Lyle gave a fleeting thought to outright asking her to stay. He didn't. Apparently she needed distance to think about what had just happened between them. Maybe he wanted that as well. He pointed. "Door in the hall."

When he heard the door close, he got up, dressed and went downstairs. Cass didn't even come into the living room where he was. Instead she went straight to her boots. It was as if she was running. Was she regretting what had happened?

She was in the process of pulling on her jacket when he placed his hands on her shoulders. "Cass."

"Yes?"

"What's going on inside that head of yours?"

She didn't look up.

Suppressing a sigh of frustration, he said, "I think we've come far enough in our relationship that we can trust each other. Why the speedy exit? At this rate you're starting to put a dent in my self-confidence."

That brought her head up. "Oh, no. It has nothing to do with you. It has everything to do with me. I don't want the staff gossiping about us. But let me assure you your ego is well deserved."

He wanted to thump his chest but he settled for a big smile. "That's good to hear. I'll walk you back to the castle." He helped her on with her jacket then pulled on his coat.

Outside the cottage Lyle took her hand. He was relieved Cass didn't try to pull free, half-afraid she would.

At the side door of the castle, she held him back when he would have gone in. "It might be a good idea for us to say goodnight here. Do you really want the staff to know the despicable things you've been doing to a resident?"

Lyle chuckled. "Despicable? What about the wicked things you did to me?"

"Wicked?" She sounded appalled.

"I like the wicked you. But I agree. We should keep this between us. There's no reason we should be the talk of the clinic, or the village for that matter." She already had enough troubling her. He didn't want her worrying about gossip.

Cass reached for the doorknob.

"You're forgetting something." Lyle brought her to him and kissed her soundly. They broke apart and he searched her face. "Sometime soon I plan to have you to myself all night."

Cass's eyes widened, as her mouth opened and closed before she shut the door between them.

Gratification filled him. She was not as unaffected by what had taken place between them as she acted.

CHAPTER SEVEN

Two days later Cass sat in the castle lounge in front of the roaring fire snuggled into one of the wing-backed chairs. She was attempting to read a book she'd found in the library about the history of Cluchlochry. What she was really doing was thinking about Lyle. She had only spoken to him briefly a couple of times since they had been together. He acted as if he was abiding by her implied suggestion they make their time in bed together a one-time occurrence. Even though she had intentionally given that impression, she missed kissing him or being held in his arms. It was driving her crazy not seeing him. But she would be leaving soon. Could her heart stand for her to take it further?

Was he waiting for her to come to him? Could she let herself do that? Would she be able not to? Indecision roiled in her.

It was a relief to have the distraction when Melissa pushed a young man in a wheelchair into the room and over beside her. At least now she had something to take her mind off Lyle.

The young man, dressed in a T-shirt and sweatpants, looked older than she guessed was the reality. He was gaunt. Dark rings beneath his eyes emphasized his lost look. One of his hands had a tremor.

"Hi, Cass. Have you met Andy Wallace?" Melissa asked as she parked the man near the fire. A small brown and white cocker spaniel jogged along beside him, coming to lie at his feet.

"No, I haven't. Hi, Andy." A week ago, could she have sounded that friendly? Being at the castle had changed her...or had it been Lyle? The thought both worried and thrilled her.

Andy nodded, then looked down at his clasped hands in his lap.

Wasn't he the patient who had been admitted the same day as she had been? In all the time she'd been there she hadn't seen him. "I've heard of you. Nice to meet you."

Melissa locked the brake on the wheelchair. She patted him on the shoulder. "I need to check on another patient then I'll be back to take you to therapy. I won't be long."

She gave Cass a quick smile and was gone.

Andy's eyes flickered to Cass with a look of uncertainty before they jerked away.

She leaned down and patted the dog. Not long ago she wouldn't have done that. "I do know Molasses. I work at the canine therapy center every afternoon so I get to take care of Molasses when she isn't with you. She's a good dog."

"Maybe when I start walking I can do that as well. The doctors keep telling me I'll walk again but I'm not sure that'll ever happen."

"Getting well takes time. I'm sure you'll get there." Who did she think she was to give encouragement when she'd been little more than a walking package of ugly emotions with a bad leg and arm a couple of weeks ago? This morning she'd even caught herself smiling when she thought of Lyle. Her leg was getting stronger and her arm was extending further. She smiled. Lyle had kissed her injuries. She had made more progress than she could have believed possible when she had arrived. For once she'd started thinking there was a future.

Andy said nothing more as he stared into the fire.

There wouldn't be much conversation unless she helped keep it going. She sensed he needed it. Wasn't that what Lyle had seen in her? The need to talk about the unseen trauma that physical therapy had no effect on? Could she help do for Andy what Lyle had done for her? Giving him an ear, just listen to him?

She raised the book in her hand. "I've been reading about the history of Cluchlochry. This is an amazing area."

He grunted.

A response. Somewhat.

"We don't have anything like this where I'm from." She waved a hand indicating the castle. "It's a special place."

"I used to spend a lot of time here," he muttered.

Cass had to lean forward to hear him. There was moisture pooling in his eyes.

"You've been to Heatherglen Castle before?"

"Yes. I grew up in Cluchlochry." His voice had grown stronger.

"It must have been a fun place for little boys. There are plenty of places to hide. Big spaces to run." The castle and grounds would be a wonderful place to spend a childhood. Would Lyle's kids one day do that? The thought of him having children with another woman caused a dull ache around her heart.

Andy's eyes took on a shadowed look. "Nick and I used to play hide and seek here all the time. I never could find him." He didn't say anything more, returning to staring at the fire. "He's gone now."

"Gone?" she prompted.

"Died in Afghanistan."

Cass sucked in a breath.

"Nick was my best friend," he mumbled.

She wasn't sure who he was talking about, but the name sounded familiar. Waiting, she hoped he'd answer her questions without her saying more.

"It should have been me who died. He should have got out of the army. Should have come home. Not gone back. I told him not to," he said, less to her and more to himself.

Cass's heart went out to him. She cringed, too well acquainted with loss. Of emotions so enormous and distressing they were difficult to live with. Hers had many fronts. Rufus being gone. What to do with her life now. Could she have a real lasting relationship with a man? Now to live with the scars. All of those were bundled into a massive ball of insecurity. She could understand the forlorn man beside her too well. That added to her discomfort. "Heatherglen was Nick's home?"

Andy gave her an odd look as if he was confused by her confusion. "Nick was Charles's older brother. Dr. Charles Ross-Wylde, the Laird."

"Yes, I've met the Laird. I know who you're talking about now. I'm sorry to hear about your friend. Losing someone you care about is hard."

"Have you lost someone?"

This was not the direction Cass had anticipated their conversation going. If she had she wouldn't have started it. Over the last few days thoughts of Lyle had managed to overtake all those ugly, sad feelings that had weighed heavy on her and she liked it that way. The pain had dulled. Maybe, just maybe, if she could share some of her pain with Andy, he wouldn't feel so alone, maybe believe that life could get better.

To her surprise, she had begun to believe that. It had slipped up on her but, yes, she did. "I have. It wasn't a person but the next thing to it. He was my partner and friend. Rufus, my dog."

Andy gave her a long searching look. "What happened?"

Cass wasn't sure she could go into the details but she'd opened the door so Andy deserved the truth. Her eyes clouded over. "We were a search and rescue team. We had just saved a child when there was a ground tremor and the wall of the building started to fall. Rufus barked, warning me. The wall fell on him. Hit me in the leg and arm." She could say this next part. Had to say it. "He saved my life and lost his."

Andy gave her a compassionate look. "I'm sorry about your dog."

Moisture filled Cass's eyes, making Andy a foggy blur. "I miss him every day. I'm not sure if I can or want to return to my job without him. It may be just too hard. But search and rescue is all I know."

Lyle walked to the lounge door when he heard Cass's voice. He halted inside the door, just in time to hear her confession about Rufus. He listened for more. She hadn't told him the entire story. No wonder she had been so devastated by what had happened to her. The loss of the dog was some of it but her fears and agony went deeper. Her world had been turned upside down. She was unsure what direction to take. The change in her life must be terrifying for her. She'd experienced a major loss of not only her dog but life as she had known it. He knew her well enough to know that, for her, losing her job was like losing her identity.

Yet she had shared her grief and feelings with another hurting person. That had to have been difficult for her. He should feel hurt that she had confided the deeper meaning of the loss of Rufus with Andy and not him, but what Lyle had just heard told him what a large heart Cass had for people.

Andy had refused to come out of his room for days. Lyle had finally convinced him to come down. On top of not wanting to interact with others, Andy refused to talk about his accident and about losing Nick. Lyle would be eternally grateful to Cass for getting him to open up, to take a metaphorical step forward.

Cass and Andy were so adsorbed in their conversation they didn't see or hear him. He shouldn't stand here eavesdropping but he couldn't move either. Thankfully that was taken out of his hands when Melissa brushed past him.

"Hi, Lyle. How're you today?" She kept going until she reached Andy.

Cass's head whipped around so that she looked directly at him. Surprise, concern and happiness ran over her features in rapid progression.

Lyle was glad to see her as well, but he was still disturbed by what he had heard and what it meant in her life. He had made less of it in his mind than he should have. He now understood why Cass acted the way she did about the dog they'd found, the sadness about her when she'd first arrived, even her not wanting to get too involved with him. Her emotions must be in turmoil. She had been and was suffering far more than he'd given her credit for.

He stepped forward as Melissa announced as she

took off the brake on the chair, "They're waiting for you in therapy, Andy. We must go."

Andy gave Cass a nod.

She offered him a wry smile. "See you soon, Andy."

Melissa rolled him back, turned him and they headed out the door.

Cass's eyes rose to meet Lyle's. "You heard?"

Lyle nodded. He didn't even try to question why she hadn't shared with him how losing Rufus had affected her. Now wasn't the time to analyze that. There might never be one. She didn't owe him anything. One hot evening together didn't mean they could or should bare their souls to one another. That was the way she seemed to want it. Didn't he as well?

Pushing herself to her feet, she said, "I'd better go."

He took a couple of steps forward, his voice going low. "I've missed you, Cass. I was coming to look for you when I heard your voice."

"Did you want something?"

"I'd like a kiss." He looked around, "But I won't do that here."

Cass rewarded him with a blush. She might be acting as if she was immune to him but she wasn't, not even a little bit.

"I'll wait until later. But I will kiss you." He stressed the last sentence.

She grinned at him. "Is that a promise, Doctor?"

Lyle's heart soared. He liked that much better than her sad look. "It is. I do have something to ask you, though. My mother rang and would like me to bring you around to Harlow House for dinner this evening. She wants to keep her promise to teach you to knit."

Cass looked away as if she was unsure. "That's not necessary."

He waited until she met his gaze again. "My mother will be disappointed if you don't come."

Cass looked down as if her shoes required her attention. "I'm just not sure that's a good idea."

"Why not? You have been invited." Lyle watched her closely. It shouldn't matter so much that she agree.

"I don't want to give her any ideas about us, with me leaving so soon."

"If that's now you feel…" He turned to go.

She reached out and grabbed his forearm. "Wait."

Lyle didn't realize until that second just how much he'd missed Cass's touch. He placed his hand over hers.

Cass's eyelids fluttered as she gave him a wary look. "I guess I could go. I'd never want to hurt your mother's feelings."

He made a *tsk*ing sound. "And here I was hoping you wanted to spend time with me. I'll meet you in the foyer at five."

She nodded.

Lyle ran his thumb across the top of her hand. "By the way, Cass, you're beautiful both inside and out. You really helped Andy out today. He needs someone to confide in, someone who understands where he's coming from. You're a special person, Cass Bellow."

Her eyes softened. Lyle had to leave before he kissed her right then and there.

A few hours later Lyle strolled into the foyer, expecting to see Cass waiting near the door. Instead he found her with a staff member and a couple of other residents, tying large red bows on the banister. The greenery had been draped the week before.

"It's really starting to look like Christmas in here." His attention was directly on Cass.

Everyone turned to him.

"Thank you," the staff member said. "I have some excellent help."

"I have one more bow to tie and I'll be ready," Cass called.

There was a happy note in her voice. That had been missing when she'd first arrived and he rather liked hearing it. Had he had anything to do with putting it there? He really hoped so. "We have time."

She moved up a step with only a slight hesitation. Soon she would be coming down those stairs as part of her graduation and be leaving him. The thought brought a wince deep within him. Did he want her to stay? Could he ask her to? He refused to do a long-distance relationship again. From experience he'd learned those didn't work. Cass's life was going all over the world, helping people, and his was staying here and doing the same. It would never work. It would be better for both of them to let go sooner than later.

Another few minutes went by before Cass came down the steps slowly, holding tightly to the rail, but she was doing it on her own. She approached him.

"You have made progress. It won't be long before you'll be going up and coming down the grand staircase instead of using the lift."

She smiled and his world brightened. "I have to admit that a few weeks ago I looked at it as if it was Mount Everest. I was halfway up before I knew it."

"You've worked hard. You should be proud of yourself." Lyle was.

"Thanks." Cass picked up her coat off a chair and slipped into it. Buttoning it, she quickly wrapped the scarf around her neck and pulled on her hat.

"Ready?"

"I am." She headed toward the front door.

Lyle followed. When they were out of hearing of the others he asked, "I thought you didn't want anyone to know about our…uh, friendship? You didn't seem to mind the others knowing you were going out with me."

Over her shoulder she said, "I told them you were testing my endurance by going for a walk with me."

"Ah, I see." He had a sour taste in his mouth. When she had suggested the other night that they keep their relationship between themselves it'd seemed the wise thing to do. Now he wanted people to know that Cass was his and she hers. Or was it really that way? "We do need to walk to my place and then take the car from there."

"Your parents live far?" She started around the castle toward the path to his cottage.

"No, but further than *you* would even wish to walk."

They were soon out of sight of the castle and Lyle took her hand. His heart thumped an extra beat when she didn't pull away. After they reached the seclusion of the large trees, he pulled her behind one and into his arms.

"I've waited too long to do this." His lips found hers.

Unsure what Cass's reaction would be, he was elated when she stepped into him and joined him in a kiss that should have melted the snow beneath their feet. They stayed like that until the wind blew and a pile of snow dropped off a branch, landing on their shoulders. They giggled like school kids then started toward his place again.

Once there, Lyle led her to the detached garage to where he kept his car. Inside it, he reached over and cupped her cheek. "I have missed you. I wished there was time to take you inside and have my way with you, but my mother is expecting us."

Cass smiled. "We all like to keep our parents happy."

He groaned. "That we do." He'd spent the better part of his life trying to do just that and was still managing to disappoint his father. If he returned to the army, he would be choosing his father's happiness over his own.

Cass looked over at Lyle as he backed out of the garage. It had been so long since she had been alone with him that she'd feared she might rush into his arms when she did have him to herself. The moment she had looked up from tying the bow to the spindle and her gaze had locked with his, her heart had galloped like a horse making the last quarter-mile.

What had he been thinking? Had he been as excited to see her? She'd left things between them as if their time together had been nothing but a nice evening. She'd been fooling herself. Being with Lyle had been more than that. She couldn't say that to him earlier in the lounge, so she was glad to have the invitation to his parents'. They would have a chance to talk. More than that, to touch.

She'd only agreed to help decorate the foyer because it gave her nervous energy an outlet. If she hadn't, she would have been pacing the floor when he arrived. It had to have been high school since she'd last been this wired up about seeing a guy. Her attraction to Lyle had tipped over into need in such a short time.

That horse had broken into an even faster gallop the second Lyle had pulled her out of sight of the castle and kissed her. She'd been back where she belonged. When the snow had fallen on them she had laughed like she hadn't laughed in far too long. Instead of having second thoughts about becoming involved with Lyle, she was running headlong into doing so. Especially by going to his parents' house.

After Lyle had driven onto the main road, he took her hand and held it as often as the narrow winding roads would allow. He drove through the village and out the other side. Soon he turned into a lane that led to a stately house that was a larger version of Lyle's cottage.

Lyle's mother greeted her by pulling her into a hug. Cass instantly missed her own mother, who she hoped to see soon. She glanced at Lyle. That would mean she would be leaving him. At that moment, she decided she would make the most of the time she had with him. She wanted this happiness to last as long as possible. The difference between misery and joy had been made clear over the last couple of weeks and she would take all the cheer in life she could grab for as long as she could have it. Right now, that meant being with Lyle.

When Mrs. Sinclair finished embracing Cass, she moved on to Lyle with the same vigor, as if she hadn't seen him in years. Done, she escorted them into a living area where the TV was on. Lyle's father didn't stand as they entered.

Mr. Sinclair did offer his hand. "Hello again, young lady."

Lyle would age well based on his father's looks, despite the older man's illness. Some other woman would get to watch that. Cass wasn't going to think of that now. "Hello. Thanks for having me."

"Glad to. Hello, son." He and Lyle shook hands.

Something about the action bothered Cass. Shouldn't they have hugged? A second of coolness seemed to surround them.

"Cass and I are going to the kitchen to have our knitting lesson," Mrs. Sinclair announced, and turned to Cass. "Unless you have changed your mind?"

"Oh, no, I would love to learn."

"Then come with me. Lyle, you watch the match with your dad while we have our lesson." Mrs. Sinclair waved a hand at him as she moved toward a door off the room.

Cass glanced at Lyle who was already settling into a chair. Maybe Cass had just been imagining things. Lyle acted as if spending time with his father wasn't a problem.

She found the more she was around Lyle's parents the more she liked them. His mother was what every mother should be—warm and open. His father was harder to get to know with his gruff voice and iron exterior, but Cass suspected he loved his wife and son deeply, and they him.

Cass followed Mrs. Sinclair into the kitchen. It, like the rest of the house, was in perfect order. The counter tops were spotless and the floor gleamed.

"Why don't we sit by the fire? We'll be warm there."

A large range sat against one wall with two rocking chairs in front of it. Beside one of the chairs was a basket full of yarn with large needles stuck in it.

Cass took the chair that didn't have the basket next to it, reasoning that it was Mrs. Sinclair's.

Lyle's mother settled into the other. "We're going to start with something simple. Just learn to knit. I think it will be all that you want to do in the first lesson. Now I'm going to show you how to start then I'm going to let you do it."

Cass eagerly sat on the edge of her seat, watching every move Mrs. Sinclair made. "That sounds fine. I know nothing about knitting."

Mrs. Sinclair's mouth formed a smile much like Lyle's. "Today you'll learn. Here are some needles and you pick out a skein of wool."

"They're all so lovely." Cass decided on a blue that reminded her of the color of Lyle's eyes. When she was gone at least she would have that to remember him by.

Lyle's mother picked up some needles and pulled out a length of wool. "The first thing you want to do is make a small loop and slide it onto one of the needles."

Mrs. Sinclair was already in her element. Cass watched intently.

"Now you bring this up around here, the tip of the needle through here and the wool around like this." The wool worked perfectly onto the needle. "Now I want you to try with your needles and wool."

Cass did as she had been shown until it was time to move the wool up and around the needle.

"Not quite, dear." Mrs. Sinclair's voice was patient. Did Lyle get that from her as well? "Let me show you." She brought the wool around and got Cass started correctly once again.

Cass had made ten rows and was proud of her accomplishment when Lyle's voice came from behind her. "It looks like you're making progress."

Cass held up what she had done. "Look, I'm actually knitting."

He smiled as if he was proud of her as well.

"She's a really good student," Mrs. Sinclair offered.

"Cass is good at anything she puts her mind to," Lyle said.

A warmth that had nothing to do with the fire spread through her. Looking over her shoulder again, Cass saw Lyle gazing at her with a twinkle in his eye. Was he thinking about their time together in bed? She gave him a shy smile then glanced at his mother to find her watching them closely. Did she see the attraction between them?

"I hate to break this up, but Dad and I were wondering how long it would be until dinner?"

Mrs. Sinclair put her work into her basket and stood. "Lyle Sinclair, you know as well as anyone that in this house we eat promptly at six. We have all your life. Gregor wouldn't have it any other way."

"Yes, once in the army always in the army." Lyle said it as fact, but there was a note of bitterness there as well.

She gave her son a direct look. "I'll have you know I don't worry about you starving when you eat Mrs. Renwick's food all the time."

Lyle's mood lightened. "I do have to be careful not to overdo it there."

Cass placed her work in the basket as well. "What can I do to help?"

"We're just having a chicken pie tonight. It's already in the oven so there's not much to do except set the table."

"Lyle and I can take care of that, can't we?" Cass looked at him.

An amazed look came to his face, but he nodded. "Yes, we can."

Over the next few minutes she and Lyle gathered what was needed. A couple of times he brushed past her, making her tingle all over. When she asked him for a fork he handed it across the table in a manner that let him trail his fingers over her palm, which started her center throbbing. She'd had no idea that setting the table could be such an erotic activity. Her eyes met his. She didn't see a flicker of desire there, but a fire burning.

His mother cleared her throat, bringing them back

to where they were. Cass dropped the fork with a clang onto a plate.

Lyle, the devil, grinned and picked it up. He put it in its place. "All done, Mum."

His mother smiled. "Thank you." She turned back to the counter to where a large bowl sat. "Oh, my goodness, we all need to give the pudding a stir. I don't want to forget it."

"Pudding a stir?" Cass gave the bowl a dubious look. "Exactly what're we doing?"

"Stirring the Christmas pudding," Mrs. Sinclair stated, as if it was a great occasion.

"I don't know what a Christmas pudding is." Cass looked into the bowl from which she had removed the cloth.

"I think they call it a fruit cake in America." Lyle moved up beside Cass.

"I have heard of them but never seen one or eaten one." Cass still studied the mixture.

"You'll have to join us for some in a few weeks." Lyle's mother pulled out a large wooden spoon from a drawer.

Cass felt more than saw Lyle tense beside her. Did it matter to him that she would be gone soon? It did her. She wanted as much time with him as possible before she left. "I'm not sure that I'll be here that long."

"Well, if you're here then you must come for a slice." Mrs. Sinclair didn't miss a beat. "You need to stir three times and then make a wish."

Lyle's mother handed her the spoon.

Wish? What should she wish for? To hurry home? For a new partner? She wasn't sure she was ready for that. She glanced at Lyle. To have him in her life always? What did she want most? Happiness. She glanced at Lyle. She felt that right now. But could it last?

It took more effort than she'd anticipated to stir the thick mixture but she managed to make the three turns. She made her wish.

"So what did you ask for?" Lyle took the spoon and started to stir.

"I can't tell you that. It won't come true." And she wanted it to come true no matter how improbable and unrealistic it was.

His mother stepped away. Lyle whispered, "Was it about me?"

Cass whispered back, "Such an ego."

"Lyle, if you'll carry the pie to the table and Cass brings the beans, I think we'll be ready." Mrs. Sinclair pulled a round golden-brown-crusted pie out of the oven. It smelled heavenly. She set it on the counter.

Lyle then picked it up and moved it to the table. His mother handed her the bowl with beans in it.

"Gregor," Mrs. Sinclair called. "Come to the table."

Lyle's father joined them, but it took him a while. He moved slowly.

Over the next hour they enjoyed good food and lively conversation. Cass looked around the cozy room. At Lyle. This was what she would like to have in her life. Lyle smiled at her. This was happiness.

"So what do you do in America?" Lyle's father asked her.

Her heart sank at the reminder. This wasn't her home. "I work in search and rescue." Did she still, though?

Gregor nodded. "Interesting work."

"It can be." She didn't really want to talk about it. "I understand you're retired military?"

He sat straighter, if that was possible. "I am. All the

men in my family have made a career in the armed forces." He gave Lyle, who had turned stony-faced, a pointed look. "I'm hoping Lyle will decide to go active again soon."

She looked at Lyle, who was pushing food around on his plate. Had she said something wrong?

"Dad, let's not get into that now."

For the first time since Cass had arrived Mrs. Sinclair had no smile on her face. An uncomfortable feeling settled around them, completely wiping out the ease of earlier.

She had said something wrong!

Lyle's request went unnoticed by Mr. Sinclair. "You need to do it soon or time will run out for promotions."

"Isn't Lyle needed here? You should have seen him in action the other night. He had two patients to see about and then me. I understand that he's the only emergency medical care around here. That's a big burden for anyone. I think there are different ways of fighting for people. You did it by being in the military and Lyle does it by caring for people when they are hurt. In my book you're both heroes."

The others looked at her, speechless. Not even Mr. Sinclair said a thing. Lyle gave her a tender look of wonderment and appreciation.

Mrs. Sinclair pushed back from the table. "I'll get those biscuits I bought at the market the other day for dessert."

An hour later Lyle was driving them back to his cottage.

"I hope I didn't say anything wrong at dinner," Cass said in a small voice. "I didn't mean to."

Lyle couldn't believe that Cass had even asked that. After her speech to his father Lyle's chest had puffed

out like a bird preening for a new mate. Few managed
to put his father in his place and Cass had done it ef-
fortlessly and had complimented his father at the same
time. Lyle looked at her like she was a queen. "You
were wonderful. The subject is an age-old sticky issue
between my father and me."

"How's that?" Her attention was focused on him.

"You could tell that I'm a disappointment to him.
He's sick. Dying, in fact."

Cass squeezed the hand he already held. "I'm sorry."

"I am, too. If I re-enlisted he'd be so happy. I could
give him that before he died. Right now, I'm letting the
family name down."

"You are not! He can't believe that. You help people.
Look how much you have helped me."

Lyle raised a brow and gave her a suggestive look.
"I don't help all the residents in the same way as I have
you."

Her lips turned up in a smirk and she poked him in
the shoulder with a finger. "And you had better not."

He was even feeling better about himself after that
statement. It was the first time Cass had indicated that
she felt any ownership of him, that he was important to
her on a level outside bed. He liked the idea of her being
jealous. She was definitely good for his ego.

Lyle pulled into his garage and turned off the engine. Twisting toward Cass he brought her to him. She
looked at him expectantly. "I thought you were perfect
tonight. Thank you for the vote of confidence. It means
a lot. Especially coming from you."

Cass gave him a tender smile as his lips slowly lowered to hers. They were as soft as he remembered. A
second later, her hands gripped his coat and pulled him

closer. She returned his kiss. He lifted her onto his lap. It wasn't until she winced that he remembered her injuries.

He let go of her and she slid back into the passenger seat. "I'm sorry again. I keep forgetting you've been hurt. That hero certificate you said I deserved should be revoked."

"I'm fine. When I make certain moves my leg lets me know it doesn't like it."

"Necking in a two-seater car would be one of those times." What was wrong with him? He forgot everything but touching Cass when she was near. He climbed out of the car and hurried around to help her out. "I'm really sorry."

She wrapped her finger around his coat lapels and pulled him to her again. "Why don't you shut up and kiss me, then take me inside?"

He brought her into his arms with a smile on his lips. "I can do that."

CHAPTER EIGHT

FOUR MORNINGS LATER Cass was still in his bed when he woke up. Lyle liked it that way. Too much. She had stayed the night after they had gone to his parents'. They had agreed to eating dinner at his place the next evening.

As he'd held her in his arms after they had made love, he'd asked, "Will you stay the night?"

She'd leaned up to look at him. "I will if you understand that this can only be a short-term thing between us. As soon as I am given a clean bill of health, I'm going home. I can't handle anything serious in my life right now. I've just gotten to where I can get out of bed without dreading it."

Lyle had wiggled his brows. "That wouldn't be because you've been in bed with me, would it?"

She'd brushed a hand low over him and his body had twitched in reaction. "You might say that. I just need things to remain easy and fun between us. I've been on emotional overload for so long. I don't think I could handle more."

"I can do slow and easy. In fact, I'd like to practice now." He'd rolled Cass on her side and brushed a feather-light finger over her hip. Lyle had been rewarded with a shiver from Cass.

The next two nights they had eaten at the castle and then walked hand in hand to his place. Lyle had tried not to question Cass's decisions. Instead, he enjoyed having her in his life. No one at the castle had asked him where she was at night and he'd offered no explanation. All he knew was that life was better than it had ever been.

What they didn't do was talk about when she was leaving. Yet both knew it was coming. Too fast for him. Did Cass feel the same way? He didn't want to ruin what they had by asking.

On Saturday morning, they were lying in bed and Cass's hand was causally rubbing back and forth over his chest when she asked, "Hey, have you ever thought about making this place more festive? Everyone else is busy decorating for Christmas but you have nothing up."

"Are you thinking I should have a tree in my bedroom?"

Her hand gave him a light swat. Which he liked more than resented. "Of course not. I was thinking of you putting one up in your living room. It looks like Scrooge lives here."

"You can hurt my feelings, you know? I'd just planned to enjoy what's up at the castle. I've never really gone in for that sort of stuff, and I go to Mum and Dad's on Christmas Day." He pushed her hair back, letting his fingers run through it. "But maybe if I had somebody to help me, I could put a few things up. Would you be willing to help?"

Cass twisted around, looking him in the face while giving him a tantalizing view of the curve of her breast and hip. She seemed to give no thought to having scars anymore. "I thought you would never ask."

Lyle chuckled.

She grinned. "So do you have any ornaments or anything to put on a tree?"

"No. I hadn't had any need for them."

"Then we'll go to the Christmas market and get some. I saw some really pretty ones made out of natural stuff in one of the stalls."

Later Cass sat at the kitchen table, having a cup of coffee, while he scrambled eggs and prepared toast. She looked up and smiled. Lyle liked this Cass much better than the one who had first arrived at the castle. He would miss her when she was gone. "I really appreciate you talking to Andy. I've been worried about him."

"Unfortunately, I think we have a lot in common." There was a dejected note in her words.

"You might be right about that." He really couldn't break patient confidentiality. "I wish you hadn't kept all that happened to you from me, but I understand why you did. I'm so sorry."

She gave him a look of appreciation then went back to her coffee. Cass would talk more when she was ready. He finished the eggs, put the toast on a plate and carried it all to the table.

"I can help you." Cass reached for the plate.

"I told you that I wanted to cook for you. If we're going to get a tree and ornaments today you need to keep up your strength." He winked. "I might have other plans for you as well."

He was rewarded with an attractive blush. She never stopped amazing him. Cass was as tough as stone on the outside but could blush like a young woman after her first kiss. He loved the two sides of her. Love! Was he falling in love with Cass?

She spooned out scrambled eggs and took a piece

of toast. "So can we go to the market as soon as we're through eating?"

"Are we in that much of a hurry?"

Cass gave him an insistent look. "We have a lot to do if we're going to get this place looking festive today."

"We have to do it all today?" He gave a theatrical groan.

She put her fists on her hips and gave him a huffy look. "We do. I won't be here much longer, and I want to enjoy it for as long as I can."

That statement stabbed Lyle with reality, but he refused to let on that her leaving would upset him. She wanted casual and he would try to give her that. He chuckled. "Where did all this newfound Christmas spirit come from?"

Cass looked directly into his eyes. "From being around you. Thank you for bringing me back from that dark place."

His heart swelled. This was what it was like to be appreciated, valued for who he was as a person. He'd not felt that in some time. He needed it. Cass had given him a real gift. "You're welcome." He kissed her, keeping it tender, wanting her to sense his gratitude, then he pulled away, "You're right, I do need some cheer."

Soon after they'd finished breakfast, they left for the village. Few people were around. The sky was dark and it was starting to spit. It would snow again before the end of the day. Cass led the way to the stall with the ornaments she had seen. There, the owner greeted Lyle, whom he had known all his life.

Lyle told Cass, "Get whatever you think I need."

She grinned. "You shouldn't have said that." Cass went about picking out ornaments and putting them into a pile on the corner of the table.

Lyle paid the man, who was grinning from ear to ear as they walked off.

"Shouldn't we stop and say hi to your mother?" Cass looped her hand in the crook of his elbow.

"Yes. She would be hurt to know you came here and didn't say hello." Lyle led her down another aisle to his mother's stall.

His mother saw them and stopped knitting to greet them. "What're you two doing here?"

Cass gave this mother a self-satisfied smile and held up the bag she carried. "We came to get some ornaments for Lyle's tree."

His mother gave him a pointed look then asked with a sarcastic note, "Lyle's going to have a tree?"

He'd not had a tree or decorated his cottage since his return home. Freya had always made a big deal out of Christmas but he had never cared one way or the other. It wasn't worth the effort as far as he was concerned. But if Cass wanted him to have a tree, he would have a tree with all the trimmings.

"He is," Cass said proudly.

His mother looked from him to her and back again. Her smile had broadened.

"We're on our way to get one right now but we wanted to come by and say hi to you." The cheerful words seemed to bubble out of her.

"Gregor," his mother called.

Lyle turned to see his father shuffling toward them. He looked more tired than usual, older.

"Hello, son. I'm glad I got to see you. I spoke to Colonel McWright a minute ago. He said you haven't been by to talk to him about re-enlisting."

That was the last conversation Lyle wanted to have

with him. "I've been busy at the clinic. I'll try to get by sometime this week."

"You need to do so. He'll be retiring soon and won't have the influence he has now. If you want that position you need to be talking to him."

The smile on Cass's face faded to an expression of curiosity and concern. Lyle wanted that smile to return. His hand went to Cass's elbow. "I'll take care of it. It's good to see you. Cass and I are putting up a tree so we need to go and pick out one before they're all gone." He started them toward the door.

"Nice to see you, Colonel and Mrs. Sinclair." Cass waved.

"Bye, Mum. Dad," Lyle called as they walked away.

Cass pulled to a halt when they were out of sight of his parents. "Are you really returning to active duty?"

"No. Maybe. I don't know. Look, we have a fun day planned and I don't want to talk about that. Let's concentrate on putting up a tree."

Cass studied him a moment then smiled brightly. "Works for me."

He would miss that smile when she returned to America. A stab of pain shot through him. This wasn't supposed to happen. He didn't, wouldn't, do long distance. It didn't work. He'd learned that the hard way. Yet he couldn't stop himself from holding onto what time he had left with her.

Cass came to another sudden stop at a stall selling Christmas-tree skirts. She fingered a navy one with silver stars sewn closer to the trunk of the tree and sloping mounds of white depicting snowy mountains. Was she thinking of the night he had found her sitting on the rock wall? Lyle smiled. Even then he had been captivated by her.

"Get it, if you want it." He pulled out his wallet.

"I wasn't asking you to buy it." She gave him a concerned look.

He gave her an indulgent smile. "I know that, but every good tree needs a skirt."

A few minutes later they left. Cass carried their purchases with a happy look on her face.

On their way back to his cottage they stopped at a place on the outskirts of the village to buy a tree. He had to remind Cass that his ceilings weren't that high when she admired a ten-foot tree. With an exaggerated expression of disappointment, she located a six-foot tree that he still hoped would fit through his doors. Cass's happiness with her choice made him keep his concerns to himself.

They made one more stop at a shop and bought a tree stand and lights. They spent the remainder of the day putting up the Christmas tree and decorating it. Done, they switched off the main lights and sat by the fire with a hot cup of tea.

Cass laid her head on his shoulder. "What kinds of family Christmas traditions does your family have?"

"You already know about the Christmas pudding. One year when I was off on the other side of the world Mum posted one to me. I hate to admit I was pretty lonely that year."

Cass said softly, "It was the year you got the letter."

For once the mention of what had happened to him didn't include pain. "It was. I sliced the pudding and shared it with the patients in my unit and we had a right fine celebration."

Lyle looked at Cass. To his amazement she had tears in her eyes. "What's all this about?"

She took his hand and tenderly rubbed it. "I just hate to think of you away by yourself at Christmas."

"Aw, honey, I'm home now. My Christmases are happy. This one will be especially so with this tree." What he didn't say was that he wished she would be there as well. He wouldn't think about that; instead he would enjoy what he had at this moment. She would be leaving soon. They had an agreement. Still the need to keep her there pulled at him.

A heavy knock at the front door broke the moment. Lyle opened it to find one of the local police officers standing there.

"Lyle, a five-year-old girl has gone missing. She wandered off from the market. We need your help to search."

"Missing?" The low sound of Cass's voice held a looming note of fear.

He forced himself to concentrate on what the policeman was saying. Cass he would soothe later. "How long has she been gone?"

"Two and a half hours." The policeman was wasting no time in giving answers.

His next question made him sick to ask but it was necessary. "Do you believe someone has taken her?"

The man's lips thinned. "Right now, no, but we're ruling out no possibilities."

"What do I need to do?"

"We've made a grid of the area." He handed him a map. "We need you to look here." He pointed to a square.

Cass came to stand in front of Lyle. "Do you have a piece of the child's clothing?" she asked in a determined voice. "I can help."

"You are?"

"This is Cass Bellow. She's trained in search and rescue," Lyle offered.

Cass let him say no more. "Time's of the essence. Do you have something or not?"

The officer glanced at Lyle. He nodded. "I can get something."

"Then we'll meet you at the market cross in twenty minutes." She made that announcement, turned and started putting on her coat.

"We'll see you then," Lyle said.

The officer looked unsure, but nodded and left.

Lyle closed the door and asked Cass, "What're you thinking?"

"One of the dogs at the center has past search and rescue training. I've been working with him. He knows me. He might be able to help." She wrapped her scarf around her neck.

Lyle had to admire her. Working with a dog on a search had to take all her fortitude. For her to even volunteer said something about what kind of person she was. "You sure you can handle that?"

"Don't really have a choice. A child is missing." She jerked her hat down around her ears and opened the door.

"Hey, wait for me." Lyle snatched up his scarf and hat and hurried after her.

CHAPTER NINE

"Komm!" Cass commanded Hero out of his pen at the canine center. She had made friends with him over the past couple of weeks so she had no trouble encouraging him to come to her. As he exited the cage she clipped on the leash. *"Fuss."* Hero walked beside her to Lyle's car.

He opened the door and Cass said, *"Komm,"* and Hero jumped into the backseat.

Less than a minute later they were on their way into Cluchlochry.

Cass clutched her hands in her lap. It hadn't been long since she'd had an assignment and worked with a dog, yet it seemed like years. She was a bundle of nerves. What if she broke down? What if they couldn't find the girl? What if...? All that fear and sadness that had held her heart in a vise had returned. If Rufus was here she'd have no doubts about locating the girl but she didn't know Hero well or his abilities. Still, she had to try.

Lyle drove faster than the speed limit, but every minute mattered. Hero sat calmly in the backseat of the car. Lyle pulled into a parking space close to the market cross. With the market over for the day, there were plenty available.

The policeman who had come to Lyle's cottage was

waiting. As soon as they joined him, he handed Lyle a small orange jacket. "I understand she was wearing this earlier today."

"So she has no coat on?" Lyle asked, concern lacing his words.

Cass shivered as much from the cold as from her fear for the little girl.

The officer's face was grim as he said, "From what her parents tell me, she's wearing a jumper, jeans and boots. We don't know if she still has gloves on or a hat, or anything like that."

"Then we need to worry about exposure as well." Cass's words were flat and to the point.

"I'll get a thermal blanket and my medical bag out of the car." Lyle wasted no time in doing so.

"May I see the jacket?" Cass reached out her hand.

The policeman handed it to her and she knelt so that Hero could get a good sniff of the clothing.

Lyle returned with a satchel on his hip, the strap across his chest. He looked at her. "Ready?"

"Yes. You have a blanket?"

He patted the satchel and clicked on a large torch.

She gave the command to find. *"Voran."*

Hero started off across the village square with his nose close to the ground. Cass followed and Lyle was close behind.

Hero led them down a side street and out into a lane. Cass remained encouraged because he acted as if he had located a scent.

Her hand stayed on the leash as they continued walking at a brisk pace. Well outside the village Hero headed off the road and onto a path.

"It looks like he's taking us to the ruins," Lyle said, walking close beside her.

Her leg began to burn as the gradient grew steeper. She would push through it; she had no choice. When she faltered, Lyle supported her with a hand on her forearm. "Let me take the lead. I know this path."

"Okay. I'll let Hero go off leash." She unclipped the dog and he moved ahead of them.

Lyle took her hand and they worked their way up the path. It became more difficult to maneuver the closer to the Heatherglen Keep ruins they climbed.

Occasionally Hero would stop and look back at them. He acted impatient for them to join him. He didn't have the same trouble with the steep terrain. Soon Cass's leg went from aching to really hurting but she wouldn't let on. She was the expert in this work. A little girl's life depended on her.

Now that the sun had gone down it was pitch black. There was no natural light from the moon. Making matters worse was the fact that clouds were rolling in. It would snow tonight.

When—if—they found the girl she could very well be hypothermic. She would need medical attention immediately. Could they find her soon enough?

Cass stumbled and Lyle caught her before she went down.

"Do you need to stop?" His concerned look touched her heart.

She shook her head. "No. We have to find her."

For a second he looked as if he were going to argue. "I don't need two patients."

"I'll keep that in mind." Cass trudged forward.

Lyle pursed his lips and nodded, then joined her.

Not soon enough for Cass they made it to the ruins. In the daylight she had no doubt the area was interesting but in the dark it had an eerie feel to it. Hero sniffed around, making a circle. Finally he stood beside a couple of huge stones and barked.

"Have you found something?" Cass said to the dog as she made her way toward him, with Lyle shining the flashlight that direction. *"Setzen."*

The dog sat.

She and Lyle were looking into a hole.

"This was the dungeon at one time," Lyle murmured.

"Looks about as much fun now. Do you see anything?" Cass searched while being careful not to lean over too far.

Lyle went down on this belly. He directed the light straight down.

"There she is," Cass cried. A small body lay curled on the ground, not moving.

She stepped closer and Lyle said, "Cass, careful! Don't fall in."

"How're we going to get her out?" Cass was already looking for things they could use.

"We'll call for help." Lyle pulled out his phone. "Damn, I don't have a signal. One of us will have to go for help. But right now we're going to have to see to her. Minutes could mean the difference between life and death."

"We're going to have to get down to her somehow." Cass paused, panic filling her. The girl just couldn't die.

"I'll climb down." Lyle was already in the process of removing his bag.

"It looks too slick to do that. You'll have to lower me. I'm the lighter of the two of us. We can use the strap on your bag. It might not be long enough, but it'll get me close enough to drop the rest of the way."

"What about your leg? It might not hold up under

that kind of pressure." Everything in Lyle's voice said that he wasn't going to agree to her plan.

Cass faced him. "That's just a chance I'll have to take. You know the path back better than me. The girl needs help now. I'm not going to argue about it anymore."

The determination in her voice must have got through to Lyle because he started unclipping the strap from his bag. With it removed, he pushed the extender so that the strap was as long as possible. "You ready?"

Cass took an end of the strap, wrapping it around her hand. "I am."

They both moved to the side of the hole. Lyle shined the light into the hole.

"There's still no movement." Cass's chest tightened. They had to get to her soon. Was she gone already?

Lyle dropped the flashlight into the hole giving them some light to work with. He then wrapped the strap around his hand just as Cass had done. She lay on her belly and crawled backward, going feet first into the hole. Lyle went to his knees, holding her under her arms as she slipped over the side.

"Feel for footholds." His voice was tight from the effort of holding her.

She did as Lyle instructed and located one. It was near the foot of her injured leg. She couldn't let the pain that shot through her slow her progress. She had to keep moving. When she was completely over the side she hung onto the strap as Lyle lowered her. She went further into the dark abyss. Thinking she had gone as far as possible, there was a sudden jerk and she was lowered further. Lyle must be on his stomach with his arms extended. She could only imagine the strain holding her was putting on his shoulder muscles. Guessing she was only a few feet from the ground, Cass let go.

She fell, hitting the ground. Pain that made her clench her jaw rocketed through her leg. She rolled onto her hip. "Huh."

"Cass?" Lyle's fear-filled voice came from above her.

"I'm fine. Harder landing than I anticipated." Cass picked up the flashlight and crawled over to the girl. She still hadn't moved. Worry leaped in Cass. Was she already gone? No, she wouldn't believe that.

Placing two fingers to the girl's neck, Cass found a pulse, but it was weak. The child's skin was icy to the touch. Hypothermia had set in. Pulling off her jacket, she wrapped it around the girl. Cass removed her hat and scarf and put them on the girl as well.

"Cass, move far to one side so I can throw the bag down. I want vitals before I leave."

"Ready." A few seconds later Lyle's bag landed with a flop a couple of feet from her.

"Check her temperature and let me know what it is. Also, can you tell if anything is broken?" Lyle was giving her more orders than she could carry out at once. He was in full doctor mode.

Cass pulled the bag to her. Searching through it, she found the thermometer. Cass positioned the flashlight so that it shone on the girl. Thankfully Lyle had a battery-powered tympanic thermometer that Cass could just push into the girl's ear. Removing the girl's clothing would only make things worse. At least she wasn't wet.

Hero barked.

"Bleib!" Cass yelled and the dog stopped barking. *"Braver hund."* She called up to Lyle's shadow as she spread out the thermal blanket. "Temp is ninety degrees Fahrenheit—that's 32 degrees Celsius. Pulse is weak.

Skin pale and cold to touch. Her breathing is shallow. I'm wrapping her in a blanket now."

"Can you do a BP?" There was an anxiousness to his voice.

"I'd rather not remove the warmth I've already given her."

"Aye. There's no question she has hypothermia."

Cass lay down on the thermal blanket and pulled the girl to her then wrapped the shiny, crinkly material around them. Maybe her body heat would help some.

Lyle's voice rang out again. "There are two heat packs in the bag. Squeeze them and put them under her arms. Don't put them against her skin."

She already knew that from her own training, but Lyle could only be frustrated by not being in the hole and the one taking care of the patient. He was a hands-on type of doctor.

"I'm leaving to call for help. Please don't take any chances. Stay put. I'll be back as soon as I can."

"Hurry."

"I will. Cass? I want your promise you won't do anything foolish." Lyle's worry laced every word.

Cass's heart swelled. He was such a good man. "Hero will be here. We'll be waiting for you."

"I'm counting on that."

Lyle hated to leave Cass but he had no choice. He had to go for help. They needed more than his to-go medical bag to save the girl's life. She needed hospital care. Right away.

Without his flashlight the walk down the rocky narrow path was slow, frustrating and dangerous. The fact that it had started sleeting only added to the difficulty.

Despite that he had to keep moving. Not just for the girl's sake but for Cass's as well.

Lyle stopped often to see if he had a cellphone signal. Everything in him pulled at him to return to Cass. As brave as she was, she still must be frightened in that black hole with a child close to death. Lyle worked his way down the hillside. He had no idea how far he would have to go before he found a signal but it couldn't be soon enough for him.

The weather was taking a turn for the worse. To complicate the conditions, the ground was slick, the path narrow and the rocks numerous. Could the situation get more dangerous?

His heart jumped when the phone connected and started ringing. Finally. The police officer answered. Lyle told him where they were and that they had found the girl. He then gave him instructions to call the hospital in Fort William and have the ambulance sent. Also, to call the clinic for the medical van. They would meet the ambulance. Every second counted. The girl might not make it if she didn't get to the hospital right away.

Lyle wasted no more words and started climbing up the hill once again. More than once he slipped as the sleet grew harder. Before he reached the ruins the sirens of help could be heard, filling the air. On flat land again at the top, he ran to the hole. Hero was still obediently sitting beside it.

"Cass!" There was no answer. "Cass?" Still nothing. Fear washed through him. What had happened to her? Had a rock fallen and hit her? All kinds of horrible scenarios played like a movie through his head. He couldn't lose Cass. He yelled louder. "Cass!"

"I'm here." Her voice wasn't strong, but it was there. Relief flooded him as if a dam had broken.

She turned on the flashlight and pointed it toward him. "I hope help is on the way. I know now why the dungeon was the least favorite place in a castle."

Lyle chuckled. "Help is on the way. Has there been any movement out of the girl?"

"No. But let me take her temp."

He waited impatiently for her report.

"It's ninety-one Fahrenheit—a little under thirty-three Celsius."

"That's progress." He would take that. "How're you doing?"

"I'd rather be cuddled up next to you."

Lyle's heart melted. He wished that too. He was in love with Cass, he realized. "Honey, I promise you I'll make that happen just as soon as I can."

"Promise?"

"You have my word on it." When he got his arms around Cass again he might never let her go.

The sounds of people hurrying up behind him drew his attention. "Over here." A group of six people headed his way. "They're down here. In this hole."

"They?" one of the rescue men asked.

"Yes. A friend of mine, a woman who works in search and rescue. I lowered her down." Guilt pricked him. He should have gone. "We'll need a rope. I'll go down."

"You're staying put. We'll need your skills up here when we get them up." Les McArthur, the leader of the group and a man Lyle had known all his life, said, and pointed to a spot near the dog. "You stand there out of the way. What's the name of the woman in the hole?"

Lyle didn't like the idea of not being the one in charge but he did as he was told, knowing his friend was right. Still, that didn't calm his nerves. "Cass."

One of the men dropped a bag on the ground and unzipped it. He pulled a rope ladder out. Securing it to a large slab of stone, once part of the keep, he dropped it into the hole.

Les walked to the edge. "Cass, it's Les McArthur. We're coming down. Rope ladder first."

"Okay."

Lyle watched as Les went over the side. Behind him was a man with a foldup stretcher strapped to his back. Soon a bright light shone from the hole. Apparently Les had a portable light in the pack on his back.

"We're going to need ropes down here," someone called from inside the hole.

Another man pulled ropes out of a bag.

Lyle shifted from side to side, not just to keep warm but in his need to do something active. "Can I help?"

"No, this will go a lot faster if you let us do our part. Then you can do yours," one of the men said. "They're going to be fine."

Cass had better be. The girl as well.

The men threw the ropes in. A few minutes later Les called up, "Ready."

Everything in Lyle wanted to go down into that hole to Cass. Instead he stood watching all that was happening with his hands fisted at his sides and shoulders braced against the sleet-filled wind that was blowing harder by the minute.

Slowly the men started hauling the rope up. Soon the stretcher with the girl on it was being laid on the ground. At her feet was his medical bag. Cass had made sure he would have what he needed. She impressed him more every day.

"Let me check her pulse. I need to tell the hospital what to prepare for." Lyle went down on his knees beside the stretcher. He wasn't going to stand on the sidelines any longer.

The child was wrapped up in the thermal blanket. On her head was Cass's hat and around her neck was her scarf. Lyle pulled a section of the blanket back. And there was her coat. Cass had nothing to protect her from the elements.

With two fingers, he checked the child's pulse. He found it, but it wasn't easy to locate. The girl needed to leave for the hospital now. As much as he hated it, he had to trust that Les would take care of Cass. His next call after the ambulance would be to Charles and Flora. They'd also see to Cass. But he wouldn't be satisfied until he had her in his arms again.

He quickly stood, putting his bag under his arm. Giving the hole that Cass hadn't emerged from a longing look he said, "Let's get her down the hill. There's no time to waste."

Cass's body shook violently. She was so cold. Where was she? In a damp, dark, freezing hole.

No, that wasn't right. She had been cold, down to her bones. Now she was in a soft place, huddled in warmth. Her eyes flickered open. It was dark outside and a fire burned in the fireplace. She could see the flames reflecting off the wall. That was the only light in the room. Her room at the castle.

She turned her head to find Lyle asleep in a chair too small for him next to her bed. He was close enough to reach out and touch. His hair was tousled, as if he had run his fingers through it more than once. He snored softly. He must be exhausted.

The last thing she had a clear memory of at the ruins was the men securing the girl to the stretcher. She'd been so cold that all she'd been able to think about was sleeping. One of the men had given her a blanket but that hadn't stopped the cold from seeping deeper. She vaguely remembered her teeth chattering as she'd stumbled down the hill with the help of one of the rescuers.

Lyle hadn't been there when she'd come out of the hole. She'd known he wouldn't be. He would be with the girl, as he should have been. Still, that didn't mean she hadn't missed having his arms around her or his heat. It would have been preferable to those of a stranger, no matter how nice they were.

At the bottom of the hill a police car had been waiting. She'd climbed into the rear seat and the officer had turned the heat up high. Despite that, she had been bitterly cold and in a daze when she'd arrived at the castle. Charles and Flora had been waiting for her in the foyer.

"Lyle called us. Gave us strict orders to give you a full examination," Charles had said, pushing a wheelchair over to her.

Cass had been glad to see it, despite saying, "I don't think all that's necessary."

"Lyle does. And based on what he told us, you earned our attention. Thanks for what you did," Flora had added.

"Hero?" Cass had mumbled as Charles had pushed her and Flora had walked beside her.

"Esme is seeing to him. One of the police officers took him to the center. I understand he's going to get an extra helping of food. Esme said she could use a person with your skills at the center."

Cass had gone in and out of awareness while Charles had been examining her. When he'd finished, Flora had taken her turn, flexing and contracting her arm and leg.

"We need to increase your therapy a bit for a few days, but I don't see why you can't be discharged on time."

Cass looked at Lyle. Discharged. At one time, all she'd wanted to do was to get home. That day would be here soon. Flora hadn't given her a specific date yet, but it was coming. Her leg and arm were much better. Despite all her efforts not to become involved, it had happened. It would be hard to leave Lyle. But she must.

She'd arrived with her emotions in a jumble and they weren't in any better shape now. In fact, her feelings for Lyle had only added to the issues. He deserved better than a woman who was so messed up. How did she even know the feelings she had for him were real? Maybe she was just reacting to her need to have someone care about her in a weak moment. That wasn't fair to him.

It didn't matter. After all, they had agreed only to a good time while she was here. Lyle hadn't said anything about wanting more. She'd made it clear she didn't. So what was she worrying about? She would leave as planned. He understood that. She would be home for Christmas.

But what if Lyle asked her to stay? Would she?

She couldn't. Heavens, she didn't know what she wanted. Taking a chance on them being together would be like jumping off a ledge. They didn't really know each other. What if it was just sexual attraction? It was best for Lyle to think of what they'd had as a nice friendship and let him move on.

It would be better for her as well. She'd learned last night that doing search and rescue was too emotionally hard for her. If that little girl had died, she would have as well. So what would she do now to make a living? Where would she end up living? There were too many unknowns.

Cass shifted. That was enough to wake Lyle. "Hey."

He sat straighter in the chair. Wrinkles filled his forehead as he studied her. "How're you feeling?"

"Better." She looked toward the window. "It's not morning?"

"No, it's still early. Do you need anything?" He leaned toward her, studying her.

"A hot bath."

"That I can handle." Lyle got to his feet.

Cass was confident he could handle almost anything.

"Let's get you into the bath. While you're there I'll go down and brew you some tea."

She grinned. "There it is again. The cure-all, but it does sound wonderful."

He started toward the bathroom. "I can tell your smart mouth isn't frozen any longer."

She giggled.

"You stay put and I'll be back for you," Lyle ordered.

"I can walk."

"Maybe so, but I'd like to carry you."

She would enjoy that. Seconds later water began running into the bath. The sounds of Lyle opening and closing cabinet doors soon followed. In a few minutes he returned to her.

"I know you've been sitting here thinking how you could walk in there by yourself but it's not going to happen." His accent became more pronounced when he was trying to make a point.

"You don't know me well enough to know what I'm thinking."

He put his palms on the bed and leaned in close enough that his nose almost touched hers. "Then deny it."

She met his gaze with a smirk. "I do. I was actually thinking how much I'd enjoy being in your arms."

Lyle's look turned to one of bewilderment as he continued to stare at her. It quickly changed to one of pleasure that included a smile spreading across his face. "Then we have a plan."

Cass pushed the covers back. Lyle placed an arm around her waist and under her legs then lifted her against his chest. The overlarge T-shirt she wore slipped up, exposing her thigh. Lyle's hand was warm and sure on her skin. She looped her arm around his shoulders and enjoyed the ride.

He sat her on the side of the tub. "Let me check the water temp before you get in."

Cass waited, watching him trail his fingers through the water. She like the tender attention from Lyle. It made her feel cherished. When had another man come close to giving her that feeling before? Never.

Jim had come the nearest, but he hadn't understood her, her job—and especially not her relationship with her dog. His idea of caring had been to tell her she should quit doing something so dangerous. He'd never appreciated what drove her. If it had been him there tonight instead of Lyle, Jim would have never trusted her enough to care for the patient while he was gone. Jim hadn't seen her as a partner, a strong person. Lyle did.

She respected him for that. Felt Lyle returned that respect. He had searched for a missing child without questioning her judgement of using a half-blind dog, then had lowered her into the hole on her directive, and cared for the girl when she'd been pulled out. Now he was looking after her. Was there anything he couldn't do?

"How's the girl doing?"

"She'll recover with a good story to tell. I understand her family went hiking up there last week. She'd lost her doll and was convinced that it was in the ruins. She went looking for it."

"I didn't see a doll." Surely she would have noticed one.

"I didn't either, so I had a new one sent to her." He said it as if it was no big deal.

"Lyle Sinclair, you're a really nice guy." She meant every word. Too nice for her to screw up his life.

"This is ready, if you are." He reached for the hem of her T-shirt and pulled it over her head.

Cass watched him but he didn't let his gaze drop below her face. He was being such a gentleman. Scooping up her feet, he placed them in the water. Cass slipped into the bath with a sigh of contentment. It rose to just below her breasts. She glanced at Lyle. His focus had fallen lower now.

"Hey." She took his hand. His gaze met hers. A flame of awareness burned in his eyes. "It feels really wonderful in here." She closed her eyes and lay back, giving him the full view.

Lyle groaned. "I'm going down for the tea. I'll be back in a few minutes."

Cass smiled, then said in her best seductive voice, "I'd much rather have you warm me up."

"I'm the administrator of this clinic. I can't be climbing into the bath with a patient." He didn't sound convinced.

"Lock the door, put out the *Do Not Disturb* sign. Live a little. Take a walk on the wild side. You know you want to." She tugged on his hand. "Mmm…it sure is nice." Cass opened her eyelids to slits. She could see the small upward curl of Lyle's lips. He was weakening. "At least kiss me."

Lyle leaned over her, his lips finding hers. She

wrapped her arms around his neck and gently pulled him into the tub. Water sloshed everywhere but she didn't care and apparently neither did Lyle. She continued to kiss him as he settled around her and brought her against him, taking the kiss deeper. When they broke apart Cass pulled at his long-sleeved shirt until her hands could wander freely over his back.

"Cass, you'll be my undoing. And the end of my job if I'm not careful." He kissed the sweet spot behind her ear.

She started working on the opening of his pants.

"How am I supposed to get out of your room without being seen in soaking wet clothes?" He sounded more perplexed than angry.

She wanted him that way. Her hand brushed across his hard manhood. "You have other things to worry about right now. I'll show you a secret passage out."

"Secret, uh?"

"First things first." She gave him an open-mouthed kiss while pushing his pants over his hips.

A few days later, Lyle sat on the couch in his cottage with his arm around Cass and her cuddled under his arm and her head on his shoulder. All the lights were off except for those on the tree. It was the prettiest Christmas tree he'd ever seen. Or maybe it was because he was sharing it with Cass. Yet he sensed something was bothering her.

She had walked home with him after work but had been more quiet than usual. Normally she told him about her day or something a dog had done during her therapy. Today had been different. They had prepared dinner of soup and sandwiches, working together like a long-married couple who knew the next move of the other. Still she'd said nothing.

Was it worry over her leaving? He'd certainly spent more time thinking about it than he found comfortable. Flora had said nothing specific about planning to discharge Cass, but he and Cass both knew the time was near. He would find out before they went to bed what was going on in that busy mind of hers.

Lyle smiled to himself. He had really come out of his respectable world with Cass's stunt of pulling him into the bath. She had added excitement to his life.

Cass had helped wring out his clothes with a grin on her face. They'd laid them to dry near the fire and climbed into her bed. Just before dawn he'd pulled the damp clothing on so he could go home and put on some dry ones. He'd shrugged into his coat, grateful it wasn't wet. Cass gave him a goodbye kiss that had been hot enough to make them both steam. He had slipped out of her room and down a back staircase, with the jubilant thought that he wouldn't be seen. The second he had put his hand on the doorknob, Charles had pulled the door open. Lyle could only imagine the dumbfounded look on his face at that moment. Charles often came in early, but Lyle hadn't realized he used the side door.

"Hey. Aren't you going the wrong way?" Charles looked beyond him as if searching for something going on.

"I was sitting up with Cass." And other things. Very nice things.

Charles's forehead wrinkled with concern. "I checked her out last night. She seemed fine. Was something wrong?"

"No, I just wanted to make sure she was okay." Lyle

made to step to past him. All he wanted was to get home and change his clothes.

A look of understanding came to Charles's face along with a grin. He gave Lyle a pointed look. "And is she?"

"She is."

Charles continued to block the opening. "Glad to hear it. Cass is a really special person. I heard what happened and how she jumped in to help."

Lyle couldn't agree more. Cass was very special. "She is special."

"Freya did you wrong. Not every girl will." Charles's words were said softly but matter-of-factly. "Maybe it's time to give someone else a chance."

Lyle had been thinking the same thing. "You're one to be talking."

"Just because I'm a bachelor it doesn't mean you should be one. Just think about it." Charles slapped Lyle on the shoulder as he went by. "Are you wet?"

Apparently his fingers had touched Lyle's shirt. "I fell in the bath."

He heard the roll of Charles's laughter as he hurried out the door.

Cass shifted beside him now. "What're you thinking about?"

He gave her shoulders a squeeze. "I was just thinking about Charles catching me leaving the other morning."

Cass smiled against him. "So he knows about us?"

"Yes. But he would anyway. The Laird knows everything that's going on in his domain."

"Do you mind?" She turned to look up at him.

"Mind? Why would I? You're wonderful, smart, beautiful, fun to be around. Why should I mind? I'm honored."

She shifted to face him and gave him a gentle kiss. "Thank you. That was a nice thing to say."

"I meant every word."

Lyle did. He wanted more moments like this with Cass. If the truth be known, he wanted her forever. Yet he wanted to do it right this time. Make no mistake. For him there could be no long-distance relationship. He didn't want to feel pressured to ask her to stay, because they would soon be separated. But could he let her go without letting her know he cared?

Cass moved away from Lyle, then turned to face him. They had to talk. She'd put it off while they'd walked to his place, through dinner, and now she had to tell him. It shouldn't be this hard—after all they had an agreement. She'd made it clear where she stood. So why was she having such a difficult time bringing up the subject?

"What's wrong, Cass? Tell me."

She clasped her hands in her lap. "I can't hide anything from you. You always read me so well. Flora said this afternoon she plans to discharge me in three days. I can start making travel arrangements. I'll be home for Christmas."

Lyle studied her a moment before he said, "I knew the time was coming. We both did."

"Yes, we did."

He had sounded resigned, while she was a ball of growing sadness. It should be easier than this.

There was a pause as if Lyle was considering what he was going to say. "If I asked you to stay, would you?"

Cass slowly shook her head. "It's a nice thought, but not realistic."

"What about it isn't realistic?"

Her chest tightened. "My life is a mess. I don't even know what I want to do for a job now. My emotions are everywhere. I fear I've used you because you were nice to me and I had no one else to turn to. I can't make a life-changing decision like staying here with you based on that. It might not end well and you deserve better."

"We can figure it all out together." His words were said softly, beseechingly.

"Lyle, I've enjoyed every minute. Well, almost every one of them." She made an attempt at humor, but his serious look didn't change. "But I have to figure out my life on my own, otherwise it would never work."

"It seems to me it's been working great up until now." He sounded mystified that she might not think the same.

"I'm just so confused. My feelings are so jumbled up right now. I have a poor history of keeping relationships alive. I'd never want to do to you what Freya did. You're a wonderful man who shouldn't be treated that way. I can't take the chance that you become like the other men in my life, and I disappoint you. I couldn't stand to see that look on your face."

Lyle watched her for a moment. There was grief in his eyes. "Do you really believe all that rubbish? After all we have shared?"

"We're good together in bed, but that was never supposed to last forever. We talked about this when we started out." She waved a hand between them. "We had an agreement. You can't change the rules now."

"The hell I can't. Why can't you call this what it is? A relationship. I care about you. I think you feel the same about me."

"And let's just say that I do, then what? I still live in America. I may return to a job that takes me all over the world. Anytime, day or night. Or what if I decide to do something else and it's still the States? Do you think we have a chance at a long-distance romance? How did that work out for you last time?"

He flinched. "There will be no long-distance relationship between us."

"So you plan to move to America to be with me?"

His face fell. "We can work something out."

She hated what she was doing to him. That she was pushing him away. "What I'm hearing is that you want me to give up everything and come here to you."

"Put that way, it sounds unfair. Still, I think we have something real here. Something that doesn't come along often in a lifetime. Come on, Cass, stop hiding behind your fear. It's easy to keep a wall up, it's harder to let go, start again. Stop being dishonest with yourself."

"Dishonest! Like you are with your father? Have you ever made it clear to him that you don't want to return to the army? Even tried to make it clear he can accept that or not, but it won't change things? That you want him to be happy, but not at the cost of your own happiness?"

Lyle looked at her as if she had slapped him. "It's complicated."

"And my issues aren't? I'm sorry. I shouldn't have said that. You and your father's issues are none of my business. But what I do know is that if you return to active duty for someone other than yourself you will be miserable. Do you really think that's what your father wants for you?"

Lyle stood. "You're right, my issue with my father isn't any of your business. It has nothing to do with us."

"I'm not sure that's true. Here you are, asking me to stay with you, yet you might be going off to who knows where with the army. What am I supposed to do? Sit here waiting for you? I thought that was the kind of relationship you didn't want. It seems to me that we both need to make some major decisions in our lives before we involve someone else in them."

The ferocity seemed to go out of him like air from an air-bag. "All I want to do is make his last days happy ones."

"I know. But is re-enlisting the right way to do that? Or would the truth be better? You deserve to be happy as well. If you make him happy, you won't be. I know for a fact you're valuable to the clinic and this area. That you're happy with the work you do now. You're thinking of making a decision, a life-altering one, based on emotion. That's not a good way to do things. I can't do that. My decisions have to be based on more than hot sex with a handsome doc. I need to think. Need to regroup." She hated to hurt him but one of them had to think rationally. "I think it's best we leave this as a nice interlude."

"Interlude," he growled with eyes blazing—and not in the way she would have liked. "An interlude. I see."

What did he see? Lyle made the word sound nasty, ugly. "That's what we said it would be."

"If that's the way you feel then I wish you the best. Since this *interlude* appears to be over, I should escort you back to the clinic." He walked into the hall and took her coat off the hook.

Cass didn't see Lyle again until three days later when she was getting into the taxi that would take her to Fort William to start her trip home. She'd cried into her pillow each night since their breakup as loneliness consumed her, then worked hard not to show her sorrow during the day. Still, she felt she had done the right thing, for both of them.

She looked longingly at Lyle. Her heart thumped in her chest. If he asked her to stay again, would she? She needn't have worried. He remained near the front door, watching her without a smile or raising a hand in farewell.

Cass closed the car door. As she rode away, she swiped at her cheek. Unable to resist one last look, she turned to see the steps empty. Lyle had gone back inside.

If the last three days had been awful, leaving Lyle was truly horrible. What would the next week or month, or her life be like when she was thousands of miles away from him? She couldn't count the number of times she'd told herself, "Stay strong."

What she had planned not to do she had done. She'd let herself take the chance of caring again. She had fallen for Lyle.

CHAPTER TEN

LYLE HAD LET Cass's words fester. He was hurt that she could so easily dismiss what he held as precious. He now understood the meaning of "It cuts like a knife." Cass's words that night had done just that. Over time he had examined them. She was right.

He had been unfair. She'd come to Heatherglen hurt and traumatized. Only a few weeks later he was making demands on her. Had he completely forgotten everything but his own needs? Cass *should* be upset with him. They both had issues to deal with before they could commit.

Lyle didn't plan to give up. He'd give her until January then he'd go after her. Surely they could find a compromise between their lives? He loved her, and he believed she loved him. There was no way he'd misread all those touches, looks and how they felt when they came together. He couldn't be that wrong.

The woman he wanted to share his life with would not only love him but support him. Cass had proved to know him better than he knew himself. She understood who he was. More than that, she complemented him. She had strength, confidence, and the largest heart of anyone he knew.

Cass was the one for him. Of that he had no doubt.

He needed to be worthy of her. Part of being that was breaking away from his father's expectations. He had only considered his father's wishes when he'd first joined the army. No matter how sick his father was now, it was time for Lyle to concentrate on his own desires. He'd lived under his father's demands for too long. Through the clinic Lyle was providing quality and necessary care for people who needed it. He was proud of that service. It didn't matter if his father felt the same way or not.

It was past time to have a frank discussion with his father. Really talk. Not dance around the issue but make it clear the direction he intended his life to go. It was with that intention Lyle drove to his parents' house that evening.

His mother opened the door. She looked surprised and pleased to see him. She glanced around him. "Is Cass with you?"

Lyle's chest tightened at the reality that she was actually thousands of miles away. He reminded himself that he would soon be going after her. "No, she was discharged and has gone home. She asked me to say goodbye to you." Cass had. Just before she'd told him the same at the castle door and had gone inside.

His mother placed a comforting hand on his arm. "I'm sorry. I could tell you really liked her."

Lyle did. More than that, he loved her. "I hope she'll come back."

"If she is as smart as I think she is, she will." His mother gave him a quick hug.

Lyle gave her a wry smile. "Is Dad home? I wanted to talk to him for a few minutes."

"He's inside, watching TV."

Lyle took a step and stopped. "How's he feeling today?"

Her look turned to one of slight concern. "He's having a good day."

"I'm glad." Lyle started toward the living room again.

"Would you like to stay for dinner?" his mother asked.

"I'll let you know in a few minutes after I've spoken to Dad." Lyle didn't look at his mother. He was sure her mouth was drawn with concern.

Lyle walked into the living room with his shoulders squared in determination. His father was watching TV. "Hi, Dad."

"Hello. This is an unexpected visit."

Lyle took a seat on the sofa instead of the closer chair so that the two of them faced each other. "Dad, I need to discuss something with you."

He turned off the TV. "Are you here to tell me you've signed up for active duty?" His delight showed clearly on his face.

"About that. Dad, I'm not going to go on active duty by choice ever again."

That joy on his father's face quickly turned to disappointment.

"I have a good job here. I'm needed and I believe I'm respected. Army life isn't for me. It never really was. I did it for you. That's not how I want to live my life. I need to do what I love and that's medicine here, at the clinic. I'm sorry if I'm disappointing you. I've known this for a long time and I've only led you to believe that I might one day go on active duty again to make you happy, and for that I apologize."

His father's look had darkened as Lyle spoke. He leaned forward and put his elbows on his knees and clasped his hands together. His expression didn't waver.

Lyle knew that one well from his childhood days when he was in trouble. "I can't say that I am pleased with your decision. It's in our family's blood to be career soldiers. I brought you up to think that way as well."

"You did. But I love private medicine more. I want to serve in another way."

His father settled back, looking both old and tired. "I see that now. I guess I didn't want to before. I grew up with my father stressing that our family fought for people by serving in the armed forces. I was given no choice, my father wasn't given one either. But we were both happy with our lots in life. It was our duty to protect. It was all I knew. All I knew to hand down to you. I never thought you would want to go another way, Lyle. I have to admit your young lady's impassioned speech did make me think, though."

Cass had done that. Lyle's ego still got a boost whenever he thought of her words.

"I heard the talk around the village about that girl going missing and what you and Cass did to save her," his father continued. "Since then others have stopped me and told me how much they appreciate you being here and the importance of the clinic. I'm proud when I hear it. I'm sorry that you're not going to return to the army but I do love you, son."

Lyle went across to his father and gave him a hug. Afterwards he called, "Mum, I'll be staying for dinner."

Cass had never known misery like the kind she'd endured on the way to the airport. Everything in her screamed to return to Lyle. But he hadn't even waved goodbye. Had she hurt him that much? She felt sick inside.

The tears had flowed the entire trip to Fort William

and then on to Aberdeen. More than once the taxi driver had looked in his rearview mirror with apprehension, but he'd said nothing.

She'd done everything she'd told herself not to. She'd let herself care. About him. The people at Heatherglen. Even Andy and that funny-looking dog, Dougal. Hero. Her emotions had been in a muddle when she had arrived at the clinic, and they weren't any better now that she'd left.

She'd known fear from when she'd almost lost her brother. She'd experienced deep loss from losing Rufus. And now Lyle was gone. This time was harder. She couldn't even breathe, the pain was so strong. Worse, she had chosen this. She wrung her hands.

She couldn't turn back. All she'd said to Lyle was true. She needed to have her act together before she made an emotional commitment to anyone, especially to him. Her parents were expecting her. It was Christmas, and they were worried about her. She had to see them first.

What her future would look like still needed to be decided. Search and rescue was no longer for her. So what would she do now? There was also her house to think about. When she had her life in order, she'd see if Lyle still felt the same. He deserved someone who knew what she wanted and had her head on straight. Only then would she return to Lyle and discuss any future they might have.

The flight home wasn't much better emotionally than her ride to the airport. She'd only found relief in the few hours she had slept. Her parents were there to meet her. They quickly enveloped her in tight hugs. She needed those more than anything at the moment. They insisted that she go to their house for dinner and stay the night.

Cass didn't resist. Right now she wanted their circle of security. With them she could just be, not think. She needed time to regroup.

Her parents' home was decorated for Christmas. Cass should have expected that. The minute she looked at their tree, her eyes filled with tears. It was all light, tinsel and glitter. It made her appreciate the simple, natural tree that stood in Lyle's living room. More than that, she wanted Lyle.

Her brother and his family came for supper the next day. With two young children, the meal was lively. Cass was glad to see them but she was so exhausted, both mentally and physically, that she excused herself early. Despite all the tears she'd shed during the day, she still wanted a good cry. She hurried to her childhood bedroom and closed the door. Minutes later she was in the shower, letting those banked tears flow.

By the time there was a knock on the door she was in bed. "It's Mom. Can I come in?"

"Yes."

Her mother entered, carrying a mug. "I brought you some tea. I thought it was too late for coffee."

That was enough to have Cass's eyes swimming once more. She'd never cried this much in her entire life. Never been this distraught. The idea she might never have a chance to share time with Lyle again had her emotionally splintered. She had to get control of herself. Showing her emotions like this wasn't her. But, then, much about her over the last few weeks was different. Like pulling Lyle into the tub. That had been so much fun, for a number of reasons.

Her mother set the tea on the bedside table then perched on the edge of Cass's bed. "I had no idea you hated tea so much, or is something else going on? What're you not telling us? Are you still in pain?"

Cass hated the fear she heard in her mother's voice. "I told you everything about my injury. I promise I'm much better. It's my heart that's broken. And I think I'm the one who broke it." She poured out her sorrow and what had happened while she'd been at Heatherglen.

Her mother held her while she cried. When she settled down her mother said, "So what're your plans now, honey?"

"I don't know. Tomorrow morning I'm going to call about my job. I'm going to resign from it. That work isn't for me anymore."

Her mother patted her leg. "Your dad will be pleased to hear that. We've worried about you being in all those far-flung places by yourself for too long."

Cass hadn't been by herself. Rufus had been with her. Now she had no one. "I've been thinking that I might enjoy training rescue dogs instead."

"That sounds like something you'd be good at. And what about that amazing doctor of yours?"

Hers? She hoped despite how she had left things between her and Lyle that he would at least speak to her when she saw him again. "Mom, he asked me to stay. I was afraid to make such a big decision when I was so messed up over being hurt, Rufus dying and not being closer to home. I didn't know what I wanted my future to look like then. I hurt him badly. I'm not sure he'll ever want me again."

"So, do you know how you feel now?" Her mother held her hand.

"I knew the minute I left the clinic. I wouldn't let myself turn around, though. I needed to come home.

To see you and Daddy." Cass looked directly at her mother. "I love him."

"Then I suggest you go back and tell him."

Cass murmured, "I don't know if he wants me anymore. He didn't even say goodbye."

"Honey, if all you've told me is true, I wouldn't worry about that. He wants you. I'd suggest you take care of business here as soon as possible then go tell him how you feel and see what happens."

"I don't know…"

She mother stood. "Our family knows better than most how easily something can be almost taken away. Grab every chance at happiness and have no regrets."

The one thing Cass had been with Lyle was happy—and at Heatherglen, too. "What about Christmas?"

Her mother shrugged. "We'll celebrate it early. Or late." Then she grinned. "Or come to Scotland."

"Oh, Mom." Cass wrapped her arms around her mother. "I love you."

Over the next few days Cass resigned from her job, packed her bags and closed up her house. She was on her way to find that happiness she wanted. And that started with Lyle.

Christmas had never really mattered to Lyle. Cass had managed to make it exciting for a while, but that had gone with her. He'd spent the last week going through the motions. To say he wasn't in a festive mood would be an understatement.

He was actually heading into the worst Christmas of his life. It was going to top the year Freya had left him, and the one when his father wouldn't speak to him because he'd said he was going inactive so he could take the job helping Charles get the clinic started.

Losing Cass was like losing an arm or a leg. He had to relearn how to function without her. Every day he forced himself to do what was necessary. People were starting to notice. The few times he had seen his parents his mother had watched him with worry and hugged him a little tighter than normal. Even Charles had made a smart remark about Lyle not looking as cheerful dry as he had wet. Lyle had snarled and stalked way.

No, Christmas couldn't go by fast enough for him. He was living for the new year. Surely he and Cass could sort something out? Find a way they could be together? If he had to leave Heatherglen and follow her all over the world, then so be it.

Now he was doing his duty as the doctor on call at the Christmas-tree lighting in the village square. He remained on the outside of the crowd around the huge tree. It was dark except for the interior lights of the businesses that surrounded the square.

As soon as he was no longer needed he would slip away to his cottage, even though he found no solace there. His home held too many memories of Cass. Their tree still stood in the living room. More than once he'd thought of taking it down but he couldn't bring himself to do it despite the fact it was a daily reminder of Cass.

Lyle stuffed his hands in his coat pockets and focused on Charles giving his Laird of Heatherglen annual Christmas speech. It was the only time Lyle smiled because he was well aware of how much Charles disliked being in the spotlight.

A movement in front of him and to the right caught Lyle's attention. *Cass?* He shook his head. For him she was like the ghost of Heatherglen. More than once he had walked around a corner and thought he'd glimpsed her. Or walked by the lounge and heard her voice. Each time he'd had to calm his rapid heartbeat as disappointment had set in. He had to remind himself she was in America.

He had laid out a plan, one he would adhere to. She would have the space and time she needed to think, and process what she wanted. Lyle was determined to give her that, even if it killed him. In January he would go after her. From there they would figure out what their future together would look like.

The person continued toward him. Lyle narrowed his eyes in the hope of seeing better. Despite his efforts not to let his heart race or hold his breath in anticipation, it didn't work. Still, in the dim light he couldn't make out any facial features.

It was a woman. She came nearer. Her walk was so much like Cass's. She held herself just as Cass did. Was his mind playing tricks on him?

Finally, she stepped close enough that he could see a scarf around her neck and a hat on her head like the one Cass had bought from his mother. Lyle remained still, sure she was a figment of his imagination.

It wasn't until she said, "Hello, Lyle," that he let himself believe and breathe. His heart raced as if he were running. It was Cass! She'd come back. Was really here. Unable to move, he stood there in disbelief.

She closed the distance between them. "Lyle?"

He put one foot in front of the other and grabbed her, pulling her against his chest. Lifting her off the ground, he was rewarded with a sigh from her as her arms tightly circled his neck. Sometime later, Lyle let her slide down his body and he stepped back. The last thing he want to do was scare her off. "Cass, is it really you?"

"Yes."

"Are you okay? Is your leg okay?" He gave her a searching look.

"I'm fine." There was a smile in her voice. "I just forgot something."

"Forgot something?" Now he sounded like an idiot. His hands shook in his eagerness to touch her. He shoved them in his pockets.

"Yes. You."

"Me?"

She watched him closely with a look of uncertainty. "Yeah, you. I was wondering if we could have that conversation about compromise you suggested."

"I'd like that. A *lot*." He pulled her to him again and kissed her with all the pent-up emotion he'd had to hold in check. It was a long and deep kiss.

The roar of the crowd broke them apart. They gave each other a startled look, then grinned. The cheer had been for the Christmas tree being lit.

Lyle looked at her beautiful, much-loved face. "I'm finished here. Where're you staying?"

"I was going to stay somewhere in the village, unless I had a better offer." Cass grinned.

"You have one now. Where are your bags?" Lyle looked around.

"At the airport, I hope. Long story that I don't want to talk about now."

Smiling, he took her hand and hurried her to where his car was parked. They needed to get away before people started talking to them. He held Cass's hand as much as the drive to his cottage would allow, afraid if he lost contact she would disappear.

As he helped her out of the car, he pulled her to him again, inhaling deeply and filling his head with her scent. "You have no idea how I've missed you."

* * *

A flutter like birds taking off filled Cass's middle. She looked at Lyle's handsome face. The one she had missed so much. "I'm glad."

"Glad?" Lyle sounded incredulous.

"Yes, I was afraid you wouldn't talk to me." She watched him for a reaction.

"Are you kidding? I'm in love with you, Cass. Nothing will ever change that."

"In love with me?" So this was what it felt like to have everything she'd ever dreamed of.

"What did you think I meant when I asked you to stay here with me?"

She lifted a shoulder in a shrug and let it fall. "I don't know. I had so much stuff going on in my head I wasn't sure what you meant."

His hands went to her shoulders. "Cass, I wouldn't have asked you to stay with me unless I meant forever."

"I should've known that. I should've heard you out. I was scared. Of myself and what you wanted."

"Come inside. We'll discuss this out of the cold. I want you to be warm and comfortable when I explain how much I love and want you." He gave her a quick kiss before he took her hand then pushed the car door closed.

Inside his cottage, Lyle helped her hang up her outer clothing. She took off her shoes, walked to the doorway of the living room and stopped. Their tree was still there.

"Is something wrong?" Lyle said from behind her.

She turned and smiled. "No, everything is perfect. I missed you and your cottage."

"I hope it was me more." There was still an unsure look in his eyes.

Cass went up on her toes and kissed him. "It was you. Almost all you."

When they separated, he called over his shoulder as he walked to the kitchen, "I'll make us some tea. We need to talk."

She liked the sound of that. They did. She needed to apologize and tell him how she felt. It was time to stop worrying about woulda, coulda, shoulda and try living. When she was around Lyle she wanted to live. She was happy. Blissfully so.

A few minutes later he offered her a mug of tea. Instead of sitting beside her, Lyle chose the chair. Cass couldn't help but pout. Maybe he was still mad at her.

"I'm sitting over here because I can't trust myself when I sit next to you. We need to talk."

Cass's heart jumped. "I know what you mean."

That brought a smile to his lips before he said, "I know I wasn't fair to you. I was so self-absorbed that I wasn't thinking about what was best for you. You were here to recover from a horrible experience, and I should've given you more room, not asked you for more than you could give. Before you left you said some things I needed to hear. I have to admit it made me angry but that didn't mean that I didn't need to hear them. Or that I didn't love you. I talked to my father. Told him in clear and concise language that I wouldn't be returning to active duty."

Cass hissed in a breath. "How did that go?"

"He didn't like it, but he accepted it. Even told me that he's proud of the work I'm doing at the clinic."

That had to have been a tough conversation for both men. She had to admire Lyle for doing it.

Lyle continued, "At least it's a positive start. I don't

think he'll ever get over it but, then, I can't live my life for him. I've got to live it for me."

"You're right. That's a hard lesson I've had to learn over the last few days as well. I knew the moment I looked out the rear window of the car for you as I was going down the drive that I was leaving behind the best thing in my life. That you held the key to my happiness. I was afraid that if I took what you offered, somewhere down the road it might be taken from me. I couldn't stand the thought of that happening. What I soon learned was that trying to live without you was far worse. I love you, Lyle."

That was all it took for Lyle to come to her. He wrapped his arms around her and gave her the sweetest kiss that held a promise that he loved her too.

After they broke apart, Lyle said, "If you don't want to live here, we can live in America, or anywhere else for that matter, as long as we are together. I can practice medicine anywhere."

"Oh, no, I would never take you away from Heatherglen. Cluchlochry. You belong here. Are needed here. I've been thinking about something Flora said. She mentioned Esme could use me at the canine therapy center. I think I would like to train dogs."

"That sounds like a wonderful idea." Lyle hugged her.

"You think you could stand to have me around all the time?" She studied his face.

He chuckled. "I can't think of anything better."

"I love you, Lyle."

"I love you, Cass."

Sometime later they were lying in Lyle's large bed in each other's arms. Cass had found the place where she belonged, where she was completely happy. "You know, there's something to the Christmas pudding thing."

"How's that?" Lyle's hand caressed her bare back over her shoulders.

"I asked to be happy." She cupped his cheek. "And I am. Blissfully so."

He gave her a quick kiss. "And I wished for you to stay longer."

"Why?"

"Because I need a date for the Christmas ball!"

* * * * *

FESTIVE FLING WITH THE SINGLE DAD

ANNIE CLAYDON

MILLS & BOON

To Charlotte
With grateful thanks

CHAPTER ONE

Up close, he looked even more…

More outdoorsy. Taller and blonder and… Just more. A two-day beard covered a square jaw, and his mane of shoulder-length hair was tied at the nape of his neck. His casual shirt and worn jeans gave the impression of an off-duty Norse god, and Flora McNeith resisted the temptation to curtsey. It was slightly over the top as a greeting for a new neighbour.

'Hi. I'm Flora. From next door.' She gestured towards her own cottage, tugging at Dougal's lead in a fruitless attempt to get him to sit down for just one moment. 'Welcome to the village.'

He looked a little taken aback when she thrust the food box, containing half a dozen home-made mince pies into his hands. It might be more than three weeks until Christmas, but the lights of the Christmas tree in the village had already been turned on, and in Flora's book any time after September was a good time for mince pies.

'That's very kind.' His voice was very deep, the kind of tone that befitted the very impressive chest that it came from. And it appeared that whatever kind of deity Aksel Olson was, language and communication weren't part of his remit. He was regarding her silently.

'I work at the Heatherglen Castle Clinic. I hear that your daughter, Mette, is a patient there.' Maybe if she explained herself a little more, she might get a reaction.

Something flickered in his eyes at the mention of his daughter. Reflective and sparkling, like sunshine over a sheet of ice.

'Are you going to be part of Mette's therapy team?'

Right. That put Flora in her place. Apparently that was the only thing that interested Aksel about her.

'No, I'm a physiotherapist. I gather that your daughter is partially sighted…' Flora bit her tongue. That sounded as if everyone was gossiping about him, which was half-true. The whisper that Mette's father was single had gone around like wildfire amongst the female staff at the clinic. Now that Flora had met Aksel, she understood what the excitement was all about.

'You read the memo, then?' Something like humour flashed in his eyes, and Flora breathed a small sigh of relief. Lyle Sinclair must have told him about the memo.

'Yes. I did.' Every time a new patient was admitted a memo went round, introducing the newest member of the clinic's community and asking every member of staff to welcome them. It was just one of the little things that made the clinic very special.

'Would you like to come in for coffee?' Suddenly he stood back from the door.

'Oh!' Aksel's taciturn manner somehow made the words he did say seem more sincere. 'I shouldn't… Dougal and I are just getting used to each other and I haven't dared take him anywhere for coffee yet. I'm afraid he'll get over-excited and do some damage.'

Aksel squatted down on his heels, in front of the ten-week-old brindle puppy, his face impassive.

'Hi, there, Dougal.'

Dougal was nosing around the porch, his tail wagging ferociously. At the sound of his name he looked up at Aksel, his odd ears twitching to attention. He circled the porch, to show off his new red fleece dog coat, and Flora stepped over the trailing lead, trying not to get snagged in it. Then Dougal trotted up to Aksel, nosing at his outstretched hand, and decided almost immediately he'd found a new best buddy. Finally, Aksel smiled, stroking the puppy's head.

'I'm sure we'll manage. Why don't you come in?'

Two whole sentences. And the sudden warmth in his eyes was very hard to resist.

'In that case… Thank you.' Flora stepped into the hallway and Dougal tugged on his lead in delight.

He took her coat, looking around the empty hallway as if it was the first time he'd seen it. There was nowhere to hang it and he walked into the kitchen, draping it neatly over the back of one of the chairs that stood around the table. Flipping open a series of empty cupboards, he found some packets of coffee and a small copper kettle, which seemed to be the only provisions he'd brought with him.

Dougal had recovered from his customary two seconds of shyness over being in a new environment and was tugging at the lead again, clearly having seen the young chocolate-coloured Labrador that was sitting watchfully in a dog basket in the far corner of the kitchen. Flora bent down, trying to calm him, and he started to nuzzle at her legs.

'Kari. *Gi labb.*' In response to Aksel's command, the Labrador rose from its bed, trotting towards them, then sitting down and offering her paw to Flora. Flora took it and Kari then started to go through her own *getting-to-know-you* routine with Dougal.

'She's beautiful.' The Labrador was gentle and impressively well trained. 'This is Mette's assistance dog?'

Aksel nodded. 'Kari's staying with me for a while, until Mette settles in. She's not used to having a dog.'

'Part of the programme, up at the clinic, will be getting Mette used to working with Kari. You'll be taking her there when you visit?'

'Yes. I find that the canine therapy centre has some use for me in the mornings, and I'll spend every afternoon with Mette.'

'It's great that you're here to give her all the support she needs.'

He nodded quietly. 'Mette's sight loss is due to an injury in a car accident. Her mother was driving, and she was killed.'

Flora caught her breath. The rumours hadn't included that tragic detail. 'I'm so sorry. It must be incredibly hard for you both.'

'It is for Mette. Lisle and I hadn't been close for some years.'

All the same, he must feel something... But from the finality in his tone and the hint of blue steel in his eyes, Aksel clearly didn't want to talk about it. She should drop the subject.

Kari had somehow managed to calm Dougal's excitement, and Flora bent down to let him off the lead. But as soon as she did so, Dougal bounded over to Aksel, throwing himself at his ankles. Aksel smiled suddenly, bending towards the little dog, his quiet words and his touch calming him.

'Sorry... I've only had him a couple of days, I'm looking after him for Esme Ross-Wylde.' Aksel must know who Esme was if he was working at the canine therapy centre. Charles and Esme Ross-Wylde were a brother and sister team, Charles running the Heather-glen Castle Clinic, and Esme the canine therapy centre. 'He's a rescue dog and Esme's trying to find him a good home.'

'You can't take him?' Aksel's blue gaze swept up towards her, and Flora almost gasped at its intensity.

'No…no, I'd like to but…' Flora had fallen in love with the puppy almost as soon as she'd seen him. He'd been half-starved and frightened of his own shadow when he'd first been found, but as soon as he'd been given a little care his loving nature had emerged. The strange markings on his shaggy brindle coat and his odd ears had endeared him to Flora even more.

'It wouldn't be fair to leave him alone all day while you were at work.' Aksel's observation was exactly to the point.

'Yes, that's right. I drop him off at the canine therapy centre and they look after him during the day, but that's a temporary arrangement. Dougal's been abandoned once and at the moment he tends to panic whenever he's left alone.'

Aksel nodded. A few quiet words to Kari, that Flora didn't understand, and the Labrador fetched a play ball from her basket, dropping it in front of Dougal. Dougal got the hint and started to push it around the room excitedly, the older dog carefully containing him and helping him play.

Aksel went through the process of searching through the kitchen cupboards again, finding a baking sheet to put the mince pies on and putting them in the oven to warm. The water in the copper kettle had boiled and he took it off the stove, tipping a measure of coffee straight into it. That was new to Flora, and if it fitted exactly with Aksel's aura of a mountain man, it didn't bode too well for the taste of the coffee.

'I hear you're an explorer.' Someone had to do the getting-to-know-you small talk and Flora was pretty sure that wasn't part of Aksel's vocabulary. He raised his eyebrows in reply.

'It said so in the memo.'

'I *used* to be an explorer.' The distinction seemed important to him. 'I'm trained as a vet and that's what I do now.'

'I've never met anyone who *used* to be an explorer before. Where have you been?'

'Most of South America. The Pole….'

Flora shivered. 'The Pole? North or South?'

'Both.'

That explained why she'd seen him setting off from his cottage early this morning, striding across the road and into the snow-dappled countryside beyond, with the air of a man who was just going for a walk. And the way that Aksel seemed quite comfortable in an open-necked shirt when the temperature in the kitchen made Flora feel glad of the warm sweater she was wearing.

'So you're used to the cold.'

Aksel smiled suddenly. 'Let's go into the sitting room.'

He tipped the coffee from the kettle into two mugs, opening the oven to take the mince pies out and leading the way through the hallway to the sitting room. As he opened the door, Flora felt warmth envelop her, along with the scent of pine.

The room was just the same as the kitchen. Comfortable and yet it seemed that Aksel's presence here had made no impact on it. Apart from the mix of wood and pine cones burning in the hearth, it looked as if he'd added nothing of his own to the well-furnished rental cottage.

Kari had picked the dog toy up in her mouth, and Dougal followed her into the room. She lay down on the rug in front of the fire, and the puppy followed suit, his tail thumping on the floor as Kari dropped the toy in front of him.

'He'll be hot in here. I should take his coat off.' Flora couldn't help grimacing as she said the words. Dougal liked the warm dog coat she'd bought for him, and getting him out of it wasn't as easy as it sounded. Perhaps he'd realise that they were in company, and not make so much of a fuss this time.

Sadly not. As soon as he realised Flora's intent, the little dog decided that this was the best of all times for a game of catch-me-if-you-can. When she knelt, trying to persuade him out from under the coffee table, he barked joyously, darting out to take refuge under a chair.

She followed him, shooting Aksel an apologetic glance. His broad grin didn't help. Clearly he found this funny.

'He thinks this is a game. You're just reinforcing that by joining in with him. Come and drink your coffee, he'll come to you soon enough.'

Right. The coffee. Flora had been putting off the moment when good manners dictated that she'd have to take her first sip. But what Aksel said made sense, and he obviously had some experience in the matter. Flora sat down, reaching for her mug.

'This is...nice.' It *was* nice. Slightly sweeter than she was used to and with clear tones of taste and scent. Not what she'd expected at all.

'It's a light roast. This is a traditional Norwegian method of making it.'

'The easiest way when you're travelling as well.' A good cup of coffee that could be made without the need for filters or machines. Flora took another mouthful, and found that it was even more flavoursome than the first.

'That too. Only I don't travel any more.' He seemed to want to make that point very clear, and Flora thought that she heard regret in his tone. She wanted to ask, but Dougal chose that moment to come trotting out from under the chair to nuzzle at Aksel's legs.

He leaned forward, picking the little dog up and talking quietly to him in Norwegian. Dougal seemed to understand the gist of it, although Flora had no idea what the conversation was about, and Aksel had him out of the dog coat with no fuss or resistance.

'That works.' She shot Aksel a smile and he nodded, lifting Dougal down from his lap so that he could join Kari by the fire.

'You're not from Scotland, are you?' He gave a half-smile in response to Flora's querying look. 'Your accent sounds more English.'

He had a good ear. Aksel's English was very good, but not many people could distinguish between accents in a second language.

'My father's a diplomat, and I went to an English school in Italy. But both my parents are Scots, my dad comes from one of the villages a few miles from here. Cluchlochry feels like home.'

He nodded. 'Tell me about the clinic.'

'Surely Dr Sinclair's told you all you need to know...'

'Yes, he has.' Aksel shot her a thoughtful look, and Flora nodded. Of course he wanted to talk about the place that was going to be Mette's home for the next six weeks. Aksel might be nice to look at—strike that, the man was downright gorgeous—but in truth the clinic was about all they had in common.

The first thing that Aksel had noticed about Flora was her red coat, standing out in the feeble light of a cold Saturday morning. The second, third and fourth things had come in rapid and breathtaking succession. Her fair hair, which curled around her face. The warmth in her honey-brown eyes. Her smile. The feeling in the pit of his stomach told him that he liked her smile, very much.

It was more than enough to convince Aksel to keep his distance. He'd always thought that dating a woman should be considered a privilege, and it was one that he'd now lost. Lisle had made it very clear that he wasn't worthy of it, by not even telling him that they'd conceived a child together. And now that he *had* found out about his daughter, Mette was his one and only priority.

But when he'd realised that Flora worked at the clinic, keeping his distance took on a new perspective. He should forget about the insistent craving that her scent awakened, it was just an echo from a past he'd left behind. He'd made up his mind that being a part of the clinic's community was a way to help Mette. And his way into that community had just turned up on his doorstep in the unlikely form of an angel, struggling to control an unruly puppy.

He'd concentrated on making friends with Dougal first, as that was far less challenging than looking into Flora's eyes. And when she'd started to talk about the work of the children's unit of the clinic, he'd concentrated on how that would help his daughter. *His daughter*. Aksel still couldn't even think the words without having to remind himself that he really did have a daughter.

'I've arranged with Dr Sinclair that Mette will be staying at the clinic full time for the first week, to give her a chance to settle in. After that, she'll be spending time at the weekend and several nights a week here, with me.'

'Oh. I see.' Flora's eyebrows shot up in surprise.

Aksel knew that the arrangement was out of the ordinary. Dr Sinclair had explained to him that most residents benefited from the immersive experience that the clinic offered, but he'd listened carefully to Aksel's concerns about being separated from Mette. The sensitive way that the issue had been handled was one of the reasons that Aksel had chosen the Heatherglen Castle Clinic.

Flora was clearly wondering why Mette was being treated differently from other patients, but she didn't ask. Aksel added that to the ever-growing list of things he liked about her. She trusted the people she worked with, and was too professional to second-guess their decisions.

'Mette and I are still working on...things...' *He* was the one who needed to do the work. He still practically a stranger to Mette, and he had to work to prove that she could trust him, and that he'd always be there for her.

'Well, I'm sure that whatever you and Dr Sinclair have agreed is best.' She drained her cup and set it down on the small table next to her chair. 'I'm going to the clinic to catch up on a few things this afternoon. Would you mind if I dropped in to see her, just to say hello and welcome her?'

'Thank you. That's very kind...' Sudden joy, at the thought of seeing Flora again turned his heartbeat into a reckless, crazy ricochet. 'I'll be going in to see her this afternoon as well.'

'Oh…' Flora shot him an awkward smile, as if she hadn't expected that eventuality. 'Would you like a lift?'

'Thanks, but Kari needs a walk.' Kari raised her head slightly, directing her melting brown gaze at Aksel. Flora appeared to be taking the excuse at face value, but there was no getting past Kari.

He'd explain. On the way to the clinic, he'd tell Kari about yet another dark place in his heart, the one which made it impossible for Aksel to get too close to Flora. He'd confide his regrets and Kari would listen, the way she always did, without comment.

Dougal had been persuaded to say goodbye to his new-found friends and had followed Flora through the gap in the hedge, back to her own front door. When they were inside, she let him off the lead and he made his usual dash into the kitchen and around the sitting room, just to check that nothing had changed while he'd been away.

She leaned back against the door, resisting the temptation to flip the night latch. Locking Aksel out was all she wanted to do at the moment, but it was too late. He was already giving her that strong, silent look of his. Already striding through her imagination as if he owned it. At the moment, he did.

But if Flora knew anything about relationships, she knew that losing the first battle meant nothing. Aksel might have taken her by surprise, and breached her defences, but she was ready for him now.

Not like Tom… Eighteen, and loving the new challenges of being away from home at university. Her first proper boyfriend. So many firsts…

And then, the final, devastating first time. Flora had gone with Tom to visit his family for a week, and found his parents welcoming and keen to know all about her and her family. But when she'd spoken of her beloved brother, they hadn't listened to anything she'd said about Alec's dry humour, his love of books or how proud Flora was of his tenacious determination to live his life to the full. The only two words they'd heard were 'cystic fibrosis'.

Tom's parents had convinced him that his relationship with Flora must end. She had desperately tried to explain. She might carry the defective gene that caused cystic fibrosis, but she might not and if her children developed the condition then it would be a result of her partner also carrying the gene. Tom had listened impassively.

Then Flora had realised. Tom had already understood that, and so had his parents. Pleading with him to change his mind and take her back would have been a betrayal, of both Alec and herself. She'd gone upstairs and packed her bags, leaving without another word.

'What do you think, Dougal?' The puppy had returned to her side, obviously puzzled that she was still here in the hallway, and probably wondering if she was *ever* going to find her way to the jar in the kitchen that held the dog treats.

No answer. Maybe Dougal had that one right. He'd been abandoned too, and he knew the value of a warm hearth and a little kindness. Flora had found a home here, and she needed nothing else but her work.

'We're going to find you a home too, Dougal. Somewhere really nice with people who love you.' Flora walked into the kitchen, opening the jar of dog treats and giving Dougal one, and then reaching for a bar of chocolate for herself.

Chocolate was a great deal more predictable in the gamut of feel-good experiences. Aksel might be bloodmeltingly sexy, and far too beautiful for anyone's peace of mind, but the few fleeting affairs she'd had since the break-up with Tom had shown Flora that desire and mistrust were awkward bedfellows. It was as if a switch had been flipped, and her body had lost its ability to respond. Sex had left her unsatisfied, and she'd given up on it.

If you could trust someone enough...

It was far too big an *if.* She'd kept the reason for her break-up with Tom a secret, knowing that it would hurt Alec and her parents beyond belief. They didn't deserve that, and neither did she. It was better to accept that being alone wasn't so bad and to channel all her energies into her work and being a part of the community here in Cluchlochry.

The next time she saw Aksel, she'd be prepared, and think of him only as a new neighbour and the father of one of the clinic's patients. When it came to thoughtless pleasure, she had chocolate, which made Aksel Olson's smile officially redundant.

CHAPTER TWO

AKSEL HAD WALKED the two miles to the clinic, with Kari trotting placidly beside him. It had done nothing to clear his head. Flora's smile still seemed to follow him everywhere, like a fine mist of scent that had been mistakenly sprayed in his direction and clung to his clothes. He was unaware of it for minutes on end, and then suddenly it hit him again. Fleeting and ephemeral, and yet enough to make him catch his breath before the illusion was once again lost.

His feet scrunched on the curved gravel drive. Castle Heatherglen Clinic was a real castle, its weathered stone walls and slate roof blending almost organically with the backdrop of rolling countryside and snow-dappled mountains. The Laird, Charles Ross-Wylde had added a new chapter to its long history and transformed his home into a rehabilitation clinic that offered its patients the best medical care, and welcomed them with a warm heart.

The children's unit was a little less grand than the rest of the building, and the sumptuous accommodation and sweeping staircases had been replaced by bright, comfortable rooms arranged around a well-equipped play area. Aksel had come prepared with a list of things that Mette might like to do, and suitable topics of conversation that might please her. But she seemed restless and bored today, not wanting to sit and listen while he read from her storybooks, and laying aside the toys he presented to her. Aksel's heart ached for all that his daughter had been through.

The awkward silence was broken by a knock at the door. Mette ignored it, and Aksel called for whoever it was to come in. Maybe it was one of the play specialists, who were on duty every day, and who might help him amuse his daughter.

Mette looked up towards the door, an instinctive reaction, even though she couldn't see anything that wasn't within a few feet of her.

'Hi, Mette. My name's Flora. May I come and visit you for a little while?' Flora glanced at Aksel and he wondered whether his relief at seeing her had shown on his face.

'Flora's our neighbour in the village, Mette.' He volunteered the information in English, and Mette displayed no interest. Flora sat down on the floor next to them, close enough for Mette to be able to see her face.

'I work here, at the clinic. I'm a physiotherapist.' Mette's head tilted enquiringly towards Flora at the sound of a word she didn't know. 'That means that I help people who are hurt to feel well again.'

'Where do they hurt...?' Mette frowned.

'All sorts of places. Their arms might hurt, or their legs. Sometimes it's their backs or their hips.'

Mette nodded sagely. She'd grown used to being surrounded by doctors and various other medical specialists, and while Aksel valued their kindness, it wasn't what he wanted for his daughter.

'Have you come to make me better?'

The question almost tore his heart out. No one could

make Mette better, and he wondered how Flora could answer a question that left him lost for words.

'No, sweetie. I'm sorry, but I can't make your eyes better.' Flora pulled a sad face, the look in her eyes seeming to match his own feelings exactly. 'You have a doctor of your own to look after you. Dr Sinclair is very important around here, and he only looks after *very* important people…'

Flora leaned forward, imparting the information almost in a whisper, as if it were some kind of secret. She was making it sound as if Mette was someone special, not just a patient or a child who couldn't be helped.

'*I've* come because I heard that you were here, all the way from Norway. I'd like to be friends with you, if that's all right?'

Maybe it was the smile that did it. Aksel wouldn't be all that surprised, he'd already fallen victim to Flora's smile. Mette moved a little closer to her, reaching out as if to feel the warmth of the sun.

'I have a little something that I thought you might like…' Flora produced a carrier bag from behind her back, giving a little shiver of excitement. Mette was hooked now, and she took the bag.

'What is it?' There was something inside, and Mette pulled out a parcel, wrapped in shiny paper that caught the light.

'Open it up and see.'

Mette didn't want to tear the wrappings and Flora waited patiently, guiding her fingers towards the clear tape that held it down. It peeled off easily, and Mette got the paper off in one piece, laying it carefully to one side, and started to inspect her gift.

A rag doll, with a brightly coloured dress and a wide

smile stitched onto her face. Mette smiled, clutching the doll tightly to her chest.

'Why don't you show her to your dad?'

'Papa, look.' Mette held out the doll, and Aksel's heart began to thump in his chest. It wasn't the gift that had made Mette smile, but the way it had been given. The way it was wrapped so carefully, and the warmth of Flora's manner.

'It's beautiful... Thank you, Flora.'

'*She's* beautiful, Papa,' Mette corrected him.

'Yes, of course. Sorry. What's her name?'

Mette thought for a moment. 'Annette.' His daughter pronounced the name with a Norwegian inflection and Aksel repeated the English version for Flora.

'That's a lovely name. It sounds even better the way you say it...' Flora waited, and Mette responded, saying the name again so that Flora could mimic her.

This was all so easy, suddenly. Mette laughed over the way that Flora struggled to get her tongue around the Norwegian pronunciation, and when Flora stretched out her arms Mette gave her a hug. So simple, so natural, without any of the thought that Aksel put into his hugs. None of the wondering whether he was going too fast, or too slowly.

But, then, Flora didn't have agonised hope to contend with. Or the feeling that he didn't deserve Mette's hugs. Aksel watched as Mette showed Flora her toys, noticing that Flora didn't help Mette as much as he did, and that his daughter responded to that by becoming more animated.

'What's that?' Flora pointed to a box of jumbo-sized dominoes and Mette opened it, tipping the contents onto the floor. 'Oh, dominoes! I *love* dominoes...'

'Would you like to play?' The words slipped out before Aksel could stop them. He wanted to watch her with Mette for just a little longer.

Flora treated the request as if it was an invitation to a tour of the seven wonders of the world. Mette couldn't resist her excited smile and gave an emphatic '*Yes!*'

'Shall we do that thing first...?' Mette took a few uncertain steps towards Flora, clearly wanting to know what *that thing* was. Aksel wanted to know too. 'Where you stand them all up in a row and then knock them down again?'

Flora started to gather the dominoes together, putting them in a pile on the floor. 'It's such fun. Your papa will show you, I can never get them to balance properly.'

That was a ruse to get him involved. But Flora could manipulate him as much as she liked if this was the result. Aksel sat down on the floor, and started to line the dominoes up in a spiral pattern, seeing his own hand shake with emotion as he did so. Flora and Mette were both watching him intently, Mette bending forward to see.

'Spirals, eh? Show-off...' Flora murmured the words and Aksel felt his shoulders relax suddenly. Maybe this wasn't so difficult after all.

When Flora walked out to her car, it was already getting dark. She'd stayed longer than she'd intended with Aksel and Mette, and the work that she'd expected to take an hour had taken two. That might be something to do with the daydreaming. Aksel's bulk and strength and the gentle vulnerability that little blonde-haired, blue-eyed Mette brought out in him were downright mouth-watering.

He was so anxious to please and yet so awkward with his daughter. Aksel watched over Mette's every move, ready to catch her if there was even the smallest likelihood that she might fall. He meant well, but he was smothering her.

Not your business, Flora. Dr Sinclair will deal with it.

Lyle Sinclair had a way of taking patients or their families aside and gently suggesting new ways of looking at things. And Lyle would have the advantage of not feeling quite so hot under the collar at the mere thought of a conversation with Aksel.

'Flora!'

Flora closed her eyes in resignation at the sound of his voice. However hard she tried to escape him… When she turned and saw him striding across the car park towards her, she didn't want to escape him at all.

'I wanted to thank you.'

He'd done that already. More than once, and in as many words as Aksel seemed capable of.

'It was my pleasure. I always bring a little gift for the children, to make them feel welcome.' She'd told him that already, too. They could go on for ever like this, repeating the same things over and over again.

'I…' He spread his hands in a gesture of helplessness. 'You have a way with children.'

He made it sound as if it was some kind of supernatural power. Flora frowned. 'Children are just…people. Only they're usually a bit more fun.'

'You have a way with *people,* then.'

It was a nice compliment, especially since it was accompanied by his smile. Something was bugging him, but she wasn't the right person to speak to about it. She had too much baggage…

Baggage or experience? Experience was something that she could use to help her get things right this time.

She'd been an impressionable teenager when she'd loved Tom, but she knew better now. There was no cosmic rule that said she had to fall for Aksel, and she could handle the regrets over never being able to trust a man enough to build a relationship. If that meant that she'd never be able to sit on the floor and play dominoes with her own child, she could deal with that, too.

Flora turned, opening the rear door of her car and dumping her bags in the footwell. Then she faced him. If all he had to throw at her were longing and regret, she'd already made her peace with them, a long time ago.

'You've said "Thank you" already, there's no need for us to stand in the cold here while you say it again. What's bugging you?'

That was obviously confronting. But the slight twitch at the corners of his mouth told Flora that challenge was one of the things that he thrived on.

He took a breath, as if preparing himself. 'My relationship with Mette's mother was over before Mette was born and we never lived together as a family.'

What was he trying to say? That he'd been an absent father who hardly knew his own child? His obvious commitment to his daughter made that difficult to believe.

'And now?'

'I can't bring her mother back, or her sight. But I'd give anything to make her happy and...' He shrugged. 'It's not working. When I saw you with her this afternoon, I saw how much it wasn't working.'

Flora thought quickly. Aksel needed the kind of professional help that didn't fall within her area of expertise.

'Maybe you should talk to Lyle Sinclair. The clinic

has a family counsellor who deals with just these kinds of issues, and Lyle could organise a session for you both.'

He shook his head abruptly. 'Mette's just fine the way she is. I won't put her into counselling just because *I* need to change.'

'Maybe it's not about change, but just getting to know each other better. Kathy uses storytelling a lot in her sessions, to make things fun. I'm sure you have plenty of stories about the places you've been—'

'No.' That sounded like a hard limit. 'That part of my life is over. Mette needs to know that I'll be there for her, always. That I'm not about to leave, and go to places that she can't.'

His heart was in the right place, but his head was way off course, and lost without a map or compass. This was something she *could* help with; Flora had grown up with a brother who hadn't always been able to do the things that she had. When Alec had been ill, she'd learned how to go out into the world, and to bring something back to share with her brother when she got home.

'Who says that you can't go together?' Flora gave an imperious twitch of her finger, indicating that he should follow her, and started to walk.

Flora seemed impatient with him, as if he was stubbornly refusing to see a simple fact that was obvious to her. On one level, Aksel just wanted to see her smile again. But on another, much more urgent level, he reckoned that Flora could be just as annoyed as she liked, if only it meant that she'd tell him what he was doing wrong. The first lesson he needed to learn was how to follow, rather than lead, and he walked beside her silently.

They reached the gravel driveway outside the clinic, and Flora stopped. 'You think that Mette doesn't know what it's like to be an explorer?'

The warmth in her eyes had been replaced by fire. Aksel swallowed down the thought that he liked that fire, and concentrated on the point that Flora seemed about to make.

'You're going to tell me different, aren't you?'

'Just think about it. She can feel the gravel under her feet, and she can hear it scrunch. If she bends down, she can probably see it. She can feel the snow...' Flora broke off, turning her face up towards the flakes that had started to drift down, and one landed on her cheek. Aksel resisted the temptation to brush it away with his finger, and it melted almost immediately.

'But she can't see any of this.' He turned towards the mountains in the distance. He'd give his own sight if Mette could just appreciate the beauty of the world around her.

'Exactly. That's where you come in. She needs someone to explore with her, and tell her about the things she can't see for herself.'

'And if it's upsetting for her?'

'Then you respond to what she's feeling and stop. Just as long as it's Mette who's upset by it, and not you.'

She had a point, and this was a challenge he couldn't resist. Aksel's head was beginning to buzz with ideas. 'Maybe I could take a photograph of them. She might be able to hold that up close and see it.'

'*Now* you're thinking... Speak to Lyle and find out whether he thinks that might work for Mette.' Flora seemed to know that she'd lit a fuse and she wasn't taking cover. She wanted more from him.

'Maybe she'd like to go this way.' He started to walk

towards the small, sheltered garden at the side of the property and found that Flora was no longer with him. She was standing still, her hands in her pockets, and one eyebrow raised slightly.

If that was the way she wanted to play it. Aksel returned to her side, holding out his arm. 'I'm going to have to guide her there, of course.'

She nodded, slipping her hand into the crook of his elbow. A frisson of excitement accompanied the feel of her falling into step beside him, and Aksel turned his mind to describing the things around them. The darkening bulk of the stone built castle. The sky, still red from the setting sun, and the clouds off to the east, which promised more snow for tonight.

She slipped so easily into a child-like wonder at the things around her. Aksel was considering asking Flora if she might accompany him and Mette when they set out on their own voyage of exploration, but he guessed what her answer might be.

No. You have to do it yourself.

'Careful…!' He'd seen her reach for a rose bush to one side of the path, and Aksel automatically caught her hand, pulling it away. 'It has thorns.'

Something that had been simmering deep beneath the surface began to swell, almost engulfing him. The thought of rose petals, wet with summer rain and vainly attempting to rival the softness of Flora's cheeks, made him shiver.

'All roses do.' She turned her gaze onto him, and Aksel saw a sudden sadness, quickly hidden. 'Will you let Mette miss the rose because of its thorns?'

That was a hard thought to contemplate. Aksel guided her hand, so that her fingers could brush the leaves. 'You must be gentle. In the summer, the rose is the softest of blooms, but the thorns will still hurt you.'

He let her fingers explore the leaves and then the stem, touching the thorns carefully. It seemed to him that the thorns of this world had done Flora some damage, but that she still chose to see roses. She had room in her heart for both Mette and for Dougal, and yet she lived alone. He wanted to ask why, but he didn't dare.

Flora looked up at him suddenly. 'What's next for us to explore, then?'

A whole spectrum of senses and experiences, none of which involved asking personal questions. Aksel took her to the trunk of an old tree, which twisted against the castle wall, and she followed the rough curves of its bark with her fingers. He explained the eerie wail of a fox, drifting towards them from somewhere beyond his own range of vision. The temptation to draw her closer, and let his body shelter her against the wind, hammered against him.

'I can hear water...' Flora seemed intent on playing this game out.

'Over here.' A small stream trickled past the flower beds, curving its way out into the surrounding countryside. Flora's excitement seemed real, and he wondered whether she was play-acting or not.

'I don't think I can get across...' Mette wouldn't be able to jump to the other side, so neither could Flora.

The temptation was just too great. He could justify it by saying that this was what he would have done with Mette, or he could just give in to it and enjoy. Right now, the urge to just enjoy was thundering in his veins.

'I could carry you.' He called her bluff, wondering who'd be the first to blink.

'You're sure you won't drop me?'

He was about to tell her that he'd carried heavier weights, over much more difficult terrain, and then he realised that Flora was looking him up and down. This was a challenge that he couldn't back off from.

'Let's find out.' He wound his arm around her back, waiting for her to respond, and Flora linked her hands behind his neck. Then he picked her up in his arms.

Stepping across the narrow stream was nothing. Having her close was everything, a dizzying, heady sensation that made Aksel forget about anything else. Her scent invaded his senses and all he wanted to do was hold Flora for as long as she'd allow it.

He wondered if she could feel the resonance of his heart pounding against his ribs. Feeling her arms tighten around him, he looked into her face and suddenly he was lost. Her gaze met his, seeming to understand everything, all of his hope and fears and his many, many uncertainties. He might be struggling to keep his head above water, but she was the rock that he clung to.

None of that mattered. Her eyes were dark in the twilight, her lips slightly parted. The only thing that Aksel could think about was how her kiss might taste.

He resisted. It seemed that Flora was too. This was all wrong, but he couldn't make a move to stop it.

'Are you going to put me down now?' She murmured the words, still holding him tight in the spell of her gaze. Aksel moved automatically, setting her back on her feet, and for a moment he saw disappointment in her eyes. Then she smiled.

'Where shall we go next?'

Their voyage of exploration wasn't over. And Aksel had discovered one, basic truth. That he must navigate carefully between the dangerous waters of Flora's eyes, and the absolute need to do his best for Mette.

'Over there.' Light was pooling around a glazed door, which led back into the castle. He needed that light, in order to forget the way that shadows had caressed Flora's face, in a way that he never could.

CHAPTER THREE

FLORA OPENED HER EYES. Sunday morning. A time to relax and think about nothing.

Nothing wasn't going to work. That was when Aksel invaded her thoughts. The night-time dreams of a perfect family, which were usually brushed off so easily when she woke, had been fleshed out with faces. Aksel had been there, and her children had their father's ice-blue eyes. The image had made her heart ache.

And she'd come so close yesterday. Almost done it…

Almost didn't matter. She hadn't kissed him and she wasn't going to. She'd flirted a bit—Flora could admit to that. They'd shared a moment, it was impossible to deny that either. But they'd drawn back from it, like grown-up, thinking people. It took trust to make a relationship, and that was the one thing that Flora couldn't feel any more.

She got out of bed, wrapping her warm dressing gown around her and opening the curtains. Not picturing Aksel at all. Actually, she didn't need to imagine he was there, because he was the first thing she saw when she looked out over the land that bordered the village. Kari was racing to fetch a ball that he'd just flung into the air, and he turned, as if aware of her gaze on him. Seeing her at the window, he waved.

Great. Not only was he intruding into her dreams, he seemed to have taken over her waking moments now. Flora waved back, turning from the window.

Somehow, Aksel managed to follow her into the shower. Wet-haired, with rivulets of water trickling over his chest. Then downstairs, as butter melted on her toast, he was standing by the stove, making coffee in that little copper kettle of his.

'If he's going to stalk me, then perhaps he should do the washing-up…' Dougal was busy demolishing the contents of his bowl, and gave Flora's comment the disregard that it deserved. Aksel wasn't stalking her. She was doing this all by herself.

The doorbell rang and Dougal rushed out into the hallway, knocking over his water bowl in the process. He was pawing at the front door, barking excitedly, and Flora bent down to pick him up. Then she saw Aksel's dark shadow on the other side of the obscured glass. She jumped back, yelping in surprise, and the shadow suddenly seemed to back away too.

She opened the door, trying to compose herself. At least the real Aksel bothered to wait on the doorstep and didn't just waltz in as if he owned the place.

'Is this too early…?' Today he was clean-shaven, with just the top half of his hair caught back, leaving the rest to flow around his shoulders. How on earth did he get such gorgeous hair to look so masculine? Flora dismissed the question for later, and concentrated on the one he'd asked.

'No. Not at all.' A cold wind was whipping through into the house, and Flora stood back from the door. 'Come in.'

She led the way through to the kitchen, and both he and Kari stepped neatly around the puddle of spilt water from Dougal's bowl. He insisted that he didn't want coffee, and that she should sit down and have her breakfast while he cleared up the mess. Flora sat, taking a gulp from her mug while he fetched a cloth and wiped up the water, washing the bowl in the sink before refilling it for Dougal.

'I assume you didn't just pop in to wipe my kitchen floor for me?' Who knew that a man could look sexy doing housework? If she wasn't very careful, she would find herself fantasising about that, too.

'No. I came to ask you a favour.'

'Fire away.' Flora waved him to a seat, and picked up her toast.

'I did some reorganisation this morning, to prepare for when Mette comes back to the cottage to stay with me.' He frowned, clearly not very pleased with the results. 'I wondered if you might take a look, and tell me what you think? I won't keep you long.'

This was where the fantasy stopped. Mette was a patient at the clinic, and Aksel was a father in need of some help. It was safer, more comfortable ground, even if it was less thrilling. Flora got to her feet.

'Okay. Let's have a look.'

Aksel picked Dougal up in his arms, and all four of them squeezed through the hole in the hedge, Flora shivering as the wind tugged at her sweater. Dougal followed Kari into the sitting room, and He led the way up the stairs. Flora was surprised when he opened the door to the left because this cottage was the mirror image of hers, with the smaller bedroom and a bathroom to the right. She followed him inside.

Aksel had obviously made an effort. There was a toy box with a row of cuddly animals lined up on the top.

A single bed stood at the other end of the room with the wardrobe and chest of drawers.

'This is nice. I can see you've covered all the health and safety aspects.' The room was immaculately tidy, which would help Mette find what she wanted. He'd obviously been thinking about trip hazards and sharp edges, and all of the wall sockets had protectors fitted.

'That's easy enough.' Aksel was looking around the room with a dissatisfied gaze. 'It's not very pretty, though, is it?'

It was a bit stark. But that could be fixed easily. 'Why did you choose this room for Mette?'

'It's the biggest.'

'Big isn't always best. In a very large room like this, Mette might find it difficult to orientate herself.'

Aksel thought for a moment, and then nodded, striding across the hallway and opening the door of the other bedroom. Inside, Flora could see a large double bed, which must have come from the main bedroom. This room too was scrupulously tidy, as if Aksel had decided to camp here for the night and would be moving on soon.

He looked around, assessing her suggestion. 'I think you're right. I'll move everything back the way it was.'

'Would you like a hand?' The heavy bedframe must have been a bit of a struggle.

'Thanks, but I'll manage. What else?'

'Well... I'm no expert...'

'Give me your next-door-neighbour opinion.' His smile sliced through all of Flora's resolutions not to interfere too much and she puffed out a breath, looking around.

'You're not here for long so you don't want to make any permanent changes. But it would be great to be able to change the tone and brightness of the light in here to suit her needs. Maybe get some lamps with programmable bulbs that you can take with you when you go?'

He nodded. 'That's a great idea. What else?'

'Taking her toy box downstairs and just having a few cuddly toys up here for bedtime might get her used to the idea that upstairs is for sleeping. If you use bright colours that she can see, it'll help guide her around the room. And what about some textures, a comforter or a bedspread…?'

He walked across to the nightstand next to his bed, picking up a notebook and flipping it open. 'Lights…' He scribbled a note. 'Colours… Textures… Bedspread.'

Flora nodded. 'If you got her a nice bedspread, then perhaps she could use it here and on her bed at the clinic. Then, if she wakes up in the night, she'll have something that feels familiar right there.'

Aksel nodded, scribbling another entry in the notebook. 'Good idea. Anything else?'

'What does Mette like?'

That seemed the hardest question of all to answer. 'Um… Sparkly things, mostly. And she likes it when I read to her. She always wants the same stories over and over again.'

'The ones her mother read to her?'

'Yes. I think they help her to feel more secure.'

'Then use them as a guide. Maybe choose some things that feature in her favourite stories.'

'That's a great idea, thank you.' He made another note in his notebook before putting it into the back pocket of his jeans and striding back to the main bedroom. 'I'll take the toy box downstairs now. If you could suggest a place for it…'

He was trying so hard. Maybe that was the problem,

he wanted to make everything perfect for Mette and couldn't be satisfied with anything less. Flora watched as he cleared the cuddly animals from the top of the toy box, trying not to notice how small they looked in his large, gentle hands.

'Oh…wait, I'll give you a hand…' Aksel had lifted the large wooden box alone, hardly seeming to notice its weight.

'That's all right. If you'll just stand aside.'

She could do that. Flora jumped out of his way, noticing the flex of muscle beneath his shirt as he manoeuvred the box through the doorway. She followed him as he carried it downstairs, swallowing down the lump in her throat. Aksel's strong frame was impressive when he was at rest, but in action it was stunning.

'Over there, maybe…?' He was standing in the centre of the sitting room, looking around with a perplexed look on his face. Flora shifted one of the chairs that stood around the fireside, and he finally put the box down, one hand rubbing his shoulder as he straightened up.

'Is your shoulder all right?' He raised an eyebrow, and Flora felt herself redden. Okay, so she'd been looking at his shoulders. 'Professional interest. I'm a physiotherapist, remember?'

'It's fine. It was just a little stiff this morning.'

His tone told Flora to leave it, so she did. 'Maybe we could move one of the lights so that when Mette opens the box she can see inside better.'

Suddenly Aksel grinned. 'Kari…'

The dog raised her head, moving from relaxed fireside mode to work mode immediately. In response to a command in Norwegian, she trotted over to the box and inserted her paw into a semi-circular hole cut into the side, under the lid. Flora heard a click and the lid swung open smoothly, its motion clearly controlled by a counterbalance mechanism.

The ease of opening was just the beginning. As the box opened, light flooded the inside of the box, and Flora could see that there were small LEDs around the edge, shaded at the top so that they would shine downwards and not dazzle Mette. The contents were carefully arranged in plastic baskets, so that she would be able to find whatever she wanted.

'That's fantastic! Wherever did you get this?'

'I made it. There was nothing on the market that quite suited Mette's needs.' Aksel was clearly pleased with Flora's approval.

She knelt down beside the box, inspecting it carefully. The lid opened easily enough for a child...or a dog...to lift it and the counterbalance mechanism meant that once open there was no danger of it slamming shut on small fingers. The lights came on when the lid opened and flicked off again as it closed, and they illuminated the contents of the box in a soft, clear light.

And the box itself was a masterpiece, made of wooden panels that were smooth and warm to the touch. It was quite plain but that was part of its beauty. The timber had obviously been carefully chosen and its swirling grain made this piece one of a kind.

'Mette must love it.' It was a gift that only a loving and thoughtful father could have made. And someone who was a skilled craftsman as well.

He nodded, looking around the room restlessly as if searching for the next thing that needed to be done. Aksel's response to any problem was to act on it, and he was obviously struggling with the things he could do nothing about. No wonder he was carrying some tension in his shoulders.

'We could go and do some shopping, if you wanted. It won't take long to pick out a few things to brighten Mette's bedroom up.'

'Would you mind…?' He was halfway towards the door, obviously ready to turn thought into action as soon as possible, and then stopped himself. 'Perhaps another time. Whenever it's convenient for you.'

Flora allowed herself a smile. 'Now's fine. I'll go and get my coat.'

Aksel had been struggling to get the fantasy out of his head ever since he'd opened his eyes this morning. Rumpled sheets and Flora's cheeks, flushed with sleep.

Yesterday had shown him how easy it would be to slip into loving intimacy with Flora, but her reaction had told him that she didn't want that any more than he did. The word *impossible* usually made his blood fire in his veins at the thought of proving that nothing was impossible, and it had taken Flora's look of quiet certainty to convince him that there was something in this world that truly was impossible.

He could deal with that. If he just concentrated on having her as a friend, and forgot all about wanting her as a lover, then it would be easy. When she returned, wearing a dark green coat with a red scarf, and holding Dougal's dog coat and lead, he ignored the way that the cottage seemed suddenly full of light and warmth again.

'Why don't you leave him here? They'll be fine together.' The puppy was curled up in front of the fire with Kari, and didn't seem disposed to move.

'You think so?' Flora tickled Dougal's head and he

squirmed sleepily, snuggling against Kari. 'Yes. I guess they will.'

She drove in much the same way as she held a conversation. Quick and decisive, her eyes fixed firmly on where she was going. Aksel guessed that Flora wasn't much used to watching the world go by, she wanted always to be moving, and he wondered whether she ever took some time out to just sit and feel the world turn beneath her. He guessed not.

For a woman that he'd just decided *not* to be too involved with, he was noticing a great deal about her. Flora wasn't content with the just-crawled-out-of-bed look for a Sunday morning. She'd brushed her hair until it shone and wore a little make-up. More probably than was apparent, it was skilfully applied to make the most of her natural beauty. She wore high-heeled boots with her skinny jeans, and when she moved Aksel caught the scent of something he couldn't place. Clean, with a hint of flowers and slightly musky, it curled around him, beckoning his body to respond.

'So… Mette's never lived with you before?' She asked the question when they'd got out of the winding country lanes and onto the main road.

'No.' Aksel couldn't think of anything to say to describe a situation that was complicated, to say the least.

'Sorry…' She flipped her gaze to him for a moment, and Aksel almost shivered in its warmth. 'I didn't mean to pry.'

'It's all right. It's no secret. Just a little difficult to explain.'

'Ah. I'll leave it there, then.'

Flora lapsed into silence. 'Difficult to explain' didn't appear to daunt her, she seemed the kind of person who could accept almost anything. He imagined that her patients must find it very easy to confide in her. All their hopes and their most secret despair. Suddenly, he wanted to talk.

'I didn't know that I had a daughter until after Mette's mother died.'

Nothing registered in Flora's face, but he saw her fingers grip the steering wheel a little tighter. Maybe she was wondering what kind of man hadn't known about his own daughter. He wouldn't blame her—he frequently tormented himself with that thought.

'That must be...challenging.'

Her answer was just the thing a medical professional would say. Non-judgemental, allowing for the possibility of pain and yet assuming nothing. Aksel wanted more than that, he wanted Flora to judge him. If she found him wanting then it would be nothing he hadn't already accused himself of. And if she found a way to declare him innocent it would mean a great deal to him.

'What do you think?' He asked the question as if it didn't mean much, but felt a quiver deep in the pit of his stomach.

No reaction. But as she changed gear, the car jolted a little, as if it was reflecting her mood.

'I'd find it very difficult.'

Aksel nodded. Clearly Flora wasn't going to be persuaded to give an opinion on the matter and maybe that was wise. Maybe he should let it drop.

'In...lots of ways.' She murmured the words, as if they might blow up in her face. Flora wanted to know more but she wasn't going to ask.

'Lisle and I split up before either of us knew she was pregnant. I was due to go away for a while, I was leading an expedition into the Andes.' Suddenly his courage failed him. 'It's a fascinating place...'

'I'm sure.' Her slight frown told Aksel that she wasn't really interested in one of the largest mountain ranges in the world, its volcanic peaks, the highest navigable lake on the planet or the incredible biodiversity. To her, the wonders of the world were nothing in comparison to the mysteries of the human heart, and she was the kind of woman who trod boldly in that unknown territory.

He took a breath, staring at the road ahead. 'When I got back, I heard that Lisle had gone to Oslo for a new job. I think that the job might have been an excuse...'

Flora gave a little nod. 'It does sound that way.'

There was compassion in her voice. Most people questioned why Lisle should have gone to such lengths to keep her pregnancy a secret from him, but Flora didn't seem disposed to make any judgements yet.

'I never saw her again. The first I knew of Mette's existence was when her parents called me, telling me about the accident.'

'That must have been a shock.'

It had changed his world. Tipped it upside down and focussed every last piece of his attention on the child he'd never known he had. '*Shock* is an understatement.'

She flipped a glance at him, then turned her gaze back onto the road ahead. But in that moment Aksel saw warmth in her eyes and it spurred him on, as if it was the glimmer of an evening campfire at the end of a long road.

'Olaf and Agnetha are good people. They never really agreed with Lisle's decision not to tell me about Mette, although they respected it while she was alive. When she died, they decided that Mette needed to know more than just what Lisle had told her. That she had a father but that he was an adventurer, away exploring the world.'

Flora nodded, her lips forming into a tight line. 'And so you finally got to meet her.'

'Not straight away. Mette was in hospital for a while. She had no other serious injuries, she was still in her car seat when the rescue services arrived, but one of the front headrests had come loose and hit her in the face. The blow damaged her optic nerves…'

The memory of having to stand outside Mette's room, watching through the glass partition as Agnetha sat with her granddaughter, was still as sharp as a knife. He'd understood the importance of taking things slowly, but reaching out to touch the cool, hard surface of the glass that had separated them had been agony. Aksel gripped his hands together hard to stop them from shaking.

'Olaf and Agnetha were naturally anxious to take things at whatever pace was best for Mette and I was in complete agreement with that. I dropped everything and went to Oslo, but it was two weeks before they made the decision to introduce me to her. They were the longest two weeks of my life.'

'I imagine so. It must have been very hard for them, too.'

'Yes, it was. They knew me from when I'd been seeing Lisle, but they wanted to make sure that I wouldn't hurt Mette any more than she'd already been hurt. Letting me get to know her was a risk.'

'But they took it. Good for them.'

'Not until I'd convinced them that I wouldn't walk in, shower Mette with presents and then leave again. That was why Lisle didn't tell me about her pregnancy. Because I was always leaving…'

Aksel could hear the bitterness in his own voice. The helpless anger that Lisle hadn't known that a child would make all the difference to him. She'd only seen the man who'd wanted to go out and meet the world, and she'd done what she'd felt she had to do in response to that.

'She must have cared a lot about you.'

That was a new idea. Aksel had been more comfortable with the thought that the only emotion he'd engendered in Lisle's heart was dislike. 'What makes you say that?'

'If the thought of you leaving was such an issue to her, then it must have hurt.'

Guilt was never very far from the surface these days, but now it felt as if it was eating him up. 'I didn't think of it that way.'

'You're angry with her? For not telling you about Mette?'

Yes, he was angry. Rage had consumed him, but he'd hidden it for Olaf and Agnetha's sake. And now he hid it for Mette's sake.

'Mette loves her mother. I have to respect that.'

He was caught off balance suddenly as Flora swerved left into the service road that led to a large car park. That was the story of his life at the moment, letting other people take the driving seat and finding himself struggling to cope with the twists and turns in the road. She caught sight of a parking spot, accelerating to get to it before anyone else did, and turned into it. Aksel waited for her to reverse and straighten up, and then realised that the car was already perfectly straight and within the white lines.

'I'd want to scream. I mean, I'd go out and find a place where no one could hear me, and *really* scream. Until I was hoarse.'

So she knew something of the healing nature of the

wilderness. Aksel hadn't told anyone why he'd taken the train out of Oslo towards Bergen, or that he'd set out alone in the darkness to trek to the edge of one of the magnificent fjords, roaring his anger and pain out across the water.

'I didn't scream, I yelled. But apart from that, you have it right.'

She gave a soft chuckle, regarding him silently for a moment. 'And then you went back home and read all the manuals? Did your best to be a good father, without any of the training and experience that most men get along the way?'

That was exactly how Aksel felt at times. He'd loved Mette from the first moment he'd seen her. But sometimes he found it hard to communicate with her.

'I've made a career out of dealing with the unexpected.'

Flora smiled and the warmth in the car turned suddenly to sticky heat. If he didn't move now, he was going to fall prey to the insistent urge to reach forward and touch her. Aksel got out of the car, feeling the wind's sharp caress on his face.

Flora grabbed her handbag from the back seat, getting out of the driver's seat, and Aksel took his notebook from his pocket, skimming through the list he'd made. 'I should get some Christmas-tree decorations as well while we're here.'

She turned to him, a look of mock horror on her face. 'You don't have any?'

Aksel shrugged. 'I'm used to moving around a lot. Whenever I'm home for Christmas, I go to my sister's.'

'Perfect. I love buying tree decorations, and if I buy any more I won't be able to fit them on the tree.' She scanned the row of shops that skirted the car park, obviously keen to get on with the task in hand. 'It's a good thing we came today, all the best ones will be gone soon.'

CHAPTER FOUR

IT WAS UNLIKELY that *anything* would be gone from the shops for a while yet. The stores that lined the shopping precinct were full of merchandise for Christmas, and rapidly filling up with people. Flora ignored that self-evident fact. It was never too early for Christmas.

Unlikely as it might be, Aksel seemed slightly lost. As someone who could find his way to both the North and South poles, a few shops should be child's play. But he was looking around as if a deep crevasse had opened up between him and where he wanted to be and he wasn't sure how to navigate it. Flora made for the entrance to the nearest store.

'What sort of decorations did you have in mind?' The in-store Christmas shop shone with lights and glitter, and was already full of shoppers.

'Um… Can I leave myself in your hands?'

Nice thought. Flora would have to make sure it stayed just a thought. She smiled brightly at him and made for some glass baubles, finding herself pushed up against Aksel in the crush of people.

'These are nice…'

'We'll take them. What about these?' He picked up a packet of twisted glass icicles.

'They're lovely.' Flora dropped a packet for herself

into the basket, despite having decided that she already had too many tree decorations.

As they left the shop, Aksel gazed longingly at the entrance to the DIY store, but Flora walked determinedly past it, and he fell into step beside her.

An hour later they'd filled the shopping bags that Flora had brought with her, and Aksel was laden down with them.

He peered over her shoulder as Flora consulted the list he'd torn from his notebook, ticking off what they already had and putting a star next to the more specialised home-support items that the clinic could supply him with. That left the bedspread.

'I saw a shop in the village that sells quilts. They looked nice.' He ventured a suggestion.

'Mary Monroe's quilts are gorgeous. But they're handmade so they're expensive. You can get a nice bedspread for much less at one of the big stores here...'

Aksel shook his head. 'I liked the look of the place in the village.'

'Right. We'll try that first, then.'

Aksel was shaping up to be the perfect shopping companion, patient and decisive. He didn't need to sit down for coffee every twenty minutes, and he was able to carry any number of bags. Maybe if she thought of him that way, the nagging thump of her heart would subside a little. It was a known fact that women had lovers and shopping companions, and that the two territories never overlapped.

It wasn't easy to hold the line, though. When he loaded the bags into the boot of the car, Flora couldn't help noticing those shoulders. Again. And the fifteen-minute drive back to the village gave her plenty of time to feel the scent of fresh air and pine cones do its work.

By the time they drew up outside Village Quilts she felt almost dizzy with desire.

A little more shopping would sort that out. Shopping beat sex every time. And this was the kind of shop where you had to bring all your concentration to bear on the matter in hand. Mary Monroe prided herself on making sure that she was on first-name terms with all her customers, and if they could be persuaded to sit on one of the rickety chairs while she sorted through her entire stock to come up with the perfect quilt, then all the better.

But Aksel wasn't going to be confined to a chair. The introductions were made and he sat down but then sprang to his feet again. 'Let me help you with that, Mary.'

Mary was over a foot shorter than him, slight and grey-haired. But she was agile enough on the ladder that she needed to reach the top shelves, and never accepted help.

'Thank you.' Mary capitulated suddenly. Maybe she'd decided that sixty was a good age to slow down a bit, but she'd never shown any sign of doing so. And when Flora rose from her chair to assist, Mary gave her a stern glare that implied no further help was needed.

Aksel lifted the pile of heavy quilts down from the top shelf and Mary stood back. Maybe she was admiring his shoulders, too.

'Your little girl is partially blind…' Mary surveyed the pile thoughtfully.

'Yes. Something that's textured might be good for her.' Flora decided that this didn't really fall into the category of help, it was just volunteering some information.

'What about a raw-edged quilt?' Mary pulled a couple from the pile, unfolding them. 'You see the raw edges of each piece of fabric are left on the top, and form a pattern.'

The quilts were rich and thick, and each square was surrounded by frayed edges of fabric and padding. Aksel ran his fingers across the surface of one and smiled. 'This will do her very nicely. Do you have something a bit more colourful? Mette can see strong colours better.'

'That pile, up there.' Mary didn't even move, and Aksel lifted the quilts down from the shelf. Flora rose, unfolding some of the quilts.

'This one's beautiful, Mary!' The quilt had twelve square sections, each one appliquéd with flowers. Mary beamed.

'I made that one myself. It's a calendar quilt…'

Flora could see now that the flowers in each square corresponded to a month in the year. December was a group of Christmas trees on snowy white ground, the dark blue sky scattered with stars.

'Not really what you're looking for.' Mary tugged at a raw-edged quilt that was made from fabrics in a variety of reds and greens. 'How about this one?'

Aksel nodded, turning to Flora. 'What do you think.'

'Do you like it?'

'Very much.' He ran his fingers over the quilt, smiling. 'I'll take this one.'

'I have more to show you.' Mary liked her customers to see her full stock before making any decisions, but Aksel's smile and the quick shake of his head convinced her that, in this instance, they didn't need to go through that process.

'I like this one, too.' He turned his attention back

to the calendar quilt, examining the different squares. 'These are all Scottish plants and flowers?'

'Yes, that's right. I design my quilts to reflect what I see around me. But this one doesn't have the texture that your daughter might like.'

'It would be something to remind us of our trip to Scotland. Perhaps I could hang it on the wall in her room. May I take this one too?'

'No, you may not.' Mary put her hands on her hips. 'My quilts are made with love, and that's why they'll keep you warm. They are *not* supposed to be hung on the wall.'

'If I were to promise to keep it in my sitting room? Something to wrap Mette in on cold winter nights and remind us both of the warm welcome we've had here. The raw-edged one will stay on her bed.' Aksel gave Mary an imploring look and she capitulated suddenly.

'That would be quite fine. You're sure you want both?'

Aksel nodded. If Mary could be an unstoppable force at times, she at least knew when she'd come into contact with an immovable object. Something had to give, and she did so cheerfully.

'You'll give this one to your daughter as a present?' She started to fold the raw-edged quilt.

'Yes.'

'I've got some pretty paper in the back that'll do very nicely. I'll just slip it into the bag and you can do the wrapping yourself.' Mary bustled through a door behind the counter, leaving them alone.

'You're sure?' Flora ran her hand over the quilts. They were both lovely, but this was a big expense, and she was feeling a little guilty for suggesting it.

'I'm sure. I'll have a whole house to furnish back in Norway, and these will help make it a home for Mette.'

'You don't have a place there already?'

'I've never been in one place long enough to consider buying a house. Mette and I have been staying with Olaf and Agnetha—their house is familiar to her and they have more than enough room. I've bought a house close by so that we can visit often.'

Flora wanted to hug him. He'd been through a lot, and he was trying so hard to make a success of the new role he'd taken on in life. She watched as Mary reappeared, bearing a large carrier bag for Aksel and taking the card that he produced from his wallet.

They stepped outside into the pale sunshine and started to walk back towards Flora's car.

'I'll give the quilt to Mette tomorrow when you're at the clinic. Will you come and help me?'

'No! It's *your* present. Aren't you going to see her this afternoon?' Flora would have loved to see Mette's face when she opened the quilt, but this was Aksel's moment.

'Yes. I just thought…' He shrugged. 'Maybe it would be more special to her if you were there.'

'It's your present. And you're her father. She can show it to me when I come and visit.' Flora frowned. 'You really haven't had that much time alone with her, have you?'

Aksel cleared his throat awkwardly. 'Almost none. I relied a lot more heavily on Olaf and Agnetha to help me than I realised.'

'And how is Mette ever going to feel safe and secure with you if you can't even give her a present on your own? You've got to get over this feeling that you're not enough for her, Aksel.' Maybe that was a little too direct. But Aksel always seemed to appreciate her candour.

'Point taken. In that case, I don't suppose you have a roll of sticky tape you could lend me?'

'Yes, I have several. You can never have too much sticky tape this close to Christmas.'

He chuckled quietly. 'You'd be happy to celebrate Christmas once a month, wouldn't you?'

Flora thought for a moment. The idea was tempting. 'Christmas is special, and once a year is just fine. It gives me loads of time to look forward to it.'

'There's that. I'm looking forward to my first Christmas with Mette.'

'You're not panicking yet?'

'I'm panicking. I just disguise it well.'

Flora grinned up at him. 'It'll be fine. Better than fine, it'll be brilliant. Christmas at the castle is always lovely.'

'Just your kind of place, then.'

Yes, it was. Cluchlochry was home, and her work at the clinic was stimulating and rewarding. Flora had almost managed to convince herself that she had everything that she wanted. Until Aksel had come along...

She felt in her pocket for her car keys, watching as Aksel stowed the quilts in the back seat with the rest of their shopping. She'd found peace here. An out-of-the-way shelter from the harsh truths of life, where she could ignore the fact that she sometimes felt she was only half living. And Aksel was threatening to destroy that peace and plunge her into a maelstrom of what-ifs and maybes. She wouldn't let him.

Aksel had spent a restless night just a few metres away from her. Even the thick stone wall between Flora's bedroom and his couldn't dull the feeling that anytime now she might burst through, bringing light and laughter. He imagined her in red pyjamas with red lips. And, despite himself, he imagined her out of those red pyjamas as well.

He set out before dawn with Kari, walking to the canine therapy centre, which was situated in the grounds of the Heatherglen Castle Estate. As they trekked past the clinic, Aksel imagined Mette, stirring sleepily under her quilt. She'd loved it, flinging her arms around his neck and kissing him. Each kiss from his little girl was still special, and every time he thought about it, his fingers moved involuntarily to his cheek, feeling the tingle of pleasure.

Esme Ross-Wylde was already in her office, and took him to meet his new charges, dogs of all kinds that were being trained as PAT dogs. For the next few weeks Aksel would be helping Esme out with some of the veterinary duties, and he busied himself reading up on the notes for each dog.

A commotion of barking and voices just before nine o'clock heralded Flora's arrival with Dougal, and Aksel resisted the temptation to walk out of the surgery and say hello. There was a moment of relative peace and then Esme appeared, holding Dougal's lead tightly.

'Flora tells me that Kari's made friends with this wee whirlwind.' She nodded down at Dougal, raising her eyebrows when, on Aksel's command, Kari rose from her corner and trotted over to Dougal. The little dog calmed immediately.

'Yes. He just needs plenty of attention at the moment.'

'I don't suppose you could take him for a while, could you? Give everyone else a bit of peace? He's a great asset when it comes to teaching the dogs to ignore other dogs, but he's getting in the way a bit at the moment.'

Aksel nodded and Esme smiled. 'Thanks. You know that Flora works at the clinic…?' The question seemed to carry with it an ulterior motive.

'Yes, she came to introduce herself on Saturday, and she's been helping me settle in. We went shopping for Mette yesterday.'

Esme chuckled. 'Shopping's one of Flora's greatest talents. Along with physiotherapy, of course.'

'We found everything that we needed.' The idea that yesterday hadn't been particularly special or much out of the ordinary for Flora was suddenly disappointing. It had been special to him, and the look on Mette's face when he'd helped her unwrap her new quilt had been more precious than anything.

'I've no need to make any introductions, then. I've been talking to the manager of a sheltered housing complex near here—her name's Eileen Ross. We're looking at setting up a dog visiting scheme there and I thought that might be something I could hand over to you. Flora visits every week for a physiotherapy clinic, maybe you could go along with her tomorrow and see how the place operates.'

'I'd be very happy to take that on. I've seen a number of these schemes before, and I know that the elderly benefit a great deal from contact with animals.' The tingle of excitement that ran down his spine wasn't solely at the thought of the medical benefits of the visit.

'So I can put this on the ever-growing list of things that you'll take responsibility for while you're here?'

Aksel nodded. He wasn't aware of such a list and wondered whether it was all in Esme's head. She ran a tight ship here at the centre, and he'd already realised that she was committed to exploring new possibilities whenever she could.

'Leave it with me. I'll have a report for you next week.'

'Marvellous. I'll give Flora a call and let her know that's what we're planning. Is an eight-thirty start all right for you?'

'That's fine. Is the sheltered housing complex within walking distance from Cluchlochry?'

Esme chuckled. 'It depends what you call walking distance. I doubt Flora would think so. You don't have a car?'

'No.'

'We have an old SUV that you can use while you're here. It's a bit bashed around and it needs a good clean, but it'll get you from A to B.'

'Thank you, that's very kind. I'll pick it up in the morning if that's okay.'

'Yes, that's fine. I'll leave the keys at Reception for you.'

CHAPTER FIVE

FLORA HAD ALLOWED herself to believe that going to Mette's room at lunchtime, when she knew Aksel would be there, was just a matter of confirming their visit to the sheltered housing complex tomorrow morning. But when she found him carefully threading Mette's fingers into a pair of red and white woollen gloves, the matter slipped her mind. The two of them were obviously planning on going somewhere as Mette was bundled up in a red coat and a hat that matched her gloves, and Aksel had on a weatherproof jacket.

'Hi, Mette.' Flora concentrated on the little girl, giving Aksel a brief smile, before she bent down towards Mette, close enough that she could see her. 'You look nice and warm. Are you going somewhere?'

Mette replied in Norwegian. Her English was good enough to communicate with all the staff here, but sometimes she forgot when she needed to use it.

'English, Mette.' Aksel gave his daughter a fond smile. If there had ever been any doubt about his commitment to the little girl, it was all there in his eyes. 'We're going on an expedition.'

'Papa says there's a river, and we have to jump across it.' Mette volunteered the information, and Flora felt a tingle run down her spine at the thought of the trickle of water, and how she'd crossed it in Aksel's arms.

Aksel flashed her a grin. 'Dr Sinclair thought that your idea was a good one.'

Okay. Flora wondered whether Aksel had shared her other ideas, and hoped that Lyle wouldn't think she'd been interfering. She'd just been trying to help...

'Don't look so alarmed. I told him that I'd asked you for some ideas and that you'd been very kind.' He smiled.

Fair enough. It was disconcerting that he'd been able to gauge her thoughts so easily from her reaction, and she wished that he'd do as everyone else did, and wait for her to voice them. But Aksel was nothing if not honest, and it was probably beyond him not to say what was on his mind.

Before she could think of a suitable answer, Lyle Sinclair appeared in the doorway, holding a flask and a large box of sandwiches. The kitchen staff never missed an opportunity to feed anyone up, and it appeared that Aksel was already on their culinary radar.

'Hello, Mette. You're off to explore with your dad, are you?' He put the sandwiches down and bent towards the little girl, who looked up at him and nodded. Lyle looked around, as if wholly satisfied with the arrangement.

'Are you going too, Flora?'

'Um... No. Probably best to leave them to it.' This was something that Aksel and Mette needed to do alone. And any reminder of the almost-kissing-him incident was to be avoided.

'Yes, of course.' Lyle beamed at her. His quiet, gentle manner was more ebullient than usual, and Flora suspected that had a great deal to do with Cass Bellow's return from the States.

'How is Cass? I haven't seen her yet.'

'She's fine.' Lyle seemed to light up at the mention of her name. 'A little achy still, she was hoping you might have some time to see her in the next couple of days.'

'How about tomorrow afternoon? Would you like me to give her a call?'

'No, that's fine, I'll let her know and get her to call you and arrange a time. In the meantime, I won't keep you. I'll see you later, Mette.' Lyle touched Mette's hand in farewell and swept back out of the room.

'What's going on there?' Aksel had been watching quietly.

'Just a little romance. Actually, quite a lot of it, from what I've heard.' Flora liked Cass a lot, and she was happy for Lyle.

'That's nice.' Aksel's face showed no emotion as he turned his attention back to Mette's gloves, picking up the one she'd discarded on the floor. Clearly he was about as impressed with the idea of romance as Flora was, and that made things a great deal easier between them.

'You're really not going to come with us?' He didn't look up, concentrating on winding Mette's scarf around her neck.

'I'll come and wave you off.' Flora grinned at Mette. 'You've got to have someone wave you goodbye if you're going on an expedition.'

Aksel put the sandwiches into a daypack and made a show of going through its contents with Mette, explaining that the most important part of any expedition was to make sure it was properly provisioned. This particular journey required three glitter pens, a packet of sweets and Mette's rag doll.

Downstairs, Mette solemnly let the reception-ist know where they were going and when they'd be back, and that they'd be documenting their journey thor-oughly with photographs. Flora accompanied them out-side, wrapping her arms around herself against the cold.

'I want to ride, Papa.'

'All right.' Aksel bent down, lifting Mette up and settling her securely on his shoulders, and she squealed with glee. He said something in Norwegian, clearly in-structing Mette to hold on tight, and she flung her arms around his head.

He was standing completely still, blinded suddenly. Flora laughed, moving quickly to remove Mette's arms from over his eyes. 'Not like that, sweetheart. Papa can't see.'

'Thanks.' Aksel shot her a slow smile, and it hap-pened again. That gorgeous, slightly dizzy feeling, as if they were the only two people on the planet, and they understood each other completely.

Flora wrenched her gaze away from his, reaching up to pull Mette's hat down firmly over her ears. The little girl chuckled, tapping the top of her father's head in an obvious signal to start walking.

Flora waved them goodbye, calling after them, and Aksel turned so that Mette could wave one last time. She watched them until they disappeared around the corner of the building, two explorers off to test the lim-its of Mette's world. Maybe Aksel's too.

Aksel had wondered whether Flora might come to say goodnight to Mette when she finished work. His dis-appointment when she didn't wasn't altogether on behalf of his daughter, however much he tried to convince himself that it was.

They had a connection. It was one of those things that just happened, forged out of nothing between two people who hardly knew each other. He could do nothing about it, but that didn't mean he had to act on it either. The days when he'd had only himself to consider were gone.

The evening ritual of reading Mette a story and then carrying her over to her bed calmed him a little. As he settled her down, cosy and warm under the quilt, he heard a quiet tap on the door and it opened a fraction.

'What are you still doing here?' Flora's working day had finished hours ago, but he couldn't help the little quiver of joy that gripped his heart.

'I've been working late. I just wondered how your expedition went.'

'We went across a big river! And back again.' Mette was suddenly wide awake again. 'Will you come with us next time, Tante Flora?'

Flora blushed, telling Mette that she would. Aksel wondered whether it gave her as much pleasure to hear the little girl call her *Tante* as it did when she called him Papa. He'd decided with Olaf and Agnetha that they wouldn't push her, and that Mette should call him whatever she felt comfortable with, but the first time she'd used Papa, Aksel hadn't been able to hide his tears.

'It means aunt. Don't be embarrassed, she calls a lot of people *tante* or *onkel*.' Flora's reluctance to be seen to be too close to the little girl in front of Dr Sinclair had been obvious.

'And I was hoping it was just me…' Flora smiled as if it was a joke, but Aksel saw a flash of longing in her eyes, which was hidden as quickly as it had appeared.

'Not usually so quickly.' Aksel tried to take the thought back, turning to his daughter and arranging the bedcovers over her again. 'Are you ready to say goodnight, Mette?'

'I want Tante Flora to say it with me...' Mette reached for the cabinet by the side of her bed, carefully running her fingers across its edge. Aksel bit back the instinct to help her, waiting patiently for her to find what she wanted by touch. The clinic staff had told him that he should let her do as much as she could by herself, but each time he had to pause and watch her struggling to do something that came so naturally to other children, he felt consumed with the sadness of all that Mette had lost.

'It's okay...' Flora whispered the words. They were for him, not Mette, and when he looked at her, he saw understanding. She could see how much this hurt, and was enforcing the message that it was what he must do, to allow Mette to learn how to explore her world.

Not easy. He mouthed the words, and Flora nodded.

'I know. You're doing great.'

Mette had found what she wanted, and she clutched the small electric light in her hand as she snuggled back under the covers. When she tipped it to one side, light glimmered inside the glass, as if a candle had been lit.

She hadn't done that for a few days, and Aksel hadn't pushed the issue, leaving Mette to do as she wanted. Maybe it was Flora's presence, her warmth, that had made Mette think of her mother tonight.

'Say goodnight to Mama.' Mette directed the words at Flora and she glanced questioningly at Aksel.

'Her grandmother gave her this. Mette switches it on when she wants to talk to Lisle and then we pretend to blow out the candle.'

'That's a lovely thing to do.' Flora's smile showed that she understood that this was an honour that Mette usually didn't share with people outside the family.

They each said their goodnights, Mette including Tante Flora in hers. Flora leaned forward, kissing Mette, and then turned, leaving Aksel to kiss his daughter goodnight alone.

She was waiting outside the door, though. The connection, which grew stronger each time he saw her, had told Aksel that she'd be there and it hadn't let him down yet.

'Would you like a lift home?'

Aksel shook his head. 'No. Thanks, but I want to go and have a word with Dr Sinclair. He said he'd still be here.'

'I can wait.'

'I'd prefer to walk. It clears my head.' It also didn't carry with it the temptation to ask Flora into his cottage for a nightcap. By the time he got home, he would have persuaded himself that the light that burned in her porch in the evenings was something that he could resist.

'I think I prefer a head full of clutter to walking in the cold and dark.' She gave him a wry smile and started to walk slowly towards the main staircase.

There was no one around, and they were dawdling companionably along the corridor. He could ask her now...

A sixth sense warned Aksel that he couldn't. Someone like Flora must have men lining up to ask her out, but she obviously had no partner. No children either. He wanted to ask about the welcome gifts she gave to all the kids at the clinic, and the quickly veiled sadness he'd seen in her eyes. But he didn't have the words, and something told him that even if he did, Flora would shut his enquiries down.

A couple of nurses walked past them, and Flora acknowledged them with a smile. The moment was gone.

'So… You're still okay for eight thirty tomorrow? To visit the housing complex?'

Flora nodded. 'I'll be ready.'

'Esme's offered me the use of one of the therapy centre's vehicles, so I'll drop in there to get the keys first thing and then pick you up.'

'Oh, great. I'll see you then.' She gave him a little wave, making for the main staircase, and Aksel watched her go.

Flora was an enigma. Beautiful and clever, she seemed to live inside a sparkling cocoon of warmth. When she was busy, which seemed to be most of the time, it was entirely believable to suppose that she had everything she wanted.

But he'd seen her with Mette, and he'd seen the mask slip. Beneath it all was loneliness, and a hint of sadness that he couldn't comprehend. Maybe he saw it because he too was searching for a way forward in life. Or perhaps the connection between them, which he'd given up trying to deny, allowed him to see her more clearly.

But this chance to work together would set his head straight. Aksel had made up his mind that it would banish the thought that Flora could be anything else to him, other than a friend and colleague. And when he made up his mind to do something, he usually succeeded.

CHAPTER SIX

FLORA SAW THE battered SUV draw up outside at ten to eight the following morning. Aksel was early, and she gulped down her coffee, hurrying into the hall to fetch Dougal's lead. But the expected knock on her door didn't come.

When she looked again, she saw Aksel had opened the bonnet of the SUV and was peering at the engine. He made a few adjustments and then started the engine again. It sounded a bit less throaty than it had before.

That was a relief. The therapy centre's SUV had done more miles than anyone cared to count, and although it was reliable it could probably do with a service. Aksel looked at the engine again, wiping something down with a rag from his back pocket and then seemed satisfied, closing the bonnet and switching off the engine. Then he walked up the front path of his cottage, disappearing inside.

Fair enough. He'd said half past eight, and that would give her time to make herself some toast. She put Dougal's lead back in the hall and he gave her a dejected look.

'We'll be going soon, Dougal.' The little dog tipped his head up towards her at the mention of his name and Flora bent to stroke his head.

When she wandered back into the sitting room, still eating the last of her toast, she saw that Aksel was outside again, in the car and that it was rocking slightly as he moved around inside it. Flora put her coat on and Dougal once again sprang to the alert, realising that this time they really were going to go.

'What are you doing?' Flora rapped on the vehicle's window, and Aksel straightened up.

'Just…tidying up a bit. I didn't realise this car was such a mess when I offered you a lift.'

He tucked a cloth and a bottle of spray cleaner under the driver's seat and opened the car door. The scent of kitchen cleaner wafted out, and something about Aksel's manner suggested that he'd really rather not have been caught doing this.

'It sounds as if it's running a lot better.' Flora wondered if she should volunteer her car for the journey, but it seemed ungrateful after he'd spent time on the SUV.

'I made a few adjustments. The spark plugs really need to be replaced, I'll stop and get some if we pass somewhere that sells car parts. They'll be okay for the distance we have to do.'

'I'm sure they will. It's not exactly a trip into the wilderness. And if the SUV breaks down, we can always call the garage.'

He grinned suddenly, as if she'd understood exactly what he was thinking. 'Force of habit. When you're miles away from anywhere, you need a well-maintained vehicle. I'll just go and fetch Kari.'

The dogs were installed on the cushioned area behind the boot divider, amidst a clamour of excited barking from Dougal. Aksel stowed Flora's bag of medical supplies on the back seat, and then gave the passenger door a sharp tug to open it. Flora climbed in, noticing that both the seat and the mat in the footwell were spotlessly clean.

'You didn't need to do all this…'

'You don't want to get your coat dirty.' Aksel looked a little awkward at the suggestion he'd done anything. He closed the passenger door and rounded the front of the vehicle.

All the same, it would have been a nice gesture on anyone's part, and on Aksel's it was all the sweeter. He clearly hadn't given the same attention to his own seat, and Flora leaned over to brush some of the mud off it before he got in.

'Anything I should know about the sheltered housing?' He settled himself into the driver's seat, ignoring the remains of the mud, and twisted the ignition key. The engine started the first time.

'It's a group of thirty double and single units, designed to give elderly people as much independence as possible. Residents have their own front doors, and each unit has a bedroom, a sitting room and a kitchenette. There's a common lounge, and a dining room for those who don't want to cook, and care staff are on hand at all times to give help when needed.'

'And what's your part in all of this?'

'I'm the Tuesday exercise lady. Mondays is chiropody, Wednesdays hairdressing. The mobile library comes on a Thursday, and Friday is shopping list day.'

'And everyone gets a rest at the weekend?'

'Kind of. Saturday is film night, and that can get a bit rowdy.'

He chuckled. 'So you just hold an exercise class?'

'No, I hold one-to-one consultations as well. I have a lady with a frozen shoulder and one who's recovering from a fractured wrist at the moment. And I also hold sessions for family members during the evenings and at weekends to show them how to assist their elderly relatives and help keep them as active as possible. Just a little of the right exercise makes a huge difference.'

'It sounds like a good place.' He manoeuvred into the drive-through entrance of the canine therapy centre and retrieved Dougal's lead from the back seat. 'I'm almost tempted to book myself in for a couple of weeks.'

'You don't strike me as the kind of person who likes a quiet life.'

Aksel shot her a sideways glance, the corners of his mouth quirking down for a moment. 'I'm leaving what I used to be behind. Remember?'

He got out of the car, opening the tailgate and lifting Dougal out, leading him towards the glass sided entrance. Dougal bounded up to the young man at the reception desk, and Aksel gave him a smiling wave. Flora wondered exactly who he was trying to fool. Everything about Aksel suggested movement, the irresistible urge to go from A to B.

'So you're not convinced that Mette will benefit from sharing your experiences?' By the time he'd returned to the car, Flora had phrased the question in her head already so that it didn't sound too confronting.

He chuckled. 'Spare me the tact, Flora. Say what's on your mind.'

'All right. I think you're selling yourself short. And Mette.'

He started the car again. 'It's one thing to take her on pretend expeditions. But I have to change, I can't leave her behind and travel for months at a time.'

'No, of course you can't. But that doesn't mean that have to give up who you are. You can be an explorer who stays home...'

'That's a lot harder than it sounds.'

She could hear the anger in his voice. The loss.

'Is losing yourself really going to help Mette?'

'I don't know. All I know is that who I used to be kept me apart from her for five years. I can't forgive myself for that, and I don't want to be that person any more.'

His lips were set in a hard line and his tone reeked of finality. There was no point in arguing, and maybe she shouldn't be getting so involved with his feelings. She sat back in her seat, watching the reflection of the castle disappear behind them in the rear-view mirror.

It wasn't fair, but Aksel couldn't help being angry. Flora had no right to constantly question his decisions, Mette wasn't her child. If she'd been faced with the same choice that he had, she'd understand.

But he couldn't hold onto his anger for very long, because he suspected that Flora *did* understand. She'd seen his guilt and feeling of inadequacy when faced with the task of bringing up a child. She saw that he loved Mette, too, and that he would do whatever it took to make her happy. And she saw that even though he was ashamed to admit it, he still sometimes regretted the loss of his old life.

In that old life, the one he'd firmly turned his back on, he would have loved the way that she understood him so well. He would have nurtured the connection, and if it led to something more he would have welcomed it. But now, even the thought of that made him feel as if he was betraying Mette. The anger that he directed at Flora should really be directed at himself.

By the time they drew up outside the modern two-storey building, nestling amongst landscaped gardens, he'd found the ability to smile again. It wasn't difficult when he looked at Flora. She got out of the car, shouldering her heavy bag before he had a chance to take it from her.

'The exercise does me good.' She grinned at him.

'All that weight on one shoulder?' He gave her a look of mock reproach. 'If I were a physiotherapist, I'm sure that I'd have something to say about that.'

She tossed her head. 'Just as well you're not, then. Leave the musculoskeletal issues to me, and I won't give Kari any commands.'

'She won't listen to you anyway, she understands Norwegian.'

'If you're going to be like that...' Flora wrinkled her nose in Aksel's direction, and then directed her attention to Kari. 'Kari, *gi labb*.'

Her pronunciation left a bit to be desired, but Kari got the message. She held out her paw and Flora took it, grimacing a little at the weight of the bag as she bent over. As she patted Kari's head, Aksel caught the strap of the bag, taking it from her.

'If you're going to speak Norwegian to my dog, then all bets are off.' He slung the bag over his shoulder, feeling a stab of pain as he did so. He ignored it, hoping that Flora hadn't noticed.

Inside the building, a woman at a large reception desk greeted Flora, and they signed the visitors' book.

'Here's your list for today. Mr King says that he has a crawling pain in his leg.'

'Okay. I'll take a look at that, then.' Flora seemed undeterred by the description. 'I'll go and see Mrs Crawford first.'

'I think you'll find she's a great deal better. She said that she'd been able to raise her arm enough to brush her hair the other day.' The smiling receptionist was clearly one of those key people in any establishment who knew exactly what was going on with everyone.

'Great. Thanks. My colleague's here for a meeting with Eileen. Is she around?'

'Yes, she's in her office.' The receptionist stood, leaning over the desk. 'Is that your dog? She's gorgeous. May I stroke her?'

'Of course. Her name's Kari.'

'I'll leave you to it…' Flora shot him a smile, and grabbed the strap of her bag from his shoulder. Aksel watched as she walked away from him. Bad sign. If she turned back and he found himself smiling, that would be an even worse sign.

Flora had gone on her way, warmed by the smile that Aksel had given her, but stopped at the lift and looked back. It was impossible not to look back at him, he was so darned easy on the eye. And the way he seemed to be struggling with himself only made him even more intriguing.

Fortunately, Mrs Crawford was waiting to see her, and Flora could turn her thoughts to the improvement in her frozen shoulder. Aksel was still lurking in the part of her brain where he seemed to have taken up permanent residence, but he was quiet for the moment.

'Your shoulder seems much better, Helen, you have a lot more movement in it now. Are you still having to take painkillers to get to sleep?'

Helen leaned forward in her chair, giving her a confiding smile. 'Last night I didn't feel I needed them so I put them in the drawer beside my bed.'

'Right. You do know that you can just tell the carer you don't need them and she'll take them away again?'

Flora made a mental note to retrieve the tablets before she left and have them disposed of.

'She'd come all the way up here. And I might need them at some other time. It's *my* medication, but they act as if it's all up to them whether I take it.'

Flora had heard the complaint before. Drugs were carefully overseen and dispensed when needed, and it was one of the things that Helen had been used to making her own decisions about.

'They have to do that, they'll get in all kinds of trouble if they don't store medicines safely and keep a record. Some people here forget whether or not they've taken their medication and take too much or too little.' *Some people* was vague enough to imply that Flora didn't include Helen in that.

'I suppose so. It's very annoying, though.'

'I know. Give the carers a break, they have to keep to the rules or they'll get into trouble.' Flora appealed to Helen's better nature.

Helen nodded. 'I wouldn't want them to get into trouble over me. They have enough to do and they're very kind.'

'Right, then. I'll write in your notes that the carer is to offer you the painkillers and ask whether you want them or not. Is that okay?' Flora moved round so that Helen could see over her shoulder. She liked to know what was being written about her.

'All right, dear.' Helen tapped the paper with one finger. 'Put that it's up to me whether I take them or not.'

Flora added the note, and Helen nodded in approval. She'd raised four children, and worked in the village pharmacy for thirty years to supplement the family income, and even though her three sons and daughter were determined that she should be well looked after now, she resisted any perceived loss of independence.

'Who's the young man you arrived with? He's very tall.' Helen's living-room window overlooked the drive, and she liked to keep an eye on arrivals and departures.

'That's Aksel Olsen. He's from the canine therapy centre at the castle. They're talking about setting up a dog visiting scheme.'

'To help train the dogs? I could help with that, but I'm not sure that many of the others could.'

'Well, those who can't help might benefit from having the companionship of an animal. Don't you think?'

Helen thought for a moment and nodded. 'Yes, I think they will. Where's he from? His name isn't Scottish.'

'He's Norwegian. The dog understands Norwegian, too. He's trained Kari as an assistance dog for his daughter.'

'He has a daughter? Then he has a wife, too?' Helen was clearly trying to make the question sound innocent.

'No. No wife.'

'Really?' Helen beamed. 'Well, he might be looking for one. And it's about time you found yourself someone nice and had some bairns of your own.'

'I'm happy as I am, Helen. I have everything I want.' The assertion sounded old and tired, as if she was trying to convince herself of something. Flora wondered how many times she'd have to tell herself that before she really believed that Aksel was no exception to the rule she lived by. That there was no exception to the rule. Fear of rejection made the practicalities of falling in love and having a family impossible.

Helen brushed her words aside. 'He's very good looking. And tall. And such a mane of hair, it makes him look rather dashing. I dare say that he'd be able to sweep *someone* off to lots of exciting places.'

'He's actually better looking close up. Blue eyes.' Flora gave in to the weight of the inevitable, and Helen clapped her hands together gleefully.

'I like blue eyes. Mountain blue or ocean blue?'

Flora considered the question. 'I'd say mountain blue. Like ice.'

'Oh, very nice. And is he kind?'

Flora had worked through her list of patients, and when she arrived back in the communal sitting room, she found that Helen had decided to take part in the exercise class today. It was a first, and Flora wondered whether it was an attempt to get a closer look at Aksel's blue eyes and broad shoulders, and make a better assessment of both his kindness and his capacity to sweep a girl off her feet.

'Right, ladies and gentlemen.' Everyone was here and seated in a semi-circle around her, ready for the gentle mobility exercises. 'I brought along a new CD, ballads from the sixties.'

A rumble of approval went round, and Flora slipped the CD into the player. Carefully chosen songs that reflected the right rhythm for the exercises.

'We'll start with our arms. Everyone, apart from Helen, raise your arms. Reach up as high as you can…' Flora demonstrated by raising her own arms in time to the music.

The response was polite rather than enthusiastic, but the music and a little encouragement would warm things up. 'That's lovely, Ella, try the other arm now. Helen, you're sitting this one out… Now gently lower your arms. And up again…'

This time there was a murmur of laughter and the response was a lot more energetic. '*Very* good. Once more.'

A sudden movement from Helen caught her eye, and Flora turned, following the direction of her pointing finger. Everyone was laughing now.

Aksel was leaning in the wide doorway, smiling, looking far more delicious than he had any right to. And in front of him Kari had obligingly raised one paw, lowering it again and raising the other.

Flora put her hands on her hips and walked over to him. Behind her she could hear chatter over the strains of the music.

'You know what this means, don't you?'

Aksel shook his head, flashing her an innocent look.

'There's a spare chair right there, next to Helen.' She may as well give Helen the chance to look him over in greater detail. 'Go and sit in it.'

'Yes, ma'am.' His eyes flashed with the ice-blue warmth that she'd told Helen about, and Aksel went to sit down. Kari trotted to her side, obviously having decided that she was the star of the show.

'Right. Let's do one more arm raise.' Flora raised her arms again and Kari followed suit, raising one paw. There was more laughter, and everyone reached for the sky.

'Well done, everyone. Aksel, I think you can do a bit better than that next time…'

Flora always kept a careful eye on everyone during her exercise classes to gauge how well they were moving and that no one was overdoing things. And this time Aksel was included in that. His left arm was fully mobile but he wasn't extending his right arm fully upwards, and she guessed that it was still hurting him. His neck seemed a little stiff as well.

Kari was loving all the attention, and when the exercise session was finished she trotted forward, eager to get to know everyone. Flora started to pack up her things, leaving Aksel to lead Kari around the semicircle and introduce her.

She'd expected that Eileen would be keeping her eye on things, and saw her standing quietly at the doorway.

'What do you think?' Suddenly it mattered to her that the dog visiting scheme was a success. That Aksel should feel useful and accepted here, rather than dwelling on all the things that he felt he'd done wrong.

Eileen nodded. 'The written plan for the scheme was very thorough and I liked the thought behind it. This is the acid test.'

Flora looked around. Kari was in off-duty mode, which meant that she was free to respond to someone other than her handler. She was greeting everyone with an outstretched paw, and receiving smiles and pats in return.

'It looks good to me. Kari certainly made everyone a bit more enthusiastic about the exercises.' Aksel had done his part in that, too. He'd joined in without a murmur, smiling and joking with everyone. His charm had contributed almost as much as Kari's accomplishments.

'It looks *very* good.' Eileen seemed to have already made her decision. 'It might be a while before he's allowed to leave.'

It was a while, and by the time Aksel had torn himself away, promising everyone that he'd return, Flora was looking at her watch. She needed to be back at the clinic for her afternoon sessions.

As soon as he was out of the sitting room, Aksel

called Kari to heel, picking up her bag and making purposefully for the reception area. He signalled a hurried goodbye to the receptionist, telling Eileen that he'd be in touch, and managed to insinuate himself between Flora and the front door so that she had no choice but to allow him to open it for her.

'How was your morning?' He gave her a broad smile. 'Did you manage to get to the bottom of Mr King's crawling leg?'

'Uh? Oh…yes, the carers keep telling him that the elastic on his favourite socks is too tight, but he won't listen. I changed them and gave his leg a rub and that fixed the crawling. You seem to have enjoyed yourself.'

'Yes, I did.'

'I see that your shoulder's still bothering you.'

'It's fine. It doesn't hurt.'

Pull the other one. There was a clear imbalance between the way that he was using his right and left arms, and Aksel seemed determined to ignore it. Just as he was determined to ignore everything else he wanted or needed. But she shouldn't push it. The clinic was full of therapists and movement specialists, and if he wanted help he could easily ask for it.

'We'll get straight back…' He dumped her bag on the back seat and started the engine. 'I saw you looking at your watch.'

'Yes, I've got afternoon sessions that I need to get back for. And if we hurry we should be back in time for you to have lunch with Mette.'

He nodded, the sharp crunch of gravel coming from beneath the tyres of the SUV as he accelerated out of the driveway.

CHAPTER SEVEN

FLORA KNEW THAT Aksel was at the clinic that afternoon, but she didn't drop into Mette's room during her break. It was bad enough that her thoughts seemed to be stalking him, without her body following suit.

Cass had come for her physiotherapy session, glowing with a happiness that matched Lyle's exactly. She'd come to the clinic as a patient, after sustaining injuries to her arm and leg during a search-and-rescue assignment. Then she'd met Lyle Sinclair. Sparks had flown, and the two had fallen head over heels in love. Lyle had been inconsolable when Cass had returned home to America, but now she was back in Cluchlochry for good. She'd spent most of the forty-minute physiotherapy session telling Flora about their plans for the future.

'The movement in your leg is a great deal better. I'm really pleased with your improvement.'

Cass sat up, grinning. 'I hardly even think about it now, only when it begins to ache. Lyle says I should still be careful...'

'Well, you don't need me to tell you that he's right, you should be taking care. But being happy helps you to heal, too.'

'Then I'll be better in no time.' Cass slid off the treatment couch, planting her feet on the floor. 'Especially as I have you to help me…'

It had been an easy session. Flora stood at the door to the treatment room, watching Cass's gait as she walked away, and Aksel intruded into her thoughts once again. Cass was so happy, and looking forward to the future, and it showed in the way she moved. Aksel was like a coiled spring, dreading the future. No wonder he had aches and pains. Tension was quite literally tearing him apart.

He might be able to ignore it, but Flora couldn't any more. His shoulder could probably be fixed quite easily at this stage, but if he did nothing it would only get more painful and more difficult to treat. This was what she did best, and if she really wanted to help him, it was the most obvious place to start.

Aksel drew up outside his cottage, trying not to notice that Flora's porch light was on. He'd decided that he wouldn't seek her out at the clinic this afternoon, and it felt almost saintly to deprive himself of that pleasure.

As he got out of the SUV, opening the tailgate to let Kari out, he saw her door open and Flora marched down the path towards him, her arms wrapped around her body in a futile attempt to shelter herself from the wind. She looked determined and utterly beautiful as she faced him, her cheeks beginning to redden from the cold and small flakes of snow sticking to her hair. Aksel decided that sainthood was overrated.

'The car sounds better than it did this morning.' That was clearly just an opening gambit, and not what she'd come outside to say.

'Yes, I changed the spark plugs.' The SUV's rusty growl had turned into a healthier-sounding purr now.

Aksel closed the tailgate and reached into the passenger footwell for his shopping bags, trying not to wince as his shoulder pulled painfully.

'And have you done anything about your shoulder? I'm not taking any excuses this time.'

'In that case…no, I haven't.'

'Come inside.' She motioned towards her cottage with a no-nonsense gesture that no amount of arguing was going to overcome. He hesitated and she frowned.

'If you don't come inside now, I'm going to turn into an icicle. You don't want to have to chip me off the pavement and thaw me out, do you?'

It was obviously meant as a threat, but the idea had a certain appeal. Particularly the thawing-out part. Aksel dismissed the thought, nudging the car door shut, and Kari followed him to Flora's doorstep. When she opened the door, Dougal came hurtling out of the sitting room to greet them.

He watched as she stood in front of the hall mirror, brushing half-melted snowflakes from her shoulders and hair. 'I appreciate the concern, but there's really no need. These things tend to rectify themselves.'

She turned on him suddenly. 'What's the problem, Aksel? You have a stiff shoulder, and I'm a qualified physiotherapist. Or are you not allowed to have anything wrong with you?'

She was just a little bit too close to the truth and it stung. He wanted to be the one that Mette could rely on completely. Strong and unbreakable. But there was no point in denying any more that his shoulder felt neither of those things at the moment.

'Okay, I…appreciate the offer and… Actually, I would like you to take a look at it if you wouldn't mind. It has been a little painful over the last few days.' He put his shopping bags down, taking a bottle of wine from one. 'Don't suppose you'd like some of this first?'

She rolled her eyes. 'No, I don't suppose I would. I'm not in the habit of drinking while I'm working.'

That put him in his place. But when he walked into the sitting room, he saw that a backless chair was placed in front of the fire. She'd been concerned about him and waiting for him to come home. The thought hit him hard, spreading its warmth through his veins as he sat down.

Suddenly all he wanted was her touch.

'Take your sweater off and let me have a look.' Flora congratulated herself on how professional her tone sounded. It was exactly how this was going to be.

She stood behind him, gingerly laying her fingers on his shoulder. 'You're very tense...'

Flora was feeling a little tense herself suddenly. The lines of his shoulder felt as strong as they looked, and there was only the thin material of his T-shirt between her fingers and his skin.

'It's been a long day.'

'What happened?'

He turned suddenly and Flora snatched her fingers away, stepping back involuntarily. She couldn't touch him when the smouldering blue ice of his gaze was on her.

'I didn't come here to tell you my troubles.'

'I know. Turn around and tell me anyway.'

He turned back and she continued her examination. There was a moment of silence and she concentrated on visualising the structure and musculature of his shoulder. Suddenly Aksel spoke.

'Dr Sinclair took me through the results of Mette's

latest MRI scan today. It's clear now that there isn't going to be any more improvement in her sight.'

'There was hope that there might be?' Flora pulled the neck of his T-shirt to one side, reaching to run her fingers along his clavicle.

'No, not really. The doctors in Norway told me that her condition was stable now, and there was very little chance of any change. It was unreasonable of me to hold out any hope.'

'But you did anyway, because you're her dad.'

'Yes. I wasn't expecting to come here and cry on your shoulder about it, though.'

'You can't expect muscles to heal when you're this tense, Aksel.'

Flora felt him take a breath, and he seemed to relax a little. As she pressed her thumb on the back of his shoulder he winced. 'It's a little sore there.'

She imagined it was *very* sore. The shoulder must be a lot more painful than he was letting on. 'You have a few small lumps on your collarbone. That's usually a sign that it's been broken recently.'

'Nearly a year ago.'

'And what happened? Did you get some medical treatment when you did it, or were you miles away from the nearest doctor?'

He chuckled. 'No. Actually, I'd gone skiing for the New Year. There was a doctor on hand and he treated it immediately.'

'Good. That seems to have healed well, but the muscles in your shoulders are very tight. I can give you some exercises that will help ease them out.'

'Thanks.' He reached for his sweater.

'I can work the muscles out a bit for you if you'd like. It'll reduce the discomfort.' It was also going to take every ounce of her resolve to stay professional, but she could do that.

'That would be great. Thank you.'

She was just debating whether it would be wise to ask him to remove his T-shirt so that she could see what she was doing a little better when he pulled it over his head. Flora watched spellbound as he took an elastic band from his pocket, twisting his hair up off his shoulders.

His skin was golden, a shade lighter than his hair. Slim hips and a broad, strong chest came as no surprise, but Aksel had to be seen to be believed. He was beautiful, and yet completely unselfconscious.

'Okay. Just relax…' The advice was for herself as well as Aksel. This was just a simple medical massage, which might make him feel a little sore in the morning but would promote healing. And she wanted very badly to heal him.

He could feel the warmth of the fire on his skin. Aksel closed his eyes, trying not to think about her touch. Warm, caressing and… He caught his breath as she concentrated her attention on the spot that hurt most.

'Sorry. I can feel how sore it must be there…'

'It's okay.' He didn't want her to stop. Flora seemed to know all of his sore points, the things that tore at his heart and battered his soul. He wondered whether all of her patients felt the connection that seemed to be flowing through her fingers and spreading out across his skin.

He felt almost as if he was floating. Disengaged from his body and the cares of the day. Just her touch, firm and assured.

'My brother has cystic fibrosis.' She'd been silent for

a while, working out the muscles in his shoulder, and the observation came out of nowhere.

'That's why you became a physiotherapist?'

'It was what made me first think of the idea. Alec's physiotherapist taught him techniques to clear the mucus from his airways, and he benefited a great deal from it.'

'It's a difficult condition to live with, though.' Aksel sensed that Flora had something more to say.

He heard her take a breath. 'I know how badly you want to help Mette, and how helpless you feel. I've been through all that with Alec. You're tying yourself in knots and that shows, here in your shoulder.'

'It's… I can't change how I feel, Flora.'

'I know. I'm not asking you to. Mette's lost a great deal, more than any child should have to. All she has left is you, and you owe it to her to take care of yourself.'

Aksel thought for a moment, trying to get his head around the idea. 'It sounds…as if you have a point to make.'

He heard her laugh quietly, and a shiver ran down his spine. 'My point is that you feel so guilty that your lifestyle kept you from her all those years that you just want to throw it all away. I can understand that, I've felt guilty about going out and doing things when Alec was ill in bed. But my mum used to tell me that if I didn't go, then I couldn't come home again and tell Alec all about it. You can share the things you've done with Mette, too. Don't be afraid to give her the real you.'

'And that'll make my shoulder better?' Flora might just be right.

'Maybe. I think the massage and exercise might help as well.'

She gripped his arm, rotating it carefully, seeming satisfied with the result. Then she handed him his T-shirt and Aksel pulled it over his head. The movement felt easier than it had for days.

'That feels better, thank you. Can we have that glass of wine now?'

She hesitated. 'It's not something I'd usually advise after a physiotherapy session. Water's better in terms of reducing inflammation.'

'Noted. Since I'm going to ignore your advice and have a glass anyway, you can either send me back to my cottage to drink alone, or join me.'

'In that case, I'd say it's my duty to keep an eye on you. I might need to save you from yourself.'

Aksel chuckled, getting to his feet.

The Advent candle burned on the mantelpiece. Another nineteen days to go. Aksel was sitting next to her on the sofa, and although they'd left as much space between them as possible, it still felt as if they might touch. Christmas was coming, and at the moment all that called to mind was mistletoe.

'Tell me about your family.' He sipped his wine, his tone lazy and relaxed now. He'd obviously forgiven her for forcing him to face the facts that he'd been so assiduously ignoring.

'There isn't much to tell. There's the four of us, and we travelled so much when I was a kid that we didn't see much of the rest of the family. Just at holiday time.'

'Where are your parents now?'

'They're in Italy. Dad's going to be retiring in a couple of years, so I'm not sure what will happen then. He always said he wanted to come back to Scotland. But my brother's married and lives in England, and they're trying for a child. I can't see my mum wanting to be too far away from a new grandchild.'

'What does your brother do?'

'He's a university lecturer. He fell in love with English literature when he went to Durham University, and then fell in love with his wife. The cystic fibrosis has slowed him down at times, but it's never stopped him from doing what he wants to do.'

'That's a nice way of putting it. It's what I want for Mette.'

'She can do more than you think. One day maybe she'll be leading you off on a trip around the world.'

The yearning in his face made Flora want to reach out and touch him. 'I'd like that very much.'

'My brother's never compromised…' Flora shrugged. 'It's caused its share of heartache, but we've faced it as a family.'

He nodded. There was never a need to over-explain with Aksel. He understood her and she understood him. That didn't mean they necessarily had to like what the other was saying, but the connection between them meant that neither could disregard it.

'So… You already know what frightens me. What are you afraid of?'

It was such a natural question, but one that was hard to answer. 'I'm afraid that the in vitro fertilisation for my brother and his wife will fail. They can't get pregnant on their own because of the cystic fibrosis. They'll deal with it, if it happens…'

'So that's a fear that you can face.' He was dissatisfied with her reply. 'What about the ones you can't face?'

'I have everything I want.' That must sound as much like an excuse to Aksel as it did to her. She had everything that she dared reach out for, and that was going to have to be enough.

'Having everything you want sounds nice.'

'I have a fireside, and a glass of wine. It'll be Christmas soon…' And Aksel was here. But however much she wanted to add him to the list, she couldn't.

'And…?' He reached out, allowing the tips of his fingers to touch hers. Her gaze met his and in an exquisite moment of clarity she knew exactly what he was asking.

She wanted to but she couldn't. Flora couldn't bring herself to trust any man enough to give herself to him. And the froth and excitement of a no-strings affair… It seemed great from the outside. But inside, when all the longing turned into disappointment and frustration, it hurt so much more than if it had never happened.

She moved her hand away from his, and he nodded. 'I'm sorry. I forgot all about my patient ethics for a moment.'

Flora couldn't help smiling. 'I thought *I* was the one who was supposed to be professional.'

'Oh, and I can't have ethics? I'm sure there's something in the patients' handbook about respecting your medical professional and not making a pass at them.' He grinned, his eyes dancing with blue fire.

He acknowledged the things that she didn't dare to. And he made it sound as if it was okay to feel something, as long as they both understood that actions didn't automatically follow.

'Fair point. Would it compromise your patient ethics to top up my glass?'

He chuckled. 'I don't think so. I'll do it anyway.'

This was nice. Sitting in front of the fire, drinking wine. Able to voice their thoughts and allow them to slip away. It was the best kind of friendship, and one that she didn't want to lose. Taking things any further would only mess it up.

CHAPTER EIGHT

FLORA HAD UNDERSTOOD his unspoken question, and
Aksel had understood her answer. Maybe she'd also
understood that in the electric warmth of her touch,
he'd got a little carried away.

She wanted to stay friends. That was fine. It was
probably the wisest course of action, and it was just
as well that one of them had kept their head. Making
love with her might well have turned into the kind of
explosive need that had no part in his life since he'd
found Mette.

Friends was good. It meant that he could seek her out
at the clinic the next day and ask her about the trucks
that had been arriving on the estate, wondering aloud
if she was interested in accompanying him and Mette
on another voyage of discovery.

'The Christmas carnival is a bit of a fixture here.
They set it up every year. There's usually an ice skating
rink.' They were walking across the grass, with Mette
between them, each holding one of his daughter's hands
so that she didn't fall on the uneven ground.

'I want to skate!' Mette piped up, and Aksel swallowed down the impulse to say no. The clinic was proving as much of a learning experience for him as it was

for Mette, and he was beginning to understand that, *Yes, let's make that happen* was the default position.

'That sounds fun.' Flora's answer wasn't unexpected. 'Perhaps you can skate with your papa.'

Okay. He could handle that. Keeping a tight hold on his daughter and guiding her around the edge of the rink. He doubted whether Kari would be all that happy on the ice.

It wasn't hard to orientate themselves as the carnival site was a blaze of light and activity. Most of the attractions were set up, apart from a few finishing touches, and Aksel recognised a few of the clinic staff using their lunch hour to try out the skating rink. The booth for skate hire wasn't open yet, and Mette was mollified with a promise that he would take her skating as soon as it was.

'We could take a look at the maze.' Flora gestured towards a tall hedge, decked with fairy lights, which lay on one side of the carnival booths.

'There's a maze?'

'Yes, it was re-planted a few years ago, using the plans of the original one that stood in the grounds. They decided to put it here so it could be part of the Christmas carnival.'

It looked impressive. Aksel bent down, explaining in Norwegian what a maze was, and Mette started to jump up and down.

'I want to go. I want to go…'

'Let's ask, shall we?' Flora approached a man standing at the entrance, who Aksel recognised by sight as having come from the village. He turned towards Aksel and Mette, waving them towards the entrance.

It was entirely unsurprising that Aksel forged ahead of them into the maze. The paths were slightly narrower than last year, the hedges having grown since then, and they were tall enough that even he couldn't see over the top now. They were all walking blind.

'Where do we go, Papa?'

He stopped, looking around. There was a dead end in front of them, and paths leading to the right and the left.

'I'm...not sure.'

'Why don't you lead the way, then, Mette? We have to try and see if we can find our way to the centre.'

Aksel shot her a questioning look, and then understanding showed in his face. 'Yes, good idea. Why don't you tell us which way to go?'

He stepped back behind Mette, who stretched out her hand, finding the branches to one side of her. Kari watched over her, walking by her side, as she carefully walked ahead, following the line of the hedge right up to the dead end, and then turning back and to her right.

'I think she's got the right idea.' Flora fell into step beside Aksel, whispering the words to him.

'Will this work? Following the wall to your right...?' he whispered back,

Flora shot him an outraged look. 'Of course it will. We'll get there if we just stay with Mette.'

'Papa...?' Mette hesitated, suddenly unsure of herself.

'It's okay, Mette. Just keep going, we're right behind you.' He reached forward, touching his daughter's shoulder to let her know that he was there, and she nodded, confident again.

Mette led them unerringly to the centre of the maze, where a small six-sided structure built in stone was decked with fairy lights. Kari guided her towards it, and she walked around it until she found the arched doorway.

'We can go inside, Mette.' Aksel was right behind

her, patiently waiting for Mette to find her own way, and he'd seen the notice pinned to one side of the arch. 'We can climb to the top of the tower if you want to.'

The tower at the centre of the maze had a curving stone staircase inside, and from the viewing platform at the top it was possible to see the whole maze, the walkways picked out by sparkling fairy lights. Mette might not be able to see them, but she could still climb, and still feel that she was the queen of this particular castle.

Aksel guided her ahead of him, ducking under the arch and letting Mette find the handrail and climb the steps. Flora followed, Kari loping up the steps at her side. The four of them could just squeeze onto the small viewing platform at the top, bounded by crenellated stonework.

'Papa! I found the way!' Mette squealed with excitement, and Aksel lifted her up in his arms.

'*Ja elskling...*' He was hugging the little girl tightly, and he seemed to have tears in his eyes. 'I'm so proud of you, Mette.'

'I'm an explorer too, Papa.'

Aksel seemed to be lost for words. Flora wanted so badly to put her arms around them both, but this was their moment. Mette had used some of the techniques that the clinic was teaching her, and they'd worked for all of them in the maze. And Aksel had found that for all his height and strength, and even though he could see, he'd not known which way to go any more than Mette had.

Flora waited while they savoured their triumph. Then she reached out, touching Mette's hand to catch her attention.

'Are you going to lead us back out again now?'

'She'd better. I don't know the way.' Aksel's voice was thick with emotion still.

Mette regarded him solemnly. 'What if I get lost, Papa?'

'You won't.' He set Mette back down on her feet, turning to guide her carefully down the staircase.

By the time they'd navigated their way out of the maze, the stallholders had almost finished setting up for the opening later on that afternoon, and the proprietor of the village tea shop was pleased to sell them sausage rolls, warm from the small oven on his stall, and made with homemade beef sausagemeat.

They wandered between the lines of stalls, and when Mette had finished eating, Aksel lifted her up onto his shoulders. Then he caught sight of it, stopping suddenly and staring at the open-sided tent.

'What's that?' He couldn't take his eyes off the large blocks of ice under the awning.

'You want to go and have a look? I'll stay here with Mette.' Flora had a feeling that this was something that Aksel would like to explore on his own.

'I…' He turned, but seemed unable to find enough momentum to walk away. Looking back, he nodded. 'Yes. If you don't mind.'

'Of course not. We can go and get some doughnuts to take back with us.'

'I'll be back in a minute.' He lifted Mette down from his shoulders and Flora took her hand, watching as Aksel strode across to the tent. She'd be very surprised if he was back in a minute.

They chose and purchased their doughnuts, and Flora looked back towards the tent to see Aksel deep in conversation with Ted Mackie, the estate manager. Ted was eyeing him up, clearly deciding whether it would be okay to let Aksel loose with a chainsaw. Flora resisted the temptation to run up to Ted, take him by the lapels of his coat, and tell him that if Aksel could be trusted to get to both Poles and back, he could be trusted with power tools. And that he really needed to do something like this.

'What's Papa doing?' Mette was unable to see her father.

'He's right over there, at one of the other stalls. Shall we go and see?' Aksel had taken the pair of work gloves that Ted had proffered, and was passing them from one hand to the other as he talked. He was tempted. Flora could see that he was *very* tempted.

She walked slowly over to the tent, wondering whether that would give Aksel time to give in to the temptation. She could see him checking out the chainsaw and running his hand over one of the large blocks of ice. Ted was nodding in agreement to something he'd said.

'Hi. We've got doughnuts.' Aksel jumped when Flora spoke, too immersed in his conversation to have noticed them approaching. Flora tried hard not to smirk.

'Oh… I suppose…' He handed the gloves back to Ted ruefully. 'I'd really like to give this a go but…'

Ted flashed Flora a glance. 'Shame. It would be good to have something to show people. It would give us a start.'

'I'd like to but…' Aksel turned, masking the regret in his face with a smile. 'We need to get you back to the clinic, Mette. You've got a play date this afternoon.'

One of the well-organised play sessions, which would help Mette to make the most of her limited sight. They were very well supervised, and Mette was already making friends at the clinic. Aksel really wasn't needed.

'If you'd like to stay here, I can take Mette back.'

'We bought you a doughnut, Papa. So you don't get hungry.'

'Thank you.' He grinned down at Mette, taking the paper bag that she was holding out towards him. 'I should come back with you, though.'

Ted had bent down to Mette and took her hand, leading her over to the blocks of ice so that she could run her hand over them to feel the icy coldness beneath her fingertips. Aksel looked about to follow, and Flora caught his sleeve.

'She can do that by herself, Aksel. Ted's looking after her.'

'I know, but…' His forehead creased into a frown. 'I'm crowding her, aren't I?'

'You're spending time with her, so that you can make a relationship. That's great.' Aksel shot her an unconvinced look. 'And, yes, you are crowding her a bit. She's learning how to explore her world.'

'And this is what the therapists at the clinic are teaching her.' He looked over at Mette thoughtfully.

'That's our job, all of us. We may have specific roles, but we all have the same aim.' Everyone who worked here on the estate was a part of that. Ted took the children on nature walks during the summer, and Mrs Renwick, the cook at the castle, held regular cookery classes for both adults and children.

'All the same, Mette's far more important than this…'

'Yes, she is. She's important to all of us, and she's just starting to feel at home at the clinic. She has a play date this afternoon, and she's going to have a great time.

You can either interfere with that, or you can stay here and make her something nice.'

He narrowed his eyes. 'Are you just saying that because you know I want to stay?'

'I'm saying this because staying's okay. Mette has other things to do this afternoon.'

Aksel was frowning, now. 'I was rather hoping that she'd learn to need me.'

Flora puffed out an exasperated breath. 'She *does* need you, Aksel. She needs you to be her father, which means you're always there for her. It doesn't mean that you have to follow her around all the time. The whole point of her being here is to learn to be independent.'

Most people would have hummed and hawed about it a bit. But Aksel had the information he needed, and it was typical of him to make his decision and act on it.

'You're killing me. You know that.' He turned on his heel, walking over to Mette.

'Ted says that I can make an ice sculpture. Would you like me to make one for you this afternoon, while Tante Flora takes you back to the castle to play?'

'Yes, Papa!' Mette obviously thought that was a good idea, too.

'Okay. What would you like me to make, then?'

Flora winced. Maybe it would have been better to give Mette some suggestions, rather than allow a child's imagination to run rampant.

'A reindeer. Mama took me to see the reindeer.'

'A reindeer?' Ted chuckled, removing his flat cap to scratch his head. 'That'll be interesting. What do you think, Aksel?'

Aksel shrugged. 'If she wants a reindeer, then… I can do a reindeer.'

'Would you like me to bring Mette back here after

I've finished work?' Flora reckoned that Aksel might need a bit of extra time to work out how to sculpt four legs and a pair of antlers.

'Um… Yes. That would be great, thank you.'

'Right.' Flora took Mette's hand. 'Shall we stay and watch Papa get started on your reindeer, Mette, and then we'll go back to the castle.'

Mette nodded, following Flora to a safe distance, while Ted gave Aksel the gloves and a pair of safety glasses. Running him through a few safety rules was probably unnecessary, but Ted was nothing if not thorough, and Aksel listened carefully. Then he turned towards the block of ice that Ted had indicated, standing back for a moment to contemplate his first move, before starting up the chainsaw.

Mette tugged her hat down over her ears in response to the noise. 'What's Papa doing?'

'He's cutting some ice off the top. To make the reindeer's back.'

Aksel had clearly decided to start with the easy part, and was making an incision on one side of the block of ice that ran half way along its length. Then he made a similar incision from the top, freeing a large piece of ice, which he lifted down onto the ground. He switched off the chainsaw, engaging the safety mechanism, and beckoned to Flora and Mette.

'See this big block he's sawn off. It's almost as big as you are.' She kept hold of Mette's hand, letting her feel the size of the block. 'I can't wait to see what it'll be like when we get back.'

'Neither can I,' Ted interjected. He was clearly wondering how Aksel was going to sculpt a pair of antlers too.

'You're *all* killing me…' Aksel muttered the words

under his breath, but he was grinning broadly. He was clearly in his element.

He bent down, kissing Mette goodbye and telling her to enjoy her afternoon. Flora took her hand and walked away, knowing that Aksel was watching them go. It wasn't until she'd turned into one of the walkways between the stalls that she heard the chainsaw start up again.

Mette had told everyone about how her papa was using a chainsaw to make her a reindeer out of ice. When Flora arrived back at the children's unit to pick her up, the nursery nurses and some of the children already had their hats and coats on.

'Are we ready, then?' Lyle was wearing a thick windcheater and was clearly intending to join the party. Flora hoped that they wouldn't be disappointed.

'Should we phone Ted first? To see if it's finished?' And possibly to make sure that the reindeer hadn't collapsed and they'd be greeted by an amorphous pile of ice.

Lyle chuckled. 'Aksel called me earlier for some orthopaedic advice.'

'He's hurt himself?' Flora hoped that Aksel hadn't overdone things and damaged his shoulder.

'No, it was more a matter of how thick the reindeer's legs needed to be to support the weight of the body. Interesting equation. I called Ted just now, and he says that it's all going rather well.'

Lyle looked round as Cass entered the room, displaying the sixth sense of a lover who always knew when his partner was nearby.

'I can't wait to see it.' Cass's green eyes flashed with

mischief. 'There's something very sexy about a man using power tools…'

Yes, there was. And there was something almost overwhelmingly sexy about Aksel using power tools. Combine that with large blocks of ice, and it was enough to melt the most frozen heart.

'You think so? I might have to have a go, then.' Lyle raised an eyebrow and Cass laughed.

They all trooped out of the main entrance to the clinic, Mette holding her hand. It was dark now and the lights of the carnival shone brightly ahead of them, people straggling along the path that led down from the castle.

The first evening of the carnival was, as always, well attended. Charles Ross-Wylde was there, fulfilling his duties as Laird and host by greeting everyone and then melting quietly away to leave them to their fun. His sister Esme had brought a couple of the dogs from the canine therapy centre, and was clearly taking the opportunity to make sure that they weren't distracted by the lights and sounds around them.

Mette tugged at Flora's hand, remembering which way they needed to walk to get to the ice sculpture. As they approached, Flora could see Ted adjusting the lights that were placed at the bottom of the sculpture to show it off to its best effect. And Aksel's tall, unmistakeable silhouette standing back a little.

He turned, seeming to sense that they were there, and walked towards them. Shooting Flora a smile, he addressed Mette.

'Would you like to come and see your reindeer?'

'Yes, Papa!'

Flora watched as he led his daughter over to the reindeer, letting her stand close so that she could see the lights reflected in the ice. It was beautiful, standing tall and proud, a full set of antlers on its head. The lights glistened through the ice, making it seem almost alive.

Over the noise of the carnival, Flora could hear Mette's excited chatter. Lyle came to inspect the reindeer and Mette took his hand, pulling him closer to take a look. Aksel stood back, leaving his daughter with Lyle and Cass, and walked over to Flora.

'That is downright amazing.' Flora grinned up at him.

'I had a bit of help. One of the antlers snapped off, and Ted and I had to re-attach it. And Dr Sinclair's anatomical knowledge was invaluable.'

'Yes, I heard about that. I'm a little more interested in *your* anatomy.' Flora frowned. She could have phrased that a little better. Somehow, a perfectly innocent enquiry about his shoulder seemed to have turned into a barely disguised chat-up line.

'My shoulder's fine. If that's what you mean.' The slight quirk of his lips showed that Aksel was quite prepared to call her bluff, and Flora decided to ignore the invitation.

'I'm glad you haven't undone the work I did on it.'

'It might be a bit stiff in the morning…'

Flora returned his smile. 'If it is, I'll be officially reporting you to Lyle for some more orthopaedic advice.' A repetition of last night was probably to be avoided.

'You make that sound like a threat.'

'Don't worry. It is.'

CHAPTER NINE

AKSEL WOKE UP the following morning feeling more refreshed from sleep than he had in a long time. It was a bright, clear day, and although his shoulder was a little sore, it was nothing that a hot shower and some stretching exercises wouldn't banish. He was ready for the day, and the day seemed that much better for the possibility that it might bring another chance to see Flora.

He wasn't disappointed. When he arrived at the clinic, after a morning's work at the therapy centre, he found that Mette was absorbed in a learning game with one of the children's therapy assistants. He kissed his daughter and told her that he wouldn't interrupt, and then wandered aimlessly down to one of the patient sitting rooms.

He saw Flora sitting in one of the wing-backed chairs by the great fireplace, which had been made bright and welcoming with an arrangement of Christmas greenery. He recognised the sandy-haired man in the chair opposite. One of the children's play leaders had told him that this was Andy Wallace and that he didn't much like to be touched, in a broad hint that Aksel should steer Mette clear of him.

Flora was leaning towards Andy, and the two seemed

to be deep in conversation. Aksel turned to walk away, but then Flora looked up and beckoned him over.

Andy didn't offer to shake hands when Flora introduced the two men but nodded quietly in Aksel's direction, clearly taking his time to sum him up.

'We're just having tea. Would you like to join us?' Flora smiled at him.

There was no *just* about it. Flora had been talking quietly to Andy, no doubt discussing the next step of what looked like a long road back to full health. Andy's leg was supported by a surgical brace and his eyes seemed haunted. But if Flora thought that it was okay for him to join them, then he trusted her.

'Thank you. Can I get you a refill?' He gestured to the two empty cups on the small table between them.

'Not for me, thanks. Andy?'

Andy proffered his cup, and Aksel carried it over to the side table where coffee and tea were laid out. He put a fresh herbal teabag into Andy's cup and reached for a coffee capsule for himself. Flora leaned forward, saying a few words to Andy, and he nodded. All the same, when Aksel operated the coffee machine, Andy jumped slightly at the noise.

'Where's Mette?' Flora turned to him as he sat down.

'She's…got something going with the play assistants. Apparently I'm surplus to requirements at the moment.' Aksel made a joke of it, but it stung more than he cared to admit.

Flora nodded, smiling at Andy. 'Aksel's not used to that.'

Andy let out a short, barked laugh. 'I can identify with *surplus to requirements*.' He nodded down at his leg, clearly frustrated by his own lack of mobility.

'It's nothing…' The comparison was embarrassing; Andy clearly had life-changing injuries.

'Don't let Flora hear you say that. She has a keen nose for *nothing*.' Andy gave a wry smile, and Flora grinned back at him.

'Nothing's a code word around here. Meaning something.' Flora's observation sounded like a quiet joke, and Aksel wondered if it was aimed at him or Andy. Probably both of them.

'In that case, it's something. And I'm handling it.' Aksel's smiling retort made both Andy and Flora laugh. He was beginning to like Andy, and Aksel pulled out his phone, flipping to the picture he'd taken yesterday and handing the phone to Andy.

'Oh, she's a bonny wee lass. What's that she's standing next to?'

Flora smiled. 'Ted Mackie has an ice-sculpting stall at the carnival. With chainsaws. Aksel made the mistake of telling Mette that he'd sculpt whatever she wanted for her, and he ended up having to do a reindeer.'

Andy chuckled. 'You made a decent job of it. Why is your daughter here?'

'She was in a car accident, and she's lost most of her sight. Anything that's more than a few feet away from her is just a blur.'

'You've done the best thing for her, bringing her to the clinic. They'll help her make the most of what she has.' Andy's reaction was like a breath of fresh air. Someone who knew the nature of suffering but didn't dwell on it, and who preferred to look at what could be done for Mette, and not express horror at what couldn't be changed.

'Thanks. That's good to hear.'

Flora had leaned back in her chair, seemingly in no

hurry to go anywhere. The talk drifted into quiet, getting-to-know-you mode. Andy had been in the army and had travelled a lot, and the two men swapped stories about places they'd both visited. Andy's story about patching up a broken-down SUV from the only materials to hand struck a chord with Aksel, and the two men laughed over it. And Aksel's story about the mystery of the missing coffee supplies made Andy chuckle.

Finally, Flora looked at her watch. 'I hate to break this up, but it's time for your physio now, Andy.' She was clearly pleased with the way things had gone. And Aksel had enjoyed their talk. Andy had a well-developed sense of humour, and he'd led an interesting life.

Andy rolled his eyes. 'Another chance for you to torment me?' He clearly thought a lot of Flora.

'Yes, that's right. I don't get paid if I can't find something to torment my patients with.' Flora gave Andy a bright smile, helping him to his feet and pulling in front of him the walking frame that stood by the side of his chair.

'I'd like to see the pictures of your expedition to the Andes.' Andy turned to Aksel.

'Sure. I'll bring them in tomorrow. Is it okay for me to bring Mette with me?' Aksel wondered if a child might be too much for Andy but he smiled.

'I'd like that. As long as she doesn't find me boring.' Andy glanced down at his leg. Aksel shook his head, sure that if anyone could see past Andy's injuries then his daughter could.

Flora broke in briskly. 'If you send me the pictures, I can print them out for you. Perhaps Mette will be able to see them better that way?'

'Thanks. I think she will.'

The two men nodded goodbye, and Flora followed as Andy walked slowly towards the doorway. She turned, giving Aksel a grin.

'If you're at a loose end, you can always go and sculpt something else. I'm very partial to unicorns, and now you have this down to a fine art it should be child's play…'

'Don't listen to her, man.' Andy called out the words. 'She's far too bossy.'

Bossy and beautiful. Soft and sweet and yet surprisingly strong. Intelligent, warm… The list just went on. Aksel had given up trying to complete it, because there was always more to say about Flora.

He called out an acknowledgement to Andy, wondering if Flora had lip-read the words that had formed silently on his lips. Or maybe she'd tapped into the connection between them and she just knew, because she shot him a look of amused surprise.

You want a unicorn…? If that was what Flora wanted, then that's what she'd get.

The ice unicorn stood next to the reindeer, and Ted Mackie had told Aksel that it had attracted both attention and admiration. He hadn't told Flora about it, even though she was the one person that it was intended to please. She was sure enough to hear about it, and he hoped she'd know it was *her* unicorn.

He'd arranged a schedule with Lyle for when he should bring Mette home. Both of them agreed that Mette was settling in well, and Aksel was anxious that she wouldn't miss any of the activities that the clinic ran for its patients.

'Are you sure you're happy with this? It's a little less than we originally envisaged.' Lyle gave him a searching look, and Aksel realised that his own attitude had changed since they'd last spoken about this. The question was less of a tug of war and more a meeting of minds now.

'I'm very happy with it. My relationship with Mette has been much better since she's been here. I have you to thank for that. She's gained a lot of confidence.' Aksel had wondered if he should say that Flora had given *him* the confidence to see that.

Lyle had nodded, smiling. 'I'm glad you feel that way. I think that your daily visits are very important for Mette, she knows that you're always there for her.'

He'd gone to the children's unit to see Mette and she'd greeted him with a hug and a kiss. When he'd asked her if she'd like to spend the day with him tomorrow, she'd tugged at the play assistant's arm excitedly, telling her that she was going to explore a new place with her papa.

Then he'd texted Flora, asking her if she was free. There had been no mention of unicorns, which had been a little disappointing, but her 'Yes' had made up for that.

Aksel arrived at the clinic just as the children were finishing their breakfast. He packed some things into his day-pack, although in truth nothing was needed. But Mette liked the idea of packing for a journey.

His shoulder had improved a great deal. The massage had done wonders and he suspected that Flora's wake-up call had something to do with it as well. He lifted Mette up onto his shoulders, perched on top of his day-pack, and felt his stride lengthen as they started the two-mile walk home, the rhythm of his steps quieting his heart. Aksel began to tell Mette the story of his trip up to a remote village in the Andes.

'Were there crocodiles, Papa?'

Not that he'd noticed. But, then, Mette's idea of a crocodile was her smiling stuffed toy. 'Yes, there were crocodiles. We gave them some chocolate so they wouldn't eat us.'

'And penguins?'

'Yes. We had to go fishing and catch them some tea, so they'd tell us the right way to the village.' If he was going to enter into the realms of fantasy, then he may as well just go for it.

'Did your feet hurt?'

'A little bit. I had a big blister on my toe.' He'd made a rookie mistake on the way back down, allowing water to get inside one of his boots, and frostbite had taken hold.

'Did it get better, Papa?'

'Yes, it got better. And when we reached the village, at the top of the high snowy mountain, the people there welcomed us and gave us food and comfortable beds, with warm quilts like yours.'

Mette whooped with joy, and the achievement seemed greater than the walk up to the isolated village, in terrible weather conditions, had been.

They had warm drinks together when they arrived back at the cottage, and Mette insisted on keeping her hat on, since she too was an explorer. Then there was a knock at the door, and Flora burst into the cottage, bringing the same sunlight with her that she took everywhere.

'I like the new look.' She grinned up at him and Aksel's hand shot awkwardly to the small plait that ran from his right temple and was caught into the elastic band that held the rest of his hair back.

'Mette's rag doll has plaits…' He shrugged as if it was nothing. When Mette had demanded that she be allowed to plait his hair this morning, it had felt like another step towards intimacy with his daughter, and he hadn't had the heart to unravel the uneven braid.

'I'm glad you kept it. She has excellent taste.' Flora obviously approved wholeheartedly. 'I hear that Ted Mackie's acquired an ice unicorn...'

Aksel wondered if she really hadn't been to see it, or she was just teasing. 'Has he?' He decided to play things cool.

'It's beautiful. I have about a million pictures of it.' She stood on her toes, kissing his cheek so briefly that he only realised she'd done it after the fact. 'Thank you.'

His cheek tingled from the touch of her lips as he followed Flora into the sitting room, where Mette was playing with Kari. Aksel decided that the hours spent sculpting the unicorn had been well worth it, and that he'd be tempted to create a whole menagerie of fantastic creatures in exchange for one more fleeting kiss.

It was agreed that they would walk down to the marketplace to see the village Christmas tree and the Christmas market. Aksel called Kari, putting on the yellow vest that denoted that she was at work now.

'Mette's already using Kari as her assistance dog?'

'No, but Esme suggested that it might be a good idea to let her see her at work a bit, just to get her used to the idea. Where's Dougal?'

'I took him up to the therapy centre, they're minding him. I didn't want him to get under Mette's feet.' Flora took a green and red striped bobble hat from the pocket of her red coat, pulling it down over her ears, and Aksel chuckled. She looked delightful.

'What are you? One of Santa's elves?'

'Right in one.' She shot him an innocent look, tugging at the hat. 'What gave me away?'

CHAPTER TEN

CLUCHLOCHRY'S MARKET SQUARE was paved with cobble-stones, and boasted an old market cross, worn and battered by many winters. The market was already in full swing, with fairy lights hung around the canvas-topped stalls, and the village Christmas tree standing proudly in one corner, smothered in lights. As this was a Saturday morning, carol singers and a band had turned out to give the market a festive air.

The band struck up a melody that Mette recognised, and she started to sing along in Norwegian. Aksel lifted her up out of the crush of people, and heard Flora singing too, in English. At the end of the carol she joined in with the round of applause for the band, and Mette flung her arms up, wriggling with delight.

'Shall we go over to the village hall first?' Flora indicated a stone building next to the church. 'There are lots of stalls in there as well.'

Aksel nodded his agreement, and Flora led the way, while he followed with Mette. Kari trotted by her side, and every now and then the little girl held out her hand, putting it on Kari's back. It was a start. Soon, hopefully, Mette would be learning to rely on Kari to guide her.

Inside, it looked as if there had been some kind of competition between the stallholders to see who could get the most Christmas decorations into their allotted space. Aksel saw a large reindeer twinkling above one of them, and decided not to point it out to Mette, in case she wanted to take it home with her.

'Oh, look.' Flora had caught sight of yet another stall that she wanted to visit. 'I heard that Aileen was here, we should go and see her knitwear. She might have something that Mette would like.'

Aksel nodded his agreement, and Flora led him over to the stall, introducing him to Aileen Sinclair, an older woman with greying hair, confiding the information that Aileen was Lyle's mother and that she did a *lot* of knitting. That was self-evident from the racks of hats and scarves, and the sweaters laid out on two tables. Aileen smiled at him, sizing him up with an experienced eye.

'I don't know whether I can find anything to fit you, hen.' Aileen seemed willing to try all the same, sorting through a small pile of chunky cableknit sweaters. 'No, there isn't much call for extra-large, and Mrs Bell bought the last one for her son. If there's something you like, we can always make it up for you.'

'Thank you.' Aksel began to dutifully look through the sweaters. 'Actually, we were looking for something for my daughter.'

Flora lifted Mette up so that she could run her hand across the fine, lace knitted children's jumpers. Aileen greeted Mette with another of her beaming smiles, producing a tape measure from her pocket, and began to measure Mette's arms.

'What colour do you like, Mette?' Flora always asked Mette what she liked rather than suggesting things to her.

'Red.' Mette had caught sight of Aileen's bright red sweater, under her coat.

'Very good choice. Maybe a lacy one?' Aileen glanced at Flora and she nodded.

Piles of sweaters were looked through, knocked over and then re-stacked, in what looked like a completely arbitrary search. Finally three pretty sweaters, which looked to be around Mette's size, were laid out on top of the others.

'What do you think, Aksel?' Flora turned to him questioningly.

'They're all very nice.' Aksel wasn't prepared to commit himself any further than that and Flora frowned at him.

'You're no help.'

'Everyone should stick to what they're good at.' And Flora was very good at shopping. She always seemed to pick out the nicest things, buying the best she could afford and yet not over-spending. That was why she always looked immaculate.

He watched as Flora encouraged Mette to run her hand across each of the sweaters to feel their softness and warmth. She picked one, and Flora unzipped her coat so that Aileen could hold it up against her and make sure it fitted properly. The general consensus of opinion seemed to be that this was the perfect sweater, and Aksel reached into his pocket for his wallet.

He was too slow. As Aileen wrapped the sweater carefully in pretty paper, sticky-taping the ends down, Flora had whipped a note from her purse and handed it over.

'Thank you. I'll get your change.' Aileen plumped the package into a paper carrier bag and gave it to Mette.

'Don't worry about the change, Aileen. You don't

charge enough for these already, I still have the one I bought from you three years ago. You'd make a lot more money if you didn't make them to last.'

Aileen flushed with pleasure. The sweaters were clearly more a labour of love than a money-making exercise.

Mette whirled around, eager to show Aksel her carrier bag, and Flora caught her before she lost her balance. He examined the bag, declared it wonderful, and Aileen bade them a cheery goodbye.

Then it was on to the other stalls. Flora was endlessly patient, letting Mette sniff each one of the home-made soaps on offer and choose the one she liked the best. The avuncular man at the fudge stall offered them some samples to taste, and Aksel was allowed to make the choice of which to buy. The indoor market was a whirl of colours, tastes, textures and smells, and Aksel found himself enjoying it as much as Mette obviously was.

'Are you hungry yet?' Flora clearly was or she wouldn't have asked the question. 'There's a pub on the other side of the green that serves family lunches whenever the market's open.'

A family lunch. That sounded good, and not just because Aksel was hungry too. He could really get used to this feeling of belonging, with both Mette *and* Flora.

'Good idea. They won't mind us taking Kari in?' Despite her yellow service coat, Kari wasn't working as Mette's assistance dog just yet.

'No, of course not. They're used to people coming in with dogs from the canine therapy centre, and they welcome them.'

Flora managed to find a table close to one of the roaring fires, and while she stripped off Mette's coat, Aksel went to the bar, ordering thick vegetable soup with crusty bread, and two glasses of Christmas punch. When he returned with the tray, Mette and Flora were investigating their purchases together. This seemed to be an integral part of the shopping experience, and Mette was copying Flora, inserting her finger into the corner of each package so that they could catch a glimpse of what was inside.

'Why don't you open them?' Aksel began to clear a space on the table between them, and Flora shot him a horrified look.

'Hush! We can't open them until we get home.'

'Ah. All right.' Aksel found that the thought of Flora and Mette spreading out their purchases for a second and more thorough inspection was just as enticing as this was. This complex ritual was more than just going out and shopping for something that met your needs. It was about bonding and sharing, and the excitement of finding a sweater that was the right colour and design, and fitted perfectly.

He was learning that there were many things he *could* share with Mette, and wondered if this would ever be one of them. At the moment, it seemed an impossible set of rules and conventions, which were as complicated as any he'd seen on his travels. It occurred to him that Mette really needed a mother, and the thought wasn't as difficult to come to terms with as it had been. He could be a good father, without having to do everything himself.

Flora and Mette were whispering together, and he couldn't hear what they were saying over the swell of conversation around them. Then Flora turned to him, her eyes shining.

'We're giving you ten out of ten. Possibly ten and a half.'

That sounded great, but he wasn't sure what he'd done to deserve it. 'What for?'

'For being our ideal shopping companion.' Flora didn't seem disposed to break the score down, but Mette had no such reservations.

'Because you carry the bags, Papa. And you don't rush, and you buy soup. And fudge.'

Aksel hadn't realised that this could cause him so much pride. And pleasure. 'Thank you. I'm...honoured.'

Mette gave him a nod, which said that he was quite right to feel that way, having been given such an accolade. Flora smiled, and suddenly his whole world became warm and full of sparkle.

'The Christmas tableau will be open by the time we've finished. And then I'd like to pop over to Mary's stall if you don't mind. I heard she has some nice little things for Christmas gifts.'

'That sounds great. I'd like that.' He wasn't quite sure what a Christmas tableau was, but he'd go with the flow. Aksel leaned back in his seat, stretching his legs out towards the fire. Making sense of the proceedings didn't much matter, he'd been voted ten out of ten as a shopping companion, and that was a great deal more than good enough.

The Christmas tableau turned out to be housed in a three-sided wooden structure outside the church. Inside were Mary and Joseph, an assortment of shepherds and three kings, along with one of the dogs from the therapy centre. Aksel wasn't quite sure how it had ended up there, but he assumed its presence had something to do with Esme, and that she'd probably had a hand in choosing its festive, red and white dog coat.

'Mette!' As they opened the gate to the churchyard,

the shortest and broadest of the three kings started to wave, handing a jewelled box to one of the other kings and ducking past the crowd that was forming around the tableau.

Mette turned her head, recognising the voice, and tugged at Aksel's hand. 'It's Carrie. Where is she?'

It was the first time that Aksel had heard Mette say anything like that. Usually she ignored the things she couldn't see, and she'd been known to throw a temper tantrum when she couldn't find something she wanted.

'She's coming over to you now, sweetheart.' Flora volunteered the information, and Mette nodded. Now that the king was a little closer, he realised it *was* Carrie, one of the children's nurses from the clinic, and almost unrecognisable under a false beard and a large jewelled hat. Her small frame was completely disguised by what looked like several layers of bulky clothes under her costume.

'Hi, Carrie. Keeping warm?' Flora grinned at her.

'I'm a bit hot, actually.' Carrie pushed her beard up, propping it incongruously on the rim of her hat, and bent down to greet Mette. 'The costume was a bit big so I've got two coats on underneath this. Along with a thick sweater *and* thermal underwear.'

'Sounds reasonable to me. You've got a couple of hours out here. The shepherds are already looking a bit chilly.'

'Don't worry about them. The vicar's brought a couple of Thermos flasks along, and we've got an outdoor heater behind the manger, that's why everyone's crowding around it. You'd be surprised how warm it gets after a while.' Carrie volunteered the information and Flora laughed.

'That's good to know. I'll make sure I'm standing next to the heater when it's my turn.'

It was impossible that Flora wouldn't take a turn, she was so much a part of the life of the village. Aksel wondered what she'd be dressing up as and decided to wait and see.

'Would you like to come and see the stable, Mette?' Carrie bent down towards her. 'We've got a rabbit…'

'Yes, please.' Mette took her hand, waving to Aksel as Carrie led her away.

'A rabbit?' Aksel murmured the words as he watched her go.

'The vicar's not afraid to improvise, and I don't think there were any sheep available.' Flora chuckled. 'And anyway, don't you think it's the best stable you've ever seen?'

It was. The costumes were great, and there was a sturdy manger and lots of straw. A couple of other children, besides Mette, had been led up to the tableau by their parents, and had been welcomed inside by the shepherds and kings. Carrie was carefully showing Mette around, talking to her and allowing her to touch everything. The place shone with sparkling lights to re-create stars, and the warmth and love of a small community.

'Yes. The very best.'

CHAPTER ELEVEN

AKSEL WAS RELAXED and smiling as they watched Mette explore the stable with Carrie. So different from the man Flora had first met. The clinic tended to do that to patients and their families. Flora had seen so many people arrive looking tense and afraid, and had watched the secure and welcoming environment soothe their fears and allow them to begin to move forward. It was always good to see, but she'd never been so happy about it as she was now.

It was hard not to wonder what things might have been like if she and Aksel had met before they'd both been changed by the world. Whether they might have been able to make a family for more than just the space of a day. But for all the hope that the clinic brought to people's hearts, there was also the understanding that some things couldn't be changed, and it was necessary to make the best of them. She should enjoy today for what it was, and let it go.

Carrie delivered Mette back to her father, and she chattered brightly about having seen the rabbit and stroked it, as they walked towards Mary's stall. It was a riot of colour. Along with a few small quilts, there were fabric bags, with appliquéd flowers, patchwork lavender bags tied with ribbon, and quilted hats with earflaps. Mary was, unusually, not in the thick of things but sitting on a rickety stool and leaving her husband and Jackie, the young mum who helped out in the shop on Saturdays, to deal with the customers.

Flora greeted her with a smile. 'Hello, Mary. It's cold enough out here…'

Mary was sitting with her hands in her pockets, and her woollen hat pulled down over her ears and brow. Most of the stallholders prided themselves on being out in all weather, however cold, but maybe Mary should consider going into the pub for a while to get warm.

Mary nodded, her expression one of deep thought.

'These look wonderful.' Flora indicated the lavender bags and Aksel hoisted Mette up so she could smell them. 'How much are they?'

Mary smiled suddenly. 'Thruppence.'

Okay…. Flora had never heard of thruppenny lavender bags being a thing, but there were three in each bundle. They'd be tagged with a price anyway. Mary went back to staring in her husband's direction and Flora wondered if maybe they'd had an argument about something.

Hats were tried on, lavender sniffed, and the fabric bags admired. They found a hat for Mette, its bright reds and greens matching her coat, and Aksel encouraged Flora to treat herself to one of the fabric bags. It would be perfect for carrying some of the smaller items that she used most regularly in the course of her job, and it would be nice to visit the residents at the sheltered living complex carrying a bag that didn't scream that it was *medical*.

Mary smiled at her, and Flora put the bag and the hat down in front of her. 'I'd like to take these, Mary.'

'Ah, yes.' Mary sprang to her feet. 'The hat's for… the little girl.'

It was unlike Mary to forget a name. 'Yes, it's for Mette.'

'Of course. Red.' Mary stared at the hat and then seemed to come to her senses. 'That's two pounds for the hat, plus three and fourpence for the bag. Fourteen and six altogether, dear.'

Mary held out her hand to receive the money. Something was very wrong. Flora leaned across, studying her face in the reflection of the fairy lights above their heads.

'Are you all right, Mary?'

'I just have a bit of a headache, dear. How much did I say it was?'

Mary *wasn't* all right. Flora glanced at Aksel and saw concern on his face too. Even if he didn't follow the vagaries of pounds, shillings and pence, it was obvious that Mary was confused and calculating the bill in coins that had been obsolete for almost fifty years.

Flora squeezed around the edge of the stall, taking Mary's hand. It felt ice-cold in hers. 'Mary, can you sit down for me, please?'

'No, dear.'

'What's the matter?' Mary's husband, John, had left the customer he was serving and come over to see what was happening.

'I don't know. Mary doesn't seem well, has she hit her head or anything recently?'

John Monroe had been a county court judge before he'd retired, and his avuncular manner covered an ability to sum up a situation quickly and take action.

'Sit down, hen.' He guided Mary to the stool, keeping his arm around her when she sank down onto it, and turning to Flora. 'She bumped her head when we were setting up the stall. She said it was nothing, and she seemed fine…'

'Okay, where?' Flora gently peeled off Mary's hat and realised she hadn't needed to ask. A large bump was forming on the side of her head.

'We need to get her into the warm, John.' Flora looked around at the crowded market. 'Go and fetch the vicar. I think that the church is the best place.'

John hesitated, not wanting to leave Mary, and Flora caught his arm. 'Go now, please.'

Aksel had dropped their shopping bags and Jackie stowed them away under the stall. Mette seemed to understand that something was wrong, and she stood quietly, her arms around Kari's neck. Jackie took her hand and Aksel bent down next to Mary, supporting her on the stool. Flora pulled out her phone.

'I'm going to call Charles.' She hoped that she wasn't overreacting but in her heart she knew that she wasn't. And she knew that Charles Ross-Wylde would rather she called, if she thought someone needed his help.

Charles answered on the second ring, and Flora quickly told him what had happened, answering his questions and breathing a sigh of relief when he told her he'd be there as soon as he could. She ended the call, and Aksel glanced up at her.

'Charles is on his way, and he's going to call an ambulance.' Flora murmured the words quietly, so that Mary didn't hear. 'This may be a bad concussion or a brain bleed, so we must be very careful with her and take her somewhere warm and quiet.'

'Fourteen and six… Fourteen…and…seven…' Mary seemed to be in a world of her own, and Aksel nodded, concern flashing in his eyes.

The vicar arrived, along with Carrie, who was red-faced and breathless from running, her beard hanging from one ear. She took Mette's hand and Aksel turned to her.

'Will you take her, please, Carrie?'

'Of course. You see to Mary, and I'll look after Mette and Kari.'

'I'll go and open up the church lounge.' The vicar was fumbling under his shepherd's costume for his keys. 'It's nice and warm in there.'

Now all they had to do was to persuade Mary to go with them. Flora knelt down beside her. 'Mary, we're going to the church.'

'Are we?' Mary gazed dreamily around her, as if she wasn't quite sure what direction that was. 'All right.'

Mary went to stand up, swaying suddenly as she lost her balance. Aksel caught her, lifting her up, and she lay still and compliant in his arms.

People were gathering around the stall, some offering help. The only help they could give was to stand back, and Flora cleared a path for Aksel. As everyone began to realise what was happening, the crowd melted away in front of them, leaving them a clear route to the church.

They walked around the side of the ancient building to a more modern annexe. The vicar was waiting for them, holding the swing doors open, and he ushered Aksel through to the quiet, comfortable lounge. There was a long, upholstered bench seat at one side of the room, and Aksel carefully laid Mary down, while Flora fetched a cushion for her head.

'Mary, love....' John knelt down beside her and took her hand, but Mary snatched it away. Aksel laid his hand on John's shoulder.

'She's confused, John. We just need to keep her calm at the moment.'

'Is there any tea?' Mary tried to sit up, and Aksel gently guided her back down again.

'The vicar's just making some. He'll be along in a minute.' His answer seemed to satisfy Mary, and she lay back. Aksel kept talking to her, reassuring her and keeping her quiet.

Flora's phone rang and she pulled it from her pocket. Charles sounded as if he was in the car, and she quickly told him where to find them.

'That's great. I'll be there soon, and an ambulance is on its way too…' The call fizzled and cut out, and Flora put her phone back into her pocket. Maybe Charles had just driven into a black spot, or maybe he'd said all he wanted to say.

'What's the matter with her, Flora?' John was standing beside her, waiting for her to end the call.

'I'm not sure, but it seems to be a result of the bump on her head.' Flora didn't want to distress John even further by listing the things it could be. 'We need to keep her quiet. Charles is on his way and the ambulance will be here soon.'

'What have I done…?' Tears misted John's eyes. 'She said it was nothing. She seemed a bit subdued, but I thought she was just cold. I was going to take her to the pub for lunch as soon as I'd finished with the customer I was serving.'

'It's okay. In these situations people often try to deny there's anything wrong with them and they'll hide their symptoms. And they'll push away the people they love most. We'll get her to the hospital and they'll help her.' There was nothing more that Flora could say. If this was what she thought it was, then Mary was gravely ill.

John nodded. 'Is there *anything* I can do?'

'Has Mary taken any medication? Did she take something for the headache?'

'She didn't say she had one. And, no, she tries to avoid taking painkillers if she can.'

That could be a blessing in this particular situation. 'No aspirin, or anything like that? Please try to be sure.'

'No. Nothing. I've been with her all day, she hasn't taken anything.' John shook his head.

'Okay, that's good.' Flora smiled encouragingly at him. 'Now, I want you to sit down and write down exactly when Mary bumped her head, and how she's seemed since. Please include everything, whether you think it's important or not.'

'Right you are.'

Maybe John knew that Flora was giving him something to do but he tore a blank sheet from one of the stack of parish magazines that lay on top of the piano and hurried over to a chair, taking a pen from his jacket pocket. Maybe the details would come in useful…

Flora knelt down beside Aksel. 'You should go and get Mette now. I can manage.'

Flora didn't want him to leave. Her own medical knowledge was enough to care for Mary until Charles arrived, but he was so calm. So reassuringly capable. But however much Mary might need him, however much Flora *did* need him, she knew that he couldn't leave Mette.

'One minute…' He got to his feet, striding towards the door. A brief, quiet conversation with someone outside, and he returned.

'You're sure you want to stay?' Aksel had obviously

made a decision and from the look on his face it troubled him a little. But he'd come back.

'Carrie's going to take Mette and Kari back to the clinic and I'll meet her there later. She's in very good hands.'

'Yes, she is. Thank you.'

He gave a little nod, and knelt back down beside Mary, taking her hand. Flora had to think now. She had to remember all the advanced first-aid courses she'd been on, and the physiology and pathology elements of her degree course. She took a deep breath.

Leaning forward, she looked for any blood or fluid discharge from Mary's ears and nose. Checked that she was conscious and alert, and noticed that her pupils were of an unequal size and that a bruise was forming behind her ear. Then she picked up Mary's hand.

'Can you squeeze my hand, Mary?'

The pressure from Mary's fingers was barely noticeable.

'As tight as you can.'

'I think I must have hurt it.' Mary looked up at her, unthinking, blank trust written on her face. It tore at Flora's heart, and she knew that she must do everything she could to help Mary.

'Let me massage it for you.' It wouldn't do her head injury any good, but it would keep Mary calm, and that was important.

'Thank you. I feel a bit sick.'

Aksel carefully moved Mary, sitting her up, and Flora grabbed the rubbish bin, emptying it out on the floor. Mary retched weakly, and then relaxed.

'That's better. I'm sorry…'

'It's okay. You're okay now.' Flora made sure that

Mary's mouth was clear, and Aksel gently laid her down in the recovery position. Flora was aware that John was watching them, and couldn't imagine his agony, but she had to concentrate on Mary.

She talked to Mary, soothing her, watching her every reaction. It seemed a very long time before the door opened and the vicar ushered Charles into the room.

John shot to his feet, watching and listening. Flora carefully relayed all the information she had to Charles, and he nodded, bending down towards Mary to examine her. Mary began to fret again, and by the time he'd finished she was trying to push him away. Charles beckoned to Flora.

'Can you keep her quiet?'

'Yes.' Flora knelt down, taking Mary's hand, and she seemed to settle. She heard Charles talking softly to John behind her, and then the arrival of the ambulance crew. Then she had to move back as the paramedics lifted Mary carefully onto a stretcher.

'I couldn't have done better myself, Flora. Well done.' Charles didn't wait for her answer, turning to usher John out of the room.

The lights from the ambulance outshone the fairy lights on the stalls in the marketplace. The noise and bustle seemed to have quietened down, and many of the stallholders watched as Mary was lifted into the ambulance and Charles and John followed.

Suddenly she felt Aksel's arm around her shoulders. As the ambulance negotiated the narrow street around the perimeter of the market square, people began to crowd around her, wanting to know what had happened to Mary.

'I'm sorry, we can't say exactly what's happened,

that's for the doctors at the hospital to decide. Mary's in good hands.' Aksel gave the answer that Flora was shaking too much to give. Then he hurried her over to Mary's stall.

'Jackie, will you be okay to pack up the stall?'

Jackie nodded. 'Yes, I've called my husband and he's on his way down with his mates. They'll be here in a minute. How's Mary?'

'I'm afraid we don't know, but Charles Ross-Wylde is with her and she's in very good hands.' Aksel repeated the very limited reassurance that he'd given to everyone else.

'Okay. I'll wait for news. Carrie came and took your shopping bags, she's taken them back to the clinic with Mette.'

'Thanks, Jackie. Are you sure you'll be all right on your own?'

'Yes, of course. Look, there's my husband now.'

Jackie waved, and Aksel nodded. He turned away, his arm tightly around Flora.

'Do you want to go the long way home? Or take the more direct route?'

'What's the long way? Via Istanbul?'

Aksel chuckled. 'No, via the clinic. I'm going to go home and pick up the SUV, then go to see Mette. I'll either walk you home or you can come with me.'

'I'll come with you.' Being at home alone didn't much appeal at the moment. 'Thanks for staying with me, Aksel. I know you didn't want to leave Mette.'

'No, I didn't. But Mette was all right and I reckoned I might be needed here.'

'Yes, you were.' Flora was going through all of the things she'd done in her head, trying to think of something that she'd missed. Something she might have done better.

'Mary's going to be all right. Largely because of you…'

'You're just saying that. I'm not a doctor.'

'No, but you used your medical knowledge to do as much as any doctor on the scene could have. You kept her quiet, you made sure she didn't choke. You acted professionally and decisively.'

'But if something happens to her…' Flora didn't want to think about it. If there was something that she'd missed, and Mary didn't survive this… She couldn't bear to think about it.

He stopped walking, turning to face her. His eyes seemed dark, and his shadow all-encompassing.

'Listen. Mary was surrounded by people, and no one realised there was something wrong. If you hadn't noticed and done something about it, this wouldn't have ended as well as it has. You were the one who gave her a chance, Flora.'

His trust in her reached the dark corners of her heart. 'You were pretty cool-headed yourself.'

'Well, I've been in a few situations before.'

Flora would bet he had. 'I don't know what I would have done without you.'

He chuckled. 'I do. You would have done exactly the same—taken care of Mary, checked all her symptoms, and acted quickly. I might not cross the line from animal medicine into human medicine, but those things are essential in any kind of emergency.'

'You make me feel so much better.' He'd lifted a heavy weight from her shoulders. Whatever happened now, she'd know that she'd done all she could.

'Mary was lucky that you were there, Flora. Never think otherwise.'

They'd reached the SUV, parked outside his cottage, and Aksel felt in his pocket for the keys and opened the door for Flora. He was clearly keen to see Mette. *She* wanted to see Mette. Both of them had found a place in her heart, and now she didn't want to let them go.

The process of winding down had taken a while, but helping Mette to unpack the bags that lay in the corner of the room had helped. Aksel had been persuaded to tell a story about his travels, and she found herself joining in with Mette's excitement at the twists and turns of his narrative.

As they were leaving her phone rang. She pulled it out of her pocket, seeing Charles's number on the display, and when she answered, she heard John's voice on the line.

She listened carefully to what he had to say, feeling the tension ebb out of her. 'That's really good news, John...'

'Words can't express my gratitude, for what you did this afternoon Flora...' John's voice was breaking with emotion.

'I'm glad I could help. Make sure you get some rest tonight, you'll be able to see her in the morning. I'll come as soon as she's allowed visitors.' Flora ended the call, aware suddenly that Aksel was staring at her, waiting to hear John's news.

'This isn't bad news, is it?'

Flora shook her head. 'No, it's very good news. We were right about it being a brain haemorrhage and Mary was taken into surgery straight away. The operation was a success, and they're hopeful that, in time, Mary will make a full recovery.'

'That's wonderful. How's John, does he need a lift from the hospital? I can go there now and take him home.'

'No, he's okay. Charles is still there and he got someone from the estate to fetch his car from the village and bring it to the hospital. Benefits of being the Laird.' A great weight seemed to have been lifted from Flora's chest, and she felt that she could really breathe again. 'John said…he was glad that I'd been there.'

'Yes. I was glad you were there, too. Let's go home, shall we?'

It seemed so natural to just nod and take his arm. As if the home that they were going to was *their* home and not two separate cottages. As they walked out of the clinic together, towards the battered SUV, it didn't seem to matter that she was leaning on his arm. Just for tonight, until she reached her own front door, she could rely on Aksel's strength and support.

CHAPTER TWELVE

FLORA HAD BEEN wondering whether to ask Aksel over for Sunday lunch, but she'd seen him set out towards the clinic with Kari by his side at eleven o'clock. She opened the refrigerator, staring at its contents. Suddenly she didn't feel like going to the trouble of cooking.

She made herself a sandwich, rounding it off with apple pie and ice cream as she watched a film on TV. Then she picked up a book, curling up on the sofa with Dougal and working her way through a couple of chapters.

The doorbell rang, and she opened her front door to find Aksel standing in the front porch. 'Shouldn't you be at the clinic?' The question slipped out before she'd had time to think.

'I went in a little early today and had lunch with Mette. I left her making paper angels with the other children.'

There was always something going on at the clinic, and Mette had obviously been drawn into the Sunday afternoon activities. 'That's good. The world always needs more paper angels.'

He nodded. 'Would you like to come for a walk?'

'A walk? I was planning to sit by the fire and make a few welcome gifts for the kids.'

'Sounds nice. A lot less chilly.' Something in his eyes beckoned her.

'The forecast's for snow later on this evening.'

He nodded, looking up at the sky. 'That looks about right. Are you coming?'

It was a challenge. Aksel was asking her to trust him, and in Flora's experience trusting a man didn't usually end well.

But Aksel was different. And what could happen on a windy, snowy hillside? Certainly nothing that involved exposing even a square inch of flesh.

'Why not? Come in, I'll get my coat.'

'You'll need a pair of sturdy shoes.' He glanced at the shoe rack in the hall.

'Even *I* wouldn't tackle the countryside in high heels. I have walking boots.' They were right at the back of the wardrobe, and Flora made for the stairs.

When she came back downstairs, his gaze flipped from her boots to the thick waterproof coat she wore and he gave a little nod of approval. As he strode across the road and towards the woods ahead of them, Flora struggled to keep up and he slowed a little.

'Where are we going?'

'I thought up to the old keep.' He pointed to the hill-top that overlooked the village, where piles of stones and a few remnants of wall were all that was left of the original castle seat of the Ross-Wylde family. 'Is that too far?'

It looked a long way. The most direct route from the village was up a steep incline, and Aksel was clearly heading for the gentler slope at the other side, which meant they had to go through the woods first.

'I can make it.' She wasn't going to admit to any doubts. 'Looks like a nice route for a Sunday afternoon.'

He kept his face impressively straight. If Aksel had any doubts about her stamina, he'd obviously decided to set them aside in response to her bravado. Perhaps he reckoned that he could always carry her for part of the way.

'I think so.' His stride lengthened again, as if he'd calculated the exact speed they'd need to go to get back by teatime. Flora fell into step with him, finding that the faster pace wasn't as punishing as it seemed, and they walked together along the path that led into the trees.

The light slowly began to fail. Flora hoped they'd be home soon, although Aksel didn't seem averse to stumbling around in the countryside after dark. She felt her heel begin to rub inside her boot and wondered if she hadn't bitten off more than she could chew.

Only their footsteps sounded in the path through the trees. It was oddly calming to walk beside him in silence, both travelling in the same direction without any need for words. Their heads both turned together as the screaming bark of a fox came from off to their left, and in the gathering gloom beneath the trees Flora began to hear the rustle of small creatures, which she generally didn't stop to notice.

He stopped at the far end of the wood, and Flora was grateful for the chance to catch her breath. Aksel was staring ahead of him at a red-gold sunset flaming across the horizon. It was nothing new, she'd seen sunsets before. But stumbling upon this one seemed different.

'You're limping. Sit down.' He indicated a tree trunk.

Flora had thought she was making a pretty good job of *not* limping. 'I'm okay.'

'First rule of walking. Look after your feet. Sit.' He was brooking no argument and Flora plumped herself down on the makeshift seat. Aksel knelt in front of her, picking up her foot, and testing the boot to see if it would shift.

'Ow! Of course it's going to hurt if you do that...' she protested, and he ignored her, unlacing the boot. He stripped off her thin sock, the cold air making her toes curl.

'You're getting a blister.' He balanced her foot on his knee, reaching into his pocket and pulling out a blister plaster. It occurred to Flora that maybe he'd come prepared for her as she couldn't imagine that he ever suffered from blisters.

All the same, it was welcome. He stuck the plaster around her heel, and then pulled a pair of thick walking socks from his pocket.

'Your feet are moving around in your boots. These should help.'

'I thought walking boots were meant to be roomy.' She stared at the socks. They had *definitely* been brought along for her benefit.

'They're meant to fit. When your foot slips around in them, that's going to cause blisters.' He slid her boot back on and relaced it. 'How does that feel?'

She had to admit it. 'Better. Thanks.'

He nodded, unlacing her other boot. Running his fingers around her heel to satisfy himself that there were no blisters, he held the other sock out and she slid her foot into it. She reached for her boot, and he gave her a sudden smile.

'Let me do it. You need to lace them a bit tighter.'

Flora gave in to the inevitable. 'Rookie mistake?'

'Yes.' His habitual honesty wasn't making her feel any better.

'You might mention that it can happen to anyone.

With new boots.' The boots weren't exactly new, but they hadn't been used much.

'It *can* happen to anyone. I let water get into one of my boots once, and lost the tips of two toes to frostbite.'

'Hmm. Careless.'

He looked up at her, smiling suddenly. 'Yes, it was. Looking at the way your teammates are walking comes as second nature because your feet are the only things you have to carry you home.'

They weren't exactly in the middle of nowhere. One of the roads through the estate was over to their right, and Flora had her phone in her pocket, so she could always call a taxi. But as Aksel got to his feet, holding out his hand to help her up, that seemed about as impossible as if they'd been at the South Pole.

She took a couple of steps. 'That's much more comfortable.'

'Good. Let me know if they start to hurt again, I have more plasters.'

Of course he did. If there was a next time, she'd make him hand over the plasters and lace her boots herself. She'd show him that she could walk just as far as he could. Or at least to the top of the hill and back down again.

As the ground began to rise, Flora's determination was tested again. She put her head down, concentrating on just taking one step after another. The incline on the far side of the hill hadn't looked that punishing, but it was a different matter when you were walking up it.

Aksel stopped a few times, holding out his hand towards her, and she ignored him. She could do this herself. It was beginning to get really dark now, and snow started to sting her face. This was *not* a pleasant Sunday afternoon stroll.

Finally they made it to the top and Aksel stopped, looking around at the looming shapes of the stones. Flora would have let out a cheer if she'd had the breath to do it.

'Perhaps we should take a rest now. Before we go back down.'

Yes! It was cold up here, but there must be some place where the stones would shelter them. Flora's legs were shaking and she suddenly felt that she couldn't take another step. She followed him over to where a tree had grown up amongst the stones, its trunk almost a part of them, and sat down on a rock, worn smooth and flat from its exposed location. Heaven. Only heaven wasn't quite so cold.

'I won't be a minute. Stay there.'

She nodded. Wild horses couldn't get her to move now. Aksel strode away, the beam of his torch moving to and fro among the stones. He seemed to be looking for something. Flora bent over, putting her hands up to her ears to warm them.

When he returned he was carrying an armful of dry sticks and moss. Putting them down in front of her, he started to arrange them carefully in two piles.

'What are you going to do now? Rub two sticks together to make a fire?' Actually, a fire seemed like a very good idea. It was sheltered enough here from the snow, which was blowing almost horizontally now.

'I could do, if you want. But this is easier.' He produced a battered tin from his pocket, opening it and taking out a flint and steel. Expertly striking the flint along the length of the steel, a spark flashed, lighting the pile of tinder that he'd made. He carefully transferred the embers to the nest of branches, and flames sprang up.

This was *definitely* a good idea. Flora held her hands

out towards the fire, feeling it begin to warm her face as Aksel fuelled it with some of the branches he'd set to one side. She felt herself beginning to smile, despite all he'd put her through.

'This is nice.' When he sat down next to her she gave him a smile.

'Better than your fire at home?' His tone suggested that he thought she'd probably say no.

'Yes. In a strange kind of way.' Flora was beginning to see how this appealed to Aksel. They'd only travelled a short way, but even though she could still see the lights of the village below her, she felt as if she was looking down from an entirely different planet. The effort of getting here had stripped everything away, and she felt unencumbered. Free, even.

CHAPTER THIRTEEN

AKSEL HAD PUSHED her hard, setting a pace that would stretch even an experienced walker. He'd wanted her exhausted, unable to sustain the smiles and the kindnesses that she hid behind and defended herself with. But Flora was a lot tougher than he'd calculated. She'd brushed away all his attempts to help her, and kept going until they'd got to the top of the hill.

But her smile *was* different now. As she warmed herself in front of the fire, Aksel could see her fatigue, and the quiet triumph in meeting the challenge and getting here. He'd found the real Flora, and he wasn't going to let her go if he could help it.

The blaze seemed to chase away the darkness that stood beyond it, illuminating the faces of the rocks piled around them as if this small shelter was the only place in the world. Right now, he wished it could be, because Flora was there with him.

'Now that we're here…' she flashed him a knowing smile '…what is it you want me to say?'

She knew exactly what he'd done. And it seemed that she didn't see the need for tact any more.

'Say whatever you want to say. What's said around a camp fire generally stays there.'

She thought for a moment. 'All right, then, since

you probably have a lot more experience of camp-fire truth or dare games, you can start. What's the thing you most want?'

Tricky question. Aksel wanted a lot of things, but he concentrated on the one that he could wish for with a good conscience.

'Keeping Mette from harm.'

'That's a good one. You'll be needing to get some practice in before she hits her teens.'

'What's that supposed to mean?' Aksel explored the idea for a moment and then held up his hand to silence Flora. 'On second thoughts, I don't think I want to know.'

'That's just as well, really. Nothing prepares any of us for our teens.'

She was smiling, but there was quiet sadness in her tone. Aksel decided that if he didn't call her bluff now, he was never going to. This wasn't about Mette any more, it was all about Flora.

'All right. I'm going to turn the question on its head. What would you avoid if you could go back in time?'

'How long have you got?'

'There's plenty of fuel for the fire here. I'll listen for as long as I can convince you to stay.'

She stared into the fire, giving a little sigh. 'Okay. Number one is don't fret over spots. Number two is don't fall in love.'

'The spots I can do something about. I'm not sure that I'm the one to advise anyone about how not to fall in love.' Aksel was rapidly losing control of his own feelings for Flora.

'All you can do is be there for her when she finds herself with a broken heart.'

The thought was terrifying. But he wouldn't have

to contend with Mette's teenage years just yet, and the question of Flora's heart was a more pressing one at the moment. He would never forgive himself if he lost this chance to ask.

'Who broke yours?'

'Mine?' Her voice broke a little over the word.

'Yes. What was his name?'

'Thomas Grant. I was nineteen. What was the name of the first girl who dumped you?'

Aksel thought hard. 'I don't remember. I went away on a summer camping trip with my friends, and by the time I got back she was with someone else. I don't think I broke her heart, and she didn't break mine.'

'If you can't remember her name, she probably didn't.' Flora was trying to keep this light, but these memories were obviously sad ones.'

'So… Thomas Grant. What did he do?'

'He…' Flora shrugged, as if it didn't matter. Aksel could tell that it did. He waited, hoping against agonised hope that if she looked into her own heart, and maybe his, she'd find some reason to go on.

'I went to university in Edinburgh to study physiotherapy. He was in the year above me, studying history…' She let out a sigh. 'I fell in love with him. I didn't tell my parents for a while, they were in Italy and I thought I'd introduce him to them first. I think my mum probably worked it out, though, and so Dad would have known as well.'

'An open secret, then.' It didn't sound so bad, but this had clearly hurt Flora. Aksel supposed that most really bad love affairs started well. The only real way to avoid hurt, was never to fall in love.

'Yes. We decided to tell our parents over the summer. We'd been talking about living together during our second year and…he seemed very serious. He even spoke about getting engaged. So I asked him to come to Italy with me for a fortnight. Mum and Dad really liked him and we had a great holiday. Alec wasn't too well that summer…'

Something prickled at the back of Aksel's neck. He knew that the end of this story wasn't a good one, and wondered what it could have to do with Flora's brother. His hand shook as he picked up a stick, poking the fire.

'You know, don't you, that cystic fibrosis is an inherited condition?' She turned to look at him suddenly.

'Yes.' Aksel searched his brain, locating the correct answer. 'It's a recessive gene, which means that both parents have to carry the gene before there's any possibility of a child developing cystic fibrosis.'

'Yes, that's right. Tom knew that my brother had cystic fibrosis, I never made any secret of it and I'd explained that since both my parents have the gene there was a good chance that I'd inherited it from one of them. Not from both, as my brother did, because I don't have the condition.'

'There's also a chance you haven't.'

She nodded. 'There's a twenty five percent chance of inheriting the gene from both parents. Fifty percent of inheriting it from one parent, and a twenty five percent chance of inheriting it from neither parent. The odds are against me.'

She didn't know. The realisation thundered through his head, like stampeding horses. Aksel hadn't really thought about it, but taking the test to find out whether she'd inherited the faulty gene seemed the logical thing to do, and he wondered why Flora hadn't. He opened his mouth and then closed it again, not sure how to phrase the question.

'When we came home to Scotland, we went to stay with his parents for a week. I told them about myself, and talked about my family. Tom told me later that I shouldn't have said anything. His parents didn't want their grandchildren to run the risk of inheriting my genes.'

'But that's not something you have to keep a secret...' Aksel had tried to just let her tell the story, without intervening, but this was too much. Anger and outrage pulsed in his veins.

'No. I don't think so either.'

'But... Forgive me if this is the wrong thing to say, I'm sure your whole family would rather that your brother didn't have cystic fibrosis. That doesn't mean it would be better if your parents had never married, or your brother hadn't been born.'

Tears suddenly began to roll down her cheeks. Maybe he *had* said the wrong thing. 'Thank you. That's exactly how I feel.'

'So they were wrong.' Surely *someone* must have told her that. 'What did your parents say?'

'Nothing. I didn't tell them, or Alec. It would have really hurt them, and I couldn't tell my own brother that someone thought he wasn't good enough. He's a fine man, and he's found someone who loves him and wants to raise a family with him.'

The defiance in her voice almost tore his heart out. Flora had stayed silent in order to keep her brother from hurt. She'd borne it all by herself, and her tears told him that with no way to talk about it and work it through, the wound she'd been dealt had festered.

'Did he listen? To his parents?'

'Yes, he listened. It probably had a lot to do with the

fact that they were funding his grant, and they threatened to withdraw their support if he didn't give me up.'

'Don't make excuses for him, Flora. Don't tell me that it's okay to even contemplate the thought that my daughter, or your brother, are worth less than anyone else.'

She laid her hand on his arm, and Aksel realised that he was shaking with rage. Maybe that was what she needed to see. Maybe this had hurt her for so long because she'd never talked about it, and never had the comfort of anyone else's reaction.

'No one's ever going to tell Mette that she's anything other than perfect. I'm not going to tell Alec that either.'

She'd missed herself out. Flora was perfect too, whether or not she carried the gene. But, still, she hadn't found out…

'You don't know whether you carry the gene or not, do you?'

She shook her head miserably.

'Flora, it's no betrayal of your brother to want to know.'

'I know that. In my head.' She placed her hand over her heart. 'Not here…'

Suddenly it was all very clear to him. 'You just want someone to trust you, don't you?'

Surprise showed in her face. 'I never thought of it that way. But, yes, if I take the test I want someone who'll stick by me whatever the result. If it turns out that I don't carry the gene, then I'll never know what would have happened if I did, will I? I suppose that's just foolishness on my part.'

It was the foolishness of a woman who'd been badly hurt. One that Aksel could respect, and in that moment he found he could love it too, because it was Flora's.

'Anyone who really knew you would trust you, Flora. *I* trust you.'

She gave a little laugh. 'Are you making me an offer?'

Yes. He'd offer himself to her in a split second, no thought needed. But he couldn't gauge her mood, and the possibility that she might not be entirely serious made him cautious.

'I just meant that you can't allow this to stop you from taking what you want from life. You deserve a lot more than this.'

The sudden anger wasn't something that Flora usually felt. There was dull regret and the occasional throb of pain, but this was bright and alive. And it hurt, cutting into her like a newly sharpened blade.

'And that's why you brought me up here, is it? To take me apart, piece by piece?' On this hilltop, with the village laid out below them like a child's toy, it felt as if she could sense the world spinning. And it was spinning a great deal faster at the thought that Aksel wanted to know what made her tick.

'I brought you here because…it's possible to walk away from the everyday. To see things more clearly than you might otherwise. And because I wanted to know why someone as beautiful and accomplished as you are seems so sad.'

No. She couldn't hear this. Aksel needed to take the rose-coloured spectacles off and understand who she really was.

'I'm *not* sad. I just see things the way they are.'

'That no one's ever going to accept you for who you are? That's just not true, Flora.'

'Well that's not my experience. And for your information, I didn't give up on men completely, I just… approach with caution.'

He shook his head, giving a sudden snort of laughter. 'I've never thought that sex was much like stopping at a busy road junction.'

Trust Aksel. But his bluntness was always refreshing. She'd been skirting around the word and now that he'd said it… They were talking about sex. And unless Flora was very much mistaken, this wasn't a conversation about sex generally, it was about the two of them having sex. Despite all the reasons why it shouldn't, the thought warmed her.

'I'm not going to have sex with you, Aksel. I can't…' Flora didn't have the words to tell him why and she buried her face in her hands in frustration.'

'You don't have to give me any reasons. *No* is enough.'

Not many men took rejection the way that Aksel did. He'd pushed her on so many other things but this was where he drew the line. His smile let slip a trace of regret, but he accepted what she said as her final answer.

It wasn't final, though. Everything they were to each other, all the things they'd shared came crashing in on Flora. She couldn't let him believe that she didn't want him. The problem was hers, and she had to own it.

'It's not you. It's me.'

'It's a good decision, Flora. We've both been hurt. I'm leaving in five weeks, and you'll be staying here.'

And despite all that she wanted him. Maybe *because* of it. A relationship that had to end in five weeks didn't seem quite so challenging as something that might end because her genetic make-up, something she couldn't change, wasn't deemed good enough.

'But I *want* to explain…'

His face softened suddenly. 'There's no better place to do that than at a camp fire.'

'After Tom left me I had a few no-strings affairs, with men I knew. I thought it would help me get over him, but…they just didn't turn out right.' Flora couldn't bring herself to be more specific than that. She was broken, and even Aksel couldn't mend her.

'They ended badly?' Aksel came to the wrong conclusion, which was hardly surprising. She was going to have to explain.

'No, they ended well, it was all very civilised. But things didn't work physically. For me, I mean…'

He was looking at her steadily. She could almost see his brain working, trying to fit each piece of the puzzle together, and when he did, she saw that too.

'I think that when two people have sex, an orgasm is something that you create together.'

Sex and *orgasm*. All in the same sentence and without a trace of embarrassment or hesitation. That made life a lot easier.

'I don't want to fake it with you, Aksel. And that's all I know how to do now.'

Tears began to roll down her cheeks. She wanted to be with him, and all that she'd lost hurt, in a way it never had before. Flora heard the scrape of Aksel's all-weather jacket as he reached for her, and she shied away.

'The way I see it is that we have a connection. I don't know why or how, but I do know that I want to be close to you, in whatever way seems right. Do you feel that?' The tenderness in his face made her want to cry even more.

'I feel it. But it's too late…' Flora made one last attempt to fight the growing warmth that wanted so much more than she was able to give.

'Maybe I just ask you to my place for a glass of wine. We put our feet up in front of the fire…'

Frustration made her open her mouth before she'd put her brain in gear. 'You don't get it, Aksel. I want wild and wonderful sex with you, and frankly a glass of wine doesn't even come close…' Flora clapped her hand over her mouth before she blurted anything else out.

The trace of a smile hovered around his lips. 'You're killing me, Flora. You know that, don't you?'

'I know. I'm sorry.'

'That's okay. You're worth every moment of it.' Aksel leaned forward, murmuring in her ear, 'Close your eyes. I won't touch you, just imagine…'

Here, alone with him on a windy hilltop, warmed by the crackling flames of a fire, Flora could do that. She could leave her anger behind, along with everything that stood between them, and visualise his kiss and the feel of his fingers tracing her skin. She shivered with pleasure, opening her eyes again.

'You're smiling.' He was smiling too. The knowledge that he'd been watching her face, knowing that she was thinking of him, sent tingles of sensuality down her spine.

'That was a great kiss. One of the best.'

He raised his eyebrows. 'So we kissed? I'm glad you liked it. Any chance I might get to participate in the next one?'

He was closer now, and Flora closed her eyes again. This time she didn't have to imagine the feel of his lips on hers. They were tender at first, like the brush of a feather, and when she responded to him the kiss deepened. She grabbed the front of his jacket, pulling him close, and felt his arms wrap around her.

Arousal hit her hard. The kind of physical yearning

that she'd searched for so many times and which had eluded her. It was impossible to be cold with Aksel.

'That was much better. There are some things I can't imagine all on my own.'

He grinned suddenly. 'I liked it much better, too.'

'Would you like…to continue this? Somewhere more comfortable?'

'Will you promise me one thing?' He hesitated.

'What's that?'

'Don't fake it with me, Flora. However this turns out is okay, but I need you to be honest with me.'

She stretched up, kissing his cheek. 'No secrets, no lies. It's what I want, too.'

The thought that Flora had trusted him enough to feel that this time might be different was both a pleasure and a challenge. Aksel kicked earth onto the smouldering remains of the fire and shouldered his backpack, holding her hand to guide her down the steepest part of the hill, which led most directly to her cottage.

Flora unlocked her front door, stepping inside and turning to meet his gaze when he didn't follow her.

'Have you changed your mind?'

'No. But it's okay for you to change yours. At any time.'

She replied by pulling him inside and kicking the door shut behind them, then stretching up to kiss him. It was impossible that she didn't feel the electricity that buzzed between them and when she gave a little gasp of pleasure, unzipping his jacket so that they could nuzzle closer, it felt dizzyingly arousing. He wanted her so badly, and she seemed to want him. The thought that he might not be able to please her as he wanted to clawed suddenly at his heart.

Maybe he shouldn't take that too personally. Flora had been quick enough to tell him that he wasn't in charge of everything that happened around him. He would be a kind and considerate lover, and if things didn't work out the way they wanted, he'd try not to be paralysed by guilt.

'I'll love you the best that I can…' The urgent promise tore from his lips.

'I know you will. That's all I want.' She took his hand and led him up the stairs.

CHAPTER FOURTEEN

HE WAS LETTING her dictate the pace. Caught between urgent passion and nagging fear, Flora had no idea what she wanted that pace to be. Aksel pulled back the patchwork quilt that covered her bed and sat down, waiting for her to come to him.

She opened the wooden box that stood on top of the chest of drawers, rummaging amongst the collection of single earrings and pieces of paper that she shouldn't lose. Right at the bottom, she found the packet of condoms.

'I have these. I hope they're not out of date...' Her laugh sounded shrill and nervous.

'Let's see.' He held out his hand, and she dropped the packet into it. Aksel examined it carefully and then shot her a grin. 'They're okay for another six months.'

'Good. Maybe we'll save one for later.' The joke didn't sound as funny as she'd hoped. In fact, it sounded stupid and needy, but his slow smile never wavered.

Aksel caught her hand, pressing it to his lips. She sank down onto his knee and he embraced her, kissing her again, and suddenly there was only him. Undressing her slowly. Allowing him to patiently explore all the things that pleased her was going to be a long journey, full of many delights.

'Stop…' She'd let out a sigh of approval when he got to the fourth button of her shirt, and he paused, laying his finger across her lips. 'Be still. Be quiet, for as long as you can.'

'How will you know the difference?' In Flora's rather limited experience, most men wanted as much affirmation as they could get.

He gave a small shrug. 'If I don't know the difference when I hear it, then I really shouldn't be here.'

Flora put her arms possessively around his neck. This guy was *not* going anywhere. And if he wanted her to fight the rising passion until there was no choice but to give in to it, then that was what she would do.

She kept silent, even though her limbs were shaking as he undressed her. The touch of his skin against hers almost made her cry out, but she swallowed the sound. Flora had never had a man attend to her pleasure so assiduously before, and while the physical effect of that was evident in the growing hunger she felt, the emotional effect was far more potent.

He moved back onto the bed, sitting up against the pillows, and lifting her astride him. Face to face, both able to see and touch wherever they pleased. She reached round to the nape of his neck, undoing the band that was tied around his hair, and letting it fall forward.

'Is that what you want?' He smiled suddenly.

'Yes.' She kissed him again. 'I want that too.'

Aksel laughed softly. 'What else?'

It was an impossible question. 'It's too long a list. I don't think I know where to start…'

'How about here, then?'

She felt his arm coil around her back, pulling her against his chest. His other hand covered her breast, and she felt the brush of his hair against her shoulder as he kissed her neck. Flora closed her eyes, trying to contain her excitement.

She couldn't help it. Her own ragged cry took her by surprise. Wordless, unmodulated, it was as if Mother Nature had climbed in through a window and stripped away everything but instinct and pleasure. She felt Aksel harden, as if this was what he'd been waiting for. If she'd known that it would feel so good, she'd have been waiting for it too.

'I want you so much, Flora…'

But he was going to wait until she was ready. Flora reached for the condoms, her hands shaking. When she touched him, to roll one on, she saw his eyes darken suddenly, an involuntary reaction that told her that he too was fighting to keep the last vestiges of control.

When she lifted her body up and took him inside, Aksel groaned, his head snapping back. And his large gentle hands spread across her back.

This time things were going to be different. No faking it, and… No thought either. She was thinking too much. Flora felt herself tremble in his arms, returning his kisses as the tension built. A soft, rolling tide that must surely grow.

He sensed it too. The fragile, tingling feeling rose and then dissipated, leaving her shaken but still unsatisfied. All the same, it was something. More than she'd experienced for a long time.

Aksel didn't question her, but as he held her against his chest she could hear his heartbeat. He wanted to know.

'It was nice… Something.'

'Not everything, though?' His chest heaved, with the same disappointment that Flora felt. Nagging frustration turned once more to hunger.

'Can we try again?' He was still inside her. Flora knew that he must feel that hunger too.

'Maybe we should stop. I don't want to hurt you.'

'You won't. I want to try again, and this time I... don't want you to be so gentle.'

He hesitated. Flora knew that she was asking a lot of him. *Just take me. Make me come.* Maybe that was too much weight of expectation to put on any man.

But she knew that he wanted to. She wriggled out of his arms, moving away from him. Bound now only by gaze.

'Don't you want me?'

'Are you crazy, Flora? You're everything any man could want, and far more than I have a right to take...'

'But I'm asking you to do it anyway.'

For one moment, she thought he'd turn away from her. And then he moved, so quickly that he'd caught her up and pinned her down on the bed before she knew quite what was happening. His eyes were dark, tender and fierce all at the same time.

'Take my hand.' His elbows were planted on either side of her, and she reached up, feeling his fingers curl around hers in what seemed a lot like a promise. Whatever happened next, he'd be right there with her.

They'd faced passion together, and then faced disappointment. The kind of disappointment that a man—Aksel, anyway—found difficult to forget. If Flora hadn't already given him a good talking to about the nature of guilt, he'd be feeling far too responsible, and much too guilty to do this.

But when he'd tipped her onto her back, she'd gasped with delight, smiling up at him and putting her hand in his when he asked her. Trapped in her gaze, entering her for the second time was even better than the first. Better than anything he'd ever done, and it felt liable to overshadow anything he ever *would* do again.

She wrapped her legs around his back, and he felt her skin against his, warm and welcoming. He began to move, and her eyes darkened as her pupils dilated. Her body responded to his, a thin sheen of perspiration forming on her brow.

Aksel watched her carefully, revelling in all the little signs of her arousal. Suddenly she gasped, her whole body quivering for a moment in anticipation and her hand gripping his tightly. And then that sweet, sweet feeling as Flora clung to him, choking out his name.

It broke him. His own orgasm tore through him, leaving him breathless, his heart hammering in his chest. When he was able to focus his eyes again, the one thing he'd most wanted was right in front of him.

'You're smiling.'

Flora reached up, her fingertips caressing the side of his face. 'So are you.'

'Yes.' Aksel had the feeling that it was one of those big, stupid after-sex smiles. One that nothing in this world could wipe from his face. 'I'm not even going to ask. I know you weren't faking that.'

The thought seemed to please her. As if she'd wanted him to feel the force of her orgasm, without having to be told.

'I loved it. Every moment.'

'I loved it too.'

Her hand was still in his, and he raised it to his lips, kissing her fingers. Easing away from her for a moment, he arranged the pillows and she snuggled against him, laying her head on his chest, so soft and warm in his arms. Aksel let out a sigh of absolute contentment.

* * *

Flora had slept soundly, and she woke before dawn. The clock on the bedside table glowed the numbers six and twelve in the darkness. Twelve minutes past six was more Aksel's wake-up call than it was hers.

But he was still asleep. And she felt wide awake and more ready to meet the day than she usually did at this time in the morning.

She moved, stretching her limbs, and his eyelids fluttered open. Those blue eyes, the ones that had taken her to a place she'd been afraid to go last night.

Afraid... The clarity of early morning thoughts wondered whether it might just be the case that she'd been afraid all these years. Afraid to give herself to a man who didn't trust her enough for her to trust him back.

But she'd given herself to Aksel. In one overwhelming burst of passion that really should have been accompanied by booming cannons, waving flags, and perhaps a small earthquake. And she couldn't help smiling every time she thought about it.

He stretched, and she felt the smooth ripple of muscle. Then he reached for her hand, the way he had last night. He was still here, with her. Still protecting her from the doubts and fears.

'God morgen.' He leaned over, kissing her brow.

He'd lapsed into Norwegian a few times last night as they'd lain curled together in the darkness. It was as if his thoughts didn't wait to be translated before they reached his tongue, and although Flora didn't know what he'd said, the way he'd said it had left her in no doubt. They had been words of love, whispered in the quiet warmth of an embrace, and meant to be felt rather than heard.

'Are you...?' Did he feel as good as she did? Did he

want this moment to last before the day began to edge it out? Flora couldn't think of a way of saying that in any language.

He chuckled, flexing his limbs again. 'I am. Are you?'

'Yes. I am too.'

All she needed was to lie here with him, holding his hand. But the sound of paws scrabbling at the kitchen door broke the silence.

'That's Dougal. He won't stop until I let him out…' Flora reluctantly tried to disentangle herself from Aksel's embrace, but he held on to her.

'I'll go. If you'd like to stay here, then I'll make you some breakfast.'

That would be nice, but even the time it took to make a couple of pieces of toast would be too long an absence. Flora let go of his hand and sat up. Even that was too much distance and she bent to kiss him again.

'I'll go. Are you hungry?'

He shook his head. 'Coffee or juice would be nice.'

She could let Dougal out, give him some food and water, and make coffee in two minutes flat if she hurried. 'Will you still be naked when I get back?'

Aksel grinned. 'You can count on it.'

She took the road into the estate as fast as the freezing morning would allow, and dropped Aksel off at the therapy centre at ten to nine, leaving him to take Dougal inside. If anyone noticed, then giving a next-door neighbour a lift into work couldn't excite any comment. She made it up to her office at one minute to nine, tearing off her coat and sitting down at her desk. Her first session of the morning wasn't until half past nine, and she could at least look as if she was at work, even though her mind was elsewhere.

Her whole body felt different, as if it was still bathed in Aksel's smile. Science told her that it was probably the effect of feel-good neuro-transmitters and hormones, but rational thought had its limitations. Aksel seemed to have no limitations at all.

When she closed her eyes, she could still feel him. He'd brushed off her suggestion that surely there wasn't anything more he might explore, and had taken her on a sensory journey that had proved her wrong. Aksel made foreplay into an exquisite art, and he obviously enjoyed it just as much as she did.

'Flora, we've a new patient....' Her eyes snapped open again to see Charles Ross-Wylde staring at her from the doorway. 'Are you all right?'

'Oh. Yes, I'm fine. Just concentrating.' Flora wondered if it looked as if she'd just spent two hours having stupendous sex. In the three years she'd been here, she'd never seen Charles show any interest in anything other than work, and he might not understand.

'Yes. Of course. As long as you're not feeling unwell.'

'No!' She could have sounded a little less emphatic about that as Charles was beginning to look puzzled. Best get down to business. 'You've a new patient for me to see...?'

The day wasn't without its victories. Andy Wallace had mentioned that Aksel had popped in, bringing Mette with him, and that they'd talked about ice carving and the long road that led across the Andes. The friendship seemed to have given Andy the final push to take his first step unaided.

Flora had tried to conceal her blushes when Andy had talked about Aksel, but he was in the habit of watching everyone closely. When they'd finished their session together, Andy had asked her to give Aksel his best when she saw him, smiling quietly when Flora had said she would.

Dougal seemed a little calmer when she picked him up from the centre, and didn't make his usual frenetic dash around the cottage. He lay down in front of the fire, growling quietly.

'What's the matter, Dougal?' Flora bent down to stroke him, and he gave her his usual response, his tail thumping against the hearth. She walked into the kitchen, wondering if he'd follow, and he bounded past her, pawing at the cupboard where she kept his food. Whatever it was, it didn't seem to have affected his appetite.

She knew that Aksel would come. He'd be late, staying at the clinic until Mette was ready to go to bed, but he'd come. She heard the sound of the battered SUV outside, and smiled. He usually walked back from the castle, but tonight he was in a hurry.

The doorbell rang and she opened the door. Aksel was leaning against the opening of the porch, grinning.

'Are you coming in?'

'Are you going to ask me in?' There didn't seem to be any doubt in his mind that she would.

'Since you're holding a bottle of wine, then yes.'

He stepped inside, and Flora took the bottle from his hand, putting it down on the hall table. Without giving him the chance to take off his coat, she kissed him.

'I thought you wanted the wine,' he teased her, kissing her again hungrily.

'Isn't that just an excuse? To call round?'

'Yes, it's an excuse. Although if you'd prefer to just sit around the fire and drink it...' Aksel seemed determined to give her the choice, even though their kisses had already shown that neither of them wanted to spend the rest of evening anywhere else than in bed.

'No. I want you stone-cold sober. Upstairs.'

Aksel chuckled. 'I'll have you stone-cold sober, too. And calling out my name, the way you did last night.'

The thought was almost too much, but there was still something she had to do. Dougal was lying in front of the fire, still making those odd growling sounds.

'Will you take a look at Dougal first?'

'Of course. What's the matter with him?' Aksel walked into the sitting room, bending down to greet Dougal.

'I'm not sure. He's eating fine, and he doesn't seem to be in any pain. But he's making these odd noises.'

Aksel nodded, trying to stop Dougal from licking him as he examined him. Then he nodded in satisfaction. 'There's absolutely nothing wrong with him. He's trying to purr.'

'What?' That didn't sound like much of a diagnosis. 'Like a cat?'

'Yes.' Aksel tickled Dougal behind his ears and he rolled on his back, squirming in delight and growling. 'When I arrived at work this morning, I went to the office to finish up my report for Esme on the dog visiting scheme. I took Dougal with me to keep him out of the way as everyone was busy.'

'And you have a cat in the office at the canine therapy centre? Isn't that a bit of an explosive mix?'

Aksel shrugged, getting to his feet. 'Cats and dogs aren't necessarily natural enemies. A dog's instinct is to chase smaller animals, and a cat's instinct is to sense that as an attack, and flee. It's all a big misunderstanding, really.'

'Okay, so there was a cat at the centre...'

'Yes, someone brought it in, thinking that they might take it. Esme wasn't about to turn it away because... Esme doesn't know *how* to turn an animal in need away. And Dougal's natural instinct seems to be to make friends with everything that moves, and so by the end of the morning the two of them were curled up together. The cat was purring away and Dougal... I guess he was just trying to make friends.'

'So now we've got a dog that thinks he's a cat on our hands.' Flora looked down at Dougal, and he trotted up to her, rubbing his head against her leg.

'Maybe he'll grow out of it.'

Maybe. It made the little dog even more loveable, if that was at all possible. And talking of loveable...

'So... Mette and Kari are at the castle, and they're both fast asleep by now. Dougal's okay, apart from a few minor identity issues.' She approached Aksel, reaching up to wrap her arms around his neck. 'That just leaves you and me.'

'And more than twelve hours before it's time to go back to work.' Aksel grinned, and picked her up in his arms.

CHAPTER FIFTEEN

THEY LAY ON the bed together, naked. Aksel had made love to her, and each time he did, it was more mind-blowing than the last. Things were going to have to plateau at some point, or Flora's nerve endings were going to fry.

'You know, don't you? When someone you're with has an orgasm.' Flora wondered whether the other guys she'd been with had known too. Maybe they had, and just hadn't cared.

'I do with you.' He grinned lazily. 'I suppose you want to know how.'

Yes, she did. Very much, because it seemed to please him so much. 'Tell me.'

'Your pupils dilate. You start to burn up, and you cry out for me. Then your muscles start to contract…'

'You like that?' Flora traced her fingertips across the ripple of muscles in his chest.

'You know I do. And you can't fake any of that.'

'Strictly speaking… I think you could try.'

'No, you wouldn't fool me.' Aksel curled his arm around her, pulling her a little closer. 'What we have is honesty, and I'd know if that ever changed.'

It was a good answer. They *were* honest with each other. It had been something that had just happened from day one. Perhaps it was that which had guided them past all the traps and obstacles, and led them here.

'Well, honestly…' Flora propped herself up on one arm so that she could look into his eyes '…you are the most perfect, beautiful man I've ever seen.'

He didn't believe that. Aksel thought that his body was a workhorse that got him from one place to another, along with anything he carried with him. Vanity didn't occur to him.

'I'd urge you to make an appointment with your optician if you think I'm perfect.'

'You have a great body. *Very* nice arms.'

'Uneven toes…' He wiggled the toes on his left foot, two of which had been amputated above the distal phalangeal joint.

'Not very uneven. You only lost the tips of your toes, and they tell a story.'

'One that I won't forget in a hurry. Frostbite's painful.'

'And the mark on your arm?'

'That's where I was bitten by a snake. In South America.'

'And this one?' Flora ran her finger across a scar on his side.

'I was in a truck that tipped over while fording a river. The current turned out to be a bit stronger than we anticipated.'

'And you have a couple of small lumps along your clavicle where you broke it. The muscles in your shoulders are a little tight because you worry. A little tension in your back because Mette loves it when you carry her on your shoulders. Most people's bodies reflect who they are, and how they've lived, and yours is perfect.'

'And you… You really *are* perfect, Flora. You're

made of warmth and love, and that makes you flaw-lessly beautiful.' He chuckled. 'Apart from that little scar on your knee.'

'It's not as good a story as yours are. I fell off my bike when I was a kid.'

Aksel reached up, pulling her down for a kiss. 'It's a great story. The scar's charming, along with the rest of you.'

Flora ran her fingers through his hair. Thick and blond, most women would kill for hair like that.

'Okay…so what's with the hair, then?' He knew that she liked it spread over his shoulders, instead of tied back, especially when they made love.

'It makes you look free, like a wild creature. Is that why you grew it so long?'

He shrugged. 'I don't know. Maybe I just never got around to cutting it. I like the sound of that, though.'

She kissed him again. 'Don't get around to cutting it, Aksel. That's perfect too.'

Aksel was happy. He felt free when he made love to Flora. And even when they weren't making love, the contentment that he felt whenever he was in her company was making him feel that maybe there was a little life left in his battered, careworn heart.

Tonight he'd be sleeping apart from Flora, though. He'd arranged to bring Mette home for the afternoon, and she'd stay the night with him at the cottage, before returning to the clinic the next morning. It had gone without saying that this was something that he needed to do alone.

He'd decided on some games, and had bought all of Mette's favourite foods. When he arrived home with her, he spread the colourful quilt on her bed, walking her around the cottage to remind her of the layout.

Everything just clicked into place, as if he'd been there all of Mette's life. She enjoyed her afternoon, and dozed in his arms as he told her the story about how crocodiles and penguins had helped him to reach the top of a high mountain in safety.

'I want to say goodnight to Mama.'

Aksel realised suddenly that in his determination to get everything right, he'd forgotten all about Mette's electric candle and had left it by her bed at the clinic. But it was important that his daughter felt she could speak to her mother whenever she wanted to. He reached for one of the Christmas candles that Flora had arranged on his mantelpiece, putting it into the grate.

'We'll use Tante Flora's candle, shall we? Just for tonight.'

Mette nodded, and Aksel fetched matches from the kitchen and lit the candle. They sat together on the hearthrug, saying their goodnights, and Mette leaned forward and blew out the candle. Aksel carried her upstairs, settled her into her bed and kissed her goodnight.

At a loose end now, and not wanting to go downstairs just yet in case Mette stirred, he went to his own bedroom and lay down on the bed, staring at the ceiling. This was the first night that he'd been completely alone with her, and it was a responsibility that brought both happiness and a measure of terror.

Aksel woke up to the feeling of something tugging at his arm. Opening his eyes, he realised that Kari had hold of his sweater in her jaws and was pulling as hard as she could to make him wake up and get off the bed. A moment later the smoke alarm started to screech a warning that made his blood run cold.

'Mette…' He catapulted himself off the bed and into her room. The bedclothes were drawn to one side and Mette was nowhere to be seen. Remembering that children had a habit of hiding when they sensed danger, he wrenched open the wardrobe doors, but she wasn't there either.

As he ran downstairs, he could smell smoke, but he couldn't see where it was coming from. Mette was curled up at the bottom of the stairs, crying, and he picked her up, quickly wrapped her in his coat, then opened the front door and ran with her to the end of the path.

'Papa. Kari made me go away from the fire.'

Cold remorse froze his heart suddenly. He could see a flicker of flame through the sitting-room window. Kari must have herded Mette out of danger, shutting the door behind them as she'd been taught. He held his daughter close, feeling tears run down his face.

'It's all right, Mette. Everything's all right. You're safe…'

The sound of an alarm beeping somewhere woke Flora up. It wasn't coming from inside the cottage, and she rolled drowsily out of bed, sliding her feet into her slippers and peering out of the window. She saw Aksel outside with Mette in his arms, Kari sitting obediently at his feet.

Running downstairs, she grabbed her coat, not stopping to put it on. As soon as she was outside, the faint smell of smoke hit her and she hurried over to Aksel.

'Are you both all right?'

He raised his face towards her, and Flora saw tears. Mette realised that she was there, although she must be practically blind in the darkness, and reached out from the warm cradle of his arms.

'Papa says we're safe.' Aksel seemed too overwhelmed to speak, and Mette volunteered the information.

'That's right. You're safe now.'

She looked up at Aksel questioningly, and he brushed his hand across his face. 'There's a fire, I think it's pretty much contained to the sitting room. Will you take Mette while I go and have a look.'

'No, Aksel. Wait for the fire brigade. Have you called them?'

'My phone's inside. Please, take her.'

It seemed that Aksel was more comfortable with dealing with the situation than he was with taking care of his daughter right now. Flora wondered how the fire had started. She took Mette, holding the little girl tight in her arms.

'Papa's just looking to see how big the fire is.' As Aksel walked back up the path, peering through the front windows, Mette craned round to keep him in view.

'It's all right, he's quite safe. He isn't getting too close, so the fire won't burn him.'

Mette seemed more confident of that than Flora felt. 'My papa fights crocodiles.'

'There you are, then. If he can fight crocodiles then a little fire will be easy...'

She watched, holding her breath as Aksel walked back towards them, his face set in a look of grim determination.

'It's just the hearth rug at the moment. Will you look after Mette while I go and put it out?'

'You should leave it, until the fire brigade gets here. We'll go inside and call them now...'

'I can put it out, there's a fire extinguisher in the kitchen. And if we leave it, then it may spread to the chimney. I don't know how long it's been since it's been swept, and I want to avoid that.'

A chimney fire could easily spread to her cottage. Flora dismissed the thought. What mattered was that they were all safe. 'No, Aksel…'

He was going anyway. She may as well accept it, and work with what was inevitable. Flora transferred Mette into his arms for a moment while she wriggled out of her own coat, wrapping it around the little girl so that his was no longer needed.

'If you must go, put your coat on, it'll protect your arms. And put a pair of boots on as well.'

He looked down at his feet, seeming to realise for the first time that he was only wearing a pair of socks. 'Okay. You're right. You'll take Mette inside?'

She was shivering, her pyjamas giving no protection against the wind. But she wasn't moving until she saw that Aksel was safe. 'If you must go, go now. Before the fire gets any worse. And no heroics, Aksel. Back off if it looks to be getting worse.'

He nodded. Giving Kari a curt command, he strode back up the path, opening the door to his cottage.

Kari was on the alert now, sniffing the air and looking around. Aksel had clearly ordered the dog to protect them, and she was taking her task seriously. Flora hugged Mette close, pulling her coat down around the child's feet.

'Papa's just going to put out the fire. He won't be a minute.' She said the words as if it was nothing. Maybe it *was* nothing to Aksel, but right now it seemed a great deal to her.

She watched as Aksel's dark figure approached the

fire. A plume of shadows emitted from the fire extinguisher and the flames died almost immediately. He
disappeared for a moment and then reappeared with a
bucket, tipping its contents over the ashes to make sure
that the fire was well and truly out.

Okay. Everything was okay, and now all she wanted
to do was to get warm. By the time Aksel reappeared
her teeth were chattering.

'Everything all right?'

'No.' He took his coat off and wrapped it around her.
'You're freezing.'

'The fire's out, though...' He was hurrying her towards her own front door, his arm around her shoulders.

'Yes. I made sure of it.' Aksel pushed the door open
and glorious warmth surrounded her suddenly. 'Come
and sit down.'

He was gentle and attentive, but his eyes were dead.
Whatever he felt was locked behind an impervious barrier.

'Stay with Mette and I'll make a hot drink.' Flora
was trying to stop shivering.

'No, I'll do that. You sit and get warm.' He picked
up the woollen blanket that was folded across the back
of the sofa and waited until Flora had sat down, then
tucked it around her and Mette. Then he disappeared
into the kitchen.

He came back with two cups of tea, and Flora drank
hers while he went upstairs to the bathroom to wash
his hands and face. When he came back and sat down,
Mette crawled across the sofa, snuggling against him
and yawning. Flora waited for the little girl to fall asleep
before she asked the inevitable question.

'What happened?'

'I was asleep upstairs. Kari and Mette were downstairs, and Kari herded Mette out into the hallway and shut the door. Then she came to wake me up.' He held out his hand, and Kari ambled over to him. He fondled the dog's ears and she laid her head in his lap.

'You taught her to do that?'

He nodded. 'I didn't even know that Mette was out of bed.'

'What was she doing downstairs?'

'From the looks of it, she'd gone downstairs and lit a candle in the grate. It must have fallen over onto the hearth rug…' His voice cracked and broke with emotion.

'Where did she get the matches from?' Aksel had clearly already tried and convicted himself, without even listening to the case for the defence.

'They were in one of the high cupboards in the kitchen. I didn't think she could get to them, but when I went back inside I saw that she'd dragged a chair across the room. She must have climbed up on it, then got up onto the counter top and into the cupboard.'

It was quite an achievement for a six-year-old with poor sight. 'What made her so determined to light a candle in the middle of the night?' Flora's hand flew to her mouth. She knew the answer.

'When I packed her things, I forgot her electric candle. So I lit a real one for her. It's all my…' He fell silent as Flora flapped her hand urgently at him.

'Don't. You're not to say it. It's *not* your fault.'

'That's not borne out by the facts.' His face was blank, as if he'd accepted his guilt without any question.

Flora took a breath. Whatever she said now had to be convincing. 'Look, Aksel, I talk to a lot of parents in the course of my work. The one thing that everyone agrees on is that you can't watch your children twenty-four hours a day. It isn't possible. But you've come up with a good second-best, and you trained Kari to watch over her.'

He narrowed his eyes. 'You're just making excuses for me.'

'No, I'm not. You let her say goodnight to her mother, Aksel, she needs to do that. And you put the matches away, somewhere that should have been out of her reach.'

'She *did* reach them, though.'

'Well, you might be able to take part of the blame for that one. She takes after her father in being resourceful. I imagine she has all kinds of challenges up her sleeve...'

'All right. You're making me panic now.'

If he didn't like that, then he *really* wasn't going to like the next part. 'You need to let her know, Aksel, that she mustn't play with matches.'

He sighed. 'Yes. I know. Her grandmother always told her off when she was naughty...'

'Yeah, right. You can't rely on her to be the bad guy now.'

Right on cue, Mette shifted fitfully in his arms, opening her eyes. 'Papa, the fire's out?'

'Yes.'

'Did you save all the crocodiles, and the penguins?' Mette was awake again now, and probably ready to play. Aksel's face took on an agonised look, knowing that the time had come for him to be the bad guy.

'Yes, the crocodiles and penguins are all fine. Mette, there's something I have to say to you.'

Mette's gaze slid guiltily towards Flora and she struggled not to react. Aksel had to do this by himself.

'I love you very much, Mette, and you know that you

can talk to Mama any time you want.' He started with the positive. 'But you mustn't touch matches or light candles when I'm not there. And you mustn't climb up onto cupboards either. You could hurt yourself very badly.'

A large tear rolled down Mette's cheek. Flora could almost see Aksel's heart breaking.

'Is the fire my fault, Papa?'

'No. It's my fault. I didn't tell you not to do those things, and I should have. But I want you to promise not to do them again.' He waited a moment for Mette to respond. 'You have to say it, please, Mette. "I promise…"'

Mette turned the corners of her mouth down in a look of abject dismay. Even Flora wanted to forgive her immediately, and she wondered whether getting to the North Pole had presented quite as much of a challenge to Aksel as this.

'I promise, Papa.' Another tear rolled down her cheek and Aksel nodded.

'Thank you.' Finally he broke, cuddling Mette to his chest. 'I love you very much.'

'I love you too, Papa.'

'What was it you wanted to say to Mama?' He kissed the top of his daughter's head.

'I forgot to tell her all about our house. And that I like my room…'

'All right. We'll go back to the clinic and find your candle. And you can tell Mama all about it.'

'When?'

'Right now, Mette.'

Mette nodded, satisfied with his answer, and curled up in his arms, her eyelids drooping again drowsily. Flora handed him the woollen blanket and he wrapped his daughter in it, leaving her to sleep. Finally his gaze found Flora's.

'Forget wrestling crocodiles. That was the most difficult thing…'

'*Have* you wrestled a crocodile?'

'Actually, no. Mette thinks I have, but that's not as dangerous as it sounds because she thinks that her cuddly crocodile is a true-to-life representation. I tell her a story about crocodiles and penguins that I met when I was in the Andes.'

'Right. Even I could wrestle a cuddly toy. I didn't know there were crocodiles in the Andes.'

'There aren't. She added a few things in as we went along. The penguins act as tour guides and show you the right way to go.'

'Penguins are always the good guys.'

He nodded, finally allowing himself a smile. 'I'm going to take her back to the clinic, now.'

'What? It's three in the morning, Aksel. Why don't you just stay here?'

'I said that we'd go now so that she can talk to Lisle. And I want her to wake up somewhere that's familiar to her.'

'But…' Flora saw the logic of it but this felt wrong. 'She's asleep. It seems a shame to take her out into the cold now when you can let her sleep and take her back first thing in the morning.'

'You heard me promise her, Flora. I'll stay the night so that I'll be there whenever she wakes up. You can't help me with this.'

There was more to this than just practicality. More than a promise. She could feel Aksel slipping away from her, torn by his guilt and the feeling that he'd let his daughter down.

Flora had to let him go. He'd feel differently about this in the morning and realise that he could be a father to Mette and a lover to her as well.

'Okay. You'll be back in the morning?'

'Yes.' He reached for her, and Flora slid towards him on the sofa. His kiss was tender, but it held none of the fire of their nights together.

'You're tired. You'll sleep in?'

If she could sleep at all. Dread began to pulse through her. What if he decided that this was where their relationship had to end? She pushed the thought away. She *had* to trust Aksel. There was no other choice.

'I'll phone in and take a couple of hours off work, I don't have any patients to see in the morning. I'll be here when you get back.'

He nodded. 'I'll come as soon as I can.'

CHAPTER SIXTEEN

FLORA WAS UP early and let herself into Aksel's cottage with the spare key that he'd left with her. The place stank of smoke, and there were deposits of soot all around the sitting room, but apart from that the damage was relatively minor. She tidied the kitchen, putting away the evidence of Mette having climbed up to reach the matches, and tipped the remains of the hearth rug into a rubbish bag. Then she brewed a cup of strong coffee to jolt her tired and aching limbs into action and started to clean.

Ten minutes after she'd returned to her own cottage for more coffee and some breakfast, Flora heard the throaty roar of the SUV outside in the lane. Running out to embrace him seemed as if it would only make the awful what-ifs of last night a reality again, and she forced herself to sit down at the kitchen table and wait for him to come to her.

When he did, he looked as tired as she felt. But the first thing he did, when she let him into the cottage, was hug her. His body seemed stiff and unresponsive, but it was still a hug. Things were going to be all right.

'I appreciate the clean-up, but I was hoping to find you'd slept in this morning.' He sat down at the kitchen table while she made him coffee.

'Your early mornings are starting to rub off on me.' It wouldn't do to tell him she'd been awake most of the night, worrying. Normal was good at the moment, even if she was going to have to fake it.

She put his coffee down in front of him and sat down. 'So how's Mette?'

'Fine. She told me that a fire's a very second-league adventure. Fighting crocodiles is much more exciting.' He smiled suddenly, and Flora laughed.

'Shame. If we could have tempted a few out of the loch then you could have done that too.'

He laughed, but there was no humour in his eyes. They were going through the motions of believing in life again, without any of the certainty.

'Aksel, I... What happened last night was a terrible accident. Mette's all right and so are you.'

'Yes. I know.' He might know it, but he didn't seem to believe it.

'You're a good father. You can keep her safe. We'll do it together, we'll go through the whole cottage and check everything... We can learn from this and make sure that it doesn't happen again.'

He looked at her blankly. 'We?'

'Yes, *we*. You're not alone with this, we'll do it to-gether.'

'*I* need to do it, Flora. When I go back to Oslo...' They both knew what happened then. When he went back to Oslo, she would stay here in Cluchlochry, and it would be an end to their relationship. Aksel couldn't bring himself to rely on her.

She'd thought about this. It was far too early to say anything, but maybe it needed to be said now. Maybe they both needed to know that their relationship didn't have to be set in stone, and that it did have a future.

'When you go back to Oslo, there's nothing to stop me from visiting, is there?' Flora decided to start slowly with this.

He looked up at her. The look in his eyes told Flora that maybe she hadn't started slowly enough.

'I just… It seems so very arbitrary, to put an end date on this. What we have.'

'We'll always have it, Flora. There's no end date on that.'

It was a nice thought. A romantic thought, which didn't bear examination. Over time, the things they'd shared would be tarnished and forgotten.

'That's not what I meant. I was thinking in a more… literal sense.' Flora's heart began to beat fast. This wasn't going quite the way she'd hoped, and she was beginning to dread what Aksel might say.

'You're thinking of coming to Norway?'

'Well… I'm a free agent. I can come and see you, can't I?'

This wasn't about Mette any more. It was about Aksel's determination to do things on his own. About hers to find someone who trusted her. It was a bright winter morning, warm and cosy inside with snow falling outside the window, but Flora could feel the chill now, instead of the heat.

He was still and silent for a moment. When he looked at her, Flora could only see the mountain man, doggedly trudging forward, whatever the cost. Whatever he left behind.

'Do you seriously think that if you came to Norway, I'd ever let you go?'

Flora swallowed hard. That sounded like a *no*.

'Okay.' She shrugged, as if it didn't matter to her. 'That's okay, I won't come, then.'

'Flora…' He reached across the table, laying his hand on her arm. The sudden warmth in his eyes only made her angry and she pulled away from him.

'I heard what you said, Aksel.' He didn't want her. Actually, not wanting her would have been relatively okay. Flora knew that he wanted her but that he was fighting it.

'I didn't mean…' He let out a breath, frustration showing in his face. Clearly he didn't know quite what he meant. Or maybe he did, and he wasn't going to say it. In a moment of horrible clarity Flora knew exactly what he meant.

Aksel wouldn't take the risk of things becoming permanent between them. She'd trusted him, and he was pushing her away now. They'd tried to be happy—and surely they both deserved it. But Aksel was going to turn his back on that and let her down.

'Don't worry about it. I know what you're saying to me. That you're in control of this, and it comes to an end when you go. Well, I'm taking control of it and it ends now. I'm going to work.'

'Flora…' he called after her, but Flora had already walked out of the kitchen. Pulling on her coat, she picked up Dougal's lead, which was all she needed to do to prompt him to scrabble at the front door.

He'd made her feel him. He'd been inside her, in more ways than just physically, and she'd dared to enjoy it. Dared to want more. When he caught her up in the hallway, and she turned to look at him, she still loved him. It would always be this way with Aksel, and she had to make the break now, for her own sanity's sake.

'Can't we talk about this?'

'I think we've said all we need to say, haven't we?

If you see me again, just look the other way, Aksel. I don't want to speak to you, ever again.'

She pulled open the front door, slamming it in his face. Aksel would be gone by the time she got home from work this evening, and hopefully he'd take what she'd said seriously. If they saw each other in the village, or at the clinic, she'd be looking the other way, and so should he.

He'd messed up. Big time. Aksel had been in some very tight spots, but he couldn't remember one as terrifying and hopeless as this.

He'd spent most of the night sitting in the chair next to Mette's bed, staring into the darkness and wondering how he could make things right. How he could be a father to Mette, and love Flora as well. He'd come to no conclusion.

Last night's fire wasn't the issue. But it had shaken him and dredged up feelings that he'd struggled to bury. Lisle's lies. His guilt over not having been there for Mette. And when Flora had spoken of coming to Norway to visit…

He knew what she'd been doing. She'd been trying to patch things up and convince them both that nothing was the matter. Flora always tried to mend what was broken, and he loved her for it. But she deserved someone better than him. Now that he was responsible for Mette, could he ever be the man that Flora could trust?

The question hammered at him, almost driving him to his knees. He'd travelled a long way, and it had seemed that he'd finally found the thing that he hadn't even known he'd been looking for. Did he really have to turn his back on Flora? Aksel couldn't bear it, but if it had to be done, then it was better for it to be done now.

He took a gulp of his coffee, tipping the rest into the sink and clearing up the kitchen. Then he signalled to Kari to follow him out into the cold, crisp morning air. As Aksel shut Flora's front door behind him, he knew only two things for sure. That this hurt far more than anything he'd experienced before. And that now he had to go on the most important journey of his life. One that he'd told himself he'd never make, and which might just change everything.

Anger had propelled Flora through the morning. But anger was hard to sustain, particularly where Aksel was concerned. When she couldn't help thinking about his touch, the honesty in his clear blue eyes, and the way he gave himself to her...

But now he'd taken it all away. As the day wore on, each minute heavy on her hands, the sharp cutting edge of her fury gave way to a dull ache of pain. She hurried home after work, trying not to notice that his cottage was quiet and dark, no lights showing from the windows.

Flora spent a sleepless night, thinking what might have been, and wondering if a miracle might happen to somehow bring it all back again. The feeble light of morning brought her answer. It had been good between them, and Aksel was the man she'd always wanted. But he couldn't handle the guilt of feeling himself torn in two directions, and Flora couldn't handle trusting him and then having him push her away.

She'd decided that she must go and see Mette, because it wouldn't be fair to just desert the little girl. Making sure that Aksel wasn't at the clinic that morning, she spent an hour with Mette, putting on a happy face even though she was dying inside, and then went back to her treatment room, locking the door so that she could cry bitter tears.

It seemed that Aksel had got the message. He knew that she didn't want to see him, and he was avoiding her too. He was perceptive enough to know that things weren't going to work out between them, and it was better to break things off now. He might even be happy about that. Flora was a claim on his time and attention that he didn't need right now.

The second time she passed his cottage, on the way to her own front door, was no easier than the first. It looked as empty as it had last night, and Flora wondered whether he'd found somewhere else to stay.

But then she'd gone to the window to close the curtains and seen the light flickering at the top of the hill, partly obscured by the ruins of the old keep. Flora knew exactly where Aksel was now. This was his signal fire, and it was meant for her.

He might have just phoned... If Aksel had called her then she could have dismissed the call, and that would have been an end to it. But the fire at the top of the hill burned on, seeming to imprint itself on her retinas even when she wasn't staring out of the window at it.

She needed something to take her mind off it. Her Christmas card list was always a good bet, and she fetched it, along with the boxes of cards that she'd bought, sitting down purposefully in front of the fire with a pen and a cup of tea. But her hand shook as she wrote. Wishing friends and family a happy Christmas always made her smile but, knowing that this year she'd be spending hers without Aksel, the Christmas greetings only emphasised her own hollow loneliness.

She gathered the cards up, deciding to leave them

for another day. Drawing the curtains apart, she saw the light of the fire still twinkling out in the gloom…

Aksel had built the fire knowing that Flora would see it. And knowing that he'd stay here all night if he had to, and then the following night, and each night until she came. However long it took, he'd be here when Flora finally decided to climb the hill.

Maybe it wouldn't be tonight. It was getting late, and the lights of her cottage had been flicking on and off, tracing what seemed to be an irregular and undecided progress from room to room. Soon the on and off of the lights upstairs would signal that Flora had gone to bed, which left little chance that she'd come to him tonight.

All the same, he'd be here. Wrapped in his sleeping bag, until the first rays of dawn told him that he had to move now, work the cold stiffness from his limbs, and get on with another day.

His fire was burning low, and he went to fetch more fuel from the pile of branches that he'd stacked up nearby. The blaze began to climb through the dry twigs, brightening as it went, and he missed the one thing he had been waiting and watching for. When he looked down toward the village again, Flora's porch light was on.

He cursed his own inattentiveness, reaching for his backpack. His trembling fingers fumbled with the small binoculars, and he almost dropped them on the ground. Focussing them down towards Flora's cottage, he saw her standing in her porch, wearing her walking boots and thick, waterproof jacket, and looking up in his direction. Aksel almost recoiled, even though he knew that she couldn't see him. And then she went back inside the cottage again.

He bit back his disappointment. It had been too much to expect from this first night. But then she reappeared, pulling a hat onto her head, and as she started to walk away from the cottage a small thread of light issued from her hand. He smiled, glad that she'd remembered to bring a torch with her.

Aksel tried to calm himself by wondering which route she'd take. The most direct was the steepest, and it would be an easier walk to circle around the bottom of the hill before climbing it. She crossed the bridge that led from the village to the estate and disappeared for a moment behind a clump of bushes. And then he saw her again, climbing the steep, stony ground and making straight for him.

He waited, his eyes fixed on the small form labouring up the hill. When she fell, and the torch rolled skittishly back a few feet down the slope, he sprang to his feet, cursing himself for bringing her out here in the dark. But before he could run towards her, she was on her feet again, retrieving the torch.

Aksel forced himself to sit back down on the stony bench he'd made beside the fire. He *had* to wait, even though it was agony to watch Flora struggle like this. He had to trust that she'd come to him, and she had to know that she would too, however hard the journey.

His heart beat like a battering ram, and he suddenly found it difficult to breathe. The fire crackled and spat, flames flaring up into the night. The moment he'd longed for so desperately would be here soon, and despite working through every possible thing she might say to him, and what he might say in reply, he was completely unprepared.

When she finally made it to the top of the hill, she seemed rather too out of breath to say anything. Flora switched off her torch, putting her hands on her hips in a stance that indicated she wasn't going to take any nonsense from him.

'It's warmer by the fire…' He ventured the words and she frowned.

'This had better be good, Aksel. If you think I came up here in the middle of the night to hear something you might have said anywhere…'

'When might I have said it? You told me you never wanted to speak to me again.'

The logic had seemed perfect to him, but it only seemed to make her more angry. 'You could have slipped a note under my front door. It's not so far for either of us to walk.'

'I trusted you to come to me.'

She stared at him. 'I really wish you hadn't said that.'

Because it was the one thing he could have said to stop her from walking away from him? A sharp barb of hope bit into his heart.

'Sit down. Please.'

Flora pressed her lips together, hesitating for agonising moments. Then she marched over to the stone slab that he was sitting on, plumping herself down on the far end so that their shoulders didn't touch.

She was angry still, but at least she was sitting down. Aksel wasn't sure where to start, but before he could organise his thoughts, Flora did it for him.

'Where have you been, Aksel? You haven't been at the cottage and Mette told me that you weren't coming in to see her today.'

'You went to see Mette?' Of course she had. Flora wouldn't let a little thing like a broken heart get in the way of making sure that a child wasn't hurt by her absence. And from the way that she seemed to hate him so much, Aksel was in no doubt that her heart was just as wounded as his.

'Yes. I made sure that you weren't there already.'

Good. Hate was a lot more akin to love than indifference was. 'I was in Oslo.'

'Oslo? For two days?'

'Just a day. I went to see Mette yesterday afternoon and left straight from there. I got back a couple of hours ago. The flight only takes an hour from Glasgow.'

She turned the edges of her mouth down. 'And it was such a long way when I was thinking of making the trip.'

He deserved that. 'I meant it when I said that I wouldn't be able to let you go, and that this is your home. I went to Oslo to talk with Olaf and Agnetha. About making this *my* home and Mette's.'

'You need their permission?' He could hear the fight beginning to go out of Flora's tone. She was starting to crumble, and if she wasn't in his arms yet, then maybe she would be if he gave it time.

'No, I don't. I'm Mette's father, and I make decisions about what's best for her, you taught me that. I wanted their blessing, and to reassure them that moving here didn't mean that they wouldn't get to see her.'

Flora stared at him. 'And…?'

'They told me that they expected me to get a house with a nice guest room, because they'll be visiting.'

A tear ran down her cheek. 'Aksel, please. What exactly are you saying?'

Now was the time. He had to be bold, because Flora couldn't be. He had to trust her, and show her that she could trust him. Aksel hung onto her hand for dear life.

'There's so much I want to say to you. But it all boils down to one thing.'

* * *

Flora had stumbled up a hill in the pitch darkness, and probably skinned her knees. If, in the process, she'd come to realise that nothing could keep her away from Aksel, she wanted to hear what he had to say for himself first.

The flickering flames bathed his face in warmth, throwing the lines of worry across his forehead into sharp relief. The taut lines of his body showed that he was just as agitated as she was.

'What's the one thing?'

'I love you.'

That was good. It was very good because, despite herself, she loved him.

'Seriously?' Maybe he could be persuaded to say it again…

'Yes, seriously. I love you, Flora.' He was smiling at her in the firelight.

'I…love you too.'

He didn't argue. Putting his arms around her, he enveloped her in a hug.

'I was so horrible to you. I'm sorry, Aksel.' The things she'd said made Flora shiver now.

'You were afraid. I was afraid too, and our fear was all that we could see. But I'd be the bravest guy in the world if you'd just forgive me.'

'You mean I'm more scary than wrestling crocodiles?'

'Much more. But the thing that scares me most is losing you.'

Flora kissed him. So much nicer than words. But even the wild pleasure of feeling him close, embraced in his fire on a cold, dark night, couldn't entirely wipe away the feeling that there were some things they really did need to talk about.

'Aksel... What if...?'

'What-ifs don't matter.' He kissed her again, and Flora broke away from him with an effort.

'They *do* matter, Aksel. I need to know. I want you to say it, because I can't keep wondering what might happen if we make a go of this, and decide to have children some day.'

'I'd like children very much. A boy, maybe. Or a girl. One or more of each would be more than acceptable...' He was grinning broadly now.

'Stop it! Don't even say that if you can't also say that there's a risk that one or more of our children might have cystic fibrosis.'

He took her hands between his. 'I know that there *may* be a risk, but only if I carry the gene as well. I love you and I trust you. It's not that I don't care about these possibilities, I just have no doubts that we can face it and do the right thing. And there are other things we need to do first.'

He trusted her. He'd take her as she was, with all the doubts that raised, and he'd make them into certainties. 'What other things do we need to do first?'

'First, I need to tell you that I intend to marry you. I'll work very hard towards making you so happy that you won't be able to resist asking...'

'What? I have to ask you?'

Aksel nodded. 'You have to ask me, because you already know what my answer will be. I'll wait.'

'You're very sure of yourself.'

'I'm very sure of *you*. And I'll be doing my best to wear you down...' He took her into his arms and kissed her. He'd answered none of her questions, but they were all irrelevant now. The only thing that mattered was that they loved each other.

'And how are you going to do that?'

He gave her a gorgeous grin. 'Close your eyes and imagine…'

Aksel wasn't sure whether he had a right to be this happy. But he'd take it. He'd stamped the fire out hastily, lucky not to singe his boots in the process, and he and Flora had hurried back down the hill. The only question that was left to ask was whether they'd spend the night in his bed or hers.

He reckoned that last night had to count towards the *wearing down* process. And then this morning, when they'd made love again, before rushing to work.

If Lyle noticed the coincidence of Aksel wanting to take Mette out after lunch and Flora asking for the afternoon off, he'd said nothing. The old SUV was now running smoothly and even though the outside left a little to be desired, it was now thoroughly clean inside and had a child seat in the back.

'Where are we going?' Flora felt as excited as Mette was.

'Wait and see.' Aksel took the road leading to the other side of the estate, through snow-covered grasslands, and then they bumped a little way across country to the half-acre plantation of Christmas trees. The larger ones, for the castle and the village marketplace had already been felled, but there were plenty of smaller ones that would fit nicely in Flora's cottage. He left Flora to help Mette out of the car seat, and opened the boot to retrieve the chainsaw he'd borrowed from Ted Mackie.

'No!' Flora clapped her hand over her mouth in horror when she saw him eyeing the plantation. 'We can't do that…isn't tree rustling some kind of crime?'

'I got permission from Charles. He says I can take whichever tree I want. Anyway, trees can't run away, so I'm sure it wouldn't technically be rustling.'

'Is it Christmas Eve tomorrow?' Mette started to jiggle up and down in excitement.

'In Scotland we can put up our tree as soon as we like, we don't have to wait until the day before Christmas Eve.'

Mette's eyes grew rounder. 'I *like* Scotland, Papa. Do we have *two* Christmases?'

'No, but there's Hogmanay.' Aksel grinned as Mette looked perplexed. 'You'll have to wait and see what that is.'

Mette nodded, and Aksel leaned towards Flora, her soft scent curling around him. 'I like Scotland, too.'

They took their time choosing, wandering through the plantation hand in hand, while Mette relied on Kari to guide her through the snow. Mette declared that she wanted a tree tall enough for her to climb up to the sky, and Aksel explained that they couldn't get one like that into the cottage. In the end, Flora settled the argument by choosing one they all liked.

'Stand back…' He started up the chainsaw, grinning at Flora, and then cut a 'V' shape in the trunk. Flora hung tightly onto Mette's hand as she screamed excitedly. The tree fell exactly where Aksel had indicated it would.

He'd brought some netting, and Aksel wrapped the tree up in it, bending the larger branches upwards. Then he lifted the tree onto one shoulder to take it to the car.

The raw power in his body never failed to thrill Flora. But there was more now. They were becoming a family.

'How long do I have to hold out for? Before I ask you to marry me?' Mette was busy scooping snow up to make a snowman, and Flora watched as Aksel loaded the tree into the car.

'Be strong.' He grinned at her. 'I'm finding that persuading you is much nicer than I'd thought. I have a few more things in mind.'

'What are they?'

'Breakfast in bed on Christmas morning. A Hogmanay kiss. Taking you back to Norway to meet my family after the New Year.'

Flora had always thought that the most romantic proposal must be a surprise. But planning it like this was even better than she'd dreamed. 'That sounds wonderful. Don't think that I won't be thinking of some things to persuade you.'

'So how long before we give in?' He leaned forward, growling the words into her ear as if they were a challenge.

'I think that decorating the tree's going to be the first big test of our resolve. Christmas Eve might prove very tempting…'

'Yes. That'll be difficult.' He took her hand, pulling off her glove and pressing her fingers to his lips.

'You'll be ready with your answer?' Flora smiled up at him.

'Oh, yes.' He wrapped his arms around her, kissing her. 'I'll be ready.'

EPILOGUE

Oslo, one year later

IT WAS THE night before Christmas Eve, and the family had gathered for Christmas. The big tree at Olaf and Agnetha's house was the centrepiece of the celebrations, and both Aksel's and Flora's parents were spending Christmas here this year. Everyone had admired the appliquéd Christmas stockings, a present from Mary Monroe, who had made a complete recovery and was back working at her beloved quilt shop three days a week.

Mette had fallen asleep as soon as her head had touched the pillow, and Aksel and Flora had tiptoed next door to their own room.

'Mum was telling me how welcome your parents have made her and Dad. They've been showing them around Oslo.' Flora slid onto the bed, propping herself up on the pillows next to Aksel, and he put his arm around her.

'I'm glad they get on so well. And with Olaf and Agnetha too.'

Flora nodded. 'I'm really going to miss this year. We did so much.'

They'd arranged a wedding and bought a house, one of the large stone-built properties just outside the village. Mette understood that her new family would always be there for her, and was gaining in confidence and exploring her world a little more each day. Aksel had been working at the canine therapy centre, after the previous vet had decided not to return from her maternity leave, and helping Ted Mackie organise adventure trips on the estate for the clinic's residents.

'I've got something to get us started on next year. I had an email from Charles this morning. He's signed the papers for the land, and it's now officially ours. We can start to build in the New Year.'

This had been Aksel's dream project, and Flora had fallen in love with it too. The small parcel of barren land, right on the edge of the estate, was no good for anything other than being ideally situated to build. Charles had sold it for a nominal amount, after Aksel had approached him with his plans for an adventure centre for people with disabilities.

'So it's a reality. That's fantastic!' Flora hugged him tight.

'Charles is as excited about it as I am. He offered to make a contribution towards the building costs, but I told him that if he wanted to do something, he could turn up and help dig out the foundations. He liked that idea much better.'

'I'm glad you decided that you weren't going to entirely give up on exploring. Even if these trips will be a little different.'

'They'll be even more challenging.' Aksel took her hand, pressing her fingers to his lips. 'And I'll never be away from my family for too long.'

'Well, maybe your family will just pack their bags every once in a while and come with you.'

He grinned. 'You know I'd love that.'

'I have something for you as well.' Flora reached under the pillow, giving him the small, carefully wrapped package.

'Am I supposed to open this now?' He grinned at her.

'Yes.' She watched as he tore the paper, then turned the little fabric crocodile with sharp embroidered teeth over in his hands.

'All right. You've given me a crocodile to wrestle…?' He'd got the message and he was smiling at the thought of whatever challenge she was going to present him with now. 'Whatever it is you have in mind, the answer's yes.'

Flora nudged him in the ribs. 'You don't know what the question is yet.'

'It'll be Christmas Eve soon. And I trust you…'

It was his trust that had brought Flora to this point. They'd talked about this, and he'd told her that she'd know when the time was right. And she *did* know.

'You said that when we decided to start a family, we'd both take the test for the cystic fibrosis gene. Together…'

A broad grin spread across his face. He knew now exactly what she wanted.

'Yes. I did.'

'Are you ready, Aksel?'

He nodded. 'I've been ready for a long time. You?'

'I'm ready. If it turns out that we both carry the gene we have lots of options. Would it be irresponsible of me to say that we don't need to decide anything now? We'll know what to do if and when we find ourselves in that situation?'

'Nope. Life's one big exploration. You can't know what's ahead of you, but if you're travelling with someone you trust, you can be sure that you'll face it together.'

This felt like the first step in a journey that Flora couldn't wait to make. She kissed him, nestling into the warmth of his arms.

'So I'm going to be a dad again.' Aksel hugged her tight. 'I'm not going to miss a moment of it this time. I'll find someone else to lead the trips...'

'Whatever happens, it won't be for a little while. And when it does, you can have both, Aksel, you don't have to choose.' Sometimes she still had to remind him of that.

'How do you do it, Flora? Every time I think that I'm about as happy as it's possible to be, you manage to make me happier.'

'Trust me Aksel. There's a lot more to come, for both of us.'

He laughed, pure joy spilling out of him. 'Oh, I trust you. Always.'

* * * * *

MILLS & BOON

Coming next month

THEIR ONE-NIGHT CHRISTMAS GIFT
Karin Baine

'We keep a few rooms made up just in case of emergencies.' Charles led her up the stairs to one of the bedrooms. She couldn't help but wonder which door led to his.

'Do you get many late-night, uninvited women calling in on you?' she teased, when he was such a stark contrast to the man who'd literally sent her packing in a previous lifetime.

'No, I don't, but sometimes we get patients arriving too late to be admitted to the clinic, so we put them up here for the night.' Her teasing fell flat with him, but she supposed his defence from her insinuations was understandable when she was accusing him of having loose morals. She knew nothing about him any more.

'I'm sure it's most appreciated. As it is by me.' She had to remember he was doing her a favour by letting her stay when she had no right to be here. Their risky behaviour in London had been her idea and as such she was fully prepared to take on the consequences single-handedly.

'Bed, bathroom, wardrobe. All the essentials.' He did a quick tour of the room before turning back to her. 'Do you need help bringing in your luggage?'

'I just have an overnight bag in the car, but I can

manage that myself. As I said, this was a spur-of-the-moment visit.'

'Ah, yes. The talk. Is this about what happened in London? I must admit it's been harder to put out of my mind than I'd imagined too.' He was moving towards her and Harriet's heart leapt into her throat at the thought of him kissing her again. She wanted it so much but that's not what had brought her here.

'I'm pregnant, Charles.'

His outstretched arms immediately fell limply to his sides. 'Pardon me?'

She sat down on the edge of the bed, wishing it would swallow her up. 'That night in London...I'm pregnant.'

Continue reading
THEIR ONE-NIGHT CHRISTMAS GIFT
Karin Baine

Available next month
www.millsandboon.co.uk

COMING SOON!

We really hope you enjoyed reading this book. If you're looking for more romance, be sure to head to the shops when new books are available on

Thursday 28th November

To see which titles are coming soon, please visit

millsandboon.co.uk/nextmonth

Ice 11|19

LET'S TALK
Romance

For exclusive extracts, competitions
and special offers, find us online: